DELICIOUS DESIRE

Grady pulled her into his arms. "I'm going to kiss you, Fortune," he said, his breath warm on her lips.

Fortune made a small sound of dismay and tried to push away. His arms, though gentle, held firm. She tilted her head back so she could look him in the eye. "I don't want you to kiss me!"

His chuckle was low, sensual and arrogantly male. "Oh, but you *do* want me to kiss you. There's magic between us, darlin'. Don't deny it. I see the sparks in those lovely green eyes of yours. I hear the catch in your breath." He kissed the pulse point on her neck. "I feel your heart pounding, too."

He lowered his head. Fortune stiffened and turned her face away, willing herself not to feel.

Grady's lips grazed her chin as she sought to deny him her mouth. She felt his responding smile against her flesh as he teased her with tender nibbles here, small tastes there, never quite reaching her mouth. His teeth gently caught her earlobe. "Mm-mm, sweet," he murmured against her neck.

Other *Leisure Books* by Charlotte McPherren:
SONG OF THE WILLOW

Love & Fortune

CHARLOTTE McPHERREN

For the beautiful ladies of my critique group.

If not for you, I'd be just a feather on the wind.

Joan Domning
Debanie Olmstead
Dana Rae Pugh
Marguerite Zody
Denise Domning
Carol Tess

Love & Fortune

Prologue

When night's veil comes on gossamer wings
The moon is full and the nightingale sings
The Gypsy fairy enchants with the Moondance

She lures poor Gajo man with sultry voice
Stealing from him any other choice
Her incantation becomes his damnation

Come unto me
Come unto me
Dance with me
Dance with me
That we may be one till the end of time

Virginia Countryside, 1864

From the evening shadows came the first silvery notes
of a violin. Quivery firelight illuminated a Gypsy woman's dusky skin as she entered the glow of the campfire.

9

The dancer was one with the music—first slow, exuding grace and sensuality, then gradually gaining tempo. She raised softly curved arms, and a myriad of gold bangles jangled to the rhythm of the mounting beat. Only her green, feline eyes were visible above the diaphanous red silk draped loosely about her head and across the lower half of her face. A red peasant blouse slipped down one shoulder, sparking the imaginations of her hushed, gray-uniformed audience. Inky tresses swirled about her undulating hips, hips that invited a man's caress.

Preparing to enjoy this unexpected spectacle, Captain Grady MacNair leaned his broad back against his saddle, one arm propped on his upraised knee. He thought it unusual for a Gypsy to hide her face but shrugged it off. Perhaps the scarf was merely an artifice calculated to add an air of mystery. If so, it was most effective.

Grady hadn't been at all happy when the Gypsy wagons had rolled off the road and asked to share their camp earlier that evening. But after searching the wagons thoroughly and finding nothing to be alarmed about, he'd relented. What harm could a motley band of six Gypsies perpetrate on 20 of Mosby's Raiders?

Any serious thoughts dispersed when Grady found himself favored with an enticing glimpse of swaying breasts beneath the thin material of the little dancer's blouse. A half-amused, half-aroused grin lifted the corners of his generous mouth. His nostrils flared at her musky scent, and his grin broadened. He boldly leaned forward as if to fill his cupped hand with her breast. Her eyes widened in sudden surprise, and she quickly danced out of his reach.

The captain's blue eyes twinkled with laughter. His gaze skipped across the fire to the shadows, endeavoring unsuccessfully to see the Gypsy that played the violin so magnificently. Whoever he was, Grady envied the man's impressive talent.

Grady's appreciative glance shifted back to the woman's slim, curvaceous figure. He wondered again about the face hidden beneath that scarf. If her body was any indication then surely she was a beauty. His groin tightened as he speculated on the availability of the little Gypsy whore. Unfortunately for him, he was just too weary to do any more than that—speculate.

He and his men had just completed a grueling and dangerous mission, relieving the Yankees of supplies en route to Sheridan's army. Tomorrow, they would ride hard to rejoin Mosby with the desperately needed ammunition and medical supplies.

Grady knew he should put an end to this evening's pleasant interlude now, but his men deserved the respite. *Just a while longer*, he thought, *then I'll send the little Gypsy to her wagon so the men can get their rest.*

The music suddenly turned especially lively and loud. One of the Gypsies tossed a tambourine to the dancer. Catching it deftly, she danced faster and faster, her colorful skirts flaring around her shapely legs.

The captain noted with amusement that every love-starved eye in camp was glued on the woman. Then before he realized her ploy, she glided up and beckoned him to join her in the circle of firelight. The men went wild. Grady shook his head and waved her away, but his men hooted and clapped, coaxed and prodded until he laughingly obliged and followed the enticing little baggage.

He heard her breath catch in shock when he caught her soft hand and swirled her round to face him. Their gazes locked, and a charge of excitement jolted through him. She'd felt it, too. He saw the proof in her startled eyes. And for one insane moment their souls entwined, both on the brink of an undefined discovery; then she released his hand and backed away.

As if nothing untoward had happened, the Gypsy resumed her dance. One dainty hand beckoned him to follow her into the sphere of firelight, and like a moth drawn to a flame, he drifted closer.

Firelight diffused through the thin scarf around her face, and he thought he detected the semblance of a smile. Curious and still confused by what he thought he'd seen and felt, Grady unconsciously lifted his hand toward the concealing silk. She gracefully pirouetted, one breast inadvertently brushing his outstretched fingertips as she spun away. He caught his breath and lunged for the scarf once more.

The woman's laughter bubbled as she again evaded his hands. She shifted, caught him off guard, and gave him a playful shove into the laps of a couple of his men. The rebels shouted bawdy suggestions to Grady as he floundered to right himself and regain a shred of dignity.

The wild music crescendoed. The dancer struck an alluring pose, then collapsed in a heap amidst boisterous cheers.

Then the violinist began a sweet, haunting melody that Grady had never heard before. He watched mesmerized as the dancer slowly lifted her head and stretched provocatively, as if awakening from a night of being well-loved. She rose to her feet, her voice ringing clear and beautiful on the cool night air. Everyone went silent and listened.

Grady was taken aback. That voice belonged in a New York opera house, certainly not here on the war-torn countryside.

Though foreign, her words needed no translation to be understood as promises of love and passion. The awed guerrilla soldiers couldn't help but lapse into dreams of the sweethearts and wives left behind in war's vengeful wake.

Suddenly the music stopped. The Gypsy's unusual eyes came to rest on Grady, and he was struck by the utter sadness he found in them. She pivoted abruptly and dashed into the oblivion of the night.

Surprised and instantly wary, Grady started to rise, but the clicking of rifles being cocked and aimed froze him in place. Very slowly he raised his hands above his head, got to his feet and turned around.

A snappy looking company of spit-and-shine Yankees emerged from the surrounding forest.

By morning it was raining hard. In the damp gloom the morose clanking of chains around his men's ankles rang in Grady's ears like a death knell.

Bogged down in muddy mire, the Gypsy caravans were having a difficult time forging their way back to the main road. Grady watched as a few Yankee soldiers lent their backs to push them out and wished the whole damn lot of them would be swallowed up by hell itself.

He eyed the shackles biting into his legs and shook his head in self-derision. *I can damn the bastards all the way to hell and back*, he thought, *but this whole mess is my fault. I should never have allowed those damn Gypsies to camp with us, if that's what they truly are. Now, because of my stupidity, the Confederacy is shy of much needed supplies and some of her best men.*

His eyes glittered angrily at the profile of the tall, darkly bearded Gypsy who approached the Yankee captain behind one of the wagons. It was the same bastard who had pleaded to be allowed to share the Rebel camp.

He'd seen nothing of the dancer since her dramatic finale the previous night and could only assume she was hiding inside one of the wagons.

He frowned, remembering the sadness in her eyes before she'd disappeared. Had she regretted her part in the charade? He shook his head in self-disgust. Obviously, he'd mistaken pity for sadness, and her pity was intolerable.

Some might call it wishful thinking, but Grady MacNair had the distinct feeling that his path would someday cross that of the Gypsy bitch, and when it did . . . But who was he kidding? He didn't even know what she looked like. Still, he'd never forget her eyes, their brilliant green color and the unusual way they tilted up at the outer corners. And then there was her incredible voice. A woman so gifted could make a fortune, and he doubted that such as she would pass up that kind of opportunity. People everywhere would come to know her. And so would he! Yes, their paths would cross again.

"Move out, you cursed Rebel dogs," a Yankee sergeant yelled, yanking on their chains.

Grady stumbled clumsily over the unaccustomed shackles. "Damnation!" he swore. Then noting that his chain had dredged up something out of the mud, he called out, "Hold up, men!"

"What is it, Captain?" a corporal asked as his captain stooped and dipped his fingers into the mud.

Grady rose up; a slow smile, the first that day, spread across his face. He cleaned the begrimed object on his gray coat and then held it up for the corporal's inspection. A small gold bracelet from which coins were suspended dangled from his dirty fingers.

"Hey," the corporal exclaimed, "ain't that bracelet like the ones that Gypsy woman was wearin'?"

"The very same, boy, the very same," Grady replied, tucking it into a pocket.

"Well, what yuh saving it for?"

Grady grinned slyly. "Someday, I'll return it to its owner."

"Quit your yammering and move on," the Yankee sergeant ordered, giving Grady's shoulder a rough shove.

Grady stifled an oath and moved out behind the corporal. He glanced over his shoulder and noted that the Gypsies had finally rolled out of sight. Then he faced front and concentrated on putting one foot in front of the other.

As they slogged through ankle-deep mud on the long road north, one of the men began singing a ditty about the beautiful, Gypsy spy to the tune of *Yankee Doodle*. Another man and then another added his own bawdy lyrics, each more outrageous than the last.

Grady held his head high and grinned. He was damn proud to be counted among these brave men. Like true soldiers, they accepted being taken prisoner as one of the misfortunes of war. Not one placed any blame on their captain's shoulders.

What rankled them all, though, was being snookered by a little Gypsy whore. And worse, she'd done it without a single shot exchanged. It was too much for a proud warrior to bear.

A true Southern gentleman would never besmirch a woman, but the verses insulting the Gypsy were a balm to soothe their manly egos. And when the Yankee sergeant ordered them to shut their filthy mouths, Grady, too, took up the tune and sang all the louder.

Chapter One

Montana Territory, 1867

Eight days on the road. Lord, her bottom hurt!

Fortune Landry's handsome Balmoral boots were ruined. The fine kid had not held up long after she'd been obliged to help push the wagon out of numerous muddy potholes. Catching another whiff of the malodorous mule skinner driving her wagon, she thanked heaven above that this horrendous journey was near an end.

The effervescent young woman gave her ebony tresses a shake, inwardly laughing at herself. Who was she kidding? If she'd had to walk knee-deep in muck from Philadelphia to Helena it was better than remaining in the suffocating confines of her parents' home. In comparison, Montana mud seemed more like a river of hot chocolate—and she loved chocolate. Besides, she'd promised her brother, Roc, that she would help him with his business, and she'd rather be hexed than go back on her word.

The wagon lurched to a sudden stop atop a small hill, and the long line of flatbed freight wagons behind them slowly creaked to a halt. The driver stretched out his arm and pointed. "There's Helena, Miz Landry. Ain't she pretty?"

"We're there?" The voice from inside the wagon resembled the soft crumpling of parchment, yellowed by time. Fortune's grandmother, Laila Fontaine, raked aside the canvas and poked her snowy head between the shoulders of the girl and the driver. Not to be left out, the raw-boned face of Ursula Price, Granny's black companion, appeared as well.

At the sight of the ramshackle mining town squatting along Last Chance Gulch, Fortune's cup of optimism drained an inch or two. She hadn't expected a gleaming metropolis, but this place was beyond imagining!

Narrow ugly clapboard buildings were huddled so close that it appeared some of the merchants had slapped a roof over the alleys, closed the open ends with doors and pronounced themselves in business. And endless lines of wagons, mules and oxen churned the crowded streets into a quagmire.

"Well, it ain't no jewel of de West but I seen worse," Ursula commented with her typical frankness.

Fortune glanced over at her grandmother, surprised at her calm expression. "What do you think, Granny?" she asked haltingly.

Laila's buoyant smile added a couple more wrinkles to her leathery nut-brown face. "Looks like that passel of people down there have been so busy setting up house, they haven't had time to hang the curtains."

The driver guffawed and cracked his whip over the heads of the mules, heading them into Helena.

A strange feeling suddenly came over Fortune as they entered town, like something or someone was watching and waiting for her. Despite the warmth of the day, icy pin prickles caused her to shiver. She glanced all around but saw nothing out of the ordinary.

"What'sa matter, gal?" Ursula asked, her eyes growing round. "You jus done shivered like a cat crossed yo grave."

"Felt like one did," Fortune said with an uneasy chuckle. "Guess I'm more tired than I realized." Shrugging off the odd sensation, her adventuresome Gypsy spirit revived her enthusiasm.

The number and variety of businesses surprised all three women. Drygood stores, clothing emporiums, groceries, carpenter and furniture stores, restaurants, doctors, attorneys, blacksmiths, stables and even a brewery lined the street.

Of course there were a few eyesores. Pigs rooting in foul-smelling slop tossed out the front door of a restaurant, and the stiff corpse of a dead horse still tied to a hitching post were a couple of the worst.

There was the usual contingent of saloons and bawdy houses too, but Fortune didn't give them a second thought. That is, until a half-dressed woman spooked their mules when she ran squealing through one set of bat-wing doors to disappear between those of a similar establishment across the road.

"Mm - mm - mm!" Ursula said. "Will you jus look at dat!"

Fortune worried that her grandmother might be rapidly revising her opinion of Helena, but the old Gypsy woman cackled and shook her head with mirth. "What a time we shall have," she said, clapping her hands together with relish.

Fortune heartily agreed. The wonderful sense of untamed freedom thrilled her Gypsy soul. It was exactly what she'd hoped for when she accepted her brother's invitation to join him in Montana.

"How much further to my brother's warehouse?" she asked the driver.

"We're almost there, ma'am. See that big white buildin' down at the end of the street? That's it."

A few minutes later the wagons entered the large open yard. Fortune noted that the warehouse had just been freshly painted and that a man stood on a ladder busily painting a new sign above the large double doors.

The driver set the brake and jumped down from the wagon. Yelling at the painter to clear away his equipment so that the freighters could unload the wagons inside, he then circled to Fortune's side of the wagon and helped her down.

As the driver headed to the back of the wagon to help the older ladies, Fortune followed along. "Is my brother meeting us here?" she asked him.

"Of course I'm meeting you here," answered a loud, rich voice.

Fortune swung around and stopped just short of bouncing into her brother's arms. "Your leg! What happened?"

"And hello to you, too, little sister," he said, laughing.

Carefully avoiding his crutches, she hugged him about his waist. "I can hardly believe how much you've changed," she said, pushing back to get a better look at him.

Roc's black wavy hair touched his collar and curled back over his ears. His beard was gone, and his dusky Gypsy skin was now an even deeper bronze. Around his dark eyes were subtle lines that hadn't been there two years ago, further evidence of his rugged outdoor life here in the West. Tall and heavily muscled, the 27 year old had filled out to a mature man.

"Well, do I pass inspection?" he asked.

Fortune nodded and grinned. "You pass—only where's your earrings?" A young Gypsy male always wore two gold earrings until he was married; then one of them went to his wife. But Roc's ears were totally bare.

Roc shrugged. "Mule skinners think earrings are just for women. I soon found the men wouldn't respect or trust me until I removed mine."

Before Fortune could comment, his brows shot up in surprise. "Granny? Ursula? What are you two doing here?"

Fortune glanced over her shoulder and saw Granny and Ursula approaching behind her. Roc handed one of his crutches to her and opened his free arm to Granny.

"I couldn't let Fortune travel to these wild parts alone now, could I?" the old Gypsy woman said, allowing Roc to tug her small frame to his buckskin-clad chest. "Besides, living in Philadelphia with your mother and that uppity Gajo she married was impossible."

Behind Granny, Fortune winked at her brother. Their grandmother had never made a secret of her dislike for their non-Gypsy father. Her dislike, however, stemmed from the man himself, not his non-Gypsy status. Grandpa Antoine hadn't been a Gypsy either, but Granny had loved him to distraction, so much so that she'd accepted being ostracized by her Gypsy band in France.

"Real reason she's here is cuz de Gypsy in 'er blood was stirrin'," Ursula interjected. "But I reckon at her age she's lucky anything stirs."

"My age?" Granny protested. "Why, I'll have you know . . ."

"Well, how are you, Ursula?" Roc injected loudly. "I see you and Granny are still nit-picking at each other, so I guess that's a good sign. Now how about a hug, sweet thing?"

Ursula's smooth mocha skin crinkled as she broke into a shattering smile. "Oh, all right," she said. "You ain't worth de pants yo wearin', but I loves you all de same." Nearly as tall as the young man, she took his remaining crutch in one hand and wrapped the other long skinny arm around him in a hearty hug.

Roc playfully pretended to struggle for breath before she released him and handed his crutch back.

"Roc," Granny interjected, "I hate to break this up, but we're plumb tuckered. Do we stay in a hotel tonight, or are you taking us to your ranch?"

"The hotel. My buggy is waiting on the other side of the warehouse. I'll take the three of you over to the International. After you've had time to bathe and rest a little, we'll have a good dinner in the hotel restaurant." He turned to Fortune. "Sister mine, if you'll hand that blasted crutch to me, we'll be off."

"Oh, wait!" Fortune said, handing him the crutch and running toward the wagon. "I left Grumpy tied to the back of the wagon. The way he hates men, I don't dare leave him here with all these freighters."

When she returned with the big droopy-eared dog, Roc shook his head in amusement. "I should have known you wouldn't go anywhere without your guardian angel. We'll have to sneak him into the hotel though. They don't cotton much to having animals in the place."

That evening, Fortune took special care with her toilette. Roc had informed them that the hotel restaurant was a popular one, and she wanted to make a good first impression on any of her brother's friends or business associates they might happen to meet. With that in mind, she passed over her comfortable, brightly colored Gypsy skirts and blouses and donned regular Gajo attire instead.

Her freshly washed hair, parted in the middle, waved off her face into a heavy braid that tucked into a pink crocheted snood. A few airy curls floated free on her high cheekbones, emphasizing the distinctive tilt of her emerald eyes.

She glanced into the mirror one last time, hoping her dress was appropriate. Though the rose pink satin was lustrous and elegant, the style was plain, a vee-shaped bodice rising to a snug demure collar of cream lace. Her cursed corset stole her breath away, but she did love the way it narrowed her 21 inch waist to 20. Despising the cumbersome bell-shaped hoops, she compromised with a flat-fronted crinoline that allowed for a pretty train-like skirt in the back. Ruched ribbon in a deeper shade of rose trimmed her bishop sleeves and skirt hem.

Fortune's colorful rings caught the light as she dabbed on the rare scent of jasmine and almond oil Granny had formulated especially for her. The aromatic potion was said to arouse the coldest of male hearts, and since most Gypsy girls married by 16, Granny considered her 19-year-old granddaughter in dire need of the perfume's mystical powers.

As Fortune corked the bottle, a light tapping sounded at her door. She opened it on Roc's smiling countenance.

"Ready, little Gyp— Fortune Landry, if we weren't related, I'd whisk you straight to the preacher and marry you. You're beautiful!"

Fortune laughed at his silliness, realizing just how much she'd missed her old partner in youthful crime. His broken leg aside, Roc cut a dashing figure in his long, navy frock coat over buff trousers. "Hm, you look pretty grand yourself," she replied. "Shall we fetch Granny and Ursula?"

"I'm afraid the two old dears have cried off," Roc informed her. "Ursula says her rheumatism is acting up, so Granny ordered their meals sent up to their rooms. Personally, I think Granny is worn out, too, but she'd die before admitting it."

"I'll get my reticule, then I'm all ready," Fortune replied. "We can check in on Granny and Ursula after dinner."

"Where's Grumpy?" Roc asked as she grabbed her bag.

Fortune bent and lifted the hem of the bedspread. Grumpy lay under the bed, his head resting on his outstretched paws. He opened one, half-curious eye then let it drop again.

"A real man-eater," Roc chuckled dryly.

"Don't be fooled by his tolerance of you. Old Grump still hates men." She straightened and patted her hair, setting her bracelets jingling.

"Uh, Fortune," Roc said, "just one thing."

"Yes?"

He reached for her arm and removed all but one of her bracelets. Then he tugged off her rings except for one on each hand. "People out here in the West are simple folks, honey. They'd take one look at all this showy stuff and think you were putting on airs."

"Oh," Fortune said, her voice reflecting disappointment. She loved her bangles and rings and the more the better. Still, she didn't want to embarrass Roc in any way. "All right, I'll try to remember not to wear so many."

Roc's progress down the hall was slow and awkward, and when they reached the head of the stairs his sister hailed the desk clerk from below to help him down.

"You never did tell me how you broke your leg," she reminded him as he made the slow, grueling descent.

One arm slung over the clerk's shoulder, Roc chuckled self-consciously. "I got into a little scuffle over a card game—fell over a toppled table and snap! Leg broke."

Fortune winced at the mental picture he painted. "You weren't drinking, I hope." For some reason alcohol affected her brother adversely, and he'd learned a long time ago to avoid it.

At the bottom of the stairs now, Roc ignored his sister's question. Handing a coin to the clerk, he motioned to her, "Restaurant is this way, Fortune. Let's eat. I'm starved!"

Later, as they finished their meal, brother and sister leaned back in their velvet-tufted chairs and caught up on each other's lives. "And so," Roc said after explaining to Fortune the trials he'd gone through the past two years in Montana, "my business has grown so much that I need someone I can trust to keep the books and oversee the warehouses when I'm out of town. That's where you come in. I don't know anyone better with figures than you."

"Well, your offer certainly was timely," Fortune answered. "I swear, Roc, after Gran sold the horse farm and we moved to town to live with Mother and Father, I thought we'd both go crazy.

"And you know Mama. She's so afraid someone will find out she's half-Gypsy. She warned the three of us to keep mum. Granny didn't give a fig for her attitude, so Mama actually tried to hide her away whenever her highfalutin friends came to tea.

"Papa wasn't much better, maybe worse. He kept pushing all the sons of his old business cronies at me. Remember Fred Bixby, the short, round man with a hundred hands? He was Papa's favorite."

"Not him!" Roc chuckled and shook his head. "I'm sorry. I shouldn't laugh." He lit a cigar and lifted one dark brow. "So tell me, how did you get Mama and Papa to agree to letting you come West?"

"Well, at first they said no, of course. Papa said Granny and Ursula were beyond help, but that he'd not allow me to go West and become some kind of frontier floozy. Then too, he's still mad at you for taking me to Virginia in '64. I pleaded and begged, but they wouldn't change their minds until . . ." Fortune chuckled mischievously. "I got the most marvelous idea. It was so simple, I don't know why I didn't think of it sooner."

She leaned over the table and whispered. "Remember Mama's annual rose garden parties?" She stuck her nose in the air in an affected manner. "So vedy proper, you know," she mocked.

Roc grimaced, remembering all too well his mother's blatant attempts to impress her friends.

"I was suppose to perform one of those stiff-necked parlor tunes," Fortune continued. "Instead, I performed the Gypsy Moondance. You know, like the one I did in Virginia during the war."

Roc's eyes widened with incredulity. "You didn't! Bare legs and all?" Fortune's head bobbed vigorously, an ornery grin splitting her face.

"Jesus, I bet Mother fainted in her soup."

"No, but the preacher's wife did."

Roc couldn't help himself and burst into uproarious laughter. "Oh, God, I wish I'd been there," he gasped between chuckles.

Fortune grinned. "Mama was so anxious to get rid of me she helped the maids pack my things. Then Granny and Ursula announced they were coming, too. Well, that made Papa so happy that he ran right down to the train station and bought our tickets to St. Louis. I didn't have to sweet-talk him too much to get him to pay for the boat tickets from St. Louis to Fort Benton."

Roc was still chuckling. "You'll be lucky if Mama ever speaks to you again," he said.

"I love Mama, Roc, but I can't live the way she wants me to. At times she was actually cruel to . . ." Fortune broke off. Time stood still. Or had it backed up? Her stunned gaze fastened on a face from the past, a face that had haunted her dreams these past three years, a face she thought she'd never see again.

A golden-haired man, nattily attired in a black frock coat, stood talking to a waiter in the restaurant entrance. "Roc, do . . . do we know that man?" Fortune stammered, knowing very well that they did, but hoping her brother would deny it.

Before Roc could answer, the stranger glanced in their direction. Fortune quickly looked away, her hand flying to her throat in speechless horror. "It can't be," she gasped in a tiny, frightened voice. But as she stole another glance from beneath her lashes, she couldn't deny what her own eyes told her was true. Her head swiveled back to Roc whose expression was suddenly closed. "It's him, the Rebel, Grady MacNair, isn't it? You must have known he was here in Helena. Why didn't you warn me?"

"Fortune, I was going to tell . . ."

"Great crystal balls and tea leaves!" she intoned in a desperate whisper. "He's coming this way."

Roc grabbed her hand and squeezed hard to retrieve her full attention. "No time to explain, little Gypsy, so pay attention. He doesn't know who we are, that is, that we were the ones—the Gypsies, I mean. Keep calm and follow my lead." He jerked her hand. "Damn it, Fortune, are you listening?"

The shocked young woman just nodded, her eyes glued to the specter approaching their table. Her stomach vaulted to her chest, or was it her heart plunging to her stomach? Either way, Fortune Landry was one scared Gypsy.

"Mr. Landry is sitting right there," the waiter told Grady MacNair with a jerk of his head to the left side of the hotel dining room.

Grady scanned the room, quickly locating his quarry. He was damn glad he'd finally cornered the man. His eyes widened, skidded to a halt and homed in for a second and very intense glance at the woman with Landry. *Hot damn! Where'd the Yank find her?*

From where Grady stood he couldn't see the color of the woman's eyes, but their unusual almond shape and the way they tilted up like a cat's gave the raven-haired beauty a mysterious exotic quality.

His discerning eye slowly slid over the satin hugging the

ample swell of bosom and tiny waist. He despaired that her lower extremities were hidden by her voluminous skirt and the white linen tablecloth.

Grady loved the ladies and the ladies loved him, but it had been a spell since one like this little filly had wandered into the territory. *Steady, boy,* he silently warned himself, *that's no wet-behind-the-ears kid she's got with her.*

An unexpected and amusing thought occurred, and the corner of his mouth tipped in a rakish smile. Wouldn't it stick in Landry's craw if he stole this beauty right out from under his nose? It seemed the least he could do to repay Landry for deliberately avoiding him these past weeks.

Beneath the table, Fortune's moist palms clutched the satin of her dress as MacNair, moving with a leisurely grace, sauntered toward them. His gaze held hers, and she'd have had to be blind not to detect the seductive gleam in his eye.

Her flesh heated as her treacherous mind played back the countless nights this man had haunted her dreams. And despite her fear, she felt a compelling urge to leave her chair and step right into his arms. Any lingering notion that the magical Moondance hadn't truly worked on that Virginia night so long ago was put to rest forever.

Dropping her lashes, she stared at her lap and took several deep breaths. Calm, she must stay calm. True, they were bonded to one another, but three years was a long time and she'd worn a concealing scarf over most of her face. Surely he wouldn't recognize her as easily as she had him—or would he?

Covertly, she watched his steady approach. Perhaps an inch or two shorter than her six-foot-two brother, his fair complexion was tanned deep gold and served to enhance his delft-blue eyes. His face was still handsome, bearing a long and square jaw with a slight cleft in his chin, but in it was a new strength and maturity.

Though still slim of waist and hip, he'd filled out considerably since the lean war days. His well-tailored coat hugged thick upper arms, broad shoulders and chest. His trousers fit his thighs with a snugness that revealed powerful muscle and sinew. Her gaze dropped lower and froze on a spot that clearly outlined his maleness.

Fortune snatched her eyes away, shocked at the path her

thoughts had taken. While she might allow for a modicum of maidenly curiosity, any kind of interest in this man, especially an intimate one, was bad for her.

Still, it wasn't easy to remain totally unaffected, not when she felt she knew the Reb so well. Heaven knows he'd intruded on her dreams with an audacious vengeance, pulling the silk from her face and sliding the clothes from her body.

MacNair came to a standstill at their table. His eyes met Fortune's, and for a heart-stopping moment he looked nonplused. Then to her relief, he just smiled and removed his black hat. A deep wave of sandy hair fell over his high forehead. Fortune sucked in her breath. The Reb reeked that renowned Southern charm, a very sensual charm.

"Evenin', Roc." MacNair tipped his head to Fortune. "Ma'am." His Southern drawl bore the slightest intonation of a soft Scot's burr, and the low mellow timbre fairly rippled over the girl's taut nerves. Without so much as a side glance at her brother, MacNair caressed her with an intimate smile and asked, "Aren't you going to introduce me to your lovely companion, Roc?"

Looking like he'd sooner be bitten by a snake, Roc's reply was curt. "MacNair, my sister, Miss Fortune Landry. Fortune, Grady MacNair."

Fortune thought she detected a surprised lift of MacNair's brows, but the expression was fleeting and she couldn't be sure. Unable to speak yet, she nodded politely.

"MacNair owns a mercantile just up the street a ways," Roc continued grudgingly.

"And don't forget," the Southerner persisted, "I'm your new partner as well."

Fortune's head snapped in Roc's direction. "Partner? You didn't tell me . . ."

"I was getting around to that," Roc interrupted. He shifted uneasily in his chair and stabbed MacNair with a hostile glare.

"You don't mind if I join you, do you, ma'am?" Not waiting for an invitation, MacNair pulled out a chair and seated himself.

Fortune's heart leaped when his knee accidentally bumped hers under the table. *Oh God, so close!* She fisted her hands to keep from reaching out to touch him. The magic binding them was so strong.

"I came here to discuss business with your brother, but I confess, Miss Landry, in view of your lovely presence, I'd much rather get to know you. What brings a gentle lady like yourself to Helena?"

His deep languid tones rolled over the vowels with a slow voluptuousness that bade Fortune drop all her defenses. *He really doesn't remember me,* she thought with relief. She began to relax, her erratic pulse receding to an uneasy calm—uneasy because her brother was giving MacNair the evil eye.

"I came here to help Roc with his business," Fortune answered, with far more confidence than she felt.

"Ah, then we'll be seeing a lot of each other. Perhaps you'd allow me to call on you soon and show you around town."

Fortune's heart fluttered. "Well . . . I . . . that is, I'm going to be awfully busy."

"I don't want you anywhere near my sister, Reb," Roc barked belligerently. "I may have to do business with you, but my sister isn't part of the deal."

MacNair's face clouded with bridled anger. "I'd say the lady is old enough to make that decision for herself, Landry."

Despite his broken leg, Roc's anger spurred him to rise. Fortune gasped in dismay, leaned across the table and grasped his hand. "Stop it!" she hissed. Her angry gaze included both men. "People are staring, and I don't care to be made a public spectacle my first day in town. Mr. MacNair, I thank you kindly for your offer, but honestly, I will be busy settling in.

"Roc, I'm going upstairs to my room now so the two of you can discuss business. I'll see you later for our own little discussion." She rose gracefully, waving her crippled brother back down to his chair when he tried to rise for her departure. "Good evening, gentlemen."

Unimpaired himself, MacNair rose quickly and caught her hand a few steps away from the table. "Miss Landry, wait. Please accept my apologies. I never meant to cause you any trouble." Using his body to block Roc's view, he bent low, gently turned her hand palm up and touched his warm lips to its center.

Fortune inhaled sharply. Something hot and intense flared to life and singed the nerve endings all the way up her arm. She didn't understand exactly what she was feeling, but one thing was sure—it was damned dangerous! Her breath coming in quick angry gasps, she jerked her hand from his and huffed, "Good evening, Mr. MacNair."

Wishing she could pick up her skirts and run all the way back to Philadelphia, Fortune drew on her last reserve of cool dignity and departed the room with queenly aplomb.

Grady stood entranced and watched her go, her exotic perfume lingering in his nostrils. He'd experienced the strangest feeling upon touching her. Like a tiny earthquake, a tremor shook his body and shifted something inside.

Hell, what's the matter with me? I just met the woman! If anything did crack and shift, it was probably my brain!

Chapter Two

"Sweet Gaia," Fortune ranted, invoking her earth goddess, "what's keeping Roc?" Catching a glimpse of her pale reflection in the mirror, she halted her furious pacing.

Her waist-length hair hung down the back of her wrapper and tangled around her face where she'd repeatedly run her hands through it. Her eyes were wide and alert and frightened. "Grady MacNair didn't know you," she told her mirrored image.

"But what if he finds out?" her image seemed to ask. "He'll shoot you—that's what!" she blurted out vehemently. Flouncing away from the mirror, she resumed pacing. Damn! If she had an ounce of sense she'd board the first stage out of Helena.

And go back to what? A mother who puts on airs and pretends to be something she isn't? A father who cherishes prestige and money more than he does his own family? A life in the midst of a society that scorns the very blood in her veins? Never! Their way wasn't hers.

Fortune's parents, Tshaya and Bonner Landry, had always been too busy climbing Philadelphia's social ladder to pay much attention to their growing children. While the Landrys partied and traveled among the *haute monde* their children, for the most part, were raised in the countryside home of Tshaya's parents.

Roc grew up helping his grandfather, Antoine Fontaine, breed horses on his farm while Granny tutored Fortune in the ways and beliefs of her Gypsy ancestors. Even old Ursula had a hand in the girl's upbringing, seasoning Fortune's knowledge with her own ancestral African beliefs.

Only when Tshaya took it in her head to impress her friends with her darling offspring did she bother with her children. But even then, these rare bouts of maternal concern were limited to seeing that Fortune and Roc were properly educated and dressed so as not to prove an embarrassment.

A sharp rap at the door brought her back to the present. "Roc, where have you been?" she asked, opening the door. "It's almost midnight."

"I know, and we must stop meeting like this," he said with an attempt at levity. Fortune didn't laugh, and he had the good grace to look sheepish. "I needed time to let my temper cool," he replied wearily. "Having a Reb for a partner is enough to madden any good Yankee."

Spying two silk brocade chairs across the room, he gripped his crutches and limped over to them. He eased into one, arranging his stiff limb before him. "I believe, sister mine, you wanted to talk?"

Fortune sat opposite him on the edge of a chair. "It's late, so I won't mince words. How long have you known MacNair was here in Helena?"

"Since before I first wrote you about joining me," he said quietly.

"Since before you . . . Then for Pete's sake, why didn't you warn me?"

"I thought if I mentioned it, you might not come. But," Roc added in defense, "I did mention that Montana's population is mostly ex-Confederates."

Fortune flashed him a peeved look. "Oh, and that was supposed to explain everything."

"Well, hell, Fortune, since the South fell, Southerners have poured into the West. And what with the gold strikes, any number of the men we had dealings with during the war could end up in Helena. We can't slink around like criminals just because we might be recognized by one of them. Remember, we were on the winning side!"

"But you knew how much the Mosby raid affected me, Roc." While Fortune had never confessed the personal nature of her dreams to anyone, her family knew the guilt she'd suffered. On her return from South Carolina she'd learned of the thousands of Confederates and Yankees dying in each other's prison camps. All she'd been able to think about was the men she'd personally condemned to die, especially Captain Grady MacNair.

Also there was the unpleasant memory of the morning after the raid. In the hopes of garnering one last look at the Rebel captain, she'd peeked out the window of the Gypsy wagon. She was sorry she had. The bitterness she'd witnessed on MacNair's face was frightening.

"Why is it that MacNair's capture bothered you so much more than any of the others?" Roc asked. "I never really understood that."

"The Moondance", she said almost to herself. She eyed him squarely, adding, "You know its significance. The Reb and I were bonded that night."

"Is that what you've believed all this time?" he asked incredulously. "Fortune, honey, you're no longer a child. Surely you don't believe all that hocus-pocus? I'm every bit as much Gypsy as you, and I sure don't. Let's face it. Many of Granny's beliefs are little more than fairy tales passed down by generations of Gypsies." He held up his hand when she would have interrupted. "It's fun to put the horseshoe above the door of our homes. It's fun to wear an amulet, and yes, I'll admit I've witnessed a few unexplainable things. That uncanny sixth sense of yours can be darn right spooky. But I also believe that we have to be practical and sensible, too."

"Just because you don't hold with my beliefs doesn't mean you have the right to talk to me as if I'm a child. Damn it, Roc, something did happen that night. Heaven knows, I didn't mean for it to." She spread her hands helplessly. "But the moon was full, and I wore red. I even sang the chant." Fortune jumped to her feet to pace restlessly. "Oh, why did MacNair have to go and touch me and look into my eyes the way he did? If he hadn't the enchantment wouldn't have been complete. But damn it, he did!" She halted and stared her brother in the eye.

"I felt the magic, and he did, too; it was in his eyes. And even though it's been three years, the bond is as strong as ever. Grady MacNair was . . . is attracted to me."

"Of course he's attracted to you," Roc reasoned. "What man wouldn't be? You're a beautiful woman. Listen, you told me you did the Moondance at mother's garden party, too. Does that mean that you left some poor soul mooning after you till the end of time?"

Fortune scowled, irritated with his mocking grin. "That was different, and you know it. It was broad daylight, I wore blue, no one touched me, and I did not sing the chant!"

"Just what are you telling me? That you think you're in love with the Reb?"

"No! Yes!" Fortune squeezed her eyes shut. "I don't know." She opened her eyes and stared beyond Roc as if trying to see into the future. "I mean . . . it's highly possible it could come to that—love, I mean. And if it does, I'll have to be honest and flat out tell him everything. I couldn't live with that kind of secret forever between us. And once MacNair knows, he'll seek God knows what kind of revenge."

Roc slapped his thigh. "Jesus, you're frustrating! If you truly believe you're connected to the man, then get unconnected. Conjure up a spell or whatever it is you do. I sure as hell don't want a Reb for a brother-in-law."

"I can't." Her voice cracked, and she sank back into her chair.

Roc's tone softened at the sight of the moisture welling in her eyes. "Why not? Not that I believe in all that mumbo jumbo, but if you do, well . . ."

"Only MacNair can undo what's been done." She sniffed, dashed a tear from her cheek and looked at her brother, adding, "Of course, ultimately it's my doing."

"Fortune, you're not making any sense."

"To undo the damage, MacNair must come to hate me unto death," she explained. "I know of only one thing that could produce that kind of hatred—the knowledge that I'm the Gypsy that betrayed him to the Yanks. Don't you see, Roc? It doesn't matter which direction I take. Every path leads to doom."

"Doom?" Roc snorted at her dramatics. "If it takes hatred to break this spell then it's probably already broken. I imagine he was pretty upset at being bamboozled by a Gypsy girl."

"It doesn't work that way," Fortune said.

"Of course not," he said. "That would be too easy, wouldn't it?"

"Stash the sarcasm, Roc." She closed her eyes and massaged her temples. "If I remember correctly, MacNair has to look into my eyes, touch me and tell me of his hatred, just like he had to look into my eyes and touch me to bond."

Roc dropped his forehead into his hand and shook his head. "This is all too preposterous."

"You may well think so, but it's all your fault."

"My fault!" her brother hooted, throwing his hands up in the air.

"Well, it is. First you talk me into stealing Granny's *vardo*. Then you talked me into joining your fake Gypsy band to spy on the Rebs and catch guerilla soldiers. And now this partnership!"

Roc slumped against the chair back with a chastened grimace. "That was sort of an accident."

"An accident? Now who's telling fairy tales? Tell me, how does one accidentally acquire a business partner?" He started to open his mouth, but she interrupted as sudden dawning settled over her features. "Wait a minute. Does this have anything to do with that card game and your broken leg?" Fortune took in her brother's guilty expression and sighed resignedly. "All right, let's have the story."

Roc shrugged. "Not much to tell. I was at the Gaiety Saloon having a drink and . . ."

"A drink? A drink! Roc, how could you? You know how you get when you take even one sip of liquor."

"For Pete's sake, give me a chance to explain, will you? I was only drinking sarsaparilla and playing cards. But it just so happens that in the middle of the evening a couple of my freighters sat down at the bar. They decided their boss should be drinking a more manly drink and had the bartender juice up my sarsaparillas. I didn't find this out until a couple days later. The men collected their wages from Slim and confessed to the prank before hightailing out of town. Guess they thought I might be gunning for them after what happened."

"Didn't you taste the difference in your drinks?"

"I might have, but I was so involved in my winning streak that I paid it little mind. Next thing I know, the Reb asks if he might join the game. I thought it would be fun to fleece him and agreed. But a few sarsaparillas later, I went from winning to losing and got surly as hell."

"What sort of man would play a drunk for such high stakes, anyway?"

Roc rolled his eyes to the ceiling with pure masculine exasperation. "Fortune, poker isn't one of your tame parlor games. It's every man for himself. If a man is dumb enough to bet what he can't afford to lose . . . well, that's his business. That aside, I still don't lay any blame on MacNair. The man heard me ordering harmless drinks, and even if he hadn't, there was no way he could have known the effect liquor has on me.

"Slim Pittman, one of my trail bosses, also played that night. He swore I played it as sober as a judge until I lost the second round to MacNair. By then I was mean drunk. I went into a rage and tried to recoup my pride and money by betting half the freight company. Slim tried to stop me, but I wouldn't listen. MacNair drew the winning hand, and that's when I threw the first punch. The two of us almost tore the saloon apart."

Fortune asked anxiously, "Have you tried to buy back the loss?"

Roc chuckled mirthlessly. "The very next day. But MacNair wouldn't sell. Said he relished being in the freighting business."

"So, you're stuck with him."

"Yeah, looks that way. But really, Fortune, I don't think you've got a thing to worry about. Your face was well-hidden that night in Virginia. And it's been three long and very eventful years since then. Hell, I can't even remember every face I saw yesterday, let alone three years ago!"

Fortune shook her head. "What you can't seem to get through that thick skull of yours is sooner or later MacNair will find out everything."

"Forget about that hocus-pocus stuff." Roc scooted forward in his chair, reached out and took her agitated hands between his own. "There's nothing to worry about, honey. As long as you don't look or act like a Gypsy, there's no reason the Reb should ever suspect you're the Gypsy girl who deceived him."

It was the wrong thing to say.

Fortune shot out of her chair, nearly tripping over his broken leg. Roc squeezed his eyes shut, waiting for the pain.

When it didn't come, he opened one eye and then the other. Fortune was glaring daggers at him, fists planted on her hips.

"Well, I guess I now know the real reason you made me remove my jewelry tonight. Didn't you hear anything I said at dinner?" she demanded. "I came west to escape lies and pretense. Damn it, Roc, I like being Gypsy!"

"Hold your horses, Sis. I feel the same way you do, but let's be honest. Most people, our parents included, have a very low opinion of Gypsies. Why do you think Mama is the way she is? It's because of the way she was taunted as a child.

"There will always be an ignorant few who hear only what they want to hear. Usually where Gypsies are concerned, it's bad—farmers coming up short a few hens, horse thievery and so on. And in case you didn't know it, horse thieving in these parts is a hanging offense."

Fortune's innate ability to see the humor in most any situation finally broke through her anxiety. "I'm not a Gypsy of the horse-thief variety," she said, smiling, "but perhaps you do have a point. I should let folks get to know me before I go off half-cocked and cause a ruckus."

"Exactly." Roc grinned, breathing a sigh of relief.

"Still," she continued stubbornly, "the pretense won't work on MacNair. Not for long anyway. You may not believe in the powers of the Moondance but I do, and believing is half the magic."

"Fortune, I warned MacNair to stay away from you," Roc said with strained patience. "If you don't encourage him, he'll never get close enough to find out anything. It's as simple as that."

To Fortune's surprise he gathered up his crutches then and made ready to leave. It was obvious he considered the subject closed.

"It's getting late and you look exhausted," he said, rising to his feet. "I want you to quit borrowing trouble and get some sleep. Things always look better by the light of day. You'll see. And by the way, I have business tomorrow so we'll be in town one more day before heading out to the ranch. I thought you, Granny and Ursula might enjoy shopping and getting better acquainted with Helena."

Fortune held the door open for her brother, knowing further argument was useless. "That sounds nice," she said perfunctorily. "Good night, Roc."

After Roc left, Fortune removed her wrapper, tossed it on the end of the large double bed and pulled the covers back. Then turning her lamp down she snuggled into the pillows and stared into the darkness.

Roc couldn't begin to imagine the half of her worry, she mused. There were, however, some things a girl just couldn't talk about with a brother—specifically, her own passionate weakness for the Reb.

Tonight, she'd seen the desire and determination in Grady MacNair's eyes. And there was no denying that he aroused something powerfully primal in her as well. If the Reb managed to get past her brother's watchful eye, who knew what could happen?

Fortune rolled over and punched her pillow. Maybe she was a fool. Maybe Roc was right. Maybe she was making too much of this situation. Maybe there was no magic. Maybe there was no attraction between herself and the Reb.

Yeah, and maybe horses fly!

A warm dewy breeze wafted through the window of the small room over MacNair Mercantile. Outside, tinkling barroom pianos accompanied gravelly voices joined in drunken song and outrageous feminine squeals. A dog barked, and a cat let loose a yowl. The report of a gun brought a sudden momentary silence. Then Helena's nighttime cacophony took up where it left off.

Grady tossed a pillow against the tarnished brass headboard and leaned back to enjoy a cheroot. Staring into the darkness, he savored the rich tobacco and contemplated the evening's surprising turn of events.

Since winning half of Roc Landry's freighting business, Grady's efforts to pin down the man long enough to discuss their partnership had proved fruitless. His efforts had been further thwarted by his own recent business trip to Fort Benton.

Under the circumstances, Grady couldn't really blame Landry for his reticence, but the fact remained that they were now partners. It was his right to contribute his opinions and share in the profits.

He hardly had been back in town this afternoon when he'd caught a glimpse of Landry disappearing into the hotel. Knowing the man kept a room there, Grady immediately made plans to waylay him at dinner.

He wasn't foolish enough to believe that he and Landry could ever be friends, but he hoped to strike an amicable working relationship. His lawyer was preparing papers that would solidify his legal title to half ownership of the freighting company, and to these Grady had added a business proposal of his own.

Grady was convinced the mercantile and freighting business could be a profitable marriage of interest. He'd intended to present that idea to Roc Landry tonight, but he hadn't counted on Fortune Landry. The moment he laid eyes on the little enchantress, all thought of business fled. And later, after she left the dining room, her brother hadn't exactly been in a receptive mood. Grady wisely postponed his business and arranged to meet the Yank tomorrow morning instead.

He smiled into the dark. Fortune. It was an odd name, and he wondered how she'd come by it. Perhaps it was only a family pet name, but it suited her. The man lucky enough to lasso her spirited heart would indeed hold a treasure worth a fortune in his arms.

Though surprised, he'd been especially pleased to learn that the girl was Landry's sister and not his mistress. It somehow made the idea of seducing her even more enticing. To his credit, though, he wasn't thinking solely with his *pistol*. He'd immediately realized a greater motivation than one-upmanship on the Yank. If he could win the sister over, she might persuade her brother to agree to the merger he planned to propose.

But business or no, he had one hell of a powerful desire for Fortune Landry which wasn't like him at all. As much as he loved the ladies—bless their ever-lovin' little hearts—he wasn't the type to fall head over heels for a pretty face. In fact, only once before had he experienced such an immediate and potent fascination for a woman.

"Yeah, and look where that got you," a mocking voice reminded him.

The Gypsy. It had been a while since he'd thought of the beautiful little whore, but this made the second time this evening. The first time had been when he approached the Landry table in the hotel, and Fortune had gazed up at him with those

unusual emerald eyes of hers. Hell, for a moment, he'd thought
he'd found the traitorous Gypsy bitch!

But he'd quickly realized his error. No loose fall of wild
raven hair swirled at her hips, but tresses of unknown quality
and length were primly constrained in a neat little net. Her arms
weren't ringed with gaudy bangles but only one bracelet with
tiny enchanting bells attached. Her dress had been conserva-
tively cut, leaving not an inch of skin bared. Clearly she was
a lady, the kind that would do any man proud.

Grady gave his head a shake. Now where had that thought
come from? Hell, he wanted to bed her, not wed her!

And yet, he had to admit, the lady exemplified his idea
of a perfect wife—beautiful, gently bred, beautiful, spunky,
beautiful, well-spoken, beautiful. Perhaps he should give this
marriage idea some consideration, he thought, amused.

Grady had goals, big ones. Montana was prime cattle country, and he didn't plan to remain a shopkeeper any longer than it
took to rake in enough profit off the gold-hungry miners to start
up his own spread. Getting married and having a few kids was
at the bottom of his priority list. First build the empire, then find
a woman and then make lots of sons to help run the place.

Grady chuckled to himself. *Hell, maybe I've been looking at
this thing all wrong from the start. The frontier does seem to
have its own order of things. And here in the territory, good
women are scarcer than a grasshopper in a hen yard. It might
be a long while before another such as Fortune Landry comes
along.*

Then too, he reasoned, *it takes nine months to make a baby.
And quite a few years before the boy—and the first will be a
boy—will be old enough to help me with the ranch. Perhaps
starting a family first is a wiser way to go. It's definitely
something to think over.*

Grady took a long drag on his cheroot. Life was strange the
way it worked out sometimes. At one time, he had thought he
would inherit his family's plantation in South Carolina, but the
war and a certain little Gypsy had danced into his life and set
him on a different path. Grady smashed his cigarette out on the
rickety bedside table and silently damned to hell the Gypsy,
wherever she might be.

But hell, there was no sense in wasting time or thought
on what might have been. Rather, Grady thought, he should

concentrate on his goals and the woman within his reach, the beautiful Miss Fortune Landry.

Throwing his legs over the side of the bed, he removed his shirt, tugged his boots off, then stood and shed his trousers. Smiling, he stretched out naked on his bed, his swollen masculinity proof of the direction of his thoughts. Whatever the outcome, there wasn't a doubt in his mind that Miss Landry would prove a delightful and worthy challenge.

Chapter Three

"You did what?" Laila Fontaine exclaimed, staring at her grand-daughter in dismay.

Fortune glanced glumly down at the unappetizing remains of her lunch. "I danced the Moondance for the Confederates," she repeated guiltily. "I know it goes against all your teachings on using magic responsibly, but Roc said I absolutely had to keep the rebels' attention occupied."

"Slitherin' serpents," Ursula exhaled deeply. "Dat oughtta done it all right."

"It did," the girl groaned.

"Fortune, are you sure the enchantment took?" Laila asked. "You were wearing red? The moon was full?"

"Did he dance with you, stare inta yo eyes?" Ursula chimed in.

"Did he touch you?" Laila continued urgently.

"Yes to all." Fortune swallowed hard. "Oh, Gran, I didn't mean for the spell to take. MacNair caught me off guard when he touched me."

"Wait," Laila said, "did you sing the chant afterwards?

Because if you didn't the enchantment wouldn't be complete."

"I had to sing it. It was the signal to Roc's men that all was ready. If they had heard anything else they would have retreated and left the rest of us in a real pickle."

"Looks ta me like you is in a bushel of trouble anyway, gal," Ursula said, shaking her head.

"Let's sort this muddle out," Laila said, shoving her plate away. "You must keep your distance from MacNair because he might realize who you are. Only that won't be easy because the two of you are bonded."

"He ain't gonna give up on havin' you," Ursula interjected. "But maybe dat be good! Iffin' he loves you, he ain't gonna hurt you none. Maybe he'll even ask ta marry up with you." She grinned encouragingly.

"Great crystal balls," Fortune said, "I hope not. I don't want a man to love me because he's under a spell. I want him to love me for me. But that's beside the point. If I ever did consent to marry the man, I'd have to tell him the truth. I couldn't keep such a secret from the man I love."

"'Pears ta me, you gotta break this here spell, cuz sure as the sky is blue, dat boy ain't gonna give up till he beds you. Den when he finds out de truth, he's gonna send you and dat brother of yo's ta meet yo Maker!"

"I agree with Ursula," Laila said, nodding her head thoughtfully.

"But Granny, you once told me the spell can only be broken by making the victim hate his bond mate unto death. The way I see it, I'd have to tell him who I am to make him that mad."

"Lordy, Lordy!" Ursula rolled her eyes. "It's hexed if you do and hexed if you don.'"

"Exactly." Fortune moaned.

"Only one thing to do," Laila said confidently. "We have to find another way to break that spell." She tapped a finger on her chin. "Now, let's see, it seems to me . . . no, that wasn't it."

"I'll help," Ursula volunteered eagerly. "Laila teached me all she knows."

Fortune's spirit lifted considerably. "Do you two really think you can conjure something up? Oh, I hope so! If MacNair loses interest in me then he'll never learn the secret and everything will be fine."

"We'll try very hard, dear, but remember," Laila warned, "I'm a Gypsy, not a witch. Ursula and I may have to try out quite a few charms and spells before we hit on the right one."

Fortune nodded her understanding, but her smile reflected her total faith in the two old ladies.

"There's just one more thing," Granny said, pointing a finger at the young woman, "and it's no small matter. You mustn't forget that you too are susceptible to the Moondance bond."

Laila paused, carefully choosing her words before continuing. "We discussed the birds and the bees a long time ago but . . . No need to blush, we're all women here and I am, after all, your Granny. Now," she continued, "there's something that I never mentioned before because you never seemed overly interested in any of those suitors your father threw at you. But the time has arrived to discuss it."

"What are you getting at, Granny?" the girl asked warily.

"Passion. One hot-blooded Gypsy has got enough for ten Gaje."

Fortune's mouth dropped open. "Granny!"

"Be quiet. This is important."

Shocked at her Granny's abruptness, Fortune snapped her mouth shut and listened.

"Being bonded as you are to MacNair," Laila continued, "the danger of your surrendering to your own passion is great."

"But, Granny, I don't think I . . ."

"Hear me out, Fortune, and don't get all het up. This is important woman to woman talk. You're bonded to the Reb, and if you're in the right place at the right time, even an innocent kiss could land you in his bed. Once lit, a Gypsy's passion isn't easily doused. So, you watch yourself, hear?"

Fortune nodded solemnly. She knew she was attracted to the Reb, but surely Granny must be exaggerating. Besides, even if what Granny said were true, there shouldn't be too much to worry about. She was only one-quarter Gypsy.

"Well, old woman," Ursula grinned at Laila, "if yo done lecturin', I wants to go have a look-see at dis here heavenly hellhole we come to."

"Good idea, Ursula." Laila grinned. "I'm all out of purple yarn. Let's put all this worrying away and have ourselves a good time." She waved her hand through the air, shooing away their troubles as she would a pesky fly. Her myriad bracelets jangled merrily.

Fortune's gaze fastened on Granny's flashy coin jewelry. "Granny," she suggested hesitantly, "I think you might have to give up wearing your bracelets."

Laila held up her bangled arm and stared at it quizzically. "What do my pretties have to do with anything?"

"Remember, I sort of borrowed them when I went behind Southern lines with Roc. If MacNair sees all those dangling coins, his memory might be tickled."

"Ah, yes, I remember now. And you lost my favorite one. Made of real gold coins, it was. Your grandpa gave it to me soon after we first met."

Fortune lowered her eyes guiltily. "Oh, Granny, I'm sorry. I didn't know it was special to you."

Granny patted her arm. "It's all right. See?" She pointed at one of the bracelets on her arm, "I still have its mate, but if it will give you peace of mind, I guess I can refrain from wearing my pretties for a while."

The young woman visibly relaxed. "Thank you, Granny." She reached over to help her grandmother with a difficult clasp. When all the jewelry was removed Laila dropped it into her reticule, then stood, ready to embark on their foray of the town.

Moments later the three women emerged on Main Street. The sky was cloudless, and yesterday's mud was drying into deep dusty ruts. Fortune lifted her face, enjoying the warmth of the sun.

"Gal, git yo nose out of de air," Ursula admonished. "Yo gonna trip over somethin' and break yo kadoolie."

Fortune giggled at the expression referring to her posterior. She'd been eight years old before she realized that there were other names for her backside besides *kadoolie*. Her mother had never allowed anyone to mention that part of the anatomy by name, saying it was just too crude.

Knowing Granny and Laila would help solve the Grady MacNair problem, Fortune threw one arm around the old black woman and gave her a squeeze.

"Now quit dat," Ursula admonished, shrugging her off. "We got us some serious shoppin' ta do. I got no time for yo shenanigans."

Fortune grinned and nudged her way between the two older women. Just to be ornery, she wrapped her arms about each woman's waist and gathered them in for a quick, stout hug.

"Ugh!" Ursula grunted. "Once a hooligan, always a hooligan, I say."

By midafternoon, Fortune and the two old ladies had inspected practically every shop in town. The stationer's shop was Fortune's personal favorite. What it lacked in selection of writing paper, it made up for in books.

Ursula was rather fond of hats and found one she simply could not do without. Not surprisingly though, Granny wasn't having any luck finding her purple yarn. It never occurred to the old dear that there wasn't much call for purple yarn in Helena, Montana.

"We ain't been in dat one," Ursula said pointing across the street. "Maybe they got Laila's yarn in dere."

Laila nodded in eager agreement and started to step down into the street.

Fortune took one glance at the sign over the mercantile, grabbed both women's arms and hauled them back onto the boardwalk. "I think not," she stated firmly. "Look at who owns that store."

"So?" Granny said, reading the sign. "Ursula and I will protect you. And if we're to work up a spell to break the enchantment we need to at least know what the man looks like."

While it was possible that Granny was right about needing to meet MacNair, Fortune wasn't fooled one whit. All Granny really cared about at the moment was finding that purple yarn.

Inhaling deeply, the young woman started to smooth her chignon. She stopped short, silently upbraiding herself. Was she primping for that man? Disgusted, she flounced across the dusty street after Granny and Ursula.

Clyde Sheety and Deke Tunney stood across the street and watched as the three women entered the mercantile. "Is that purdy gal the one?" Clyde whispered unnecessarily.

"Yeah," Deke Tunney replied. "Looks a fancy piece, don't she?" He spat out a wad of tobacco juice. "But I know different."

"You sure it's her, Deke? She don't look like no Gypsy I ever heard tell of."

Deke grabbed his companion by the shirt front. "Dimwit, you ain't never even seen a Gypsy so how would you know? I say it's her, and it is." He shoved the smaller man away with disgust and focused on the women. "It was on account of her and that brother of hers that my brother, Cal, died in that stinkin' prison, and I got me this," he said, rapping his wooden leg on the boardwalk. "They're gonna pay a mighty high price for what they done."

"But Deke, they weren't the ones what shot you in the leg, was they?"

"No, but it was cuz of them that it happened. I already kilt the varmint that shot me and the sawbones that hacked my leg off, too."

"What you gonna do now, Deke? Kill 'em both? Cuz if you are, I sure wouldn't mind havin' me some of what's under that fancy dress afore you do. I ain't never had me a woman that fine."

Deke Tunny glanced down at Clyde with little emotion. What brains Clyde had were in his britches. A couple years back Deke had saved his worthless scalp from the Sioux, and the ignorant bastard had followed him around ever since. But that suited him just fine because for as little as a bottle of whiskey and an occasional woman, Clyde would slice a man's throat, quick as lightning.

"I ain't gonna kill 'em outright," Deke told his partner. "The rest of the men are in this for the money, but I want them Landrys to suffer, just like I did."

"Does that mean I get ta have the woman?" Clyde asked, eagerly rubbing his crotch. "I know how to make a woman suffer long and hard."

"Yeah, sure. Soon as I'm done with 'er. Now, go tell Joe to get that carriage ready. No sense waitin' to commence the sufferin'." He chuckled evilly.

The bell on the mercantile door tinkled as the women passed over the threshold, and Fortune blinked, adjusting her eyes to the dim interior. A combination of disappointment and relief washed over her when she realized Grady MacNair was nowhere in sight.

Instead, a tall, gangly young man with freckles stood behind a counter. "What can I do you for, ladies?" he said with puppy-dog eagerness.

"We'd just like to browse a little, sir," Fortune replied.

"You're welcome to, ma'am. My name is Angus McPheany. If you need anythin' just holler."

"Thank you, Mr. McPheany. We'll do that," Fortune told him, smiling.

So, she thought, glancing around the store, this is Grady MacNair's place. She did a slow turn, inhaling the rich aroma of tobacco and leather pleasantly blended with that of coffee, cheese, dried fruits and pickled fish. Every nook and cranny was filled to capacity.

On one side of the room was a counter of groceries and behind it a door Fortune assumed led to a storeroom. On the opposite wall she saw shelves piled high with dry goods. Hardware hung from hooks on the wall, and above her head, hanging from the rafters were hams, slabs of bacon, cooking pots and lanterns. Standing on the hardwood floor about the room were brimming barrels of sugar, flour, vinegar and molasses.

Fortune noted large glass jars of hard candy strategically placed by the cash register where a tired whiny child would plague his mother for some as she paid her bill.

In the center of the store was a large unlit potbellied stove. She pictured miners cozied up to its warmth, sharing the latest gossip during the cold winter months. Grady MacNair, she decided, was indeed an astute businessman.

Standing at the yard-goods table, Ursula's turbaned head was bent over some bright solids and prints. Granny made a sound of delight, and Fortune glanced over to find her hugging several skeins of red yarn.

"It's not the purple I'd hoped for," Laila said, "but I'm just as fond of red. It will do."

Fortune smiled and was about to pick up a lovely comb when she felt a prickle down her spine. She slowly pivoted.

Grady MacNair stood framed in the doorway of the store-room. It was uncanny, the way she'd sensed him before seeing him. She'd never experienced such a thing with any other man. Could he have been the reason she'd had that strange feeling of portent on entering town yesterday? It was possible; they were bonded, after all.

One corner of the Reb's mouth lifted in a lazy smile of greeting. Then the audacious devil winked, and to her horror, she felt herself blushing.

MacNair's eyes never left off his casual perusal as he sauntered further into the room. "Good afternoon, Miss Landry. I'm pleased that you stopped by—surprised, but pleased." He stepped close and lowered his head near hers. "Would I be remiss in nurturing the hope that you've forgiven last night's transgressions?" he whispered next to her ear.

One of Fortune's dark brows winged up. *The rake! Butter wouldn't melt in the man's mouth, but, oh Lord, it was such a nice mouth.* She remembered his warm lips against the palm of her hand the previous night and couldn't help wondering what it would be like to have those lips touch hers. The illicit daydream made her body throb with the excitement of the utterly forbidden.

She gave herself a mental shake. What was wrong with her? *Sweet Gaia,* she thought, *was Granny right about Gypsy passion? Well, forewarned was forearmed,* she told herself determinedly. Not for a minute would she let herself be taken in by this Reb!

Her hands played nervously over the skirt of simple beige calico until she finally managed to find her tongue and reply to his sally. "I simply brought my grandmother and her companion in to shop, Mr. MacNair. Nothing more."

"Is this the young man you were telling me about?" Granny broke in, sidling up to the couple.

Thankful for the interruption, Fortune detached her gaze from MacNair's amused one. "Yes, Granny," she said, "this is Mr. MacNair, Roc's new partner. Mr. MacNair, this is my grandmother, Mrs. Laila Fontaine, and this lady," she indicated Ursula who had joined them, "is Miss Ursula Price."

Laila's smile was warm as she offered her hand to the Reb. Lifting it, he bent his head and kissed the air near it in a gentlemanly fashion.

Fortune's eyes widened as Ursula's hand shot out and plucked a couple of hairs from the back of MacNair's bent head.

The Reb popped up, a befuddled expression on his face. He reached a hand to his nape and frowned questioningly at Ursula.

Her answering smile was all innocence as she snatched up

his hand and shook it. "How-de-do, Reb!"

Fortune smothered a giggle.

MacNair still looked confused but shrugged and smiled back. "Miss Price," he said politely, "it's a pleasure."

Laila's hand fluttered to her chest, her smile almost coquettish. "Is that a bit of a Scotch accent I detect, Mr. MacNair?" she twittered.

Fortune glanced away for a second time and covered her twitching mouth. Granny was playing her part to the hilt.

The Reb's face broke into a boyish grin. "Yes, ma'am. Actually it's a combination of Scotch and Irish. My mother was as pure Irish as my father was pure Scottish."

Granny chortled at that. "Must have made for a lively relationship, hey, sonny?"

Sonny? Granny never called anyone sonny.

"Aye, me laidy, make no mistake o' that," MacNair replied, laughing.

Good grief, Fortune thought vehemently. *He really is a ladies' man of the first water!*

"Miss Landry?"

Fortune started and glanced up at him. "Sorry, Mr. MacNair, I guess I was woolgathering."

"I was just wondering if you'd allow me the chance to redeem myself. I'd like to call on you sometime, if that's all right."

"Oh, I . . . that is, my brother . . . he wouldn't like . . ."

"So nice of you to make the offer, sir," Granny interrupted, "but we're leaving for my grandson's ranch tomorrow. Perhaps another time, hm?"

MacNair opened his mouth to reply but shut it as the door slammed open so hard that it bounced off the wall. A grimy boy of about 12 strutted in holding onto the hand of an equally grimy little girl wearing torn britches.

"You git, Book Tabor," Angus yelled at the boy. "You ain't comin' in here no more and stealing crackers out of the barrel." He halted his tirade and wrinkled his nose in distaste. "Whew! Where you young'uns been anyway? Looks and smells like you been rootin' with them pigs up the street."

The boy scowled. "It ain't no never mind of yers, iffin' I'm dirty, you 'ol freckle-faced pickle puss," he snarled. "My ma sent me for some flour."

"Yeah," the female mite in pigtails asserted. "We wants fouer!" Then as if in afterthought, "Peaz!"

Fortune smiled and noted that Grady MacNair was trying hard not to laugh.

"You got money, boy?" Angus asked, oblivious to his boss's amusement.

"Ma said put it on the bill."

"Can't do that," Angus said. "She ain't paid 'er bill since that no-good pa of yours up and ran out on 'er two months back."

Fortune couldn't help herself. She stepped forward like a protective mama hen. "Mr. McPheany," she admonished, "is it necessary to speak ill of these children's father in front of them?"

Angus glanced at his sober-faced boss then back at his pretty adversary. "These ragamuffins is always runnin' round causing trouble, miss. And their ma ain't paid her bill. It's considerable, too."

"Fouer, peaz!" the little girl demanded again. When her brother gave her thin little arm a jerk and hissed something into her ear, the female urchin stuck her tongue out at him.

Grady subdued the smile tugging on his own lips. "It's all right, Angus. I've made special arrangements with Mrs. Tabor. See to it the children have what they came for."

The boy threw Grady a grateful glance then flung the grumbling clerk an I-told-you-so sneer.

Grady turned his attention back to the ladies. "I was wondering if . . ."

"Hey, come back here, you little sneak!" Angus yelled.

Fortune, Granny, Ursula and MacNair looked up in surprise as all hell broke loose.

The pigtailed Tabor shrieked with delight, kicked Angus in the shins and shoved her brother down as she scrambled toward the door with a handful of hard candy.

Cursing, Angus limped after the child, stepping over the boy and a split bag of flour.

Fortune darted past the clerk, not so much in an attempt to catch the candy thief as to protect her from Angus.

The child dashed off the boardwalk into the busy street with Fortune right behind her. Neither female heard Angus's alarmed warning or saw the careening carriage that suddenly launched out of nowhere.

There were shouts; a woman screamed. Fortune sensed the danger in time to hurtle her body, arms outstretched, toward the child.

The horse whinnied shrilly, reared and pawed the air. As the ground came up to meet her, Fortune felt a sharp pain lance through her forehead. Then the world went black.

"The lady saved the kid's life," someone commented.

Grim-faced, Grady shoved through the milling crowd and knelt to gently examine Fortune Landry's crumpled form. Finding only a small laceration on her forehead, he gathered her with great care into his arms and carried her into the mercantile. The little Tabor girl shuffled along behind him, her chin resting on her chest.

Grady couldn't take his eyes from Fortune Landry's still features. Streaked with dirt, her face was turned into his broad chest. Thick black lashes brushed her pale cheeks and her long raven hair hung unraveled over his arm. *My God, but she's beautiful!* He sucked in a ragged breath, trying to ignore the press of her soft breasts against his chest and his body's passionate reaction. Now wasn't the time for such inappropriate emotions.

Though blood oozed into her hairline from the injury, Grady had seen enough head injuries during the war to know that this one wasn't serious. Still, his heart wrenched at the sight of her wound, and he pulled her closer to his body, wishing he could somehow absorb her pain. In his concern, he didn't once question his intense emotions.

When he entered the shop Grady noted at once Laila Fontaine's ashen pallor. "It's just a scratch, ma'am," he told her, "not nearly as bad as it looks."

Both old women followed Grady up the stairs to his living quarters. He gently laid the girl on his bed, careful to preserve her modesty by straightening her skirts over her slim legs.

The little Tabor girl had followed at a wary distance and now scrubbed at her tearful dirty cheeks. "Dead!" she sobbed. "Dead."

"Naw, honey chile," Ursula said taking the child aside. "She ain't dead. She'll be jus fine."

Laila moved closer and hovered over her granddaughter. Grady backed away, feeling a bit awkward. "I'll fetch water and clean cloths and send someone for Doc Holly, Mrs. Fontaine."

He hurried down the stairs then, ordering Angus to fetch the doctor as he headed for the water pump out back.

"Tabor boy already went after the doc," Angus called after him. "They ought to be back any minute."

When Grady returned upstairs, Laila Fontaine had loosened Fortune's dress collar. He set the basin of water on the bedside table, then pressed the distressed little woman into a chair. His smile was kind, but his voice firm. "Please sit, ma'am. You're as pale as a ghost, and I don't think I could handle two unconscious ladies."

He dipped the cloth into the water and with infinite care cleansed the dirt and blood from the cut on Fortune's head. Laila slid her chair back, silently and very curiously watching his gentle ministrations.

Grady's big hands trembled as he cupped the young woman's fine-boned face with one hand and tenderly examined the scratch with the other. She felt so damn fragile. His stomach rolled at the thought of her narrow escape. *If it's the last thing I do, I'll find the irresponsible bastard who did this to her,* he vowed to himself. Fortune's eyes fluttered opened, and his hand froze. "Welcome back," he said, smiling down at her.

She blinked up at him, confused. Grady stepped back so that she could see her grandmother.

"Granny?" Her eyes flew wide, and she bolted upright. "The child!" she gasped. Clutching at her head, she collapsed back onto the pillows.

"Hush now, Fortune. The child isn't hurt, thanks to you," Laila soothed. She beckoned the little girl to her side.

At Ursula's urging, the girl moved haltingly until she reached the bed. "Dere now, you see," the black woman soothed the sobbing urchin. "De pretty lady ain't dead. She's jus been sleepin'."

Fortune smiled at the little girl before her gaze wandered back to Grady. She lifted her fingers and winced when they contacted with the cut on her head. "What happened?"

"You're very lucky, Miss Landry," he answered. "When you and the girl ran out in front of that carriage, the driver managed to rein in just in time. The horse reared up and one of its hooves glanced off your forehead."

"That driver oughtta be hoss whipped," Ursula put in, edging closer to the bed. "He mustta been drunk, drivin' like a madman through de middle of town like dat."

"Where's the driver now?" Fortune asked. "Was he hurt?"

"Don't waste your strength worrying about that bas . . . that man," Grady said. "The polecat spun that carriage around and hightailed it in the opposite direction. A few men took out after him, but I doubt if they caught him. He was striking a bullwhip at anyone who got too close. But don't worry. I aim to find out who was driving that carriage."

Surprised at his vehemence, Fortune laid her hand on his arm. "It's all right, Mr. MacNair, I'm sure it was an accident, and the man regrets his carelessness."

Grady thought to remind her that if the man were truly remorseful he'd have returned to apologize and ask after her welfare. But he held his peace. She'd been through enough for one day. He glanced toward the doorway then as Doc Holly thumped up the stairs and into the room.

"Dang it," the doctor wheezed. "I'm getting entirely too old to run like that." The short rotund man smiled kindly at Fortune. "You must be my patient. Glad to see you awake, young woman. It's a good sign. Book Tabor said you and a horse had a run-in." Doc Holly nodded to Ursula and Laila. "If one of you ladies would care to stay and assist, the rest of you can clear outta here while I make sure this young lady has no broken bones."

Ursula took the little girl by the hand. "Me and this young'un will go see iffin we can find Roc," she told Fortune. "I reckon you better ride back in de carriage to de hotel."

Grady turned to leave but was pulled up short when Fortune caught his hand. "Thank you," she said, staring at the blood-stained cloth in his hand.

The dimple in his chin deepened as he smiled and executed a deep bow. "Always glad to be of service to a damsel in distress."

He straightened and followed Ursula and the little girl to the door. But before descending the stairs he granted himself one last look at the beautiful woman on his bed. He knew very little about her, but in that moment Grady made up his mind. Fortune Landry would be his!

Chapter Four

Fortune could hardly contain her excitement. After two days of enforced bed rest, she was finally on her way to Roc's ranch, her new home. Dressed in a plain yellow shirtwaist, dark green riding skirt and boots, she reached down and patted the neck of her sleek black mare. Roc had given her the animal early that morning, and Fortune knew the mare was prime horseflesh. If there was one thing her brother knew well, it was horses, and this fine animal was strength and beauty in motion.

Riding alongside her brother, she followed his gaze as he glanced over his shoulder and checked the progress of the slow-moving wagon behind them. One of Roc's freighters handled the reins while Granny and Ursula sat on either side of him, chattering.

"Have you decided on a name for the mare?" Roc asked, swinging round in his saddle.

Fortune grinned. "Uh huh, thought of a perfect name."

Hearing the mischief in his sister's voice, Roc's expression was amused and wary. "Nothing weird, I hope."

52

She flung him a sisterly look of disgust. "I named her Magic."

"Oh," he said, "that's not too bad." At her continued scowl, he laughed. "Well, with a dog called Grumpy in the family, you can hardly blame me for expecting the worst."

They laughed together then, and Fortune rejoiced in the sound of it. It was so good being with Roc again. They might not agree on the validity of magic but they'd shared too many adventures together to let anything ever come between them.

They rode along silently a while, Fortune taking in the beautiful scenery around them. Roc had exaggerated Helena's attributes but hadn't overstated the breathtaking beauty of the Montana territory.

Mountain streams, clear and cold, abounded. The bright green slopes were generously sprinkled with lavender lupine, wild, yellow daises and purple violets. Paintbrush and asters sprang up between immense boulders. And all around, looming like white-haired guardian angels, were the magnificent Rockies.

"Fortune," Roc interrupted her reverie, "there's something we need to discuss."

She cocked her head to one side. "You sound so serious," she teased.

"Yeah, well, that's because I am. Remember that business I had to take care of a couple mornings back?" At her nod he continued. "It was with the Reb. He offered to give me back half of his fifty percent interest in the freighting company."

"What? But that's wonderful, Roc. Why would he want to do such a thing? And why such a glum face? I would think you'd be happy."

"Sure, but MacNair didn't make the offer out of any liking for me," Roc said sarcastically. "As you might guess, there's a catch. That damn Reb came up with a business deal, and though I hate to admit it, it's a damn good one. I'd be a fool not to take him up on it."

"Then what's stopping you?"

Roc stared off down the road. "You."

"Me?" Fortune exclaimed. "What do I have to with it?"

"Let me explain the offer before I go into that. Then you'll understand. The Reb wants me to take twenty-five percent of the freight interest back and invest its value to finance half of a new mercantile in Fort Benton. He'd finance his share of the new operation with the bank."

"A sweet deal for him," Fortune commented wryly. "He retains twenty-five percent ownership in the freight business, gains fifty percent ownership in a new mercantile and risks none of his own money. And he'd get a bigger return on the goods sold in both shops because he'll save on freighting costs.

"On the other hand," she continued, "your seventy-five percent of the freighting company allows you to wield the greater power in the running of the company. Also, the goods sold in Fort Benton will yield you a healthier profit. Instead of the usual smaller wholesale profit, you'll receive retail. In a sense, you'd both eliminate the middleman."

Roc studied her with surprise and no little pride. "Not bad, my clever sister. Granny told me how well you managed the sale of the horse farm, but I had no idea you were so savvy. Quite a little businesswoman I've just taken for a partner." He grinned.

"Did you say partner? I thought I was merely a bookkeeper."

"Making you a partner is the least I can do if this deal goes through because a lot depends on you."

"And why is that?"

Roc cleared his throat, obviously uncomfortable. "First, promise to hear me out and don't interrupt." At her slow nod he continued. "I want this deal, but before I lend my name to paper next to MacNair's, I need to know what kind of businessman he is. I'd like you to go over his mercantile accounts."

"That doesn't sound like much of a problem. You can bring his accounting to me, and I can go over everything in your office at the warehouse or out at the ranch."

Roc grimaced and pulled a little too tight on his steed's reins. The animal threw back its head and pranced a couple steps sideways. Easing back, he brought the horse under control.

"I take it there *is* a problem," she said warily.

"Yeah. You see, MacNair tells me he's a lousy bookkeeper and that his books are slapdash at best."

"Just how bad are they?"

Roc shrugged. "I haven't seen them, but I'm counting on you to put them to rights and give me a report."

Fortune reined Magic off the road and came to a dead stop. "If his accounting is a shambles, I'll have to work very closely with him. Roc, you promised me I'd not have to have anything to do with MacNair."

"Hold on there, Sis. I don't like the idea any more than you do, but I need you with me on this."

"Hire another bookkeeper, Roc. I won't do it."

"Aw, Fortune, the least you could do is give it a try. Besides, in auditing MacNair's business, you'll learn something about the mercantile trade. And if I'm going to be in the business that's important. That's why I . . ."

"Why you made me a partner," the girl finished for him. "Seems to me, MacNair isn't the only one that makes offers with a catch."

"All right, I admit it, but if he's as lousy at keeping books as he intimates, you'll have to keep the books for the Fort Benton store, too. That is, providing I take him up on his offer." Roc tipped his hat lower on his forehead and adjusted his stiff leg in the special stirrup Slim had rigged for him. "I know it means more work than what you counted on, Fortune. I thought, though, that the partnership might compensate you."

"Great crystal balls and tea leaves, Roc! You're throwing me into the lion's den."

"Fortune," Roc pleaded, "please?"

"You know, brother, sometimes I could just slap you."

She sighed resignedly and stared at the hard ground beneath her. She had agreed to come to the territory to help, hadn't she? *Yes,* said a little voice, *but you didn't count on running into Grady MacNair, let alone on having to work side by side with the man.*

Roc needs you, she told herself. *You'll just have to be strong.* When Grumpy trotted up between Rock and Fortune's horses an idea occurred to her. Gran and Ursula would have to work faster and harder to find a spell to break the bond, but in the meantime, she had Grumpy. The only man the dog tolerated was Roc. MacNair wouldn't get within five feet of her with Grumpy at her side.

Feeling a little better she focused on Roc. "If not for the fact that it's in your best interest to retain the controlling share of the freighting company, I'd refuse to do this," she stated.

"Then you'll help?" he asked, a hopeful smile blooming on his dusky face.

"Yes, I'll do it. But if MacNair's memory is triggered or something else goes wrong and he withdraws the offer, don't try laying the blame at my door."

"Nothing bad is going to happen, Sis," he assured her. "I promise."

Fortune shivered, remembering Granny's warning about Gypsy passion. *Oh, if he only knew what could happen!* Being cooped up with Grady MacNair's seductive charm for several weeks could very well ignite an already highly flammable situation. *Well, if I have to, I'll just tie Grumpy to my leg.*

"What's going on here?" Granny called as the wagon caught up to Fortune and Roc. "Something wrong?"

"No, Gran." Fortune smiled back. "Roc was just pointing out a few of the sights."

Following Roc's lead, Fortune nudged her horse onto the road and turned her mind back to her new home.

Nestled in a cool grove of aspens, the L-shaped log ranch house resembled something out of one of Granny's fairy tales. Fortune's mother would have called it crude, but for the Gypsy girl, who had grown up on folklore and tales of enchanted cottages, it was love at first sight.

While the wagon driver helped Roc down from his horse, Fortune tied Magic to the hitching post in front of the house. Grumpy sidled up to her, gave her hand a generous lick, then rested on his haunches as if he too wanted to inspect the place.

"Mmm," Ursula said, as she and Laila joined Fortune, "dat's one fine house."

Fortune nodded absently as her gaze wandered over the structure. A porch spanned the narrow front of the house and wrapped around the inside of the L. A stone chimney ran up the north side with two more rising from the back of the house.

To the left and separated by a clump of trees was a longer rectangular building that Fortune assumed was a bunkhouse. The stables, corrals and a large carriage house were strategically situated far enough from the living facilities to be inoffensive. Beyond the outbuildings lay a grassy pasture supporting a large herd of mules and a few horses.

At Grumpy's growl, Fortune glanced up to see several freighters emerging from the bunkhouse. She recognized most of them from her recent trek from Fort Benton. Talking soothingly to her pet, she smiled and waved at the men. They did the same before heading off toward the pasture.

"What are you waiting for?" Roc chuckled coming up behind the women. "Go look inside."

The stark nudity of the sitting room gave Fortune pause. Not so much as a rug graced the dusty pinewood floor. Nor were there any curtains at the smudged windows. Only the huge stone fireplace on the north wall broke the rustic austerity of the room.

Roc followed behind the three women, an anxious expression on his face. "I'm afraid I'm not much of a hand at decorating," he apologized. "Mostly, I live in the kitchen or out of my bedroom."

Aware how very much Roc wanted them to love his home, Fortune gave his arm an affectionate squeeze. "It's lovely, Roc. And it's very considerate of you to wait and let the three of us have the fun of decorating it."

"Oh my, yes!" Laila added happily. "I'll set my rocker on the braided rug I brought along right there in front of the fireplace."

"Well, come on," Ursula prodded, "let's have a look at de rest of de place."

The sitting room narrowed into a smaller dining area. "Oh, that's the perfect spot for my rosewood china cupboard," Laila commented, pointing to a vacant corner. "Too bad I couldn't bring my dining table. Ah well, in time, in time. Is that where the bedrooms are, Roc?" she asked indicating a hall off the dining room.

"Yes, there are four. I'll show them to you. Each of the bedrooms has a rear door onto the back porch," he added, leading them down the hall.

The first three bedrooms were bare with the exception of a small single bed in the first one and a fireplace in the second. "This is my room," Roc said, stepping inside the fourth and largest. It had a fireplace and was furnished with a large brass bed, a chest of drawers and a desk. But like the rest of the house, the windows were curtainless.

"We're going to have to do something about obtaining more beds," Fortune told her brother as they moved back up the hall.

"Taken care of." He smiled smugly. "After leaving you ladies at the hotel that first day, I headed straight over to Olaf Jorgensen's Furniture and Carpentry and ordered two more big beds. We were lucky. Olaf had one of the beds on hand. He said he and his sons could have another finished for us in a few days."

"Don't worry about the sleeping arrangements," Fortune said. "For now, we can use our bedrolls. The three of us got quite used to them on the trip from Fort Benton."

Roc scowled. "Fortune, you wound a man's sense of honor. I'll not have any of you sleeping on the floor. I'll sleep in the bunkhouse with the boys. Granny and Ursula can share my big bed, and you can take the smaller one in the first bedroom."

"All right, but only if it doesn't pain your leg."

"It'll be fine. Hell, this splint is due to come off soon anyway."

"Can we see the kitchen now?" Laila asked. "It's probably where we women will spend most of our time."

The kitchen was a nightmare!

A large rectangular table, big enough to accommodate at least 12 big men, sat squarely in the middle of the room. Stools and chairs were scattered around it, some tipped over. The tabletop looked as if it hadn't been wiped clean in an age, and at one end dirty tin plates and cups were stacked high. The countertops on either side of a dry basin were likewise hidden beneath an array of dirty pots and pans.

Ursula checked out the stove in one corner, her interested expression deteriorating to one of revulsion. "Hell fire, boy, dere must be a pound a grease on dis here stove. Don' nobody ever clean it?"

Roc shrugged. "I leave that to Nubbins Smith. He cooks for me and the men. Guess the kitchen isn't something I ever give much thought to except when I'm hungry."

"Leave it to a man," Laila said, shaking her head. "No furniture, no rugs, no curtains, but he doesn't forget about filling his belly!"

Roc tried in vain to hide his smile. "I'm sorry about the mess, Granny," he said. "I'll get Nubbins in here to clean it up."

As they turned to have a look out back of the house, Fortune discovered a small well-stocked pantry next to the back door. "Well, at least we won't go hungry." She smiled cheerfully.

"Don' matter none ta me," Ursula grumbled. "I ain't eatin' nothin' outta dis here kitchen till it's done cleaned up good." So saying she stepped out on the back porch.

"Look," Laila exclaimed with pleasure as she joined Ursula, "the porch runs the whole length of the back of the house."

"And dere be a good place for a garden on de edge of them woods," Ursula pointed out.

"Ursula and I brought our herb seedlings with us, Roc," Laila explained. "You don't mind if we plant them along with a vegetable garden, do you?"

"Of course not, Granny." He slung his arm around her narrow shoulders. "This is your home now. You can damn well do any damn thing you want here. No one is going to tell you otherwise. Not even me. You're the boss."

Fortune saw the tears well up in Granny's eyes and felt a lump in her own throat. After Granny had moved in with her daughter, Tshaya had let her mother know in no uncertain terms that she was intruding and would have to abide by *her* rules. The old lady had never really said so, but Fortune knew she'd been deeply hurt.

Fortune lifted her gaze to the distant horizon. An enchanted cottage on the edge of an enchanted forest surrounded by mystical mountains. *Yes*, she thought, *it feels like home*.

Chapter Five

Grady MacNair left the main road and turned down the narrower trail to the Landry place. It hadn't been difficult getting the directions, not with half of Landry's freighters in town drinking the saloons dry. The ranch was only a half hour from town by horseback. Convenient, since he hoped to return to Helena this afternoon with Miss Fortune Landry in tow.

Grady had met with Roc in town yesterday and learned that Fortune had agreed to audit the mercantile books. Now, he not only had a foot in the doorway of a profitable business deal but in the lady's door as well.

After the meeting with Landry, Grady had hurried back to his mercantile to hide his neat and precise ledgers in his private quarters over the store. Then he dug out a box of neatly bundled and dated records that already had been recorded in those ledgers. It had taken all of five minutes to dissemble the bundles, toss the loose papers like a salad and heap them back into the box.

He chuckled to himself. It would take a great deal of time to sort out the jumble, time he planned to spend wooing Fortune

60

Landry. The tactic would make for only a minor delay in the building of the new store in Fort Benton, but it would aid his courtship plans immensely.

Ever since the carriage accident, he'd stumbled around in a lusty daze. He couldn't even go to his room at night without remembering how Fortune had looked on his bed.

Last night had been another sleepless night, so this morning he decided to take matters into his own hands. He'd fetch the little lady back to town himself and, once there, commence courting her good and proper.

The air was redolent with the scent of living green things. A gentle breeze frolicked in the treetops, the soft flapping of leaves sounding remarkably like the patter of rain. Standing at the river's edge, Fortune dug her toes into the spongy earth and lazily swatted at a pesky fly.

She'd been at the ranch three days now and each one grew hotter than the preceding one, but here in the woods it was quiet and many degrees cooler. It was cooler yet when a girl wore absolutely nothing beneath her outer garments.

Feeling deliciously wicked, Fortune scooped the hem of her faded red skirt and tucked it into her waistband. Then she waded into the water, gasping at the first chilly rush over her bare legs. Splashing water over her thighs, she cared little that her skirt was getting spattered as well. It was pure heaven, and she wished that she'd brought a towel so that she might discard her clothes and go for a swim.

Retracing her steps to the rocky shore, she knelt down and palmed water over her face, allowing it to trickle beneath the neck of the loose peasant-style shirt Granny had made her. Then noting that the ends of her loose hair were getting wet she slowly stood, sorry to quit the enjoyable pursuit.

Fortune chose a grassy spot under a tree, sat down and leaned back against its smooth white bark. A tiny wood spider crawled over her toe and disappeared in the grass. She smiled. For a Gypsy to see a wood spider outside was especially good luck. Glad for this private moment, she raised her knees and let the bulk of her skirt bunch in her lap so that her legs could dry in the gentle breeze.

The past days had been busy with unpacking and setting up housekeeping. During the hubbub of activity Roc escaped back to town to meet a freight train due in from Salt Lake City. Fortune knew he also planned to talk business with MacNair, but she didn't want to think about that or anything else right now. She'd come for a peaceful moment alone.

Her eyes drooped closed as she listened to the forest's ambience—the trilling birds, the soft skitter of a chipmunk up a tree, the perambulating of a bee.

Grady drew his dark bay gelding to a halt before the Landry ranch house and dismounted. Tossing the reins over the hitching post, he climbed the porch steps by twos. The front door was propped open so he knocked on the frame. "Hello, anybody home?" No answer.

A wiry, little sawed-off fellow ambled around the corner of the house. "Hey there, stranger," he said, stopping to tilt his tattered hat back on his head, "you lookin' for the ladies?"

Grady pivoted and tipped his hat to the old man. "Sure am. I'm Grady MacNair. Came to call on Miss Landry. Is she about, Mr. . . . ?"

"Smith, Nubbins Smith." The old man scratched vigorously at something under his shirt. "Last I recall, I saw Miss Landry headin' down to the river. Her grandmother and that crabby old black woman be out back in the garden."

"Much obliged, Mr. Smith." Grady smiled. "If it's all right, I'll just take a gander around the house here and go find Miss Landry."

"Makes no nevermind to me. It's them two old ladies out back you gotta watch out for." Without bothering to explain his comment, Nubbins Smith shuffled off toward the bunkhouse.

Grady left the porch, cursing his luck. He supposed he'd have to run the gauntlet past the two old women before he got the chance to talk to Fortune alone. When he reached the back corner of the house he heard the women's voices growing louder as they approached. Engrossed in their argument, neither saw him standing there.

Quicker than a fox with a hound on its tail, Grady slipped back in the shade and flattened himself against the rough-hewn logs. As soon as the old ladies disappeared inside, he darted across the open yard and into the woods. A triumphant grin on his face, he stopped just inside the wooded shelter to catch his breath.

In no time, Grady found a well-worn path that he accurately guessed would lead him to the river. Out of habit from his soldiering days, he moved through the trees without a sound. He spotted Fortune through a break in the foliage and froze at the fleeting sight of long, shapely legs disappearing beneath her skirt.

He watched mesmerized as the young woman's head turned this way and that as if listening. He hadn't made a sound and she couldn't possibly see him, yet it was obvious she sensed she was no longer alone.

Dispensing with stealth, he brushed limbs aside and burst into the clearing. "There you are," he said, smiling. "Mr. Smith told me I'd find you here."

Fortune started but not because he'd surprised her. No, she'd awakened somehow knowing he was near, but she'd forgotten how handsome he was.

A sun-streaked lock tumbled over Grady MacNair's forehead as he politely removed his hat. His blue plaid shirt emphasized the breadth of his strong, square shoulders and the black silk scarf at his neck was tied at a jaunty angle. The lethal weapon strapped low on his denim-clad hips banished the benign shop-keeper and lent MacNair an air of danger.

Suddenly Fortune felt very feminine and very vulnerable. She started to rise. "Mr. MacNair, I . . ."

"No, please, don't get up," he interrupted, waving her down. "I'll join you. And please, let's dispense with the formalities. We are, after all, business partners. Call me Grady."

Leaning back against the tree, Fortune strived for nonchalance as she nodded her assent.

Grady made himself comfortable, squatting down beside her and crossing his legs Indian style. One of his knees bumped her thigh. Instant heat shot up Fortune's leg. And had she not known he was perfectly aware of his gaffe, his devilish grin would have given him away.

Refusing to grant the Reb knowledge of his effect on her, she inched away. Unfortunately, the distance did little to douse the fire racing through her blood.

Grady swallowed hard, his eyes glued to the soft sway of her breasts beneath the loose shirt as she scooted away. *Damn, she was naked under there!* On the heels of this thought came the reminder that he *had* intruded on her privacy. And from the looks of her damp hair, she'd obviously sought that privacy to bathe.

"I'm sorry if I caught you at a bad time," he said, "but there's something I . . ." He interrupted himself, lifting his nose to the air. "Lord, you smell good, woman. Like flowers and sunshine. What do you call that perfume?"

"It hasn't a name, really," Fortune replied self-consciously. "Granny makes it special for me." *And I'll be careful not to wear it again around you,* she silently added. The man didn't need any further encouragement.

"Kind of sneaks up on a fellow, real tantalizing like, if you know what I mean," MacNair drawled with a suggestive grin.

Fortune sniffed primly. "I'm sure I don't care to even guess at your meaning, Mr. MacNair. You should go. It's highly improper for the two of us to be here alone."

"Grady," he corrected. "We agreed, remember?"

"All right. Grady."

Her icy tone cooled Grady's ardor a little and reminded him of his purpose for coming. "I talked to your brother yesterday, and he told me that you've agreed to have a go at my accounts."

"Oh, is that why you're here? You've brought your book-keeping to me?" Fortune asked, sounding relieved.

"No. Wish I could." He didn't blink an eye at the lie. *All's fair in love and war,* he silently vowed. "It would be darn foolishness to haul that mess all the way out here. I'd like you to get started as soon as possible, though. That's why I'm here. I was hoping you'd accompany me back to town this afternoon."

"My brother wouldn't like that at all."

A wicked gleam in his eye, Grady leaned close. "Do you always do what big brother says, like a good little girl?"

"Of course not," she blustered. Then her face was awash in embarrassed astonishment. "You're deliberately baiting me, aren't you? You thought I'd jump on a horse and follow you to town just to prove my independence. Well, I'm not that gullible, Mr. Mac . . . Grady."

Grady's blue eyes danced. "It was worth a try, but don't worry. My motives are purely business. The sooner you finish the audit, the sooner your brother and I can set up business in Fort Benton."

Remembering how he'd kissed her palm that first night at the International, Fortune didn't believe him one whit. *But damn, that smile of his would charm a hen into a fox's den!* "I understand your eagerness to get started, but for the sake of peace and harmony in my family, I'll wait until Roc sees fit to escort me himself." *Chicken,* a little voice in her head accused. *Damn right, I'm chicken,* she silently answered.

Grady shrugged. "I guess you have to do what you feel is best." *Damn,* he thought, *she's a tough one to crack.*

He let the conversation lapse for a moment, wondering how he was going to court her with the antagonism between himself and her brother standing in the way. He'd tried the direct approach, simply asking if he might call on her, and that hadn't worked. Perhaps another tack?

"Fortune," he finally said, "I need your help. If this partnership is to work, your brother and I have to overcome our differences. What is it that Roc hates most about me? The fact that I bested him at cards, or the fact that I'm an ex-Rebel?"

Surprised by the uncomfortable turn of the conversation, Fortune was momentarily struck dumb. "Well, maybe a little of both," she finally replied.

"I can understand his anger over the card game, but it was played fair, Fortune. It's important to me that you believe that. I don't cheat. Hell, I've never had to. I've always had the luck of the Irish with cards and wo . . . with cards. As to the other," he continued quickly to cover his blunder, "I have no love for the Yanks, but for the sake of our business together I'm willing to try to get along with Roc. Can't he do the same?"

Fortune knew exactly what MacNair had been about to say but overlooked it in light of his serious question. "Roc's a fair man, Grady, but the war took its toll on him."

"The war was hard on a lot of men, Fortune," he said bitterly.

"I know," she said so softly he almost didn't hear. She searched his eyes. "Was it very terrible for you?" Under the circumstances it was a dangerous question, but one she felt compelled to ask.

Grady looked away, his expression stony. "Some had it worse. The war actually ended for me in '64. I was taken prisoner and sent to Point Lookout, Maryland—just a flat stretch of land, not a single blade of grass. My men and I existed in open tents without blankets or even a pile of hay to sleep on. The food, what there was of it, wasn't fit for pigs. A close friend of mine died for lack of proper medical treatment and proper food."

His words carried a sharp bite, reinforcing Fortune's conviction that he must never learn her and Roc's secret. "I'm sorry," she murmured.

"I was one of the luckier ones," he continued, the tension easing from his face. "I was in prison only a short time before the Yanks came looking for volunteers to fight Indians out West."

Fortune's head jerked up. "I don't understand. You mean they let you go free?"

"Not really. You might say I exchanged one kind of hell for a lesser one. You see, when the War Between the States broke out, most of the Western forts were abandoned or seriously depleted. The Cheyenne and Sioux took full advantage of the situation. Lincoln was persuaded that Confederate prisoners might be put to better use subduing the tribes than rotting in prison. Volunteers were promised they'd not have to fight fellow Southerners, so I swore an oath of allegiance and signed up with the Galvanized Yankees."

"I don't recall ever hearing about Galvanized Yankees."

"I don't imagine Rebels turned Indian fighters took any precedence over the war in Union papers. It was a rough tour of duty though. We, that is the First Regiment, nearly starved that first winter at Fort Rice. Even so, I felt better off fighting Indians than I did in that stinking prison."

"How did you come to be in Montana?" Fortune asked, fascinated with all this man had been through and overcome.

"H Company—that was me and nine other men—was detached north to Fort Benton to control the trade with the Indians between that point and Fort Union. After mustering out, I stayed on."

"You panned for gold, then?"

"Some, but I found out the real money lay in helping the miners spend it." He smiled. "Mining is a long shot, but everybody's got to eat."

He took her hand in his bigger one and adroitly turned the conversation back to its original topic. "So, how 'bout it? Will you help me smooth things out with your brother?"

"I don't know if I can."

He cocked a brow. "What is it, lass? You don't hate me too, do you?"

"Of course not," she stated softly, and she meant it with all her heart. "You were fighting for a cause you believed in. Nobody can fault you for that. But you must understand that I didn't have to watch my comrades fall under Rebel guns, like Roc did. And you said yourself that you have no love for Yankees. Be honest, Grady, can you really put the war behind you?" Fortune knew she was tempting fate again, but she couldn't help herself. She had to know how deep his resentment ran.

His thumb circled the back of her hand as he mulled over his reply. "I disagree with the North's politics," he finally said, "but I've met a few Yank soldiers who weren't so bad. I guess it's like you said. They were fighting for what they believed in." At her skeptical expression, he chuckled. "Oh, I'll admit there's a couple of Yanks I wouldn't mind getting my hands on."

"Yes?" she prompted unsteadily, trying desperately to mirror his lighter mood. "Like who?"

He shrugged and smiled. "Nobody you'd know, lass. Now, will you at least try to work on that stubborn brother of yours?"

"I'll try, Grady. But you might as well know that I've never been much good at changing Roc's mind once it was made up."

"That you'll try is all I ask." Still holding her hand, he rose and helped her to her feet. "I suppose I better get you back up to the house before someone discovers my horse out front and comes looking for us."

Fortune lowered her gaze to her hand which he still held. She tried to pull it away, but he held it fast and she gazed up at him.

Grady knew he risked ruining his chances with her by moving too fast. But damn, when she looked up at him like that, her eyes all wide and innocent . . . Well, what was a man to do, if not kiss her senseless?

He pulled her into his arms. "I'm going to kiss you, Fortune." he said, his breath warm on her lips.

Fortune made a small sound of dismay and tried to push away. His arms, though gentle, held firm. She tilted her head

back so she could look him in the eye. "I don't want you to
kiss me!"

His chuckle was low, sensual and arrogantly male. "Oh, but
you *do* want me to kiss you. There's magic between us, darlin'.
Don't deny it. I see the sparks in those lovely green eyes of
yours. I hear the catch in your breath." He kissed the pulse point
on her neck. "I feel your heart pounding, too."

He lowered his head. Fortune stiffened and turned her face
away, willing herself not to feel.

Grady's lips grazed her chin as she sought to deny him her
mouth. She felt his responding smile against her flesh as he
teased her with tender nibbles here, small tastes there, never
quite reaching her mouth. His teeth gently caught her earlobe.
"Mm-mm, sweet," he murmured against her neck.

Her breathing became erratic, and her breasts tingled where
their sensitive tips lay pressed to his chest. Her bid for freedom
grew more and more feeble. *Oh Lord,* she thought, *why can't
he be hideously repulsive?*

She inhaled sharply when his adventurous caress slid just
beneath one breast and rested there while his thumb strummed
her nipple through the thin material of her peasant blouse.

His tongue flicked over her lips then again retreated to the
sensitive curve of her neck.

Pearls of sweat broke out on Fortune's forehead. Despite all
her efforts, her treacherous body quickened with each gentle
onslaught.

The heady sensation of Grady's mouth and hands on her flesh
shattered Fortune's valiant efforts not to feel. *Not feel?* she cried
inwardly. *Sweet Gaia, every inch of me is aching with want
of his touch!* Slowly, her arms crept up his chest and locked
about his neck. Then leaning into the hard planes of his torso,
she closed her eyes and lifted her face to his, silently begging
him to kiss her as he'd promised.

The invitation was all he'd been waiting for. Grady's mouth
covered hers hungrily. He coaxed her lips apart and tasted
deeply of her sweetness. And with very little tutoring, her
tongue spiraled around his, surprising and pleasing him with
her eager response.

Fortune knew she should put an end to this madness. But
Lord, it was true what Granny said of hot-blooded Gypsies.
Even now, though newly awakened, her passion ruled her, body

and mind. She clung to Grady, her fingers sifting through his soft golden hair. Like a wild thing, she was hot and needful of what she instinctively knew only he could give. She moaned into his mouth.

The girl's abandon and the sensation of her taut breasts pressed against him sent Grady beyond all control. He grasped her behind, lifted her and edged her up against the tree. Holding her there with his body, he let her feel his rock-hard desire pressing against her.

Something on the periphery of Fortune's mind registered a discordant noise. Then she heard it, a low menacing growl. Her eyes flew open and searched the clearing. Standing a few yards away, Grumpy was poised to attack the man molesting his beloved mistress.

At her sudden inattention, Grady tilted his head back and scanned Fortune's face. Seeing her fear and misjudging the cause, he cursed himself and immediately slacked his hold.

"No!" She clutched him fiercely to her. "Don't let go of me. Not yet."

"What . . . ?"

Grumpy growled again, louder. Grady slowly turned his head. The sight of viciously curled canine lips over razor-sharp teeth instantly quelled his passion. "Jesus!" he hissed, not daring to move. "I hope you're on friendly terms with that beast."

"He's my pet. Don't make any sudden moves or he'll take you," Fortune warned. Slowly, she lowered one of her arms and held out her hand to the dog. She made soft unintelligible noises, and the animal edged closer. "That's a boy, Grumpy. It's all right. He's a friend."

Grumpy nudged her hand with his big head. Then Fortune reached for Grady's hand, twined her fingers in his and slowly lowered their hands toward the dog. The animal sniffed at their hands, then circled round and sniffed at Grady's legs. Seemingly satisfied, he sat back on his haunches and stared curiously.

Careful to make no sudden moves, the couple disengaged, but Fortune kept hold of Grady's hand. She crouched down to the ground, tugging the Reb down with her. Then she set their entwined hands on Grumpy's head. Grady took her cue and freed his hand from hers to pet the dog. The dog allowed

it, but his low steady growl made it obvious he still didn't trust
the man.

Fortune let out a deep sigh of relief. "It will be all right now.
He won't hurt you unless you try to touch me again."

"Is he always like this, so protective of you?" Grady asked,
finally daring to breathe.

"Always, especially around men. He hates them. I've never
known why, but it's my guess that before I found him, he'd
been badly abused by a man, maybe several."

"I take it his name is derived from his sweet disposition,"
Grady surmised archly. "How long has he been with you?"

"I found Grumpy two years ago, not far from my grandmother's horse farm. He was lying on the side of the road
dying. And yes," she smiled wryly, "his name is indicative of
his personality." She stood, and Grady slowly followed suit.

"And now he associates love and care with you," Grady
interjected. He made to rub her cheek with the back of his
hand, but Grumpy growled and he thought better of it. "Fortune,
I'm sorry I got so carried . . ."

"Don't," she interrupted. She lowered her lashes self-
consciously. "I shouldn't have let you kiss me. I acted like
a . . . Forgive me, if I led you on. I didn't mean to. The two
of us—it's not meant to be."

"How can you say that when . . ."

A third voice cut Grady off. "Fortune, you out dere, gal?
Now don' go scarin' an 'ol woman. Dere's a man runnin' loose
round here somewheres. Answer me, gal."

"I'm right here, Ursula," Fortune called.

Ursula crashed through the trees like a bull moose. "Oh,
dere you are." She noticed Grady and scowled. "So, Reb, it
was you who come snoopin' round. How'd you get past me
and Laila?"

"Ursula," Fortune said trying to be patient, "Mr. MacNair
came to talk to me about auditing his accounts. Remember? I
mentioned that to you and Gran at dinner a couple days ago."

"Well, he shoulda done it up ta de house. Dat's de proper
way, ain't it?"

"We were just coming up to the house," the girl explained.
"Besides, I had an excellent chaperon."

Grumpy growled at Grady, and Ursula cackled with glee.
"Guess you did at dat, chile. Come along now," she said

turning towards the house. "Company isa comin' down de road.
Nubbins says it's a George-gan-son feller with the furniture."

"Jorgensen," Fortune corrected with a smile.

"Ain't dat what I jus said? Now come on, we bes get on upta
de house. And dat goes for you too, Reb."

Ursula stomped off in the direction she'd come, the two
young people following right behind her without a word.

Fortune stared at Ursula's back, her mind reeling with the
folly she'd just committed. True, Grady had seduced her into
wanting his kiss, but she'd lost all control. And if Grumpy
hadn't come when he had . . .

What was the matter with her? *Well, you know what's wrong
with you*, that now familiar little voice taunted. *It's the magic!*
Yes, Fortune thought, the magic. And it was the magic that
made him kiss me that way. A pain she'd never experienced
before shot through her heart.

The young woman gave a harsh swipe at a lock of hair.
*Why should you feel hurt? You knew all along his attraction
for you wasn't real. And when the bond is broken and he no
longer wants me, will I no longer want him as well? Will the
hurt go away?* Fortune told herself it would and prayed that
she was right.

Chapter Six

"Oh, there you are," Laila said from the back door as Ursula and the young couple came across the backyard. "Why, Mr. MacNair, is that your horse we found out front?"

"Yes, ma'am. I came to have a word with Miss Fortune about getting started on my mercantile accounts."

"Well, no more of that now," she told him. "Nubbins says Olaf Jorgensen is coming down the road with our new beds. Here." She handed Grumpy's leash to Fortune. "You better tie up your dog."

A full-throated "Whoa!" and the crunch of wagon wheels on gravel announced the carpenter. Anticipation lit Laila's face as she turned and hurried back through the house.

Fortune finished tying Grumpy to the porch and trekked around the side of the house to the front yard behind Grady and Ursula.

A lumberjack of a man with graying blond hair leaped from his perch on a wagon seat then helped his tall, plump wife. On the opposite side, a handsome blue-eyed Viking in denim overalls jumped down.

72

Other than Nubbins, who had once again evaporated into thin air, Grady was the only one present who knew the Jorgensens well enough to perform the introductions. "Olaf," he said, holding out his hand, "good to see you. I hear you brought some furniture for these folks."

"Ya, Ya," Olaf said, smiling good-naturedly as he gave Grady's hand a vigorous shake. "You have met my wife, Helga, ya?"

"Sure have," Grady replied. "A pleasure to see you again, Mrs. Jorgensen."

Helga's apple cheeks puffed out in a smile. "The same to you, Mr. MacNair. I just had to come to welcome our new neighbors."

Grady turned to introduce Fortune and the older ladies. That's when he noted the youngest Jorgensen nimble-footing it straight for his woman. *Damnation!* he silently cursed, curling his hands into fists at his side. *I ought to kick that claim jumper ass over teakettle!*

Fortune was caught off guard when the blond Viking boldly strode up to her and began pumping her hand. "And you must be Fortune, Roc's sister, ya?" he said with a wide, winsome smile. "Roc said you were pretty, but he didn't do you justice. I'm Eric and still unmarried!"

Fortune burst out laughing and withdrew her hand. The hand-some Swede was outrageous and entirely likeable. "Pleased to meet you, Eric the Unmarried." Out of the corner of her eye she saw Grady shoot a steely glare at the Viking's back, but before she could guess its cause, the Reb abruptly pivoted away and continued the introductions. "Olaf, Helga," he began with strained politeness, "as you heard, this is Miss Fortune Landry." Fortune smiled, greeting each of the older Jorgensens respectfully.

"And this," Grady continued, entirely ignoring Eric's presence, "is Fortune and Roc's grandmother, Mrs. Laila Fontaine, and her friend, Ursula Price. Ladies, this is Olaf and Helga Jorgensen. Olaf makes the finest furniture in the West."

Olaf nodded proudly, and Helga came forward and shook Laila's hand effusively. "Welcome!"

"Thank you," Laila replied. "Now won't you all please come inside and join us for something cool to drink?"

The men declined, preferring to tackle the job of setting

up the beds first, but Helga gladly accepted and followed her
hostesses into the kitchen.

Fortune poured drinks for everyone then settled down to
become acquainted. The women gossiped and laughed over the
clamor of the men as they hauled in the beds and hammered
them together.

"Ladies," Grady interrupted from the doorway a half hour later, "Mr. Jorgensen says Roc purchased a surprise. He and Eric
are bringing it in now, if you'd like to come see what it is."

The women followed Grady into the sitting room. Then while
he held the door open Eric and his father struggled through with
a piece of furniture hidden beneath a cloth cover. They set it
down in the middle of the room and whipped the cover off with
a flourish. Fortune gasped in delight. "It's beautiful!" Sweeping
her hand over the dark brandy velvet settee, she admired the
serpentine oak piece across its back. "This is lovely. I've never
seen anything quite like it."

"Eric carved the wood himself," Helga bragged proudly.

Fortune glanced up at the tall young man. "You're truly
gifted, Eric." At the scuff of a boot toe, she glanced up and
glimpsed Grady's irritated expression. *What's wrong with the
man?* she wondered. *Jealous? Surely not.*

"Well, we can't leave it dere," Ursula said, breaking into
Fortune's thoughts. "We gotta find a place for it."

The next half hour, Eric and Olaf were put through the paces
of furniture arranging while the others watched and laughingly
took turns offering ridiculous suggestions. The rocker being the
only other piece of furniture in the sitting room, they naturally
had to try out every other available spot.

Grady barely managed to hide his seething jealousy behind
a frozen smile and took no part in the tomfoolery. At one point,
however, Eric shot him a cock-of-the-walk smirk that bore all
the earmarks of a challenge. The Reb knew then that he'd been
found out and dropped all pretense at politeness.

The plump Helga interrupted the horseplay, announcing that
it was time to sample the welcome meal she'd brought along.
Fortune, Granny and Ursula helped her fetch several aromatic dishes of food from the wagon. In a matter of minutes,
they'd warmed them on the stove and spread the small feast
on the table.

Grady reached the kitchen first, but Eric elbowed past him

and claimed the only seat beside Fortune. Swallowing an acid remark, the Reb yanked out a chair across the table from them.

Why, he is jealous, Fortune realized, observing Grady's ugly expression. Unaware of Eric's recent maneuvers, she found the Reb's attitude unreasonable and proceeded to ignore him during the meal.

Just as dessert was served, Olaf Jorgensen lifted his glass of water and announced in his bold Swedish brogue, "I propose a toast—to good food and good folks to share it with. It makes a man happy."

"Skol!" Eric shouted.

Crash! Grady MacNair's glass met Eric's with shattering force. The others reacted with a startled silence then erupted in laughter—all but a water-soaked Fortune, that is. Her mouth thinned with displeasure as she stabbed the Reb with a glare of emerald fire.

Feeling more than a little sheepish, Grady silently cursed himself and used his cloth napkin to sop up the mess on the table. *Christ,* he thought, *what's the matter with me? I'm acting like some jealous, wet-nosed kid.* After all, Eric wasn't really a bad sort. And who could blame the man for being attracted to a woman as beautiful as Fortune?

"But look what we've done," Eric crooned apologetically, calling attention to Fortune's soggy condition. Using his napkin, he dabbed at her bodice.

For Grady it was the last straw. His conciliatory mood vanished. *I'll be damned if I'll sit back and let that big dumb Swede paw my woman!* Leaning across the table, he ripped the cloth from the startled Swede's hand. "Enough!"

Eric's complexion flushed with anger. His chair scraped the pinewood floor, and as he stood up abruptly it tipped over.

The two young men circled round to the end of the table and faced off like two roosters at a cockfight.

Olaf rose to protest, but his voice was drowned out by the others as their objections joined his.

Eric braced his feet apart and drew back his fist. Grady lifted his arm to block the punch when a bewildered voice asked, "What's going on here?" Fists froze within a hair's breadth of jutting masculine chins.

Seven pairs of eyes slanted toward the doorway between the

kitchen and dining room where Roc Landry stood, feet braced apart, arms crossed over his chest. "Well?"

The stillness erupted into a chorus of explanations.

Fortune vaulted up from the table and propelled herself at her brother. "It's all a misunderstanding, Roc. You see . . ."

"Just two young men sniffing after the same girl," Olaf explained.

Grady was hopping mad and felt no compulsion to explain himself to anyone. Instead he accused Eric directly. "Damn it, you put your filthy hands on her!"

"If you hadn't smashed your glass into mine none of this would have happened," Eric shot back angrily.

"And if you hadn't been moving in on . . ."

Eric's fist clipped Grady's jaw and sent him stumbling backwards.

"Fat's in the fire now," Ursula hooted, scooting her chair back from the table. With an exclamation of exasperation, Laila followed the black woman's good example.

Giving his head a shake, Grady roared back to life and slammed a fist into Eric's belly.

Eric cannonballed into the wall next to the stove and slid to the floor amidst the clanging and banging of dislodged pots and pans. Immediately, he was up again, giving as good as he got.

The Reb launched a strong uppercut. Eric's body skidded down the length of the kitchen table, scattering food and dishes in his wake. Grady sailed across the table and landed atop the Viking in a flurry of driving, bloody-knuckled punches. Then they both rolled and dropped to the floor. Just as they regained their footing, Grady slipped in spilt apple strudel and down they went again.

"Olaf, you big dolt," Helga cried, tugging on her husband's arm, "this has gone too far! I demand you stop this at once!"

"Nothing's going to stop them now, woman," Olaf replied, shaking her off. "Might as well sit back and enjoy the fun." With that he began to weave back and forth, punching the air as if fighting in his son's stead. "Atta boy! Get 'im!"

Fortune winced with each crack of bare knuckles against flesh and bone. Unable to differentiate between the blood and wild raspberry jam staining their clothing, her stomach lurched. If the fight weren't stopped soon, she was going to humiliate herself. She glanced up at her brother, dismayed to find that he too was enjoying the ruckus. "Roc," she threatened, "I swear if you don't stop them, I will!"

Roc simply swept her out of his line of view and shouted, "Clean him down to bedrock, Eric!"

"Give 'im a good lickin', Reb!" Ursula yelled. At Fortune's stunned stare, Ursula shrugged. "Somebody's gotta root for de boy."

Clicking her tongue in disgust, Fortune turned her pale face back to the fray. Her gaze met Granny's across the room, and they nodded to one another in silent accord. Hugging the perimeters of the fight, first Fortune and then Granny found their weapons.

Pot in hand, Fortune clobbered the first brawler who stumbled in her direction. With a fleeting look of shock, Eric hit the floor like a felled ponderosa pine.

The Reb's sudden burst of laughter at the sight ended with an abrupt grunt. Then he too hit the floor.

Granny lifted her skillet and gave it a loud smacking kiss. "Dealing with men isn't easy," she sighed, "but it's woman's lot in life so we must be firm. And now," she said, stepping over Grady's prone body and waving the skillet at the other men, "wipe the sulks off your faces and get those two galoots out of my kitchen before I decide to deal with the two of you."

Fortune winked at Helga over Granny's shoulder as Roc on his crutches held the door open while Olaf dragged first one and then the other unconscious man outside to the well.

Helga began apologizing, but Fortune held up a staying hand. "I'm the one that's at fault," she said, "and I've never been so humiliated in my life."

"You aren't to blame for Eric's stupidity," Helga replied disgustedly as she wiped potatoes off the wall. "He had no business touching your . . . well, he shouldn't have, that's all."

"Oh, it wasn't his fault," Fortune told her. "Eric was just trying to be helpful. That blasted, Southern polecat of a Reb started the whole thing. He acted jealous from the very moment Eric shook my hand—as if he had a right!"

A twinge of guilt flicked at Fortune's conscience. She'd allowed Grady freedoms that no lady should permit a man, other than her husband. Sweet Gaia, no wonder the man acted possessive!

"Damn fool men," Laila grumbled. "There's nothing ruffians like better than a good fight. Makes them feel manly or some such nonsense. It's beyond me why such big, strong bodies hold only tiny, childish brains."

Fortune chuckled at her Granny's truisms, but Helga grabbed a broom and snorted in annoyance. "Look at this mess."

For a moment all four women paused in their cleanup and took in the battle scene—tumbled chairs, broken dishes, food splattered everywhere. The momentary quiet was broken when a thick blob of gravy dripped off the ceiling and fell to the floor with a soft kerplop.

A bubbly sound escaped Fortune's throat. She covered her mouth, but the laughter trickled between her fingers anyway. Soon they were all laughing and trying to top each other's disparaging remarks about the male gender.

The female camaraderie gave Fortune an excuse, if only temporarily, to forget the guilt over her outrageous behavior toward the Reb. She was also able to console herself with the knowledge that after tonight Grady MacNair would no longer be a problem—providing, of course, Granny's Riddance spell worked.

Chapter Seven

Midnight. Somewhere in the stygian cloaked mountains, a wolf howled at the Gypsy moon. By its scant glow the three women silently negotiated the forest trail. Overhead a doleful breeze sighed and breathed life into the gnarled arms of the tall, eerie beings that by day were merely trees. An owl hooted, and Fortune shuddered. Owls always brought ill tidings. She hurried along, but thorny shrubs snagged her skirts, making haste hazardous.

A damp mist off the river caressed the women's faces as they reached the clearing. A safe distance from the foliage Fortune dropped the logs she'd carried from the house and pulled her shawl more snugly around her shoulders. Ursula kicked a few dry leaves over them, and Granny lit the fire. Chilled, the three women huddled close to the crackling yellow flames.

Laila wore a red *diklo* or scarf on her head, as did Fortune. Both women's necks were weighted with beads and magic amulets. The firelight reflected on the gold bangles adorning their arms. And as all three held their hands out to the warmth of the fire, their shadows loomed tall and wavered like the bodiless spirits of crooked crones.

For once, struck dumb, Ursula watched warily as Laila slowly raised her arms skyward.

The old Gypsy's bracelets jingled like wind chimes as her body began to sway to the hypnotic singsong intonation of her cracked voice.

> "In our oneness of life we are a part of Gaia.
> She is composed of the four elements: water,
> fire, air and earth, as our bodies are
> comprised of the same."

Fortune closed her eyes, seeking to open herself to the energies of the universe, but unlike other times, it wasn't easy. When she tried to clear her mind, Grady MacNair's vaporous image intruded. He seemed to be laughing at her puny efforts to dispel him from her life. *Concentrate, I must concentrate.* There. He was gone. Her body began to sway. Lifting her arms to the moon, her lilting voice joined Laila's.

> "Dance my dance and I dance with you.
> Hold me and I hold you.
> Know life and the wheel turns.
> Be one with Gaia.
> Be one with Gaia."

"Do you have the paper with Grady MacNair's name on it?" Laila asked Fortune.

The young woman nodded solemnly and dug a small scrap of paper from her skirt pocket. Ursula crept forward and handed a consecrated white candle to Laila who held its wick to the fire. Fortune then burned the paper in the candle flame, while Ursula caught the ashes in a small dish that shook with her trembling.

Fortune watched as Granny bent close to the fire and opened the small leather bag which hung at her waist. From the *putsi*, she extracted the strands of Grady MacNair's hair that Ursula had plucked from his head. She handed them to her granddaughter who then burnt them over the dish of ashes. The scent of scorched hair wafted upward and dissipated on the wind as quickly as the hair joined the ashes.

Then the cooled ashes were carefully deposited in Fortune's cupped hand. The ground mist swallowed her feet as she drifted to the river's edge. She lifted her offerings to the night breeze and chanted the spell of Riddance.

"Winds of the North, South, East and West,
Take this man's love on a new quest.
Let Grady's heart be open and free,
And let him dwell not on me."

The young woman waited until airy fingers carried away every particle in her palm. Then with a sigh of relief, she retraced her steps to the campfire.

"It is done," Laila said. "Now we must wait and see."

Fortune shivered, but it was less a reaction to the damp chill than to her own fear—fear that the spell might not work, fear of newly awakened passions and fear of the man who aroused them. The tie binding Grady to her was so strong, the mere memory of those few moments in his arms made her body burn with the yearning to mate. She shivered again. *If the spell is working, why do I still feel this way? Shouldn't I feel indifferent toward him now?*

"Do not think on it," Granny said as if reading her thoughts. "You must believe in the magic or its power will be too weak to do what we ask of it. Now, we best go back to the house. It's late."

The woods crowded in on Fortune as she followed the two old women on the narrow path. Granny was right, she thought. She must have faith in the magic. *It will work. It will work.*

Over and over again, she repeated the words in her head. Suddenly, a niggling little voice taunted, *"But do you really want to give up the thrill of his body demanding yours? What if he's the only one who will ever be able to fire your Gypsy passion?"* Fortune stumbled and would have fallen but for Ursula's sturdy form directly in front her.

"What's a matter, gal?" came the black woman's startled whisper. "You near spooked me white! You still in a trance?"

"No, of course not," Fortune whispered into the dark. "I

tripped over a tree root is all." Ursula grunted and together they pressed on.

It will work. It will work, Fortune told herself. *It better work!* In two days time, she'd be in Helena auditing Grady MacNair's accounts.

Chapter Eight

Fortune stood just outside the International Hotel and waved to Roc as he headed down the street with Grumpy. Roc was on his way to leave Grumpy at the warehouse before seeing Doc Holly to have his cast removed. From there he planned to look into the possibility of renting or purchasing a house in Helena. Their continued renting of hotel rooms was becoming expensive and impractical.

While Roc was seeing to the house hunting, Fortune had her own chores to see to, and since they had arrived in town much later than intended, time was short. She rummaged in her reticule for the shopping list Granny had given her. Glancing over it, she saw the large quantities necessitated a wagon to haul them back to the ranch. Roc would have to see to that problem tomorrow.

In the meantime, she'd purchase the supplies at MacNair's mercantile and inform him of her intent to start auditing his books tomorrow morning.

A disturbed frown marred Fortune's face as she tucked the list away. Today's meeting with MacNair would prove one

way or another if the Riddance spell had worked. She pulled
a tiny watch from the skirt pocket of her puff-sleeved frock
and gasped at the time. It was already past 3:30. As much
as she dreaded the confrontation with the Reb, she could no
longer put it off.

Beneath Fortune's high collar lay her amber stone, and she
touched it now for luck. Then giving each of her lacy, fingerless
mitts a tug, she rested her gay little parasol on one shoulder and
set off down the boardwalk.

The sound of muffled childish laughter reached her ears as
she strolled past a saloon. *Odd,* she thought, *what would children be doing in a saloon?* Without giving her unseemly action
a thought, she stood on tiptoe and peeked over the bat-wing
doors. A familiar prickle danced down her spine, but before
she could react, he was at her side.

"See anything interesting in there?" Grady MacNair drawled.

Fortune dropped down on her heels and swung round so fast
she nearly poked Grady MacNair's eye out with her parasol.
Caught interloping where no true lady would, Fortune babbled,
"Oh, Mr. MacNair, I . . . er, I didn't see you coming. And no,
I didn't see anything. That is, I don't make a habit of this,
but I could have sworn I heard children laughing inside this
saloon."

She twirled her parasol on one shoulder, her mind traveling
an entirely different avenue than her words. *Damn,* she thought,
this isn't how I planned our meeting. Granny had specifically
instructed her to grasp the amber amulet and repeat the Riddance chant just before facing him. Supposedly, this small ritual
would strengthen the spell.

Unaware of the young woman's inner turmoil, Grady easily
glanced over the saloon doors from his superior height. "Don't
see any children in there," he said turning back to her and
admiring the way the spring-green material of her dress clung
to her figure.

Fortune studied his black eye, deciding it detracted very little
from his handsome features. He turned and smiled down at
her, and little goslings marched down her arms. *Sweet Gaia,
that wasn't suppose to happen anymore, was it?* Definitely not a good sign, she thought. "Well," she replied aloud,
"I feel a little foolish. Guess my ears were playing tricks
on me."

He tipped his black hat back on his head, and his smile widened to a grin. "Maybe not," he said, staring over her shoulder at something behind her.

Swirling around, she followed his gaze. Four little wriggly bodies were struggling out from underneath the boardwalk. She immediately recognized the Tabor children as two of the four scrambling to their feet.

"I got more than you," the Tabor girl clamored pridefully.

"Do not!" yelled the other female ragamuffin.

"Do, too!"

"Do not!"

"Ah, shut up," Book ordered. "Me and Joe got the most, and that settles it." The boy glanced up then and spied Fortune and Grady. "Howdy, Mr. Grady, Miss Landry. How's the lump, Miss Landry?"

"Lump? Oh, you mean my head," Fortune said, laughing. "I'm fine, thank you." Curious, she asked, "What in heaven's name were you doing under the saloon, Book?" At her side she heard Grady chuckle knowingly.

A grin lifted the boy's dirty lean cheeks. He loosened the drawstring on a small leather pouch and held it up for her inspection.

Remembering the slithery things Roc used to keep in such bags, Fortune approached cautiously and peeked inside. "I don't see anything but dirt."

"Naw, it ain't dirt," Book said. "Poke your finger in there."

At her shoulder Grady challenged, "Go ahead, you might be surprised."

"That's what I'm afraid of," Fortune said wryly.

"Hell—I mean heck—nothin's gonna bite yuh," the boy added.

Fortune glanced up at Grady. "You two better be telling the truth." Grady just smiled and nodded at the bag Book held up. Warily, she dipped her finger inside then quickly yanked it out again. Bright yellow specks dusted the tip. "Gold?"

"Sure is," Book boasted.

"But I don't understand," she said brushing the grains back into the small bag.

"She's dumber 'n a sheepherder." The boy called Joe guffawed.

"No, 'ers got a lump!" Book's sister said as if that explained everything.

Grady's burst of laughter was quelled by a discreet jab from Fortune's parasol in his solar plexus.

"Whatdayuh 'spect, Joe?" Book rolled his eyes at his friend. "Miss Landry's a girl." All sympathy now, he addressed her, "Beggin' your pardon, ma'am. I reckon you can't help bein' female."

The Gypsy girl grinned. "No, that's true. I had nothing to say in the matter. And since I'm so feebleminded," she gave Grady a don't-you-dare-say-a-word look, "could you tell me how that gold got under the saloon?"

"Oh, it ain't just under this here saloon," Book explained. It's under all of 'em. See, the miners pay for their drinks in gold dust. The saloon keeper's gotta weigh it, and some of that dust sifts between the boards of the floor and onta the ground underneath the place. Me and Joe staked our claim on the Gaiety here. Anybody tries jumpin' it, and we whup their butts. 'Scuse the language, ma'am."

Fortune grimaced and sought out Grady's reaction. He shrugged. "Mining under the saloons is one of the biggest pastimes for the youngsters in Helena. They've all pretty much staked their claims on a particular saloon."

Fortune opened her mouth to comment but felt a firm tug on her skirt. Book's sister stared up at her with big blue eyes, but before the child could voice a word Book rebuked her. "Tish, look what you done to Miss Landry's purdy dress."

The little girl's mouth formed an "oh" as she eyed a grimy handprint on the green material. She lifted her anxious gaze to the beautiful dark-haired lady and swallowed hard. Fortune's heart melted. "It's all right, sweetheart," she said stooping down on her heels. "I was going to wash this old dress anyway." Tish grinned, and Fortune asked, "Is there something you want to tell me, honey?" The child bobbed her head vigorously. "Well?"

"Ma's gotta baby in 'er belly."

Fortune felt her cheeks go hot at the little girl's blatant announcement. Then remembering that the children's father had deserted his family two months ago, sympathy for this poor family nearly overwhelmed her. But for the child's sake she only smiled. "How nice. You'll have a brand new baby brother or sister."

"No, it ain't nice," Book refuted belligerently. He roughly snatched up his sister's hand and started to drag her away. "Come on, flap jaw, we gotta git."

As Grady took Fortune's elbow and helped her to rise, she called out, "Book, wait, I . . ." But it was too late. All four children scurried down an alley like little mice seeking refuge from the barkeeper's cat.

Fortune sighed deeply, "The poor dears. How could a man simply take off and leave his wife and children like that?"

Grady laid a comforting hand at her waist. "I'm afraid it's all too common here in Helena. Montana territory has the highest divorce rate in the nation."

"But that's scandalous!"

He nodded grimly. "It's a fact though. The only good side of the story is that women are in high demand and usually find themselves quickly remarried. I heard tell of one woman who had four husbands in as many years."

"Good Lord!" Without conscious thought of her action, she turned to him and laid one small hand on his blue flannel-clad forearm. "Is there anything that can be done to help the Tabors?"

"I'm not sure," Grady replied distractedly as he stared down at her slim, feminine fingers griping his arm. He forced his glance to meet her eyes and cleared his throat. "I did give Mrs. Tabor a job clerking a few hours a week so she and the children won't want for enough to eat. And I know she takes in laundry and mending from the miners when she can. Unfortunately, the Chinese have most of the laundry trade in this town. They'll work for next to nothing."

"I doubt she can keep working so hard in her delicate condition."

"Yeah, guess you're right. I could tell the church ladies when they come into the store, but Irene Tabor wouldn't cotton to charity." He paused, scrutinizing her. "Why are *you* so concerned? I mean, most young women are too busy thinking about their beaux or planning tea parties to worry about a couple of dirty kids they hardly know."

"I came West to escape all those meaningless social customs," Fortune said more sharply than she intended. Then more gently she added, "How could I not be concerned about Tish and Book? They're innocent children, helpless against the whims of a father who has abandoned his responsibility to them. That's reason enough."

Grady nodded, sensing the explanation had roots that went much deeper. He couldn't help wondering about the girl's parents, but her sudden bright smile made him forget the question he was about to voice.

"I better be on my way," Fortune said, giving the parasol on her shoulder a nervous little twirl. "I've a lot to do this afternoon, and the day is almost gone."

Grinning, Grady removed his hat and placed it over his heart. "May I be of service, ma'am? Perhaps I might escort you?"

In spite of her anxiousness to be away from his virile presence, Fortune laughed. "Thank you, but I wouldn't want to keep you from your own errands. Besides, I'm on my way to the mercantile to fill my grandmother's supply list. I'm sure we'll meet again later." *And I'll have time to repeat the Riddance spell,* she reminded herself.

Grady lifted his hands, palms up, "I wasn't doing anything that can't wait, and I could find everything on that list of yours much faster than you can."

Unable to bring herself to be out-and-out rude, Fortune stifled a groan. Nothing was going according to plan. Common sense demanded she refuse his company, but he was being so damned charming. And what about the Riddance chant? She couldn't very well repeat it in front of MacNair. Well, maybe the spell had worked without the chant. The Reb's inborn southern charm made it difficult to discern between his good manners and the effects of the Moondance. Well, time would tell.

Misreading the young woman's distressed expression, Grady laid a hand at her waist and gently urged her down the boardwalk. "Come on, I promise not to throw you over a counter and ravish you. Though I'll admit," he added with a wink, "it would be tempting."

Fortune stopped short. *So much for the Riddance spell!* She faced the Reb stiffly, taking her disappointment and frustration out on him. "If your past actions are any example, I am not very reassured, Mr. MacNair." To her exceeding satisfaction the muscles in his jaw went taut.

"Excuse me, ma'am, but your actions spoke loud and clear. Lady, you were hot!"

His searing reply hit its mark. Fortune stared into his icy blue eyes in shocked surprise, then suddenly ashamed, dropped her lashes. "You're right, of course. I did behave badly that day. It was as much my fault as yours. But you must understand, I was just curious. That's all." In the next breath she squared her shoulders and looked him straight in the eye. "It won't happen again."

As if he hadn't heard her last statement, Grady's mouth tilted in a doubtful smile. "Curious, huh? Well, Sugar, you haven't learned half of what I have to teach. However, if you ever get curious again, I'm willing to conduct another lesson."

Fortune's temper threatened to erupt, but there was more at stake here than exposing her past. There was the freighting company and Roc's need to regain controlling interest. Still, her anger seeped out. "Mr. MacNair, let's get something straight right now. If we're to get any work done in a reasonable amount of time, we must keep our relationship strictly business. Do I make myself clear?"

Grady's hot gaze bathed her trim figure appreciatively. "All right, partner. While at the store we'll keep things strictly business." He surprised her then by letting the subject drop and, cupping her elbow, urged her toward the mercantile.

Damn southern devil, Fortune silently fumed. How could he look at her with that rakish gleam in his eye and expect her to trust his words? Then the young woman remembered Grumpy. She smiled like a gambler with an ace up her sleeve.

At the mercantile, Fortune conveniently remembered another errand and left Grady to fill the supply list. She escaped to the stationers where she lingered for well over an hour. Then she strolled down the street to the bakery. There, she toyed with a pastry and sipped a cup of coffee, fortifying herself for the return to the mercantile.

The bell over the door tinkled as she walked in. Grady stood up from behind the counter and smiled. "Your purchases are stacked and waiting in the back room. You're going to need a wagon though. Is someone coming by with one?"

"Roc will come in the morning if that's all right," Fortune replied. At his nod, she glanced down at the bill he'd prepared and paid him what was owed. Then preparing to leave, she settled the handle of her closed parasol over her wrist. "Oh," she said, glancing back up at him, "I almost forgot. I'll be coming in early tomorrow morning to start auditing your books."

"Good, I'm anxious to get started. Would you care to take a look at what you're letting yourself in for?" He chuckled. "My desk is in the back room."

"Thanks, but no. I'm meeting my brother for dinner. If I'm late, he'll worry."

Glancing out the window at the waning light, Grady pulled a watch from his pocket and grimaced at the time. "It's later than I thought. The miners will be filling up the restaurants and saloons. I'll walk you back. Where is it you're staying, the International?"

For a moment, Fortune didn't answer. She couldn't; her mouth had gone dry at the sight of MacNair's unusual watch chain. *Great crystal balls and tea leaves!* It was Granny's coin bracelet, the one she'd lost three years ago in Carolina. He'd obviously found it and kept it. But why? What could it mean? Did the bracelet serve to remind him of unfinished business with a certain wild Gypsy girl?

"Fortune, is something wrong?" Grady asked, replacing his watch and stepping closer with an expression of concern.

Fortune barely heard him as she struggled to regain her composure. "I . . . er, no, I'm all right. I just went dizzy for a moment." Her smile was tremulous. "Guess I've gone too long between meals."

The Reb's stance relaxed. "You're sure?"

She managed a small smile. "Quite, thank you."

Grady retrieved his hat and gun from behind a counter. Buckling the holster low on his hips, he doffed his hat and opened the door for her.

The bracelet! He has the bracelet, Fortune silently screamed.

"Are you sure you're all right?" he asked again, staring down at her. "You look downright pale."

"Fine. Just fine. You needn't go to the trouble of escorting me to the hotel."

"I was a gentleman a long time before becoming your partner, Fortune, so whether or not it's businesslike, I will see you safely home." He reached for the doorknob and hesitated, staring down at her. "What are you clutching there at your throat?"

Fortune dropped the good luck amulet as if it burnt. In her distress she'd unconsciously pulled it from beneath her collar.

Grady lifted the oddly shaped piece of amber and bent to study its strange markings.

His lips were mere inches from hers. She inhaled sharply, bringing his clean masculine scent to her nose. The need to escape warred with the insane urge to outline his mouth with the tip of her tongue. *Sweet Gaia, it's that damn Moondance at work again!* Fortune gave herself a mental shake and would have retreated but for his hold on the amulet. "It's just a necklace Granny once gave me," she finally answered.

"What do these little pictures mean?"

"Oh, I don't know. Lots of things, I guess. Granny is from the old country, France to be exact. She still holds with many of the old beliefs—you know, good luck charms and the like."

He gazed down at her, his smile playful. "How 'bout you? Do you believe in such things?"

Gypsies believed lying to a Gajo was no sin, but Fortune was heartily sick of having to lie about her heritage. And sticking to the truth as nearly as possible might save her from tripping over her own lies later. "Yes I do." At his amused smile, she added, "Go ahead and laugh if you want to, but I'll have you know truly intelligent people don't discount such things."

"Is that a fact?" Grady said in mock sobriety.

"It is." *Sweet Gaia, first the bracelet, now the amulet.* Anxious to escape, she whirled around. "Shall we be on our way? I'm going to be late." Without waiting, she rushed out the door.

Once outside, Fortune was heartily glad of his company. The thought of slipping past dark alleys and dodging rowdy miners was more than a little daunting.

As they strolled down the boardwalk toward the hotel, Grady rested his hand on the butt of his army issue Remington. He might have pulled a shady trick to aid his courting of Fortune, but he hadn't exaggerated the dangers of the streets at night. Already, the saloons were loud and lively.

He stole a sidelong glance at his lovely companion. Working alongside her day after day was definitely going to test every ounce of his willpower. But he'd made her a promise and he'd hold to it. At the store their relationship would be strictly business.

Of course, nothing was said about after working hours. And he planned to show her, undeniably, that it was more than mere curiosity that spurred her response to him. Grady smiled to himself. Fortune Landry was proving to be a whole lot more than a pretty face. On one hand she was intelligent, brave and caring. On the other, she was a feisty little beauty who believed in, of all things, magic charms. And he had a notion that he hadn't even begun to scratch the surface of this odd little package of womanhood.

At the Red Dog Saloon, Grady's reverie was shattered by a crack of gunfire. A woman screamed. In one slick motion Grady drew his gun and shoved Fortune behind him against the building.

Bullets whizzed around them as a gunman and his pursuers blasted their way out of the saloon doors. A bullet went wild and struck the wall only inches above their heads. Fortune buried her head against Grady's back and locked her arms about his waist. "Get down," he ordered. Before she could comply, another bullet zinged by. This time Grady heard Fortune gasp in pain. With a curse, he shoved her into the opening of a narrow alley and pressed her to the ground, shielding her with his own body.

As quickly as the ruckus had begun, it was over. The only reminder was the dead man sprawled on the street and the gunpowder fouling the air.

His senses still heightened from their close encounter with death, Grady suddenly became aware of his leg between Fortune's thighs and the soft press of her breasts against his chest. Instantly he went hard. He was contemplating stealing a kiss when he suddenly remembered the stray bullet and her gasp of pain. "Darlin', were you hit?"

Fortune shoved against his chest. "No. Now kindly get off me, will you? You're flattening me like a flapjack!"

Relieved, Grady started to rise.

"Oh, stop!" Fortune grabbed his belt and tugged him down again. "Don't move! My dress is snagged on your belt buckle."

Leaning slightly to one side, Grady groped around trying to find the loose end of his belt so that he could unfasten his buckle and free her. "Damn, I can't see a thing."

"Good Lord, MacNair, hurry up! What if someone sees us like this? They'd think . . . Oh, God." With that she went for his buckle herself. Her fingers immediately came into contact with something else entirely—something long, hot, hard and still growing! She yelped and jumped.

"Damn it, woman, will you hold still for just one minute? You give a man a real pain, you know that? I think I've just . . ." He fumbled around with the wadded material. "Got it!" He quickly helped her to her feet.

Fortune gasped at the unsightly rent at the waistline of her dress. Bunching the shredded material in her fist, she did the best she could to hide the damage.

"You ready?" he asked.

"Yes, let's get out of here."

He took her arm, but she winced and gasped. "You are hurt," he said almost accusingly. "Why didn't you say so?"

"It's nothing serious, just a splinter, I think. One of those bullets chunked out a piece of wood and it flew into my arm. It's too dark to see anything here so we might as well go on to the hotel."

A few minutes later Grady opened the door on the International's empty lobby. He immediately took Fortune aside to examine her arm. Standing behind her, he bent down for a closer look.

"See anything?" she asked.

"You were right. You've got one hell of a splinter in your arm."

"Can you pull it out? It stings something awful."

"Hold on a minute." Grady whipped a small knife out, and Fortune went white. "Be still," he ordered.

"Ouch!"

"It's out, darlin'. Feel better now?"

She pivoted around. "I'd feel fine if you'd stop calling me darlin'." She cranked her head at an awkward angle trying to get a better look at her arm. "Are you sure you got it all? It still stings like . . . I'm bleeding!" She gazed up at him in horror and immediately waxed sickly green. She started to droop.

"Whoa there, little lady," Grady said, lifting her into his arms.

"Please, you can put me down. I'm all right."

"Sure," he said, locating the nearest settee and sitting with her on his lap. "If you aren't the damnedest woman I ever knew," he muttered, with a wondering shake of his head. "You step in front of a racing carriage to save a kid, and weather getting shot at without so much as a peep. But at the first sight of a speck of blood you swoon."

"I only swoon at my own blood," she corrected with a sniff. "Though I'll admit any kind of blood makes me queasy." She squirmed in his lap, trying to sit up.

Grady's arousal flared again. For the second time that night, she'd cocked his pistol with absolutely no intentions of allowing him to shoot it! She might be innocent of her effect on him, but a man could only stand so much torment.

MacNair started to help the girl from his lap. At that same moment, the desk clerk came down the stairs. Taking in Fortune's disreputable attire and her intimate position on Grady's lap, the man glowered a censoring glare down his thin pointed nose. "We don't put up with any goings-on in this hotel, Miss Landry. I suggest you take your friend down the street to the Red Dog Saloon."

Fortune gasped in outrage and scooted off Grady's lap. In three long strides Grady had the desk clerk by the collar. "Apologize to the lady, you slimy little bastard."

"I believe this is where I came in last time," Roc Landry said, entering the hotel door. "What goes here, Sister Mine? And what happened to your clothes?"

Ignoring her brother, Fortune ran to Grady's side and tugged on his arm. "Let go of the man; he can't possibly apologize. For God's sake, you're choking him to death."

Grady reluctantly did as she asked. The smaller man tugged his tie loose, rasped an apology, then faded behind his desk.

"Fortune," Roc said, reminding her of his presence.

"Don't be such a bother," she admonished. "It was all a mis . . ."

"Oh, another misunderstanding," Roc finished wryly. "I should have known. Is your dress part of the misunderstanding, too?"

Knotting the gaping waistline in her fist, Fortune replied testily, "No, that was something else entirely." As quickly as possible she proceeded to tell her brother what had happened.

"A regular knight in shining armor, aren't you, Reb?" Roc commented at the story's end.

Grady hooked his thumbs in his gunbelt and smiled arrogantly. "Guess so, Yank."

"Stop it, both of you," Fortune admonished. "Roc, I'll meet you in the dining room after I've changed." She turned to Grady then. "Good evening, Mr. MacNair. I'll see you first thing tomorrow morning."

"Evening, ma'am." Grady tipped his hat and started for the door. He halted when Fortune caught his arm.

"Wait, I . . ." What could she say? The man had shielded her from harm and defended her honor all in one night. Standing this close, her recent urge to outline those sensuous lips of his reasserted itself with all the fire of her fervent Gypsy passion. She should thank him, shouldn't she? Darting a sidelong glance at her brother's unhappy face, she took a deep breath and refocused on Grady. She lifted one hand to his shoulder, drew him down to her height and brushed a soft kiss on his cheek. "Thank you," she whispered. Shaken, she stepped back quickly. Then fearing Roc's reaction to her impulsive act, she scurried up the hotel stairs and didn't look back.

A silly grin on his face, Grady rubbed his cheek where her lips had kissed him. He turned round and ran into Roc's dark angry gaze. Passing him, he smirked. "Milady seems to like Reb knights."

Chapter Nine

Grady's face lit up when he unlocked the mercantile door and found Fortune Landry smiling up at him. "Good morning, you're here bright and early."

"I told you I would be," she replied with alacrity, indicating with a nod the ledger held under one arm.

Grady ignored the ledger, surveying instead the prim gray skirt and the snowy shirtwaist she wore. Recognizing her sober attire for the obvious ploy it was, he smiled to himself. He doubted she'd be so cheerful if she realized that the simple lines of the schoolmarmish garb actually accentuated her feminine curves. Even her hair, skinned back in a bun, served only to make her big green eyes loom like lustrous jewels.

Inhaling deeply, he tried to catch a whiff of the enticing perfume she usually wore, but his nose met with disappointment. No doubt the scent's elimination was as purposeful as her garb. "It looks like you came well-prepared," he said, stepping aside so she could enter.

Lifting one hand from the concealing folds of her skirt,

Fortune tugged on a long leather strap and hauled a reluctant Grumpy into view.

The Southerner's welcoming smile floundered. *Shit! The man-hating mutt!* The sly little vixen's angelic demeanor didn't fool Grady one whit. Was she using the dog to make sure he kept his promise, or was the dog her brother's idea? Both seemed likely conclusions, but now that he was certain Fortune wasn't immune to his advances, he'd not let a dumb dog get in the way of his plans. He'd have the finest ranch in the territory, and he'd be damned if he didn't have the finest lady to go with it!

As Fortune eased past him into the store, he slammed the door shut behind her and slapped the open sign outward. *You've won a battle, Miss Landry, but not the war.*

Fortune winced at the slam of the door. Calling forth every ounce of her feminine charm, she graced him with a lamblike smile. "I hope you don't mind that I brought Grumpy. I could hardly leave him at the hotel all day, poor thing. He won't cause a bit of trouble, that is, he never makes a mess inside."

"I don't allow animals in the store," he groused, crossing his arms across his chest.

"Oh, I understand, but I plan to take him to the storeroom with me. He won't cause any trouble back there. You did tell me that's where your office is, didn't you?"

"Yes, but . . ."

"Fine." Though she didn't dare show it, Fortune was beginning to find the situation terribly funny. Where did all that dazzling Southern charm get to? Hastily averting her smile, she ever so daintily glided around Grady's stubborn, wide-legged stance and proceeded into the back room.

Grady ground his teeth together and followed right behind her. He watched unhappily as the dog crawled under the desk and Fortune set the ledger on top of it and sat down. Then grabbing an extra chair, he slammed it down next to her. Before he could sit, she asked, "Aren't you forgetting your ledgers?"

"Ledgers?" Remembering the disreputable state of his accounts eased Grady's temper, and he smiled. "Oh, sure, my bookkeeping." He sauntered over to a dark corner. Hefting a large cumbersome box, he carried to the desk and set it before her.

Fortune frowned. "These are your records?"

"Yes, they're all here—I think."

The girl stared at the overflowing box and blinked in dismay. "But . . . but didn't you write these transactions down somewhere?"

"What for? The money is in the bank and all the information is in the box somewhere."

"I see." But she didn't see at all. It didn't make sense. Everything about the astutely run mercantile had led her to believe he'd exaggerated the condition of his accounts. "You weren't joshing when you told Roc your records were slapdash, were you?"

"Slapdash? No, ma'am. I believe the term I used was meyess," he drawled out, exaggerating the Southern pronunciation. Grady silently congratulated himself. It tickled him immensely to witness her dismay, especially since she'd seen fit to bring her damn dog.

"Mess? This is a disaster. I don't know how you've stayed in business this long with these kinds of records."

He tapped his head. "It's all right up here."

"That's a bunch of . . . Oh, never mind." She reached into the box. "Thank goodness these are dated," she commented, thumbing through a handful of receipts. "What's this mean?" She held out a sales slip and pointed at a notation at the bottom.

"S.D.—J.B.," he read aloud. "That one's easy. Sales due on Jed Beamer's account. You see?" he said, grinning. "This won't be too hard at all. Every receipt and bill of sales is initialed according to what it pertains to. It's my own little invention. Abbreviations take less time."

The man is daft! Fortune picked up a few more pieces of paper and stared dumfounded. "Oh, Lord," she groaned, "I'll never figure these out."

"I'll help you, Sugar. Oh, sorry, strictly business. I'll remember from now on, Miss Fortune. What I started to say was that all you have to do is ask. I've got the abbreviations right—"

"I know, I know," she said tapping her head. "You've got them all up here. I was hoping some of this work could be done in Roc's office, but now . . ." She sighed in exasperation. "Well, I suppose there's no help for it." She yanked her chair out and sat down hard.

Grumpy's low growl froze Grady in place when he bent to take a seat in his own chair. Fortune hid a smile as she reached down and coaxed Grumpy out from underneath the desk to the side opposite Grady.

Scowling with a resurgence of anger, Grady eased into the chair with great care. "You didn't have to bring the dog for protection. I promised to behave like a gentleman, didn't I, lass?"

Fortune was all innocence. "But I told you why I brought my dog. I couldn't leave him at the hotel. As it is, I'm breaking the rules by sneaking him in at night."

Vexation shadowed Grady's features, and Fortune knew he didn't believe a word she'd uttered. Well, so much for feminine charm. Abruptly she changed the subject.

Reaching into the box she slapped a handful of receipts down in front of him. "Now," she said, methodically, "you can help me separate these papers by date. Later we'll separate them further by transaction."

The butternut-colored dog rested his big square head on Fortune's thigh and stared across her lap at Grady. The Reb grumbled in disgust and reached for the papers Fortune had handed him. His hand accidentally collided with hers. She started in surprise. The dog growled. Grady cursed. "Damn mutt! Keep it up and I'll turn you into a eunuch!"

Suddenly a harassed-looking woman burst into the back room like a whirlwind. Acknowledging her presence, Grady kept a wary eye on Grumpy and stood.

"I'm sorry if I'm late, Grady," the woman gasped, mistaking the remnants of anger on her boss's face. Not giving him a chance to correct her assumption she chattered on. "That Joe Billings boy and Book were out all night. Book didn't get home till just a half hour ago, and let me tell you, I was fit to be tied. He wouldn't tell me where they'd been either. Now what's a mother to do with a boy like that?" Licking her fingertips, she plastered a few wiry chestnut hairs into her chignon then negligently tossed her shawl over a hat tree behind the door.

Grady drove his long square-tipped fingers through his hair. As much as he liked Irene, he was in no mood for her prattling. Reminding himself that the poor woman was not the one responsible for his ill mood, Grady mustered a half-hearted smile. "You're right on time, Irene. And I wouldn't worry too much about Book. He's a typical boy. But if you like, I'd be happy to have a word with him."

"Oh, would you, Grady? He does need a man's firm hand,"

she said, tying a long white apron over her plump middle. "He's of an age where he thinks women, especially his ma, don't know a whole lot." As if she'd just noticed Fortune, she asked, "And who might this be?"

"Remember the lady I told you about," Grady asked, "the one who pushed Tish out of the way of that runaway carriage?"

"Oh, yes!" Irene came forward and took Fortune's hand. "Miss Landry, it's a pleasure."

"Miss Fortune," Grady interjected, "this is Mrs. Irene Tabor."

"Please just call me Fortune," the younger woman said, smiling.

Irene Tabor's face glowed with warmth. "All right, Fortune it is, and you call me Irene. Goodness, you're as pretty as Book and Patricia said, and I'm so beholden to you for saving my little Tish. Book says you were so brave."

"Children tend to exaggerate," Fortune said, laughing, "but thank you for the compliment. Mr. MacNair has spoken very highly of you, and I've been anxious to meet you."

Irene sent Grady a grateful smile. "Grady has been a good friend to me and the children," she said. When the bell over the front door tinkled, her hazel eyes whisked to the front of the store. "Well, time to earn my pay. Perhaps we can lunch together and become better acquainted."

"Thank you, I'd like that very much." Fortune watched as the woman left to help the early-bird customer.

The walls of Jorgensen Carpentry reverberated with the sound of saws, hammers and sanding tools. Particles of sawdust floated in the sunlight streaming though the big front windows. Roc Landry inhaled the scent of freshly cut lumber and varnish as he limped to the back of the shop.

"By Odin's beard, Roc!" Eric exclaimed glancing up from his workbench, "You got rid of your cast, but you look like you just lost your best friend. What's the matter? Your leg still hurting?"

Leaning against a wall adjacent to the bench, Roc replied solemnly, "My leg is fine, just a little weak. I do have something I need to talk to you about, though."

Eric laid his tools aside and dusted his hands off on his overalls. "Come back to Pa's office, where we can hear each other without shouting."

The sounds of carpentry muted as Eric pulled the office door closed behind them. Resting one hip on a desk filmed with sawdust, he asked, "What's the problem, Roc? A pretty girl got your insides twisted out of sorts?"

Roc relaxed into a chair facing Eric's battered face. "It's Fortune."

"Fortune or the Reb?" Eric asked with a shrewd lift of one blond brow.

Roc's chuckle was cynical. "Both, I guess." He hesitated, wondering how much he should reveal. Eric was already cognizant of his Gypsy blood and his spy missions during the war. He didn't, however, know about Fortune's part in one of those missions. Still, Roc trusted the big Viking. If he called one man "friend", that man was Eric Jorgensen. And considering what he was about to propose, Eric deserved to know everything.

Inhaling a deep breath, Roc told him of Fortune's brief career as a spy and the Reb's part in it. Then he explained Fortune's superstitious belief in the Moondance.

Dumbfounded, Eric shook his flaxen head. "You mean she really believes in magic? She believes that she and the Reb are bound together in some kind of love spell?"

Roc nodded. "That's about the size of it. But don't go thinking that Fortune is some kind of crazy, because she's far from it. She's just a little eccentric in this one thing. You have to understand, Eric, that our grandmother practically had full rein over her while she was growing up, and Granny filled her head with all kinds of Gypsy folklore."

"Well, I guess we Swedes have our share of beliefs in fairies and such, too." He smiled. "And I can certainly understand Fortune's fear of the Reb learning who she is. But what's this you're saying about her being attracted to MacNair? Under the circumstances that surprises me."

"I said she *thinks* she's attracted to him. Don't forget, she believes herself entrapped by the Moondance, too. For my part, I'm not convinced she's actually attracted to the man. She said something the other day that stuck in my mind, something about believing being half the magic. Fortune believes! Therefore, it follows she imagines she's falling in love with the Reb."

The corner of Eric's mouth lifted in an ironic grin. "This is the darndest situation I've ever heard of, but I got a feeling you've thought of a way out of it."

Roc's expression relaxed in a sly smile. "Maybe. I figure if Fortune were to fall in love with another man, it would solve the problem, don't you think?"

"Well, sure but . . . Wait, you want me to be the other man?"

Roc nodded, glad that Eric grasped his plan so quickly. "She already likes you and thinks you're good-looking, too," Roc said encouragingly.

Eric looked pleased to hear it.

"She is a beautiful woman," Roc continued. "Surely you wouldn't mind . . ."

Eric laughed and stretched his arms wide. "Mind? What healthy man would mind those green eyes of hers and all that black hair, not to mention that figure?"

Roc's head jerked up at that, and he regarded his friend seriously. "I don't want her ill-used, Eric. I'd kill any man that took advantage of her—and that includes you, my friend."

Eric's feet hit the floor in objection. "I'd never do that, Roc. And for your information, I planned on courting the lady long before this conversation. I've never met a woman like Fortune."

The big Gypsy grinned then and grabbed the Swede's hand in a hearty handshake. "Eric, you don't know how much it eases my mind to hear you say that. And once Fortune falls in love with you, she'll come to realize this Moondance nonsense is nothing more than a fairy tale.

"It'll make my life easier, too. I'm not afraid of the Reb, yet having him for a partner does put me in a precarious position. I've told Fortune there's little danger, but if through some misguided sense of honor she were to reveal our identities to MacNair, who knows what the man might do? And even if he weren't vengeful, I don't relish having a Reb for a brother-in-law!"

Eric nodded agreement. Both had fought hard and long on the side of the Union. "Don't worry. The worst you'll have to suffer is a big Swede for a brother-in-law."

The two men laughed, then put their heads together to map out a sweeping courtship.

When Fortune parted with Irene Tabor after lunch she left the mercantile and headed for Roc's warehouse. It was a fair distance in the opposite direction from the mercantile, but

Grumpy's energetic tug on the leash kept her to a quick pace. In no time, she found herself in her brother's office.

Roc glanced up from his desk and smiled in surprise. "I didn't expect you until this evening. Is everything all right? Did the mongrel do his duty? That damn Confederate didn't try anything, did he?"

"If you'll stop shooting questions at me like a Gatling gun, I'll tell you." Fortune chuckled, taking a seat in a tattered settee.

"Sorry. I was worried for you, that's all."

"Well, thanks, but Grumpy did an admirable job. If MacNair so much as looked cross-eyed, Grumpy leapt up and growled furiously. The Reb got so mad that he threatened the poor dog. Oh, that reminds me, what's a eunuch?"

"Where did you hear that word?" Roc asked with a lift of one dark brow.

"It's what MacNair threatened to do to Grumpy."

Roc roared with laughter. When he calmed down he answered her question. "A eunuch is a man that's been rendered incapable of . . . Well, you know, don't you?"

"Oh, you mean he can't have sex."

"Fortune!"

"Oh, for gosh sakes, why the fuss? Nobody is around to hear, and you *are* my brother."

Roc cleared his throat, clearly uncomfortable discussing sex with his sister. "And how did the bookkeeping go?"

"Fine, though I'm sorry to say that MacNair's books are as reprehensible as he said they were. It'll take a long time to sort out everything."

"And yet you're calling the day done?"

"Yes. I had lunch with a new friend, then decided to have a look at your books. After all, I came to Montana to help you."

But the freight books weren't the real reason Fortune left the mercantile. Working at Grady's side all morning had been a grueling test of her will power. Every touch, every heated glance set her Gypsy blood at full boil. When Irene Tabor appeared for lunch, Fortune had practically fallen over Grumpy getting out of the back room.

"Come to think of it," Roc said, interrupting her thoughts, "maybe it is a good idea we work together this afternoon. After next week I won't be around to answer your questions."

"You're leaving?" Fortune sat forward in surprise. "Where are you going?"

"We're heading for Salt Lake City."

"But for how long, and why you?"

"Fortune," Roc said patiently, "I told you when you arrived that I'd be gone much of time. That's why I sent for you, remember?" At her nod, he continued. "I'll be gone for around eight weeks, depending on the trail, the weather and lady luck."

"But what about the new store in Fort Benton?" she asked.

Roc grinned. "You're my partner now, so you handle it. If Grady proves honest and free of debt, go ahead with the deal. I'll see to it that Harry Arlington over at the bank knows you're to have access to the business accounts."

"You'd really trust me to do all that?"

Roc's smile was both loving and knowing. "It's what you've always wanted isn't it?"

"Yes, but—"

"Then it's all yours, Sister Mine. I'm sure MacNair will provide the know-how in setting up the Fort Benton store, so don't worry about that part of it. All you have to do is look out for the Landry interests."

Swiveling around in his chair, Roc bent down to dial the safe combination and commented over his shoulder, "I saw Eric Jorgensen today. He's quite taken with you. I didn't think you'd mind so I accepted a dinner invitation from him on your behalf. He'll be by the hotel at six o'clock." Roc shut the safe and turned around, placing an armload of ledgers on the desk. Next to them went a stack of bills of lading. "I believe," he continued, "he's taking you to Chang's. It's one of the few Oriental restaurants outside Chinatown, and the food is delicious." He glanced up from the ledgers and frowned. "Why the dour face? I know this looks like a lot of work but . . ."

"It's not the work, Roc. You're repeating our father's mistake. I wouldn't let him choose a man for me, and you're not getting away with it either."

"Fortune, you should know me better than that. I know how you hate others meddling in your life." Veiling his eyes with downcast lids, he flipped through the papers on his desk with a suspicious fervency. "I'd think after what happened out at the ranch Eric's feelings for you would be obvious," he commented offhandedly. "You seemed to like him."

"If Eric wishes to court me, then he should be man enough to ask me himself," she said, studying her brother. "But really, Roc, don't you think I've got enough to cope with right now, without having to keep Grady MacNair and Eric from killing one another? In case you haven't noticed, MacNair is still very interested in me."

Roc glanced up and scowled. "Oh, I noticed all right, and you didn't exactly discourage him with that damsel-in-distress kiss last night."

Fortune grimaced guiltily but offered no explanation. She'd already berated herself, and it was now a moot point.

"The way I see it," Roc continued, "if the Reb has any pride at all, he'll back off when he finds out you're enamored of another man. And that is what you want, isn't it?"

"Yes, but—"

Roc interrupted and forged ahead. "Didn't you say that the Reb had to hate you to undo the magic of that Moondance?"

Fortune cocked her head to one side. She knew Roc didn't believe in the Moondance and wondered what he was up to. Playing along, she answered, "Yes, that's right. If Grady comes to hate me, the spell will be broken."

"Well, speaking as a man, I can tell you that if the woman I loved gave another man even a passing glance, I'd be mad as hell."

Fortune considered that a moment. "Being mad isn't the same as hating, but you might have something there."

Satisfied that he'd accomplished what he'd set out to, Roc motioned to an extra chair. "Let's get started. I have to leave soon and pick up those supplies you purchased at MacNair's mercantile. I promised Granny I'd be back at the ranch for supper.

"Oh, before I forget, I have good news. I may have located a house. John Ward, my lawyer, is looking into it. I should know something by the time I return to town Friday. Now," he said opening a ledger, "this looks like as good a place to start as any."

The bat-wing doors of the Red Dog Saloon fanned open, admitting Deke Tunney and Clyde Sheety. After the clean night

air, the pungent aroma of stale beer, tobacco and unwashed
bodies assaulted Deke's bulbous nose, but he was too preoc-
cupied to notice much. He panned the smoky bar for the two
men he'd come to meet. He found them at a dark corner table
at the back of the room, jabbed Clyde in the ribs and pointed.
"Over there," he said, hobbling to the table on his wooden leg.
Clyde shuffled along behind.

As Deke reached the table, one of the men hailed a waitress
and yelled for another bottle and two more glasses. "Frank,
Eli," Deke greeted each. He dragged off his hat and kicked
a chair out from the table. He gestured to Clyde to sit next to
him. "Well, whatcha learned, boys?" Deke asked anxiously.

Frank, a dark-haired, huskily built man of over six feet,
grinned and displayed a mouthful of rotting teeth. "Me and
Eli hired on with Landry like you told us to. We head out for
Salt Lake City sometime next week. And get this, Roc Landry
is making this trip."

Deke slapped his thigh in glee. "Good, good. This is what
we've been waitin' for. Damn, but it's right accommodatin'
of Landry to leave town. You'll have to be twice as careful,
though. Landry ain't no fool. Make sure all the trouble you
cause looks like accidents."

Eli leaned his tall, gaunt form back in his chair and brushed
a muddy brown lock off his forehead. "Don't worry, boss. Me
and Frank can handle it. We'll see to it Landry has nothin' but
bad luck all the way to Salt Lake."

"Fine." Deke grinned. "The boys will be at Blood Rock
waitin' for you on the return trip. You two are to make sure
that Landry's wagons can't make a run for it when the boys hit
the train. Understood?" He took the bottle and glasses offered
by a frowsy redhead and waved the woman off.

"Can I go with 'em, Deke?" Clyde wheedled, grabbing the
bottle and pouring a drink. "I can drive a team real good. You
know I can." He swigged down the whiskey, wiped his bristly
chin with the back of his hand and poured himself another.

"Not this time, Clyde." Clyde's face clouded with disappointment. "I've got another job for you, a very important one. You
want to be here to help me with the girl, don't you?"

Clyde grinned and licked his lips. "Do I get to have 'er
now?"

Deke grimaced, wondering if he wasn't making a mistake

letting his halfwit shadow perform such an important job. "Not yet. That comes later. We're gonna have a little fun with 'er and 'er brother first, remember? For now, I'm lettin' you set the Landry warehouse afire."

"When?"

"Just as soon as that Gypsy bastard of a brother of hers leaves town."

Chapter Ten

Standing behind the mercantile counter, Fortune smiled and thanked Mrs. Pritchard for her purchase. Business had been brisk all morning, and when Angus left to help a farmer load his wagon, Fortune jumped at the opportunity to lend Irene a helping hand with the customers.

Except for the failure of the Riddance spell, the past three days had gone well. In the mornings she worked at the mercantile, the afternoons at the freight office.

She didn't always accomplish as much bookkeeping at the store as she would have liked, but she was gaining an invaluable knowledge of the everyday workings of a mercantile. And of equal importance, she'd made lots of new acquaintances.

Customers were always poking their heads into the back room to gossip with Grady or coax an introduction to her out of him. At first, Fortune fretted over the interruptions, but she soon came to enjoy the constant comings and goings and the lively gossip.

Hildy Stevens, on hearing about Ursula's rheumatism, immediately wrote down her guaranteed-to-cure-or-kill recipe of green tea, whiskey and herbs. Sarah Barkly offered the warning that while the Widow Harkins presented a ladylike mein, she was anything but. Why, everyone knew the widow invited her male borders into her bed! Fortune learned that the mayor suffered from gout, the sheriff kept a Chinese mistress, and that the only meat in the soup at Joe's Soup House consisted of roaches.

Yes, Fortune mused, Helena was beginning to feel like her home. The people here were real. As in so many other mining camps, fortunes were made and lost with equal rapidity. Therefore, a person's wealth didn't count for much, not like it did with her mother's hoity-toity friends back east.

The bell over the door tinkled, jarring Fortune from her thoughts. She smiled at the wizened old miner who shuffled in. His name was Twig, and whenever the shabbily dressed old fellow sauntered into the store, things were sure to get lively.

"Howdy, Kitten," he called out to her. "How's my little cat-eyed gal today?"

Fortune laughed. She'd met Twig two days ago, and he'd promptly nicknamed her Kitten because she had green eyes that tilted like a cat's. "I'm just fine," she answered cheerily. "Anything I can get for you today?"

"Nope." He chuckled. "Just come in to pester you all." He spat a wad of tobacco toward the spittoon resting at the foot of the potbelly stove. "Damn," he grumbled, "missed again. Eyesight's gettin' worse every day." Wiping a brown dribble from his lips with the back of his hand, he turned and focused faded blue eyes on Fortune. "Where's that ornery Reb today?"

"Oh, he's around here somewhere—unloading supplies out back, I think."

Irene finished helping the mayor's wife choose a bolt of material and turned to Twig. "You gonna play us a tune on that new Jew's harp you bought the other day, Twig?"

"Yeah, give us a tune," Angus encouraged, entering the front door.

Twig bobbed his shiny pate. "I reckon I kin do that," he answered with a nonchalant shrug.

Fortune hid an amused smile. Everyone who'd been a Helena citizen more than a week knew the old man loved to show off his talents.

Twig shuffled over to one of the chairs stationed around the potbelly stove and made a show of getting comfortable. Then

placing the Jew's harp at his mouth, he began to pluck out a few
twangy notes. "Plays right good, don't it?" he cackled, glancing
up at his audience. He played again, this time a complete song.
Angus grabbed a pair of wooden spoons and rapped against his
thigh in time with Twig's next song.

Fortune closed her eyes and swayed with the music. How she
missed singing and dancing! It had been so long. And music,
any music, had always been an inspiration to her Gypsy soul.

Hearing the music, Grady came out of the back room, set
down a bag of flour and relaxed against the doorjamb. His
prim business partner immediately caught his eye. She stood
there clapping her hands and tapping her toe to the music. It
was very obvious that she was enjoying the music. But there
was something very intriguing about her today. It was as if
she'd shed her prim facade like an unwanted skin and exposed
a totally different person.

She glazed up at him, and he knew then what it was he was
seeing. Her green eyes sparked with it—the zealous soul of a
free spirit. Seeing her in this new light fascinated him, and without conscious thought, he slowly made his way toward her.

Grady barely noticed when more passersby came in to enjoy
the impromptu entertainment. And he only nodded to the blacksmith when the man whipped out his harmonica and played
along with Twig.

Stamping out the rhythm with one booted foot, Twig led into
Oh, Susanna. Fortune let go a surprised "Oh," when Grady
caught her up in his arms and swung her into the middle of
the store. He let her go just long enough to perform a deep
bow, then caught her up in his arms again.

To his delight, his prim and proper partner made no attempt
to vanquish her free-spirited side. Far from it! Fortune tossed
her head back and laughed with sheer abandonment and joy.
The sound was like no other Grady had ever heard. It literally
frothed and bubbled with her lust for life.

Grady whirled Fortune around flour barrels, tables of dry
goods and farm implements. Her hair worked loose and rippled
down her back like lustrous black velvet. As she laughed her
tilted green eyes shone with her delight in the music, the
dancing and something more.

Excitement, Grady thought, a lifetime of it! He was startled
when it dawned on him that until this very moment, he hadn't

truly known the woman in his arms. But he wasn't displeased. What man would be? If only he could figure out why she'd kept this wonderfully earthy side of herself locked away.

Saturday dawned early. Fortune yawned, stretched and swiped a long strand of ebony hair from her sleep-glazed eyes. Reluctant to leave her snug nest, she buried into the bedcovers and stared up at the ceiling of her hotel room. She smiled to herself, mindful of the events of this past week.

She couldn't think about the mercantile without Grady entering into her thoughts. As he'd promised, Grady had remained a perfect gentleman all week. Even the temporary slip of her self-discipline a couple days ago hardly bothered her. After all, she'd been safely chaperoned by a small crowd. Besides, it was the most fun she'd had for a long time.

But though Grady's hands had otherwise never touched her, his insidious Southern charm did. To her dismay, Fortune had actually found herself longing for him to forsake his promise, to take her into his arms and satisfy the strange yearnings that plagued her more and more with each passing day. And constantly reminding herself that their attraction wasn't real did nothing to sway her wild Gypsy passion.

And then there was the sweet, lovable Viking. Every evening, Eric came to the warehouse to escort her to dinner and then back to the hotel. His company was always pleasant, and he was fast becoming a good friend. Fortune found his attentiveness flattering, but his stolen kisses roused none of the passion evoked by the Reb's mere touch. She wished with all her being it had been otherwise, because Eric deserved no less than all a woman had to offer.

Grumpy's snort retrieved Fortune from her musing. She watched as the big hound padded to her bedside. His tail thumped eagerly against the bedside table as he let loose with one sharp and impatient yip.

"All right, boy," the girl said laughing. "I know it's getting late and you want to go out." Resignedly, she threw back the sheets and reached for the wrapper draped over the footboard.

Once up and moving, Fortune began to look forward to the day's activity and hastily performed her morning ablutions. Roc had returned to town yesterday with Granny and Ursula in tow and was taking all three of them to view a house this morning. He'd been extremely vague in his descriptions so she'd counseled herself not to expect too much.

She drew her hair back with a primrose ribbon that matched her lawn dress, then reached for the tiny pocket watch laying on the dressing table. After checking the time, she dropped it into her reticule and took one last glance in the mirror. Assured that she was completely buttoned, tied and combed, she leashed her eager pet and hurried down the back stairs to meet Roc and the two elderly ladies.

Roc drove the carriage down Cutler Street past a Methodist church and reined to a stop in front of a Italianate villa-styled house. Having expected little more than a crude, two or three room log cabin, Fortune gasped in astonishment at the lovely home.

The two-story house hosted a center gable with a double door entry. To the left of the doors was a porch, to the right an arched bay window. A tall three-window cupola crowned the roof of the opulent structure.

The tall weeds and junglelike rose garden lent the stately dwelling a forlorn feeling, but Fortune was undaunted. "Oh, Roc, it's perfect! I never expected such—"

"Have a look inside before you draw any conclusions," he interrupted, avoiding her eyes. "You see, ah, this place was a—" Roc stopped when he realized Fortune had already left the carriage and headed up the path to the door. Amused, he shook his head, leapt to the ground and secured the horses to a hitching post. As curious and as excited as Fortune, Granny and Ursula helped each other from the carriage and joined the younger woman on the porch.

"Looks like a backbreaker ta me." Ursula grumbled, staring up at the house. "It'll take a heap a work ta keep dis monster lookin' like somethin'."

"Well, it has a nice rose garden," Granny said, trying to sound optimistic.

Ursula eyed the weed-infested, five-foot-tall rose bushes with skepticism. "Ugh," she grunted. "Looks more like a briar patch ta me."

"The choice was limited to this or a bedbug-infested miner's shack," Roc said, stepping up on the porch. He produced a key and unlocked the door.

Fortune bustled ahead of the others, stopping just inside to let her eyes adjust to the dimness. When she could see clearly again, she gaped thunderstruck. Scarlet and purple assaulted her senses.

Over her shoulder, she blinked up at Roc. He shrugged apologetically. "Well," he started, clearing his throat, "the place—"

"Looks like a hohouse to me," Ursula blurted in her forthright way.

Granny laughed at her grandson's bleak expression. "That's it, isn't it?" she said, slapping her well-padded thigh with glee. "This was a whorehouse. Well, I must say the soiled doves had good taste. My, but I do love red and purple!"

Ursula grunted and rolled her eyes.

Fortune laughed, turning in a slow circle and taking in the outlandish red-flocked wallpaper and garish gold-embossed fixtures. From where she stood, she could see not only the entryway but part of the parlor and dining room, all finished in the same bawdy colors. "Minus the wallpaper, I can live with most of this," she finally commented. "Why, with the walls painted white, it will be rather cheerful, don't you think?"

"Indeed," Granny agreed happily.

"Hmm, Gypsies!" Ursula mumbled, eyeing the other two women as if they were minus the good sense they were born with.

"Well, what are we waiting for?" Fortune asked. "Let's go exploring." While Ursula and Granny took their time intricately detailing each room and its contents, Fortune tugged Roc from room to room, sometimes exclaiming in horror, sometimes in shock, but always in fascinated delight.

The ground floor accommodated a good-sized parlor, a small library, a large dining room and a kitchen. Off the kitchen was a large pantry, and across from that were servants' quarters. After glimpsing all the rooms downstairs, Fortune returned to the entryway and ascended a beautiful redwood staircase.

At the top was a long hallway lined with six bedrooms and one washroom. All the rooms were small and hideously gaudy except for the spacious master suite at the east end of the hall.

"This must have belonged to the . . . er . . . Madame," Fortune stuttered as her brother followed her into the room. A little embarrassed, she shied away from looking directly at him and found something else to comment on. "Roc, look at that bed! Have you ever seen one that big? And look at the cupids on the headboard," she said going to the bedside. "Aren't they cute?" Reaching out, she tested the quality of the mattress. Then, unable to resist, she laid down on the room's crowning glory.

Light reflected in her eyes, and she glanced up at the ceiling. She sat straight up. "Sweet Gaia, will you look at that! Now why do you suppose anyone would put a mirror on the ceiling?" When her question met with silence, she removed her gaze from the mirror to her brother. "Roc?"

Her brother did an about-face and bolted for the door.

"Wait! Where are you going?" Fortune leaped from the bed and chased after him. In the hall she snared his arm and yanked him to a reluctant halt. "What's wrong with you? Why didn't you answer my question?"

Her brother's black brows knit in grouchy discomfort. "For Christ's sake, Fortune, use your head—a mirror above a whore's bed, a bed in which she entertained customers?"

Fortune flushed. "You mean she . . . they . . . watched?" Roc gave a curt nod. "Great crystal balls and tea leaves!"

"Does this change your mind about the place?" he asked hesitantly.

"Of course not! Oh, I'll admit the mirror is a shock, but I certainly wouldn't let something so easily remedied shade my opinion of the entire house. When can we move in?"

"Well, that depends. The place isn't cheap, but as you've seen it's not exactly what most women are looking for in a home."

"Unless you're a Gypsy," his sister quipped with a grin.

"Well, be that as it may, some say the place is evil and contaminated."

"That's the silliest thing I've ever heard. Whoredom doesn't rub off. And if there is evil inside these walls, well, that can be dealt with easily enough."

Roc chuckled. "I don't want to hear about how you intend to do that, but be prepared for a few raised eyebrows among Helena's ladies."

Fortune laughed then asked, "Why do you suppose the girls all left?"

"Remember that Methodist church we passed up the street?" She nodded.

"Well, the church caused a real ruckus about having a devil's den in their very midst. Seeing as how they were here first, they finally talked the town council into closing the place down. The story is that the Madame was so mad, she up and took her girls, headed for San Francisco and left the bank holding the mortgage. The bank wants it off their hands, and the church, of course, wants decent people in the neighborhood. But thus far there have been no takers."

"And people really believe it's tainted?" Fortune asked incredulously.

"Suffice it to say that I'm positive I can talk the price down to an affordable one."

"Then I'll take it."

"Are you sure, Sister Mine? People are bound to talk."

"Oh, pooh!"

"It's an awfully big house, and you'll be here by yourself most of the time," Roc reminded her. "That bothers me a lot. A woman alone isn't safe in a mining town."

"I know, but I have that all figured out."

Roc arched a brow. "You do?"

"Yes, from the moment you stopped the carriage in front of this place, an idea began to take shape in my mind. Remember that family I mentioned, the Tabors?"

"Yes."

"Well, I'm going to ask Irene if she and her children would like to move in with me. She's too proud to take charity so I thought I'd hire her as my housekeeper and cook. It'll be the perfect solution for both of us." Fortune threw her arms around her brother's waist, almost squeezing the breath out of him. "Oh, Roc, I'm so happy, I could dance a jig. Things couldn't have worked out better."

Roc laughed and disengaged himself. "Whatever you do, don't do any more of those spellbinding jigs," he teased. Fortune shook her head, too excited to let the reminder of the Moondance shadow the moment.

Brother and sister found Granny and Ursula downstairs in the parlor, lifting sheets off the furniture. Ursula sneezed from the accumulated dust and cursed.

"Well, what do you think so far, Gran?" Fortune asked, spreading her arms wide to indicate the house. "Isn't it wonderful?"

"Oh, yes," the old Gypsy agreed, uncovering a settee of purple silk damask.

Though the room was cluttered with an overabundance of furniture, Fortune noted with satisfaction that all the pieces matched, the framework done in dark laminated rosewood, the upholstering in purple. Purple velvet festooned the windows in elegant swags. In front of a large fireplace made of Montana boulders, two settees faced one another with a low rectangular table centered between. Small elegant parlor chairs interspersed with divans were artfully arranged to form cozy conversational circles.

"We won't need all this furniture," the young woman commented.

"Exactly my thinking," Laila piped up. "If you've decided to take this place and you don't mind, I might appropriate a few pieces for the ranch."

Fortune caught her brother's eye. "If Roc can get the price down, I'm definitely taking it. So you'll be more than welcome to pick and choose the pieces you want."

"What are the bedrooms like?" Granny asked, glancing out the parlor doors toward the stairs. "Anything in them we might use at the ranch?"

"I didn't take a careful look, but I doubt it. Except for the master suite they're shabbily furnished and every bit as shocking as the red wallpaper is down here."

"You wants a shock, get a sight of dat fat nekked woman painted on de wall in de dining room," Ursula exclaimed. "Don know how a body could eat starin' at dat thin'."

"Well, let's have a look upstairs," Granny said, prodding the old black woman toward the stairs.

Ursula left the room with Laila, still muttering under her breath. "Neber in all my born days thought ta set foot in a hohouse, let alone live in one. Lordy! Lordy!"

Chapter Eleven

When Fortune entered the storeroom of the mercantile Monday morning Grady was hard at work unloading a freight wagon just arrived from Fort Benton.

"Good morning, partner," he said with a grin. Adding a crate to the growing stack along one wall, he pivoted round and nearly tripped over a growling Grumpy. His ready smile bent at the corners. "I thought you said this mutt wouldn't get in my way."

"Sorry, just got here," Fortune sang out cheerily. She sashayed to the desk and called Grumpy to her side. Ignoring Grady's low grumblings, she arranged her russet skirts, sat down and opened a ledger. She tried to concentrate on the columns of numbers, but for some reason found herself stealing surreptitious peeks at her grouchy partner. Despite the dirty apron that covered his clothes, there was something about him this morning that reeked with animal magnetism.

As he stomped in and out of the building, Fortune became more and more intrigued. The sleeves of his dark blue shirt were rolled up above his elbows, exposing biceps that flexed with the weight of the crates and lumpy burlap bags. And when he turned his back on her to stack a crate, she couldn't help noticing the way his denim trousers stretched over his slim-hipped buttocks. Enjoying her private pursuit, the young woman smiled to herself. She couldn't recall ever studying a man's backside before, but Grady MacNair definitely had a nice one.

And wouldn't he be shocked if he could read your thoughts, she admonished herself. Focusing on safer climes, Fortune shifted her gaze to a rebellious lock of hair that always tumbled over his forehead when he was hard at work. It lent his face a mischievous boyish quality, and she wondered what he'd been like as boy. A little hellraiser, no doubt.

Fortune studied the strong masculine lines of his face, admiring not for the first time the dimple in his chin. Her roaming eyes came to rest on his sensuous lips. As she sat there staring, a slow grin grew on those lips, and to her horror, she realized she'd been caught gawking. Heat suffused her cheeks. Her eyes darted back to the ledger on her desk. Without looking up, she abruptly announced, "I have to leave early today. Roc found a house for me, and I'm moving my things in this afternoon."

Grady grinned at the girl sitting across the room with her nose buried his ledger. Then the meaning of her words struck him. "I didn't know you were looking for a house," he said, approaching her desk. "If you need an extra pair of strong arms," he opened his wide, "I'm all yours."

Fortune glanced up, unable to keep from smiling at his sudden playfulness. "Thank you, but it's not necessary. The house comes furnished so all I have to do is move in a few personal items. Besides, Eric Jorgensen has volunteered to help, and Roc, Ursula and Gran will be there, too." Seeing Grady's abrupt halt and ensuing scowl, she realized her mention of Eric had not been wise. At a loss to correct the damage, she again bent over her paperwork.

Damn that Swede! Grady silently cursed. He grabbed a chair next to Fortune, flipped it around backwards and straddled the seat. Resting his crossed arms over the back, he leaned forward. "Damn it, Fortune, I'm your partner—and your friend, too. If you would've let me in on your plans, I'd have been happy to help you in any way possible." Grady knew he was taking his irritation over Jorgensen out on Fortune, but he couldn't help it.

"I'm sorry, Grady, but I didn't even see the house until Saturday morning. And this is the first time I've seen you since Friday."

"Oh." Grady forced himself to calm down and refrained from reminding her that she'd obviously had time enough to impart her news to Eric Jorgensen. Damn, he was behaving like a jealous fool. Well, he wasn't jealous. No, but he was plenty mad! That damn Yankee Swede was trying to horn in on the woman he'd decided to claim for himself. And after the war he'd promised himself that he'd not let a Yank or any other man take anything that belonged to him—not ever again!

"I suppose a house in town will be more convenient," he said evenly.

"Yes, it will. Roc can give up his room at the hotel, and of course, Granny and Ursula will stay with me when they're in town. You know," she added, steering him clear of what had turned out to be an awkward subject, "I'm surprised you haven't moved into larger quarters. I don't know how you stand living in that tiny room upstairs."

Grady shrugged, but he decided that maybe now was a good time to enlighten her about his plans for the future. A woman like Fortune would naturally want a man that could take care of her, and he wanted her to know that he had every bit as much—no, more to offer than Jorgensen did. "Haven't you ever heard of the frugal Scotsmen?" he asked with a cocky smile. "That room upstairs doesn't cost me a dime. And I've got plans for every penny I own."

Grateful for the return of his good humor, she asked, "You mean the Fort Benton store?"

"No. I'm using your brother's and the bank's money for that. But as soon as it's on its feet, I'll invest in a ranch. Then I'll have plenty of leg-stretchin' room."

"I didn't know that you . . ."

He winked. "There's a lot of things you don't know about me—yet."

I know a whole lot more than you think I do, Fortune thought. But aloud she asked, "What about the mercantiles? Will you keep them after you acquire the ranch?"

"For a time, but only until the ranch is self-supporting. To tell you the truth, I hate being cooped up in this store. I was raised to love the land. I like the sun and wind in my face all day."

Fortune had sensed this about him. Often she'd thought the clerk's apron incongruous with Grady's tall muscular frame. He seemed more in his element sitting atop a horse, a brace of guns strapped on his hips. However, until now, she'd credited his soldiering days for this perception. "So the mercantile will finance this dream ranch of yours?"

"Not a dream. It will be fact. By the time the mines play out and the miners leave, I figure to be well-situated on the biggest and best-run ranch in the territory."

"You seem awfully sure of yourself."

"Have to be. This isn't the civilized East. It takes more than money to conquer the land here in the territory. I've got the gumption and determination. The money will come."

"Don't forget know-how," Fortune put in. Though Fortune knew more about Grady than he realized, she was surprised at her desire to learn even more. She cocked her head to one side. "You said you were raised to love the land. Were you raised on a ranch, Grady?"

"No, but I know enough to get started. I learned a lot riding herd for the army. The posts kept small herds to feed the soldiers. I figure what I don't know, I'll learn, same as any other man. I'm not too proud to hire good men who can teach me."

"Your family were farmers then?" she probed.

A smile warmed Grady's expression, and a faraway look drifted into his delft-blue eyes. "Pa would have been insulted to hear himself called a farmer. He preferred planter. We owned a cotton plantation near Charleston. Oakridge, it was called. When I close my eyes I can still see my home sitting up on the hill it was named after. It was a big white house with stately columns across the front. Mother had roses planted round the entire house. A long drive wound from the road to the front door, and big granddaddy oaks shaded the whole thing." He chuckled. "Broke my arm twice learning to climb them."

Grady met Fortune's intent gaze, a smile still on his lips. "Folks around Charleston called it MacNair's Lair. I think Pa secretly liked the name better than Oakridge. Sounded more Scottish, don't ye ken," he added in heavy brogue.

"Pa was a rough, hard-drinking and hard-working man. But he never was ashamed to show his affection for me, and he sure did love my mama."

Fortune thought of her own parents. Did they love each other as much as Grady's parents apparently had? They seemed so absorbed in their own interests and in impressing others. Still, she'd like to think that they at least cared for one another a little. She'd never given it much thought, but perhaps she should have. Maybe it would have helped her to better understand them.

She gave herself a mental shake and returned her thoughts to the present. "You loved your home very much, but you never returned, did you?" When he spoke, she heard the sadness and loneliness in his reply, but none of the expected bitterness.

"There was nothing to return to. Pa died at Vicksburg. I lost Mother soon after. They said she died of pneumonia, but what really took her was a broken heart."

"No brothers or sisters?"

"An older sister, but she died before I was born."

"I'm sorry. And Oakridge?"

"Gone. Sold for taxes before I was mustered out of the army. Even if I'd been there, I wouldn't have had the money they said I owed on the place."

"My God, you've lost so much," she said almost to herself. "But if you love the South so much, couldn't you go back?"

"I can *never* go back." This time Fortune did hear the sharp edge of bitterness in his tone. "In the South I'm considered a traitor, Fortune. Most Galvanized Yankees are."

"I'm sorry, I didn't realize." Without conscious thought, she reached out in a gesture of compassion, laying her hand over his where it rested on the chair back.

Grady stared down at her small hand then reversed the position so he held hers in his. He gave it a gentle squeeze and let go. "Sorry," he smiled sheepishly. "Sometimes I get downright maudlin when I get to talking about the war and home.

"Hell," he said, shaking his head in amusement, "how did we get on this subject? We were discussing your new house. You were very lucky to find a decent place in Helena."

Fortune set her pencil down and smiled mischievously. "There's some in town who might argue about it being decent. The house is on Cutler Street, just down the street from the

Methodist Church. You've probably heard about it.''

Grady started to shake his head, then stopped and stared at her. "Surely you don't mean the notorious Madame La Bell's place?''

"Roc didn't mention the former owner's name but, he did say the house used to be a . . . Let me see, how did Ursula put it? Oh, yes! House of joy.''

Grady threw his head back and whooped with laughter. "That's one way of putting it. Your brother actually consented to let you buy a whore—er, a house of joy?'' he asked doubtfully.

"Good gravy, Mr. MacNair, don't tell me I've shocked you,'' she exclaimed, her laughter joining his.

"No—well, maybe just a little. It's just that, well, most of the ladies in this town wouldn't go near the place, let alone live there.''

"So my brother tells me. In fact, Roc said something about using that very reason to drive the price down.''

"That sounds like your brother,'' Grady returned dryly. "As darn right unfriendly as he's been, I hate to hand him a compliment, but he's blessed with business acumen.''

"Yes, and on that note, I think I better get busy on these books or I'll never get away from here today.'' Fortune took up a receipt and made a notation.

Grady slowly stood. "There's just one more thing I'm dying to know,'' he said, laughter evident in his tone.

Hearing the mischief, Fortune smiled but didn't bother to look up from the ledger. "And what might that be?''

"Are you going to keep the mirror over the bed in the Madame's room?''

Fortune's pencil lead broke. She didn't know which shocked her more, that he'd dared to ask her such a question or that he'd been in her bedroom—no, not her bedroom—the Madam's bedroom! "You . . . you've been there?''

Grady shrugged, then asked again, "Well?''

An unreasonable spark of jealousy touched off Fortune's temper. "What kind of crude question is that to ask a lady anyway?''

Taken back by her sudden enmity, yet unable to control his mirth, Grady held up both hands as if to ward off a blow. "Hey, I'm sorry. But moving into a bordello didn't seem to offend you, so I didn't think my question would."

At Fortune's continued scowl, his laughter broke off, and his voice took on that low melodious drawl that always made her heart beat like a tom-tom. "But maybe you weren't offended. Maybe you were wondering how I knew about the mirror. Are you jealous, sweetheart?"

He ducked as her pencil flew past his head. Emerald fire flashed from her eyes, and fury reddened her skin. *And this,* Grady thought in awe, *is what she'll look like when I make love to her—rosy and full of fire—magnificent!*

"Jealous!" Fortune ranted. "Me, jealous of you?" That Grady had stumbled on the very heart of the issue escalated Fortune's anger tenfold. "Don't flatter yourself, MacNair. And don't call me sweetheart!" She shoved her chair back and stood.

Grady reached for her shoulders, intending to press her back into her chair, but Grumpy snarled and leapt to all fours.

The Reb instantly released his beautiful partner and wisely backed off. "Damned mutt is a hellhound!"

The comment broke through Fortune's ire, and she almost but not quite cracked a smile. She *had* sounded jealous even to her own ears. Absently stroking Grumpy's head, she admitted, "Perhaps I did overreact a little. Truce?"

"Truce," he replied in bewilderment. *Damn,* he thought, *how the hell did she do that—go from one mood to the next without so much as the blink of an eye? Women!* he thought. *Who could figure them?* Shaking his head, Grady left to finish unloading the wagon out back.

Fortune seated herself and again attempted to give her attention to the ledger in front of her. She found a new pencil and began ruffling through the paperwork. *So,* she silently mused, *the Reb's been in a bordello. And not just any bordello, but mine. And he didn't deny sharing the Madame's bed either! Well, who cares?*

You care, answered a taunting voice in her head.

No. It's the magic. I only think I care about the brute, but I don't—not really. I just wasn't using my head, that's all. Most virile, unmarried men like Grady MacNair patronized those kinds of places. Or so she'd gathered from snatches of conversation she'd overheard among Roc's men during her travels with them.

But did it have to be my bordello he debauched himself in?
"Damn Rebel rake!" the girl cursed aloud to the room. "He's
making me crazy."

Returning with a large crate in his arms, the Reb caught
Fortune's words and paused in the doorway. *So I'm making
the lady crazy, huh?* A smile hovered on his lips. *Hot damn,
I can't wait to make love to this little crazy lady in that bed!*

Fortune poured herself into her work, unaware of the bustle
in the store until a harried Irene poked her head through it.

"Fortune, honey, can you give me a hand? Angus is busy,
Grady is loadin' a customer's wagon, and I got five or six
customers out here gettin' as cross as snappin' turtles."

Fortune laughed and pushed back from the desk, glad for
the chance to stretch her legs. "Of course, I'll help." In an
exaggerated stage whisper she added, "Besides, it's been a
day or so since I heard the latest gossip. Wouldn't want to
get behind now, would I?"

Two hours later, a weary Fortune leaned across the countertop,
glad for the temporary lull. Irene handed her a cup of the blackest
coffee the girl had ever laid eyes on and pulled up a couple tall
stools. "Whew," she sighed. "A body would think this stuff is
free the way people been swarmin' in here today."

Fortune nodded absently, thinking that now was a perfect
time to approach Irene about moving in with her. She sipped her
coffee and turned to the other woman. "Irene, there's something
important I've been wanting to discuss with you."

"Oh?"

"Yes, I desperately need your help."

"Well, if it's at all possible, you got it."

Fortune proceeded to explain about her new home, purposely
saving the whorehouse part for last. Not that she believed for a
minute that Irene was a prude, but on the other hand, why take
any chances?

"I adore the place," she was saying, "but you see it pres-
ents me with a couple problems as well. My brother will be
gone a good deal, and Granny and Ursula prefer living at
the ranch. They'll only stay at the house when they're in
town to shop. So you see, most of the time I'll be rambling
around that big place all by myself, and Roc worries about my
safety."

"As well, he should," Irene broke in. "Why, when word gets out that you're living by yourself, men will come swarmin' like bees to honey."

"That's what Roc said. But I do have what I think is a wonderful idea. I know it's presumptuous of me to ask, but I was wondering if you and the children might consider coming to live with me." She rushed on to allay any objections Irene might voice. "There's plenty of room, and I know we'd get along splendidly."

Irene hooted. "The offer is temptin', but, girl, you don't know what you're lettin' yourself in for. I love them little rascals of mine, but I'm their mother and it comes natural. Even so, I'm the first to admit they ain't angels. 'Sides, as nice as your offer sounds, there's no way I could live off you."

"Live off me? Did I say anything about living off me?"

"Well, no, but . . ."

"Irene, I'm a lousy cook and an even worse housekeeper. And if I don't find a companion to live with me, Roc is going to back out on buying the house for me." This was a fib, of course, but any Gypsy worth her salt knew a little lie for a good cause was not a sin. "I know and like you, Irene. I don't want to hire a stranger to live in my home. Besides, I think it most unlikely that I could pay anyone enough to live with me. Even you may not want to."

"How can you say that?" the older woman protested. "You're a respectable young woman. Why, I heard several ladies invitin' you to their homes today. They wouldn't be askin' if they questioned your morals."

"They may not think I'm so respectable when they hear where I'm living. Now keep in mind," she rushed on, "that it's a big gorgeous house."

Irene crooked an amused brow. "And?"

"Well . . . Oh fiddle! I might as well come right out and say it." Fortune leaned closer and whispered in Irene's ear. "It used to be a house of joy."

Irene's mouth dropped open. "House of . . . ? Oh, no! Oh, my, yes!" She roared with laughter, drawing odd stares from a couple across the room. Then for Fortune's ears alone, she joked, "You brazen hussy, you. You've gone and bought La Bells's whorehouse, haven't you? You know I've always wanted to see the inside of one of those places. Hell, honey, I bet you

could sell sightseein' tickets to every old prude from here to
Salt Lake City!"

"You don't mind, then? You'll come live with me?" Fortune
asked anxiously.

"Well . . ."

"Free board and room for you and the children, and all I ask
is that you help me with meals and housework. I'm getting off
cheap, Irene, and you know it. I'd have to pay anyone else to be
my companion, and she probably wouldn't cook or clean. You
can even keep your part-time job here in the mercantile, if you
like. And of course, I'll pay you for housekeeping. Whatever
it takes to get you to agree, just name it."

Tears gathered in Irene's eyes. "Fortune Landry, don't think I
don't know what you're up to, you sweet girl. I should turn you
down, but when it comes to my kids I have no pride, and what
you're offering is a godsend. I've been worryin' about how I
was gonna take care of my babies come winter. And . . . and
you see . . . there's another on the way."

Fortune threw her arms around Irene's shoulders for a heart-
felt hug. "Oh, Irene, a baby. I love babies. We'll be like one
happy family. And don't you dare suggest I'm offering you
charity. Believe me, I plan to get my money's worth, and when
you see my house you'll understand what I mean." She bent
close and whispered in Irene's ear again.

"No!" Irene gasped in delight. "Really? Over the bed?" At
Fortune's nod, Irene chuckled, "I can't wait to see it."

Outside, Grady tossed a bag of flour into Duncan Lawson's
wagon. Duncan, a fellow Southerner and a frequent customer,
had become a good friend over the past year. "How's Sue Ellen
and the kids, Duncan?" Grady asked the hulking farmer.

Only a few years Grady's senior, Duncan laughed. "Well, I
guess Suzie's doin' fine, considerin'. We're expecting another
baby in October."

"Congratulations. This is number four, isn't it?"

"Yeah." Duncan grinned, adjusting his hat over thick brown
hair. "Sure hope this one's a son." He leaned over conspiratorially and nudged Grady in the ribs. "That little black-haired filly
you got working for you is mighty pretty, friend. Ever give any
thought to gettin' hitched one of these days? It ain't half bad
havin' a good woman waitin' round to warm your bed at night."

Grady wiggled his brows slyly, not bothering to correct Duncan's assumption that Fortune worked for him. "I've been giving it more than just a thought. Trouble is, the lady has a man-hating hound for a pet, and he goes everywhere she goes. Let me tell you, that mutt cools a man's ardor faster than a snowstorm in May."

"Hell, I'd get rid of the dog." Duncan laughed.

"I couldn't harm the animal. She loves him too much."

"Naw, I didn't mean you should kill 'im or nothin'. Just get rid of 'im for a while, that's all."

"Yeah, and how do you propose I do that?"

"What is it every male craves, be he man or beast?"

Grady's face lit up. "A bitch in heat! Hot damn! Now why didn't I think of that?"

"Working side by side with a female as pretty as that one clogs a man's brain real bad," Duncan replied, shaking his head in mock pity. "Why, I'll bet you ain't even invited that little gal to the Fourth of July celebration yet. You know it's comin' up in a couple weeks."

Grady shook his head. "I clean forgot about it."

"Better get to it before some other feller beats you to it."

"I just hope I'm not already too late. Eric Jorgensen has been sniffing around Fortune since she hit town."

"Well, you ask her real sweetlike, cuz I've got three bitches out at the farm. If one is in heat over the Fourth, I'll bring 'er to town with me and the family."

Grady grinned and slapped Duncan on the back. Then the two of them put their heads together and made their plans.

Grady entered the mercantile with a big smile on his face. He spied Fortune finishing up with a customer and looked surprised. "You still here? Thought you were leaving early. Do you realize what time it is? It's near one o'clock."

"Oh, good gravy, I've missed lunch. Granny and Ursula will be fit to be tied."

"Fetch your things from the storeroom and meet me out back," Grady told her, stripping off his apron as he headed in that direction himself. "I'll take you to the hotel in the wagon. It'll be faster."

Fortune didn't waste time arguing. After retrieving her bag and her dog, she slipped out the back door of the warehouse.

While Grady finished hitching his horse to his delivery wagon, she urged Grumpy inside the wagonbed and secured his leash to one of the wood slats. Then she stood waiting for Grady's assistance into the wagon.

Grady gave the horse's flank an affectionate pat and stole a glance at Grumpy tied up in the rear of the wagon. Lady luck must be riding his shoulder today for he hadn't expected this opportunity to present itself so quickly. But it had, and he wasn't one to waste an opportunity. Oh, he knew getting a yes to his invitation wouldn't be easy. The vixen avoided him at every turn, but maybe with the right kind of persuasion, who knows?

Tipping his hat back at a rakish angle, Grady strolled over to Fortune and set his hands on her waist as if to lift her into the wagon seat. But once he'd captured her, he turned her to face him instead.

Fortune stared down at Grady's hands, now firmly clasped on her hips, and jerked her head up. "Just what do you th . . .?" Her voice died away at the sight of the hungry gaze that met hers. She immediately backed out of his hold, only to come up against the wagon. Nervously she demanded, "What are you doing?"

Grady planted his hands flat on either side of her. "Why are you always so jumpy, darlin'?" he drawled softly. "Don't you know I'd never harm a hair on that pretty little head of yours?" He caressed her cheek then with the back of his hand, as if to smooth away the misgivings etched on her face.

His touch fired Fortune's Gypsy passion. Unconsciously, she reached for her amulet.

Grady noted her action and frowned. Did she think she could use that damn thing to make him disappear?

"I *am* afraid," she said, pushing his hand away form her face with her free hand. "Please, I don't want you to touch me like that—and don't look at me that way either. It scares me."

"That's not fear I see in those lovely green eyes." Cupping her chin, he tilted her head back and dipped his head to hers. "Lord, woman, you got me so hot!" His kiss was gentle but firm in its demand that she let him in. And she did.

A thrill swept through Fortune as she savored Grady's warm tangy taste. How she wished she dared to surrender to it! But therein lay the danger, and she couldn't allow herself the luxury.

"You promised," she gasped, twisting her mouth from his and bracing her hands against his chest. "You promised business only!"

Grady smiled tenderly, his fingers exploring the texture of her jet hair from temple to crown and loosening it from its prim chignon. "I've kept my promise, Fortune, and will continue to do so—when we're working. But we're not working now."

Fortune's whole scalp tingled, and she barely registered the meaning of his words beyond the sound of his deep-timbred drawl. Yet, somehow, she managed to gather up the last threads of her willpower. Grasping his hand where it rested at the back of her head, she drew it away. Then she uttered a bold-faced lie. "Grady, I don't feel for you what you seem to imagine I do. I . . . I don't want you in that way."

"The hell you don't." He chuckled softly and ran his hands up her arms. "These goose bumps on your arms weren't caused by the chilly weather, darlin'."

"Why you arrogant . . ." He imprisoned her in his sinewy arms, and the rest of Fortune's reply was lost in his potent kiss. His male essence invaded her senses, unleashing primitive urges that rendered all thoughts of escape superfluous. Her tongue mated with his, and she moaned into his mouth. Her hands inched up his chest, grabbed handfuls of his shirt and pulled him against her breasts.

In the throws of his own erotic agony, Grady forgot all about issuing an invitation to the Fourth of July celebration and was heedless of the low growls emanating from the wagonbed. He reacted only to Fortune's fervor.

Grady lifted Fortune against the wagon and gyrated his swollen member against that sensitive place between her thighs. *God, if he could only be inside her!* The wagon slats creaked behind her, and he was reminded of the rhythmic creaking of a bed during the mating of a man and woman. The thought jolted him to his senses and reminded him where he was and why he'd begun this delightful interlude.

Damn, what was the matter with him? One kiss and he lost his head like some horny kid with his first woman. Never in his vast experience had a woman had so much power over him. It was as if she'd cast some kind of spell over him.

Lifting his face a scant few inches, Grady smiled down at Fortune's dazed expression. At least he had the satisfaction of knowing that he did to her what she did to him. "Come with me to the Fourth of July celebration, darlin' lass. Just this once, grant me a boon and say yes." He kissed her again, gentle and loving. "Say you will, darlin' girl." He began raining urgent kisses on her eyes, nose and cheeks. "I won't stop until you say yes."

Fortune didn't want him to stop. At this point her will was not her own, and she'd grant him the world if he but asked. "Yes!" she breathed barely above a whisper. Then a little louder, "Yes, I'll go with you."

An ear-splitting Rebel cry rent the air as Grady released her abruptly and tossed his hat over their heads. Then he yanked the startled girl back into his arms for a quick buss across her swollen mouth.

Stunned, she said nothing as he laughingly collected his hat and helped her aboard the wagon. But as he went on about what a good time he was going to show her, Fortune started coming to her senses.

My God, what had she done! Had she told Grady MacNair that she'd attend the Fourth of July celebration with him? *Great crystal balls and tea leaves, I already told Eric I'd go with him!*

A triumphant grin on his handsome face, Grady gave a shake of the reins and commanded the horses forward. *Now*, he thought, as he steered the wagon between buildings and onto Main Street, *if Duncan just remembers to bring one of his bitches, I'll have Fortune all to myself for a whole day.*

Fortune's mind spun. Damn! MacNair had gotten her drunk on his kisses and weaseled her into giving him a yes when she should have said no. He'd known she'd refused him under normal circumstances and also had known he could stir her to mindless passion. He'd seduced her, damn him! What impudence! What arrogance!

But wait. Was it possible his attitude was a product of the Moondance? She couldn't be sure, so how could she condemn the Reb for such behavior? She couldn't. It wouldn't be fair, not when the enchantment was her fault to begin with. Damn the Moondance! Something had to be done about it, and the sooner the better! Before Granny and Ursula returned to the ranch they had to come up with another Riddance spell. That's all there was to it.

For now, she'd tell Grady she'd made a mistake, that she wasn't free to attend the Independence Day celebration with him. She detested doing so, but tell him she would. With a determined lift of her chin, Fortune swiveled on the wagon seat and faced him.

He smiled at her—a warm, tender smile—a special smile.

I will tell him, she told herself. *I will. But not today. I'll wait for a better time.*

Chapter Twelve

Fog. Mist. It's cold here, Fortune thought. But where is here? It's so dark. Sweet Gaia! There's something, something evil here!

Slowly she rose, her movement sluggish as if she were moving through quicksand. This wasn't her bed, her room! What was the matter with her? Had she been drugged?

And what happened to her nightgown? She hadn't worn her Gypsy skirts for a long time, yet she had one on now.

Was she dreaming? Her situation felt real, yet not. Nothing was quite in focus. Damn, but this was scary!

Take a deep breath. Keep calm and look around. A log cabin, dingy and small. No tables. No chairs. Just the cot and the dust motes floating in a filmy light streaming in from a tiny broken window over the cot. Good, escape will be easy.

Escape? Yes. The evil that pervaded this place was like a living thing, slimy and cold against her nerve endings. She didn't like this place.

Someone's coming! She leaned over the cot and peered out the window. A man in Confederate gray. He was getting closer.

132

Who is he? Can't see his face. Sweet Gaia! He has no features. There's nothing but fog. How could that be? Run! Must run for her life! The man was coming for her. She didn't know how she knew; she just did.

Running through the trees. The cold mist was clammy on her face. She couldn't see the ground. It was like running on a cloud. She didn't know where she was, where she was going.

Something snagged her skirt. She must hurry, free herself! She was screaming, but there was no sound. A disembodied hand with a manacled wrist clutched her skirt hem. She yanked it free. Oh, God, bloodied faces, bodies, limbs, reaching out to her. She ran.

She could hear her heart pounding. Her chest was heaving, and it hurt so bad. Was he still coming? She glanced over her shoulder. God, yes! There he was!

Her foot caught on something, and she hit the ground hard. Maniacal laughter, his laughter. She rolled over in the cold, damp bed of leaves. The faceless Confederate stood over her, emanating malice.

What was that? Roc's voice. He was calling to her from the misty depths of the woods. Her tormenter lifted his gun. No! Not Roc! Don't shoot him. She heard no explosion even though the Confederate had pulled the trigger. "Roc," she called. No answer.

The faceless specter leveled the muzzle of the gun at her heart. She squeezed her eyes shut. Nothing. No sound, no pain. She opened her eyes. He was gone!

But what was that crackling sound. Fire! All around her! She must get up. Her ankle. Oh, sweet Gaia, no! It was sprained. The smoke, she couldn't breathe. Her throat burned. Yellow tongues of fire were getting closer, growing hotter and hotter. Fortune screamed and screamed and screamed, but not a sound came out.

"Fortune! For God's sake, wake up!"

Like a drowning victim reaching for a lifeline, Fortune groped wildly for the owner of the arms shaking her awake. Her eyes fluttered open and focused on her brother's anxious face. "Roc? Oh, Roc!" Sobbing she threw her trembling form into his arms.

"It's all right, Sis," he crooned, cradling her close. "It was just a dream."

"Slitherin' serpents! What's goin' on?" Ursula grumbled, scurrying into Fortune's room as she fumbled with her wrapper's sash.

Laila rushed in on Ursula's heels, took one look at her granddaughter's glazed eyes and gasped, "You've had one of those dreams, haven't you?"

"Now, Granny," Roc began.

"Don't you now-Granny me, young man!" Laila wagged her finger. "You can't deny the girl has a gift, not after that time she saved your hide."

"A coincidence, Gran," Roc sighed impatiently.

"Please," Fortune interrupted, shrugging out of her brother's arms, "let's not start that debate tonight."

Ursula's eyes darted around the room suspiciously. "You don reckon der's haunts in dis here hohouse, do you?"

Laila rolled her eyes heavenward. "Every corner of every room in this house has been sanctified with magical herbs. And garlic hangs over the front and back doors. No demon would dare cross our threshold."

Roc stared at his grandmother and shook his head, but wisely, he kept his opinions to himself. Instead, he turned to Fortune and asked, "Is something troubling you, Sister Mine? Is that why you had the dream?"

"I don't know. I suppose that could be it. But . . ."

"But?"

"Oh, Roc, it was so real. There was a Confederate soldier chasing me. He had no face. I think he shot you. And he was going to kill me. Only then he didn't. Instead I was surrounded by fire." Fortune shuddered and hugged herself.

Her brother smoothed her mussed hair from her face. "A man in a gray uniform, huh? Sounds to me like you've got yourself worked up over MacNair. Has he been bothering you?"

"No, he's done nothing. And the man in my dream wasn't Grady. At least I don't think he was. I know this sounds crazy, but it was as if I could feel the man's emotions. He didn't feel like Grady MacNair. He felt like someone else, someone mean and vile." Fortune swallowed over the lump in her throat. "And Roc, it *was* one of *those* dreams."

Laila had listened intently to Fortune's rendition and mused,

"One must be on guard when a fire is dreamed of, but it's not usually a sign of tragedy or death. Yet you say you feared for your life?"

Fortune nodded. "What do you make of it, Gran?"

"I hate to admit it, but I'm not sure what it means," Laila answered. "That you should be cautious is the only conclusion I can draw for the moment."

Roc frowned. He was a practical man who didn't believe in magic, ghosts or witches, but he had to admit that on at least one or two occasions, his little sister had spooked him with these curious dreams of hers. "Listen, honey, I'll have one of my freighters keep an eye on the place while I'm gone to Salt Lake."

"No, it's all right. Irene Tabor and her two children are moving in tomorrow, and Granny and Ursula will be here for another day or two. I won't be alone."

"Are you sure? It's easily arranged."

"We'll be fine, Roc."

"Promise me, you'll call on Eric if you need him," Roc gently insisted.

"I will."

Satisfied, Roc rose to his feet. "I better get back to bed myself. I'll be pulling out for Salt Lake in just three hours."

"Fortune, dear," Laila said, "would you like me to fix you a cup of tea before I turn in?"

"Thanks, Gran, but no. I'll be all right now. Sorry I woke you up."

"Bah, I couldn't sleep anyway."

"And she keeps me up too with all dat pacin' of hers," Ursula complained. "Makes me dizzier than an owl hoot, and I ain't even in the same room. When she do sleep, she snorts like a hog rootin' for dinner."

"You old dried-up prune," Laila retorted. "All that hot air coming out of you is making this room stuffy. Come on now, let's get of here and let the girl get back to sleep." The old ladies said their good nights and continued their bickering down the hall.

Roc and Fortune shared a smile. He bent down and pecked her cheek, then picked up the lantern he'd brought into the room. At the doorway, Roc turned to his sister one last time. "Good night, little Gypsy."

"You will be careful on this trip, won't you?" she asked. "I feel . . . I don't know, but I think someone means us harm."

"I'll be careful. I always am. Now get some rest."

Fortune nodded, but she worried he hadn't taken her warning seriously enough.

Hours later she was still awake, and when she heard Roc preparing to leave, she tiptoed from her room.

At the bottom of the stairs she heard him in the kitchen, probably having a cup of coffee before departing. She was in luck. Smiling with satisfaction, she found his saddlebags at the front door, removed her amulet from around her neck and tucked it inside. Then blowing a kiss toward the kitchen she scrambled back up the stairs.

"Vervain, what's that?" Ursula asked, as she sat down at the dining room table.

Breakfast dishes washed and put away, Ursula, Laila and Fortune had gathered at the table to discuss a new Riddance spell.

During breakfast Granny had made Fortune repeat what she could remember of her dream. Unlike Roc, Granny wasn't convinced the gray uniformed man in Fortune's dream was Grady MacNair. She'd reasoned that if Grady was under the spell of the Moondance, he couldn't possibly be the one wishing Fortune harm. On the other hand, perhaps the dream predicted that MacNair was about to find out Fortune's secret. In either case, it was decided they should cast another Riddance spell this very night.

"Vervain is a magical herb," Fortune replied to Ursula's question.

"Well, I neber heard of vervain," Ursula said. "Do it even grow around here?"

"Of course it does, you old fool," Laila replied. "What do you think verbena is? Didn't I just point it out to you, not a week ago? I even picked some. You're getting senile, Ursula. I've said it before, and this proves it."

"Ugh! Senile, my foot! You was gonna pick dem violets till I showed you they was de wrong weed. You need specs, and if dat ain't a good sign of bein' senile, I don know what is."

"Verbena isn't a weed, you ol' reprobate," Granny shot back. "It's an herb like Fortune said. And as for wearing specs, Gypsies don't wear them. We . . ."

"Dat's right, I forgot," Ursula interrupted as she placed her finger beneath her left eye and drew the lower lid down. "You Gypsy folks got de third eye. Too bad it ain't good for nothin' but seein' spooks."

Laila tossed Ursula a singularly disgusted look. "I've told you over and over again, it's the past and the future we can see, not spooks."

"You still can't tell de difference 'tween de violets and de weeds," Ursula snorted, clearly determined to have the last word.

Fortune's soft laughter earned her perturbed scowls from both old women. "You two are in high form this morning, but I think we better get on with this discussion before Irene and the children get here."

"Well, as I was saying earlier, before I was rudely interrupted," Laila said, curling her nose at Ursula, "the spell I found requires vervain leaves. I dried the ones I found last week and have them with me in my herb bag. Tonight we'll build a big fire out back and cast the spell."

"Do you think we should ride out of town a ways, Granny? We wouldn't want to be caught by any of our neighbors. And don't forget Irene will be here."

"If your friend Irene is like most pregnant woman, she'll sleep like the dead when she hits the bed at night."

"And what if someone gets nosy and wants ta know what yo doin' burning at midnight?" Ursula challenged.

"Why we simply tell the busybodies we're burning the evil beds once used by the soiled doves. We can even say a little prayer and tell them it's some kind of grand exorcism." Laila cackled at this last, and Fortune wondered if the dear old rascal hoped someone did come along.

"Only one thin' wrong with dat plan," Ursula snorted. "You don know no prayers. Yo almost heathen."

"Heathen! I'll have you know I was baptized five times in five different churches, one of them Roman Catholic."

"I know. I heard de story a thousand times," Ursula grumbled. "And I was with you when you snuck yo granbabies out of de house ta three different churches."

"Well, then, I fail to see how you can say I'm a heathen," Laila huffed. "I've been saved on numerous occasions."

Fortune crossed her eyes in an expression of exasperation and vexation. Baptizing their children many times was a safety precaution practiced by many Gypsies to doubly protect the vulnerable little ones from evil. But over the years she'd grown weary of hearing Granny and Ursula argue the benefit of multiple baptisms. "Granny, Ursula, the spell?" she reminded them.

"Oh, uh, yes, where was I?" Laila sputtered. "Now I remember. Will the fire out back be all right with you, Fortune?"

"I think it will have to be. I'm not much for driving through Helena and into the country in the middle of night. Roc says all kinds of ruffians prowl the streets at night, and I've already experienced the truth of it once."

"Then it's settled. Now, I suppose we'd better start cleaning out the rooms upstairs."

As they started to rise someone knocked at the kitchen door. Fortune experienced a familiar tingling on the back of her neck, but since she was expecting Irene and not Grady, she brushed it off. "I'll get it, Gran. It has to be Irene." She hurried from the dining room into the kitchen and yanked open the door.

Grady was wearing a gray shirt, and Fortune's heart nearly stopped. Then almost as quickly, a calm settled over her. She sensed none of the malevolence from Grady that she'd felt emanating from the man in her dream. Quite the contrary. The dashing rake was looking at her like she was a piece of his favorite cake.

"I'm here, too," Irene chirped, peeking out from behind the Reb's tall figure.

Fortune gave herself a mental shake and forced herself to look away from Grady and smile at Irene.

"Irene needed a hand moving her things," Grady explained with a jerk of his head to the wagon that sat in the backyard. "Is there some place in particular you'd like me to set this box?"

"Oh, forgive my manners. Come in." Holding the door, Fortune backed out of the way. "Ah, let's see, the box, yes, set it over there in the corner for now."

"What's that wonderful smell?" Irene asked, sniffing the air as she followed Grady inside.

Grady removed his hat and also sniffed. "Smells too good to be the garlic I saw hanging over the door out there."

For a moment Fortune went blank. Then remembering something Granny had once told her about the magical herbs, she smiled. "What you're smelling is Granny's dried herbs and flowers. She says they keep the insects out of the house."

"And the garlic over the door?" Irene asked curiously.

One thing Fortune very much enjoyed in common with her ancestors was the act of shocking the daylights out of a Gajo. She bit her lower lip and said in all seriousness, "Well, that's a little harder to explain."

"So are you going tell us what the garlic is for or not?" Irene asked, clearly impatient with the intrigue.

"It keeps the vampires out of the house."

Irene looked at Grady. Grady looked at Irene. They both turned to Fortune.

"Vampires?" Grady finally asked.

"Bloodsucking monsters," Fortune said, watching their expressions with glee.

For a moment her explanation met with stunned silence. Irene looked utterly repulsed, and Grady disbelieving. Then Grady started to laugh. "Irene, I think we've just been duped."

"Oh! You're just joshing us, right?"

"No," Fortune replied. "It's quite true, and a word of warning. To Gran it's serious stuff, so don't tease her about it."

Fighting against laughter, Irene just nodded and tried to regain her composure.

"Bloodsucking monsters?" Grady whispered doubtfully in Fortune's ear. "Surely *you* don't believe in that nonsense."

"Well, I've never seen one, and I admit it sounds farfetched but . . ." Fortune shrugged. "Who can say?"

Out of the blue a piece of memory flashed into Grady's mind. "Gypsies," he said aloud.

Fortune stomach lurched in alarm. "Gypsies?"

He shook his head in self-mockery. "Oh, I was just thinking out loud, that's all. During the war, my men and I were captured by some spies who appeared to be Gypsies. I remember seeing garlic hanging over the doors of their wagons. I wonder if Gypsies share the same belief about vampires."

Flustered and more than a little sick to her stomach, Fortune stammered, "I . . . er, I really don't know."

"Fortune, who is it? What's the commotion about?" Laila called. She and Ursula sauntered into the kitchen and spied Irene and the notorious Reb of the Riddance spell. "We heard laughing, so I'll assume everything's just fine."

Grateful for the interruption, Fortune put one finger against her lips to warn the other two against telling Laila what she'd just divulged. "Mr. MacNair has brought Irene's furnishings in his wagon, Gran. And Irene was sharing a funny tale about the children." The girl proceeded to introduce Irene to her Grandmother and Ursula.

"Pleased to meet you at last," Irene greeted the old ladies. "Fortune told me all about you."

"Mrs. Landry, Miss Price," Grady said, nodding to Laila and Ursula. "Nice to see you again."

Ursula and Laila politely acknowledged Grady's greeting.

Fortune noticed Irene peeking into the bedroom off the kitchen. "I thought you might like to have that room, Irene, unless you prefer sleeping upstairs."

"I was hoping this one was mine," Irene confessed. "It'll be real handy." There was a thumping at the door, and Irene's hand shot to her mouth. "Gracious, I forgot about the younguns. I told 'em to wait in the wagon till Grady and I made ourselves known. And here I stand jawin'."

Grady opened the door. The disgusted look on Book's face immediately brightened at the sight of Fortune. "Hi, Miss Fortune. This sure is a great house. Which room's mine?"

Fortune laughed, but before she could answer Book's question, little Tish whined at the door. "Lemme in, damn it!"

Grady hid a smile as Irene jerked open the door for her daughter. "Watch your mouth, or you'll sleep in the stable with the horses tonight."

Tish stomped in, spotted Fortune and made a beeline for her. Hugging Fortune's leg through mounds of petticoats and a blue calico skirt, the little girl popped her thumb in her mouth with a happy sigh.

Fortune introduced both children to her grandmother and Ursula. Then turning to Irene, she said, "I'm afraid we haven't had time to clear out the mess in Book and Tish's rooms yet, and it will have to be done before we move their things in."

Grady stepped forward and snapped her a smart salute. "Captain Grady MacNair at your service, Sugar. Point me in the right direction, and tell me what's to be done."

Irene giggled and winked at Fortune. Fortune flushed. Laila scowled.

"Don sound like no bad man ta me," Ursula muttered in

Laila's ear. She ignored Laila's jab in the ribs and sashayed up to Grady. "Come on, Johnny Reb," she said, "I'll show you de way."

Behind Ursula they all trooped up the stairs to inspect the two spare bedrooms at the opposite end of the hall from the master suite. The children chose between the rooms, and Grady went to work clearing them of their rickety furniture and suggestive art pieces. Book had wanted to keep the picture of the naked lady on his wall, but Irene boxed his ears and told him to behave.

By midday the rooms had been cleared and thoroughly scrubbed. "Guess we can start bringing in the beds," Irene said, glancing around the room that was to be Book's.

"Not we," Grady corrected. "Me. You shouldn't be lifting anything heavy. Come on, Book," he said, heading for the door, "you can help."

Book puffed up like a little peacock. "Sure, Grady. We men can take care of the important work, huh?"

Grady ruffled the boy's hair and grinned as they left the room.

Fortune swiped at a drooping strand of hair and sighed. "Well, the rooms still need painting, but at least they're clean."

"Honey, this is a castle compared to where we came from," Irene expounded. Then her breath caught on a sob. "I just can't thank you enough for all this."

"Now, none of that," Fortune smiled.

Irene sniffed and waved her hand in the air dismissively. "Don't mind me. Every time I get in the family way, I burst into tears over the slightest thing."

"Come on then, let's go see if Granny and Ursula need a hand in the kitchen. Neither one particularly enjoys cooking anymore."

After a late afternoon meal, Irene helped the two old ladies in the kitchen while the children went outside to play. And Fortune headed upstairs to find Grady.

She found him on his knees pounding Tish's bed together. The familiar shock of hair that always fell over his brow when he was hard at work lay there now. She resisted the urge to stoop down and brush it back.

Unaware that she was smiling, Fortune admired the cut of his long square jaw, his broad shoulders, his steady hand, the way his thick thigh muscles shifted under his kneeling weight.

Hearing the soft swish of skirts Grady glanced over his shoulder. The warmth of her admiring smile heated his blood. "Hi, darlin'." His drawl was low and intimate, embroidered with passion.

Raw physical desire swept through Fortune like a Kansas prairie fire. For one perilous moment, she was tempted to throw herself into his arms. Her feet took her two steps farther into the room before reason prevailed. She inhaled a deep, steadying breath and doused her flames with cold reality. Grady MacNair wasn't for her—not now, not ever. And she better say what she had come to say and leave.

Grady was far from immune to the passion that simmered in Fortune's emerald eyes. Yet even as he rose to take her in his arms, her lusty expression hardened into grim determination.

"Grady, don't." Fortune sidestepped his arms and shook her head. "Please, we have to talk."

It wasn't the first time he wondered what she was running from. Why did she deny her feelings for him? Was she frightened of all men, or was it just him? The thought that she might fear him pierced his heart deeper than he'd ever care to admit.

Determined to assuage her fear, whatever it might be, Grady ignored the stiffening of her body as he lifted her hand and touched the back of it to his cheek. "What's on your mind, honey girl?"

Fortune pretended indifference and snatched her hand away. "Don't. I can't concentrate when you do things like that. And I need to because there's something I must discuss with you."

Grady chuckled low, knowing she didn't realize that she'd just admitted that he *did* have an effect on her. "I'm sorry," he said, sounding anything but. "Go ahead and say your piece."

Fortune fidgeted, rolling her skirt into pleats between her fingers. She spoke softly, staring at a hole in the floor. "I know that I promised, but I can't go with you to the Fourth of July celebration."

"What did you say?" he asked, hoping he'd heard wrong.

Her resolute gaze met his. "I can't go with you to the celebration," she repeated.

For a moment Grady's face showed only surprise. Then it

collapsed into anger. "Is that damn Swede behind this?"

"No!" She paused uncertainly, then the words rushed out. "But he did ask me first, and I accepted."

Grady's eyes narrowed angrily. "The hell you say! Why did you agree to go with me then?"

"Because . . . I . . . that is . . . Damn it, MacNair, you tricked me, and you know it. I couldn't help myself. The way you kissed me, the way you . . ." Fortune clapped her hand over her mouth.

The transformation in Grady's expression was miraculous. "So you feel nothing for me, huh?" He grinned with arrogant male triumph. "Come here, darlin'." He spread his arms wide and strode toward her.

"Oh, no, you don't!" Fortune threw her hands up and backed away. "Stay where you are. I'll not fall for that sham twice."

"What sham? You want me as much as I want you."

"That may be, but I don't *want* to want you!"

That made Grady laugh. "Why fight something that feels so good? Tell Jorgensen you've changed your mind, that you're going with me."

"I'm not going with either one of you, Grady. I'm taking Gran and Ursula instead."

"Well, I'll escort all three of you then."

"I'm afraid that won't work either. You see, when I turned Eric down, he offered to do the same."

"Well, tell him no, damn it!"

"Grady, I'm not spending the Fourth with either one of you. I'll not have you two at each other's throats over me. It was embarrassing enough at the ranch. I certainly won't risk being humiliated before the whole town of Helena."

Grady understood her side of the awkward situation, but contrary to what she might believe, he wasn't about to take no for an answer. For that matter, he doubted that the Swede was either. So, he thought, with resignation, it's war. He smiled to himself. This was one war a Reb would win. Miss Landry might not arrive at the celebration on his arm, but she damn sure would leave on it!

"All right, Fortune," he said, "maybe I'll get lucky and see you there."

Suspicious of his quick capitulation, Fortune nonetheless was relieved. "Thank you for understanding."

"Grady!" Book Tabor nearly trampled Fortune as he stampeded into the room. "A man! I saw him!" The boy gulped for air. "He was 'cross the road lookin' at the house through one of them spyglass things. I sneaked up on 'im, but he knocked me down and ran!"

"Are you sure he was looking at this house?" Fortune asked.

"Course, I'm sure," came the indignant answer.

"Probably someone who hasn't heard this is no longer a whorehouse," Grady concluded. "But I'll check it out anyway. Come on, Book, you can show me where he was watching from and which direction he ran. Maybe we can find him and teach him some manners."

Book pivoted round and ran down the hall to the stairs. Grady started to follow, stopped and brushed a kiss on Fortune's forehead. "See you later."

Grady and Book returned just before dark. In the entryway, all four women stood waiting to hear what he found out. "I'm sorry," he said, shaking his head. "We didn't find the man. I checked the place where Book saw him watching the house, but he left nothing behind. Book and I even hit the saloons, but evidently our Peeping Tom wasn't thirsty.

"I doubt there's anything to be alarmed about, but if it would ease your minds, I'd be glad to keep an eye on the house tonight."

"We appreciate the offer, Mr. MacNair, but with four women, young Book here, and one man-eating dog, I think we'll manage just fine," Laila replied confidently.

Ursula laughed. "Yassir, we got us a fine supply of fryin' pans in yonder kitchen, too. We'll just pass 'em out at bedtime."

Grady winced and slapped his hat over his head. He remembered all too well his own experience with one of Laila Fontaine's skillets. "Well then, ladies," he said, "I'll take my leave. Please don't hesitate to send Book if you need me."

Under her grandmother's watchful eye, Fortune saw Grady to the door. He slipped her a surreptitious wink and was rewarded with an instant smile.

Fortune watched until he mounted his horse and rode away. When she turned from the door, only Granny remained, the rest of the household having gone to the kitchen to find something to eat. "It's been a long eventful day, hasn't it?" Fortune sighed.

"That it has, dear, and I think we should postpone the Riddance spell till tomorrow night."

"Sounds like a good idea to me. I'm very tired."

"Come along then. Let's join the others and have a bite to eat."

"And pass out the skillets?"

Laila laughed softly.

Chapter Thirteen

Day had long waned, and night shrouded the house as if in a
ghostly mystery. Nothing stirred, but for the creaking of the
settling structure or the moan of a fitful sleeper. All doors
were closed and rooms darkened except one on the second
floor. From beneath that one door a meager light glowed.

Inside, one candle held the stygian gloom at bay, casting
shadowy apparitions in the corners of the room. And standing
in the aura of the candle like a sculpture of a naked goddess,
Fortune stared back at her pale image in the mirror.

She was always anxious before casting a spell, but tonight a
sense of foreboding had come over her, leaving her chilled and
clammy. She scrubbed at her bare arms, trying to raise a heat
that would burn away fear's chill. It didn't help. Somewhere,
lurking in the night, evil was afoot, and she feared it might be
her dream come true.

Her loose hair fell over her buttocks as she gave her head
a shake. She must try to blank out all thoughts but those
pertaining to the magic at hand. Reaching for the long, red
satin cloak lying at the foot of her bed, she swirled it around

her shoulders, then quietly crept down the dark stairs. She glided on silent feet as she moved through the house to the back door.

The night air was warm, humid and ominously still. A small bonfire at the far corner of the property beckoned the young Gypsy like a lighthouse on a rolling black sea. Though the grass was cool and wet underfoot, her skin perspired beneath the satin cloak as she moved toward the light.

Granny and Ursula's silhouettes swayed against the firelight, and Fortune could hear Granny's opening chant to the earth goddess.

"In our oneness of life we are a part of Gaia
She is composed of the four elements: water,
fire, air, and earth, as our bodies are
comprised of the same."

Then, but for the crackling of the fire, all was quiet as Fortune joined the two old ladies. It was eerie how not even a cricket chirped.

Draped in simple dark capes of serge, Granny and Ursula slipped to either side of Fortune while the girl's voice joined her grandmother's in the last of the opening chant.

"Dance my dance and I dance with you.
Hold me and I hold you
Know life and the wheel turns.
Be one with Gaia.
Be one with Gaia."

As the last word was spoken, Laila turned to her grand-daughter, lifted her arms and settled a new amulet made of a sea shell around her neck. "To replace the one you gave your brother," she explained. "You should not go unprotected."

Fortune smiled her thanks, gave the shell a kiss and let it slip out of her hands to hang between her breasts. Then tugging her cloak around her, she lifted her gaze to the star-studded sky. The moon was on the wane, perfect for tonight's particular spell. Praying for success, she shifted nervously. The slick satin slid over her nipples, instantly ripening them to awareness and evoking sensual memories—Grady's tongue twining with hers, Grady's hand kneading her breasts, Grady's hard arousal pressing against her feminine mound. Silently cursing, she rearranged the teasing material and ended its sensual torment.

Damn! It was becoming more and more difficult to resist her body's affinity for Grady's. And it didn't help matters that in his ignorance of the Moondance, Grady was actually assisting rather than resisting its power. The bond had to be broken!

Laila's bangles clinked softly and brought Fortune out of her reverie. As the girl watched, her grandmother spread the vervain leaves on the ground before the fire. It was time.

With renewed determination, Fortune stared into the fire, and let herself be mesmerized by the dancing pictures deep within the flames. Her body swayed in time to their dance. She closed her eyes and still saw the pictures against her lids.

She felt Ursula's brief touch as the old woman reached around her and slid the cloak from her shoulders.

In stark contrast with her creamy nakedness, Fortune's midnight hair swayed with the movement of her body. She opened her eyes. Then with uninhibited grace, she glided towards the compelling flames.

A few feet from the flames Fortune knelt and retrieved the vervain leaves. She rose and retreated a few paces as Laila came forward and tossed a blue powder into the fire. Orange and blue flames leapt high. And like a ghostly lover, blue smoke curled up and out, wrapping the Gypsy girl in diaphanous arms. Nearing the fire again, she threw in the dry leaves one by one. And she called out.

"Grady MacNair! Begone!

Here is my bane
Take it and soar
Depart from me now
That you offend no more!

Grady MacNair! Begone!"

Fortune edged away from the smoke and fire. Ursula joined her, covering the girl's nakedness with the satin cloak. "Is dat all der is ta it?" she whispered.

The girl nodded. "Yes, and let's hope it works this time."

"It's a very strong spell," Granny assured her as she started kicking dirt into the fire.

Ursula helped but waved Fortune away when she made to aid their efforts. "You ain't wearin' no shoes, girl. 'Sides, yo Granny says you can't touch dis fire's ash in any way or the spell won't work."

When the fire was safely banked, the terrible sense of foreboding fell over Fortune again. "Granny," she asked softly, "do you feel it?"

"Feel what, child?"

Fortune shook her head. "It's gone now. Perhaps it was my imagination."

"What, Fortune?" Laila probed. "What did you feel?"

"Evil."

Ursula's eyes popped wide. "Lordy, I knowed there was haunts round here. Yassir, I surely did!"

"Hush up," Laila said in disgust. "She's not talking about haunts or shades."

If possible poor Ursula's eyes got wider. "Only thin' could be den is demons and ghouls."

Fortune patted Ursula's arm. "It's all right, Ursula. I was just having a bad feeling—you know, like when you feel something awful is about to happen."

"Oh, well, dat ain't so bad den, is it?"

Amusement chased Fortune's own misgivings back into the shadows. "No," she admitted, "I guess it isn't so bad as ghosts and ghouls."

The threesome silently retraced their steps to the house. Fortune felt good about tonight's spell. She'd felt the magic more than she had the first time. Perhaps this one would end her troubles—as well as end the delicious pleasure and pain of the desire that so often haunted her body.

Chapter Fourteen

As Laila pushed open the back door of the house, a terrified shriek from inside sent her careening backward onto Ursula's toe.

"Ow-o-o!" the black woman howled. "Get off my foot, you ol' heifer."

"Heifer!" Laila screeched indignantly.

"Hush," Fortune ordered. "You'll wake everyone within a mile." Hesitantly, she stuck her head around the door, then stepped inside. A lantern suddenly flared, blinding her.

"Fortune? Is that you?" came Irene Tabor's voice from behind the bright glow. Laila and Ursula scurried into the house behind Fortune. "Good Lord, it's all three of you."

"Irene," Fortune said, "could you do something about that lantern? I can't see a thing."

"Oh, sure, honey." Irene hastily set the lamp on the kitchen table, and Fortune clutched at her red cloak, hoping the woman hadn't noticed how disheveled she was, but on second glance at the bewildered housekeeper, the girl forgot about her own ludicrous state of dress and almost laughed.

150

A knotted belt at the waist of Irene's bulky wrapper lent her matronly figure the comfy appeal of a pillow pinched in the middle. Bare ankles and wide flat feet poked out at the bottom. Her red, sleepy eyes were barely propped open, and her hair stuck out like spokes on a wagon wheel. In all, the poor woman resembled an inmate from a madhouse.

"You three near scared my drawers off," Irene said on a high note. "What were you doin' in the backyard this time of night anyway? Did Book wake you? Were you running after him?"

"Book?" Laila asked in surprise. "Isn't he in bed?"

"No, damn it! Excuse my language, but that boy will be the death of me. Lately he's taken to sneaking out nights to prowl with a friend of his. Looks like he's taken off again tonight. A while ago, I heard a noise and went to check his room. I was on my way back to bed when you pushed the door open and scared the wits outta me."

"Sorry," Fortune apologized. "We were out back burning that horrible old furniture we found upstairs. Book must have left by the front door because we certainly didn't see him."

"You were doin' what? Burning at this time of night?" Irene asked, looking even more confused. She eyed Fortune's red satin cloak and bare feet skeptically. "And doin' such a dirty chore dressed like that?" she added, pointing at Fortune. "If you don't mind my sayin' so, I think you're leavin' out the best parts of this tale."

Fortune tossed Laila a pleading look. But instead of coming forth with the agreed-upon explanation, the old Gypsy just yawned sleepily and headed out of the kitchen. "I'm tired Fortune, dear. You explain everything to Irene, will you?"

"But Granny, you said that . . ." Fortune started.

"Good idea," Ursula interrupted, hurrying after the departing Laila. "You explain everythin', gal."

Irene gave the old women a curious glance as they left the kitchen then turned back to Fortune with a raised brow. "This oughtta be real good. Settle yourself into a chair, and I'll fix some coffee while you talk. Might as well take that wrap off, too. It's plenty warm in here."

"No!" Fortune blurted. "I mean . . . well, the costume beneath is just so hideous, it's embarrassing." Before Irene could interrogate her further about her clothing, Fortune asked abruptly, "Ah, shouldn't we change and go look for Book?"

Irene's shoulders drooped a little. "No," she sighed, setting the coffeepot on the stove. "He's safer out on them streets than you and I would be. He'll be home by dawn and then he'll get his comeuppance. Damned if I know what I'm gonna to do with that little hell-raiser." She leaned against the cupboards then, facing Fortune and crossing her arms beneath her ample bosom. "Now, tell me, what were you really doin' out in the yard."

Fortune pulled a chair out and sat down at the table. Living in the same house, Irene was bound to discover that her younger friend was no ordinary young lady. She made a decision she prayed she wouldn't regret. "First, there's something you should know, Irene," Fortune began. "I'd have mentioned it earlier, but to tell the truth, I was afraid of your reaction."

"Afraid?" The coffee boiled, and Irene quickly poured them each a cup.

Fortune murmured her thanks for the coffee, using the moment to formulate her thoughts. She blew softly at the steaming brew and took a cautious sip. "Before I say one more word, you must promise not to tell a living soul what I'm about to reveal to you."

Irene's eyes rounded with excitement. "Boy, this must be really good. Okay, I promise not to tell. Now talk!"

"Granny is a Gypsy. And so am I."

Irene's mouth opened and shut several times, but no words came out. Then she began to laugh softly. "If that don't beat all. Gypsies, huh?"

Fortune let out a deep breath she hadn't realized she'd been holding. "You really don't mind?"

"Hell, no. Keeps things interestin' But what's that got to do with tonight?" Irene sipped her coffee and studied the girl on the other side of the table over the rim of her cup.

"We were casting a Riddance spell."

"Wait a minute," Irene held her hands up expressively. "Are you telling me you were doin' magic? I thought Gypsies told fortunes."

"Well," Fortune laughed, "we do on occasion, but we know magic as well. Mind you, we aren't witches. No need to worry on that account."

The housekeeper gave her head a shake. "Come on now, you don't really believe in that nonsense, do you? You're just kidding me, aren't you?" Fortune stiffened, and Irene hastily added, "Now don't go gettin' your tail up in the air. It's just that I've never held with that spooky stuff. Trust in yourself, I always say." She leaned across the table conspiratorially. "Just what were you tryin' to get rid of anyway?"

Fortune stared into her coffee cup and tried to sound nonchalant. "Oh, the usual, evil spirits and the like. I was perfectly satisfied that the herbs we spread around the house were sufficient, but Granny said we couldn't take any chances since the house had been occupied by such evil women."

"You mean those herbs ain't really good for keepin' the bugs outta the house like you said?" Irene asked, clearly disappointed.

"Oh, that much was true. But they also keep evil spirits out of the house."

"Oh, well, that's good to know—that they keep the bugs away, that is." She chuckled. "I guess you could call bugs evil little critters, too, huh?"

Fortune smiled. "I hope you're not upset with me for not telling you everything to begin with. It's just that . . . well, lots of people look down on Gypsies."

"Naw, makes no never mind to me. I sure am surprised that you believe in magic though. A smart gal like you doesn't need to depend on such nonsen . . . Sorry, what I'm tryin' to say is, you don't need magic to make your way in this world. Why, you're smarter than most men, girl."

"You sound like Roc. But that's okay. He and I have agreed to disagree. But Irene, it's important that you keep your promise. Don't tell anyone I'm a Gypsy, especially Grady."

"Why especially Grady? Jehoshaphat, girl, anyone can see he's smitten with you. And if he's the kind of man I think he is, it won't make a bit of difference in his feelin's for you."

"I have my reasons for not wanting him to know."

Irene shrugged. "If that's the way you want it, I won't tell a soul, honey." She drained her cup and stood up. Well, I'm for bed. I'll be sleepin' with one ear listenin' for that little beggar of mine. And when I get my hands on that boy . . ." She left off there, making a wringing motion with her hands. She started to leave, then stopped abruptly and regarded Fortune with an amused glint in her eye. "Just what are you wearing under that wrap?"

Fortune shook her head and grinned. "That's one secret I'll keep to myself." She stood quickly. "Good night, Irene."

Fortune made a fast exit.

Glad she'd confided in Irene, Fortune pulled back the sheets on her bed and climbed in with a weary sigh. Now, she could at least relax in her own home without hiding behind the constant vigilance of secrecy and lies.

But as her dark head lay back on the pillow, Irene's words came back to her. *"Trust in yourself, I always say."* Fortune stared into the darkness. Was she depending too much on magic? Could it be possible that the Moondance had nothing to do with Grady's desire for her? Oh, if she could only believe it! But then what good would it do? She could never let herself love him without telling him who she was. And of course, that would be the end of everything.

Magic. Perhaps she *had* been too dependent on its powers. But magic got her into this situation with Grady, and right now magic seemed the only way out of it.

Fortune woke abruptly. *Morning already?* she wondered fuzzily. *Is that a bell ringing?* She sat up slowly and rubbed her eyes. The bedroom was still dark as was the sky outside her window. Groaning, she flopped back into her nest of pillows. Obviously someone was up to high jinks, ringing the church bell at this time of night. Fleetingly, she wondered if that was where Book Tabor and his friend were at this very moment.

Finally the clanging stopped, and Fortune closed her eyes again. Perhaps the pranksters had been caught, she thought vaguely as she drifted off.

Excited voices floated up the stairs. "A hex on them," she hissed, sitting up again. Wait, she knew those voices. Apparently Book has been caught sneaking back into the house. She smiled, thinking Irene would rest easier now, and so, she hoped, would she. She lay back again and closed her eyes.

The bedroom door slammed open. "Sweet Gaia, now what?" she shouted at the intruder.

"Fortune! Get up! Fire!" Irene shrieked, her arms flailing about her body. "Your brother's warehouse is on fire. Book came runnin' to tell us. Hurry!"

Without a word, Fortune leaped from the bed. Not caring that Irene still stood there, she whipped off her nightgown and hurriedly dressed, dispensing with cumbersome petticoats and underclothes and donning only the outer necessities.

"The alarm from the watchtower on the hill has been sounded," Irene rattled on. "Book said the whole town's leavin' their beds to help. Oh Lord, I hope it don't spread." She whirled round to leave the room. "I better get dressed and go with you."

Fortune pivoted and snared her arm. "Irene, no. The baby. You can't. Stay here. I pray to God no one's been hurt, but if so I'll have them sent here. You, Granny and Ursula can handle that, can't you?"

"Of course. I'll get bandages and water ready just in case." Fortune barely heard this as she tore down the stairs.

Book had her mare saddled and ready to go. Fortune mounted, and the boy lifted his hand to be lifted up behind her. "Please, Miss Fortune, let me come. I can help." Knowing the boy would follow her whether she took him along or not, she lent him a hand up. Then kicking her heels into Magic's belly, they raced through town and down Main Street toward the bright glow in the sky.

Fortune reined in at a scene of devastating destruction. Magic pranced about nervously as Book and Fortune slid to the ground. Book led the skittish mare to a hitching post a safe distance away, but Fortune could only stare in stupefied fascination at the ravenous inferno.

Flames lit the night and lashed at the back of the warehouse, and even from this safe distance she could feel the terrible heat. People were running everywhere, shouting orders and carrying water. But amidst the seemingly chaotic scene, she discerned a surprising orderliness.

Soot-blackened men and women formed bucket brigades at the well. Several stout men manned a fire wagon, pumping water and handling long hoses, and a few brave souls ran in and out of the warehouse rescuing whatever they could carry.

Though an empty lot separated the Rattler Saloon from the warehouse, dandified gamblers and satin-garbed girls worked tirelessly to splash its walls with water. A troop of young boys doused the roof.

The efforts all around her suddenly spurred Fortune into action. The front of the warehouse hadn't yet caught fire, and she was determined to save Roc's important business papers.

*   *   *

His scarf tied over the lower half of his face, Grady toted an unconscious man across his shoulders from the back of the burning building. A brief flash of color caught his eye. He glanced up just in time to see Fortune, skirts hiked up to her knees, running toward the far front side of the warehouse. Cursing loudly, he loped across the freight yard and left the injured man at a wagon attended by Doc Holly and a young woman. Then he charged in the direction Fortune had taken, dodging bucket brigades and rescued wares.

At the warehouse office door Fortune almost lost her nerve. The flames! The heat! My God, it was just like her dream. *Don't panic!* she admonished herself. *Do what you have to do and get out.* She yanked several times on the habitually stubborn door before it finally flew open. Smoke rolled out at her as she propped the door open with a stone. Then, girded by sheer determination, she plunged into the murky interior.

Light from the many lanterns shining through the front window lit the room just enough so that Fortune could discern the shadowy outlines of the furniture. The fresh air coming through the door helped, if only a little, to disperse some of the acrid smoke.

Deciding this was what hell must be like, the girl wasted no time. She crouched down before the safe, and though she knew the combination by heart, not until the second try were her fumbling fingers successful in opening it. Then wadding the hem of her skirt in one hand, she scooped the contents of the safe into the skirt. With a sigh of relief, she stood to leave.

The door suddenly slammed shut. With nowhere to go the smoke rapidly thickened, burning her lungs and stinging her eyes. She was beginning to feel a bit woozy, which frightened her into further action. If she didn't get out of here fast, she knew she'd pass out, and she didn't wish to contemplate her fate if that happened.

She began kicking and pounding on the stuck door and nearly dislocated her shoulder butting up against it. It wouldn't budge. She stared back over shoulder through the blinding smoke. Somewhere, on the other side of the room, was the door into the main warehouse. Perhaps she could find it, but could she find her way out of the warehouse in all this smoke? Panic threatened her vanishing composure, and sweat dripped down her brow and into her eyes. She blinked and swallowed a sob. Sweet Gaia, had the dream foretold her own death? She opened her mouth to scream, but thanks to the smoke, the only sound at the back of her neck. A sudden peace eased her. Exhausted, she quit her worthless efforts against the door and waited.

The door was abruptly wrenched open, and Fortune fell into a pair of welcoming arms.

"Fortune, you foolish lass! Are you alright?" Roughly peppering her face with kisses, Grady murmured gentle admonishments as he edged Fortune away from the building. She raised her eyes to his beloved face. His blue eyes were ringed with soot and grime, but she thought it the most beautiful face she'd ever beheld. She realized that the calm, the sense of being safe that had overcome her hysteria, had been Grady. She'd felt his presence as she had since the very first day she arrived in Helena.

Grady wanted to crush Fortune closer, and except for her tenacious hold on the skirt full of papers, he would have. "Answer me, Sugar. Are you all right?"

Fortune started to nod but abruptly found herself roughly torn from his arms.

"Fortune, what's happened? What are you doing here?" Eric Jorgensen yelled above the surrounding commotion.

Fortune smiled up at Eric's concerned and equally dirty face. She started to answer but again could only croak. Then, to her dismay, her knees failed her, too.

Both men made a grab for her. Since she refused to let go of her bundle, Grady on one side and Eric on the other lifted her between them and carried her to the safety of the medical wagon. Both men eyed each other disdainfully before reluctantly handing the girl over to the doctor's capable hands. With no excuse to remain, they hurried back to the burning building to save what they could.

As Grady and Eric rejoined the fire fighters, a man raced from the smoky building. "Jorgensen, your pa—a beam fell on 'im. I tired to free 'im, but it'll take a couple strong men to heft that beam."

Eric stared at the smoke belching from the gaping double doors of the warehouse. "Where?" he demanded anxiously.

"I'll show you." Someone threw water over the three of them.

Grady and Eric each grabbed a bucket of water and, following the man, were instantly swallowed up by the swirling, choking smoke.

Fire was already licking at the beam that lay across the unconscious Olaf. Grady tossed his bucket of water at the flames while Eric doused his father's clothing with his. A cry of alarm was the only warning either man had when another beam came hurtling down at them. Grady's body plowed into Eric's, knocking him out of the beam's fiery path.

His breath knocked out of him, but otherwise unharmed, Eric was instantly on his feet and lifting one end of the timber that pinned his father. With Grady's aid, Olaf was finally freed and carried to safety.

After washing her throat down with water and resting for a short time, Fortune left her brother's papers in one corner of the medical wagon and joined the other women in one of the bucket brigades. Now, three hours later, the fire was almost out and the danger past. There was little left of the warehouse, but as Fortune made her way back to Doc Holly's wagon, she gave silent thanks that no one had died fighting the blaze.

Fortune leaned wearily against the wagon's side. "You're welcome to take the injured men to my home to recuperate, Doc," she said, her voice still a little rough. "My grandmother and housekeeper are there and are prepared to take care of them."

"That's real nice of you, Miss Landry, but Jim over there is already recovering from that knock on his head, and Joe," he added, indicating the man in front of him, "can go home, too. Eric's ma already fetched Olaf home."

"Mr. Jorgensen is hurt?" she exclaimed in alarm. "How bad is it?"

The portly doctor glanced up at her concerned face and smiled. "He's got a broken leg and he inhaled a lot of smoke, but he'll be right as rain in no time."

As relief washed over her, Fortune became aware of the sooty face of the man with the head injury. The doctor had mention only his first name, and his identity hadn't at first registered. But now, studying his face, she realized that he was Jim Fetters, Roc's night watchman.

As she watched, Fetters scooted off the end of the wagon and seemed intent on leaving. "Mr. Fetters, wait," Fortune called, stepping to his side. "Are you sure you're all right? Do you have someone to look after you when you leave here?"

"Thanks, ma'am, but I kin take care of myself," Fetters said, shuffling his feet. "T'weren't no real harm done, 'cept maybe for a hell of a headache." He grinned. "Somebody whomped me good."

Fortune froze. "You were on duty then when the fire broke out?"

"Yes, ma'am. I heard a noise at the back of the buildin' and went to have a look. Somebody had piled some rags on the ground, doused 'em with coal oil and set it afire. I was tryin' to stomp it out when I got hit over the head."

Terror gripped Fortune's heart. Then it was true! Someone was out to harm the Landrys! "Did you see who it was?" she asked anxiously.

"No, I didn't. I'm purely sorry I let you down, ma'am."

"Let me down?" she exclaimed. "Mr. Fetters, you could have been killed. You didn't let me down in the least. I just pray that you'll continue to want to work for Landry Freighting."

The big man snorted and grinned. "Course I'm still workin' for yuh, ma'am. And I'll be roundin' up a crew tomorrow to start cleaning up this mess."

"I can't thank you enough, Mr. Fetters. Perhaps you'd better go get some rest now." As the night watchman nodded and headed up the street, the Gypsy girl began to tremble. *The fire was intentional; my dream is coming true!*

"Fortune, is something wrong?" Grady asked, approaching her.

She swung around and found him standing there with Eric and Book. Exhaustion etched his face. "Yes, but we'll discuss it later."

"How's Pa?" Eric interjected anxiously.

"Doc Holly says he'll be fine, Eric. Your mother has already taken him home."

Eric nodded. "I better head that way myself. Ma might need my help." Shifting his attention to Grady, he extended his hand. "Well, Reb, I hate admitting this, but you'll do to ride the river with."

Grady chuckled, accepting the compliment and Eric's hand.

"I guess I'd say the same for you, Swede. Too bad we've staked a claim on the same woman, but maybe after I've made her mine, we can think about being friends."

"Oh, I'm sure we can be friends all right, only it'll be me that claims the lady."

"I guess we'll just have to see about that now, won't we?" Grady's mouth smiled, but there was a challenge in the hard glitter of his eyes.

Eric and Grady's hands dropped apart as they turned toward Fortune, determination stamping their expressions. *Lord,* she thought, *on top of everything else, this is all I need.*

It was quite plain that Eric was torn between accompanying Fortune and going home to help his mother with Olaf. In the end he gave in to practicality. Fortune, after all, did have Grady MacNair and Book to see her safely home.

Grady lightened Fortune's load by taking on a portion of the papers she'd rescued from Roc's office. Book rode behind Grady, and for the weary threesome it was a quiet ride back to the house.

Irene cooed and fretted as she hustled her son upstairs to a waiting tub of hot water and lye soap. Grady asked if he might have a word with Fortune and didn't object when Laila and Ursula trailed them into the parlor.

Tired as he was, Grady couldn't help noticing that Fortune and Irene had obviously been busy peeling off the red wallpaper. The entryway walls were completely bare, and the underlaying gray was yet to be painted. Two walls in the parlor had undergone the same treatment.

Granny and Ursula seated themselves on a purple settee. Grady and Fortune eyed each other's sooty clothes, exchanged bone-weary smiles and remained standing.

Grady got straight to the point. "Fortune, how did you get into the office? Through the warehouse?"

"No, the side door. I was afraid to go through the warehouse for fear I'd get lost in all that smoke. Why do you ask?"

"Because when I got to the door, I had one hell of time getting it open."

"The door sticks badly, but before I went inside I propped it open with a rock. While I was busy emptying the safe, it slammed shut." She paced before the window thoughtfully. "Someone must have come along, thought the door should be shut and removed the rock."

"Or they saw you go in and did it deliberately," Grady added gravely. "We found evidence pointing to the fact that the fire was deliberately set. Whoever set it might have been trying to kill you."

Laila gasped, her hand flying to her heart.

Fortune only nodded thoughtfully. "Jim Fetters, the night watchman, told me someone started the fire."

"That's what was bothering you earlier then?" he asked. At her nod, Grady continued. "I found Fetters unconscious behind the warehouse. That's when we realized the fire had been set. What else did he say?"

"He said he went to investigate a noise and discovered a pile of burning rags. He was hit from behind while trying to stamp it out."

Her voice trembling with the fear she felt for her granddaughter, Laila said, "Then maybe someone did shut you in the office on purpose, Fortune."

Fortune thought of the faceless Confederate soldier in her dream and shuddered. There wasn't a doubt in her mind that an enemy existed, but she could hardly explain her reasoning to Grady. Instead she said, "Roc is a Yankee. Most of the freighters are ex-Confederates. I suppose any one of them could have it in for my brother."

"But why Roc in particular?" Grady wondered aloud. "There's other Yanks in Helena, including Eric Jorgensen's family." He shook his head. "No, whoever fired the warehouse either has a personal grudge or is possibly an angry competitor."

"I think we're all too tired to think about it any further today," Laila interjected. "I suggest we get some rest and tackle the problem later with a clear head."

Grady took Fortune's hands in both of his. "Your grandmother is right, Sugar. You look exhausted, and I know I could use a couple hours sleep, too. I'll have a talk with Eric later this afternoon. Perhaps Roc shared something with him that he didn't want you to worry about. I'll stop by later if I find out anything. All right?"

Fortune nodded grimly. "Thank you, Grady, for all your help tonight. I don't like to think about what may have happened if you hadn't found me."

Aware of their lack of privacy, Grady brushed a chaste kiss

on her cheek. After bidding Laila and Ursula a good night, he took his leave.

"Come, dear," Laila sighed at her granddaughter's back. "I have a bath waiting for you in your room."

"Thanks, Gran. Sounds wonderful." She gave each of the old ladies a hug and started up the stairs.

"It didn't work, did it?"

"What?" Fortune pivoted on the steps and glanced down at her grandmother.

"The spell—it didn't work."

Fortune sighed. "It's hard to tell. Grady is a Southern-bred gentleman."

Laila shook her head. "It wasn't a gentlemanly gleam I saw in his eyes, dear. I think he's deeply in love with you."

Fortune turned her face away so her grandmother wouldn't see her tears. "It's not a true love, Gran. We both know that."

"What you gonna do now?" Ursula asked.

"I don't know, but I don't have time to dwell on it now. Someone could have been killed tonight. I have to find out who set that fire."

Chapter Fifteen

Fortune leaned back in her chair, closed her eyes and rubbed her temples. She'd never worked so hard in her life as she had this past week after the fire.

The day after the disaster she sent her grandmother and Ursula back to the ranch with Roc's handyman, Nubbins Smith. Laila had protested that she and Ursula might be needed, but in the end she relented. And once the two old dears were no longer underfoot, the young woman was able to concentrate on setting the Landry freight business back on its feet.

Men had worked day and night to clear away the warehouse rubble and prepare the site for the new building. Though Eric was a furniture maker, his carpentry skills were well-rounded, and Fortune had gratefully accepted his offer to oversee the rebuilding of the warehouse.

Grady extricated Roc's blackened safe from the debris and hauled it in his wagon to the mercantile. Since then the freight business had operated out of the mercantile's back room, and while Fortune sorted through Roc's business papers, Grady followed her precise instructions and finished bringing the mercantile bookkeeping up to date.

As he'd promised, Grady talked to Eric about Roc's possible enemies. Unfortunately, the Swede had nothing to impart that might help solve the who and the why of the fire.

Regardless of who started the fire and the reason behind it, Fortune decided that it was imperative Roc be warned. A telegraph could be sent to Salt Lake City, but her brother wasn't due to arrive there for many days yet. Rather than leave him vulnerable and unsuspecting in the interim, she hired five idle mule skinners to catch up with the slow-moving mule train. A single man would have done to carry the news and the warning, but she reasoned that Roc might need the extra guards.

"Fortune?"

Fortune started out of her reverie and glanced up at Grady.

He settled on the corner of the desk. "What were you thinking about? You looked a thousand miles away."

"Nothing and everything," she replied.

Reaching across the desk, he caught her chin. "You've done all you can do to warn Roc, and he's no green tinhorn. And," Grady said, chuckling, "if he thought you thought otherwise, he'd be one riled Yank." This last earned Grady a smile.

"You're right, of course. But putting worry aside is a lot easier said than done."

"Well, here's something that might cheer you." He grinned like a boy who'd just been given his first pony. Then reaching inside his leather vest, he extracted a small packet of folded papers and tossed them on the desk before her. "The bank loan for my share of the Fort Benton store. Yesterday I took all our figures over to Harry Arlington at the bank. He had these papers ready for me this morning."

Grady then reached into another pocket and extracted a thicker packet of papers. "Our lawyers have finished drawing up the terms of partnership. These need only your signature to make them legal. You did say Roc gave you power of attorney, right?"

Fortune nodded and unrolled the official-looking papers. After reading the personal note from her lawyer, she picked up a pen, shot Grady an audacious smile and signed with a flourish.

Grady scooped them up and moved toward his safe. "This calls for a celebration, wouldn't you say, Miss Landry?"

Fortune laughed as he tossed the papers into his safe. He spun around, held one finger up, indicating she should wait a moment, then disappeared into the store. Within a few moments, he returned with two chipped cups and a bottle of wine.

"Excuse the poor glassware," he teased, setting the cups on the desk. He poured them each half full and came around to her side of the desk. Fortune rose as he handed her a cup. "A toast, partner, to the new partnership of Landry and MacNair! May it become all and more than our expectations."

Fortune's emerald gaze locked with the magnetic blue of his over the rim of the cup as she sipped deeply. Never taking his eyes from her, Grady set his cup aside, reached for hers and set it next to his. "Let's seal this bargain properly," he said huskily. And before she realized his intent she was in his arms.

From under the desk Grumpy growled, but at a silent hand command from his mistress, the dog ceased and curled up for a nap.

Nibbling on her soft pliant lips, Grady's mouth teased them apart. As her tongue met his, he switched their positions and pulled her into his lap as he sat down in her chair.

Fortune rested her cheek against one broad shoulder and closed her eyes. What would it hurt, just this once, to give in to her feelings for him? She was tired and worried and needed to be held. He felt good—so big and strong and safe. He smelled good, too, like lime, leather and man.

Her wicked mind started visualizing his naked body lying over hers, and an ache she was becoming well-acquainted with uncurled in her most private place. She inhaled sharply. Of their own volition her fingers found the open vee in his shirt and weaved through the light mat of chest hair. She heard his quick intake of air as she released a couple buttons and slipped her hand deeper into his shirt. Tilting her head back, her slumberous feline eyes melded with the blue heat of his.

"I like it when you touch me, darlin'" he murmured. He shifted so that the crook of his elbow rested on the desk and cradled Fortune's head. Her hand slid to the back of his head encouragingly, and he bent his head, whispering her name and adoring her with his lips.

Fortune moaned into his mouth. Never had she felt so cherished. Lust and passion were both exciting emotions, but shared with this rare brand of tenderness, they were incomparable.

Grady nuzzled the warm, soft woman in his arms. She fired his blood, but in her sweet surrender, he sensed a need beyond mere physical satisfaction. Thus he banked his swelling desire to plunder the treasure she so prettily offered. Instead, the hand that would have gladly ripped off her clothing, kneaded one breast with gentle possessiveness.

"Ahem!"

Startled, Fortune's head popped up and bumped Grady's chin. He simultaneously stiffened to attention and started to stand. Fortune let go a shriek of surprise as she slipped, fanny first, through the space that opened up between his knees.

From her ignominious position between Grady's legs, she cuffed his calf. Then she peaked under the desk. All she could see was the hem of Irene's faded lavender skirt in the doorway. She groaned, raised her knees and buried her face in her rumpled skirts.

"Sorry, Grady," Irene stuttered. "That little man from the Landry ranch, a Nubbins Smith, is out here askin' after Fortune. Seems there's some kind of trouble."

Embarrassment forgotten, Fortune scrambled out from behind the desk with the aid of Grady's offered hand.

"Send Nubbins back here," Grady replied.

With an amused cursory glance at Fortune, Irene nodded and disappeared.

Fortune hurriedly slicked back her hair and smoothed her skirts before Nubbins, covered with dust and sweat, scurried into the room. "You gotta come, ma'am! Somebody's gone and poisoned the stock with moldy feed. Miz Laila said you knew what to do. I got two men walkin' 'em, but we got six animals that need tendin' to."

Suddenly all business, Fortune instructed the little man. "Scrounge up any of Roc's men you can find in the saloons and head them out to the ranch. Grady and I will fetch Eric Jorgensen on the way out of town. We'll need big strong men for what must be done." Her shoulders snapped around toward Grady. "Let's go. If we hurry, maybe we can save a few mules."

"Anything I can do?" Irene asked, appearing where Nubbins had just stood.

"Thanks, Irene, but no. I'll need Grady's help, and we may not be back till morning."

"Don't you worry none, Grady," Irene said. "Angus and I will handle things here and lock up the place tonight."

Grady and Fortune saddled their horses and headed to Jorgensen's. There was little said on the swift ride to the ranch.

Laila met Fortune, Eric and Grady in front of the house. "I got catnip and peppermint tea in some buckets, and I'm fixing more," she said by way of greeting. "Your grandfather swore by it for colicky stock. The hard part will be getting it down the poor beasts' throats."

"Tell us what you want us to do, Fortune," Eric said.

They all glanced up then as Nubbins rode in with three more men. As soon as Nubbins and the others joined them, Fortune asked, "Could any other animals have gotten into the bad feed besides those six over in the corral?"

"No, ma'am, just them six. They got into the feed afore I discovered it, but I managed to keep the others away."

Fortune grimaced. The mules were matched spans, expensive, well-broken, and used to working with one another. If she failed to save them, they stood to lose money and precious time breaking in new spans. She inhaled deeply and faced the three men Nubbins had found. "One of you follow Granny, fetch the medicine and bring it to the corral. We're going to have to ear the animals and drench them. Then we walk them and pray they don't die."

Grady and Eric followed Fortune to the corral where two other men were walking mules. Two mules were down on the ground kicking at their cramping bellies.

"What is this drenching you're talking about?" Eric asked. "Have you ever done it before?"

"Drenching is pouring fluid down the animals' throats," Fortune answered, "and no, I've not personally drenched an animal. I'm not strong enough. But I've watched Grandpa and Roc doctor horses for this problem."

Following Fortune's instructions, Eric and Grady and the others worked tirelessly. One man grabbed the colicky animal's ears and pulled back, forcing the head on a straight angle with the throat. Another grabbed its tongue and pulled it to one side while a third poured the muscle-relaxing medicine down its throat. The mules were hurting and cantankerous, and it took every ounce of the big men's strength to perform the lifesaving task. Once the medicine was down, the long vigil of walking the animals began. "We mustn't let any of them lie down or their insides will get all twisted up," she told them.

Fortune insisted on taking her turn walking the animals. One mule died late that afternoon, but by that evening it appeared that the others would survive.

Admiration and respect glowed in the eyes of the freighters for their boss's pretty, dark-haired sister. Though they had always given her the respect due a lady, they now accepted her as one of them. Despite her self-consciousness, Fortune knew it was the highest praise a mule skinner could give when one of the hulking men offered to teach her how to use a bullwhip.

Weary to the bone and in dire need of a bath, she was exceedingly grateful for the hot bathwater Ursula had prepared for her. Grady and Eric joined the other men at the river to bathe, then headed up to the house where a hearty meal awaited them.

In the kitchen Granny and Ursula dished up heaping plates of beef and potatoes to the men. But when Ursula went to see what was keeping Fortune, she came back alone. "Dat li'l gal is sound asleep, and I don have it in me ta wake 'er."

"Let her be," Laila advised. "I reckon she needs the sleep more than the food." She turned to Eric and Grady. "You two might as well bed down in the bunkhouse with the other men tonight. And if you don't mind, I think Fortune might like you to hang around in the morning to help her straighten out this mess. Poor dear. First the fire and now this."

"I'd be happy to help any way I can, ma'am," Grady drawled.

"Same goes for me, Mrs. Fontaine," Eric replied.

"Good. Now if you'll excuse us, Ursula and I will leave you men to your meal. These old bones aren't used to long days like this one. Nubbins," she said, gaining the man's attention, "please see to it that Mr. MacNair and Mr. Jorgensen are made comfortable in the bunkhouse."

It was late the next morning when Laila went to Fortune's room and found the girl getting dressed. "Did you sleep well?"

"Granny, how could you let me sleep so late?" Fortune complained, pulling a brush through her hair. "There's so much to do." She tossed the brush down, grabbed a bright red ribbon and tied her hair back at her nape. "Has Nubbins checked on the mules this morning?" she asked sitting down and pulling on a pair of serviceable boots. "Are Grady and Eric still here? I didn't even thank them for all their help."

Laila sighed in exasperation and rested her fists on her narrow hips. "Now, calm down," she said crossly. "Everything is well in hand. I didn't live on a horse ranch with your grandfather all those years and not learn a thing or two, young lady."

Fortune rose, a chagrined look on her face. "Sorry, Gran. It's just that I've so much on my mind, and I'm worried. Everything is going wrong. It's as if all our magic and good luck charms have been hexed by an evil eye."

"I know, I know. But dear, you really *are* doing a fine job."

"Granny, how can you say that? Roc trusted me to take care of things, and no sooner is he gone than his warehouse burns down. And now this . . . this horribly cruel abomination. If this keeps up he'll have no business to come home to."

"Oh, bother! You didn't set that fire, and you didn't poison those mules out there. And if you think having Roc here would have made a difference, you're wrong. Now come along and have something to eat. Grady and Eric are out at the corrals waiting for you. They've been having a look around the place to see if they could figure out how this happened. After you've eaten, and not until then, you can fire all those questions at them."

Grady watched the gentle sway of Fortune's hips as she made her way across the dusty yard. A wide red sash added color to the heavy, dark cotton skirt and white shirtwaist she wore. Out of the corner of his eye he saw the Swede slick back his hair and offer Fortune a lady-killer grin. Grady silently cursed, but he knew now wasn't the time to put the Swede in his place.

"Grady, Eric," Fortune greeted them, "I'm sorry I kept you waiting. Gran should have gotten me up."

"Eric and I used the time well," Grady replied. "We checked the outbuildings—even rode out a ways and circled the property. I'm afraid we didn't find a thing that would lead us to the man or men who poisoned your stock."

"We was lucky at that," added Nubbins, joining them at the

corral. "They coulda poisoned the horses, too."

"Nubbins," Fortune started hesitantly, "you're sure this was a deliberate act and not a terrible accident? Mind you," she added, carefully choosing her words, "I know how careful you are about your job, but well, sometimes things happen."

"No, ma'am. Weren't no accident of mine or any of the men. That hay they was fed was moldy. Our feed has been kept dry in the barn."

"He's right," Eric interjected. "The Reb and I checked your feed supply. There isn't any of it bad except for that moldy stuff we raked up yesterday."

Fortune nodded. "I don't want you to think I was implying you were negligent, Nubbins. I guess, I was actually hoping a mistake had been made. Then I wouldn't have to face up to the fact that someone is trying to put Landry Freighting out of business."

"No offense taken, ma'am. I know you got a powerful responsibility, what with Roc bein' gone 'n all."

Fortune smiled gratefully at the old ranch hand and looked at Eric and Grady. "What now, gentlemen?" she asked, sounding at a loss. "Do I station guards here at the ranch?"

"I think that would be wise," Grady responded, casually resting one boot on a low rail. "In fact, I already took the liberty of assigning guard duty to some of your men. Hope you don't mind."

"Of course not. After all, you're a partner in this firm, too, and right now I'm darn glad I don't have to face this alone. I don't mind telling either one of you that I'm a little afraid. Not for myself," she quickly qualified, "but for Granny and Ursula here at the ranch as well as Roc out on the trail. We have no idea to what lengths our enemy is willing to go to."

"I'd be happy to drive your grandmother and Miss Price into town for you," Eric offered.

Fortune shook her head. "I've already discussed it with them, and they refuse to budge until next week, when they plan on coming to town for Independence Day." She smiled and added, "You have to understand. Granny and Ursula are very set in their ways. This is their home now, and heaven help the man that tries to oust them from their little kingdom."

"In that case, perhaps they'd allow Nubbins or one of the other men to guard inside the house at night," Grady suggested.

"Granny won't like it, but I'll try to convince her," Fortune assured him.

"I'll make sure guards are posted at the warehouse site, too," Eric said. "But don't you think there also should be guards at your house in town?"

"Surely whoever is doing these things wouldn't be so bold as to try entering my home. Besides, my home is well-protected."

Eric looked puzzled at that, but Grady knew exactly what the feisty little baggage was referring to. "If you think that garlic over your doors is enough protection, you're sadly mistaken. These aren't evil spirits we're dealing with, Fortune, but living, breathing, flesh and blood."

Fortune scowled up at him. "I won't have my house turned into an arsenal or a guardhouse, Grady. And I wouldn't be so quick to discount something you know nothing about."

Having finally picked up on the gist of what they were talking about, Eric pulled the piece of straw he'd been chewing out of his mouth and spoke up. "For once, I'm in agreement with the Reb, Fortune."

"Eric, you know nothing about my mag . . ."

Eric grinned sheepishly. "Ah, as a matter of fact, I do. Roc confided to me your, ah, belief in magic and charms and such. Look, Fortune, you agreed easily enough that a guard should stay in your grandmother's house."

Fortune wondered what else her brother had revealed about her to Eric. Pushing that thought aside, she pressed her point. "It's different with Gran and Ursula," she finally replied. "They're very old. On the other hand, I can take care of myself, and I will not have men tramping through my home. People are scandalized enough by the fact I live in a former bordello. They'll get over that, but if I allow men to hang around at all hours, they're bound to get the wrong idea."

Grady tapped Eric on the shoulder and whispered something in his ear. Eric nodded and faced Fortune again. "For now, we'll agree not to post guards in the house. But you have to promise to let us do as we see fit if anything happens that might jeopardize your safety."

"Oh, all right," Fortune bit out grudgingly.

Grady, Eric and Fortune headed back to town after the noon meal. When they reached Helena, Eric left them to check on the building preparations for the warehouse. Grady escorted Fortune home, then headed back to Main Street with the intentions of hiring a couple of trusted men to keep an eye on Fortune's house—from a distance, of course. After accomplishing that, he planned on investigating the Landrys' competitors to find out which ones were most likely to play dirty.

Chapter Sixteen

The Fourth of July had come to Helena. It mattered little to the large Confederate population that this was a Union celebration. After all, the South, like the North, had fought long and hard to win their freedom from the Brits.

Fortune, Granny, Ursula, Irene and Tish strolled along the street, stretching their necks in every direction and trying not to miss a single thing. With Grumpy along, the crowd was no problem at all. People took one look at the big ugly dog and moved out of his way.

Bugles tooted off key, guns banged, and miners, cowboys and gamblers ballyhooed. Ladies sported lavish hats and new frocks in a rainbow of colors. Children with sticky peppermint rings around their mouths shrieked in delight at the unusual sights and sounds. The aroma of hops combined irreverently with the bake goods being offered by the good ladies of the Methodist Church. The little boys competed to see who could steal the most food off their tables.

As the women passed the Red Dog Saloon, a bellowing temperance preacher disparaged the demon alcohol. Across

173

the road a medicine show spieler pitched his alcohol-ladened nostrums amidst cavorting strong men and scantily clad female acrobats. Farther up the street, people gathered on the boardwalk around a strange-looking chair, while an itinerant dentist entertained by pulling rotten teeth.

A commotion caught Fortune's attention when a group of men began yelling profanities. Apparently a few rowdy miners were challenging some freighters to an impromptu mule race down Main Street. The young Gypsy and her companions shrieked and ran for safety right along with everyone else as the burly men and their mules commenced the race.

Fortune and Irene kept a firm grip on the rambunctious Tish, who periodically lifted her feet off the ground so that she could swing like a little monkey between them. Fortune didn't mind at all and in fact liked indulging the child's fancies—mainly because it meant she, too, might indulge in them.

"Lordy, Lordy! Ain't seen the likes of dis since I left N'Orleans," Ursula declared, laughing and walking next to Laila just behind Fortune and Irene.

Book Tabor came running so fast he nearly plowed into his mother. "Ma, come quick! They're 'bout to start the sack race up past the Landry place."

"Oh, my, we wouldn't want to miss that, would we?" Irene said, winking at Fortune. "Come along, Tish." The small clutch of females promptly switched direction and trooped up the street.

"Hey, where are you all going in such a hurry?" a familiar voice called.

"Sack 'n run, Grady! Sack 'n run!" Tish giggled, jumping up and down excitedly.

An instant smile broke out on Fortune's face at the sight of Grady MacNair. The moment she'd seen how much fun this day would be, she'd regretted not being able to spend it with the good-natured Reb. Of course Eric was lots of fun, too, but it was Grady who held her heart.

Held her heart? Fortune stumbled and let go of Tish. Grady's strong hand caught her arm.

"You all right?" he asked solicitously. Grumpy nudged his way between the couple and snarled. "Nobody asked you, hellhound," Grady said.

Fortune's gaze never left his handsome, smiling face as she ordered her pet to calm himself.

"Come on, you two," Irene called from just ahead. "Book wants to enter the race."

Grady laughed and threw his arm around Fortune's waist. Granny and Ursula caught up with them then, and Granny bestowed a reproachful scowl on her granddaughter.

Fortune gazed straight ahead, pretending not to be aware of her grandmother's irritation. *Damn*, she thought. *I've concocted Riddance spells, worn my charms and said my chants. And I've avoided the Reb to the point of rudeness. Is it my fault that none of our plans have worked?*

More and more she questioned the magic of the Moondance. Oh, she still believed that she and Grady had bonded that long ago night, but these recent failures were enough to shake anyone's faith. Perhaps her magic wasn't truly responsible for what took place that night. Could there have been some other force at work? Fate?

Then again, maybe this was wishful thinking on her part. Because if destiny were involved, there was a very real possibility that despite all the lies and secrets between them, she'd get to keep Grady.

As Fortune and her companions arrived at the site of the sack race, she retreated from her confusing thoughts. It was too glorious a day to spend brooding.

Grady moved to stand between Laila and Fortune, but suddenly the old woman shrieked, "Get off, get off! You'll be my death, you nasty Gajo!"

"What?" Grady asked, holding his hands high and wide as if to show himself innocent of any wrongdoing.

"He's stepped on my shadow. Oh, I'm a dead woman. He stepped on my shadow."

Fortune grasped Laila's arm and urgently whispered, "Granny, you're making a scene. Stop it! You called Grady a Gajo. Sweet Gaia, you'll give us away."

"But he stepped on my shadow. It's terrible bad luck."

"Yes, yes, Granny, I know it is normally. But he didn't mean to, and it really can't be avoided in this crowd."

Ursula put a consoling arm around Laila, and the little old Gypsy calmed down.

Grady tugged Fortune aside and bent close so he wouldn't

be overheard. "Would you mind telling me what that was all about?"

"It's like she said," Fortune explained. "You stepped on her shadow. It's the worst kind of bad luck, but only when it's done on purpose."

"I see," Grady replied. "Fortune, I thought your grandmother liked me but lately I'm not so sure."

"No, no, don't mind Granny. She gets cranky is all. Her age, you know."

He gave her waist an affectionate squeeze. "I hope that's all it is. She may be little," he added with a chuckle, "but to tell you the truth I'd hate to be on her bad side."

"Fortune, Fortune," Tish cried, nabbing the young woman's attention, "I wanna race, too!"

"Gets pretty rough out there, little one," Grady told her, patting her head.

"Too rough for you, Reb?" came a male voice.

As one, Fortune and Grady glanced over their shoulders. "Eric." Fortune smiled. "I'm glad you made it. Book is going to race and we're here to cheer him on."

Eric smiled at Fortune, but his expression hardened as he repeated his earlier challenge to Grady. "Well, Reb, too rough for you?"

"Eric, it's just a game."

"Hell no, it's not too rough for me," Grady snarled in Eric's face. "How 'bout you, Yank?"

"Grady, Eric, please . . ."

"Let's go," Eric said laconically.

When Grady and Eric joined the ranks of sack racers, a number of drunk freighters and miners also decided to have a go at it. And despite the fact that Eric's challenge had been anything but good-humored, Fortune had to laugh at the resulting sideshow.

While the drunks managed well enough getting one leg in the sacks, they found it extremely difficult to keep their balance long enough to get the other leg in, too. Finally with the aid of their compatriots they managed to bag themselves and hop or, in some cases, tumble into line. Bets were quickly made and money exchanged.

"Ain't neber seen so many growed men make such crack-brains of demselves," Ursula commented, shaking her head.

"Hush, now," Laila said crossly. "And this time, don't you dare root for the Reb."

Ursula's brows raised in surprise, and she turned to Fortune. "Ugh," she grunted, "the ornery ol' coot is actin' like she swallered a bone crosswise cuz her magic didn't work. Dat's all dere is ta it."

"It's time," Irene interjected, excitedly.

"Ladies and Gents," a loud voice announced, "when the gun goes off the race shall begin. The winner shall receive a free pie from the church booth."

The gun went off, and a roar went up among the spectators. Men and boys hopped, hobbled, tumbled and rolled. Hats were lost and shirts were torn, while creative curses thickened the air. Fortune laughed till her sides hurt.

She saw Eric pause and laugh when one of the tipsy miners knocked Grady to the ground. But in the next instant Grady deliberately rolled over and over right behind Eric until finally he bowled the big Swede off his feet.

In the end, Book tied the race with a skinny gambler. They flipped a coin to see who got the pie, and Book got lucky. "I won, Ma," Book said, running up to his mother with a toothy grin on his face. "Here's the ticket for the pie. I gotta go now. Me and Joe wanna watch the weight lifting contest."

Grady and Eric strolled up then, brushing twigs and dirt from their grass-stained clothes. "Where to next, ladies?" Grady asked, completely ignoring Eric.

"Let's go to the weight lifting contest?" Book piped up.

"Come on," Eric said, slinging his arm around Fortune's shoulders. "I've signed up for this one, and I plan to win." Grumpy growled, but Fortune decided her pet must be getting used to Eric and Grady's presence because he was no longer baring his teeth at them.

Eric guided Fortune down the street, leaving Grady behind to fume.

"Well," Irene goaded Grady, "you gonna just stand there and let that man steal your girl?"

Grady started to reply, then spotted someone waving at him. He smiled and waved back. "I'll join you in a while, Irene," he replied enigmatically. "There's someone I must speak to."

Irene tugged on Tish's hand and headed for the contest with Laila and Ursula. Book spotted a group of his friends and went off on his own.

*   *   *

Grady joined Duncan Lawson at the bake sale stand. "You're late, Grady." Duncan mopped his sweaty brow with a bright red kerchief then tucked it down the front of his overalls. "You were supposed to be here a half hour ago."

"I know. I'm sorry, Duncan. I sort of got roped into the sack race."

"The sack race," the farmer hooted. "Well, did you at least win then?"

As an answer, Grady held up his grass-stained elbows. Then glancing down at the black dog next to Duncan, he asked, "That ugly mutt there the bitch?"

Duncan grinned and ran a beefy hand through his tousled brown hair. "Shore is, pard."

"She isn't much to look at, is she?"

"Hell, Grady, that doesn't make any never mind to a randy hound."

"Guess not." Grady chuckled. "'Sides, the beau I have in mind for her isn't much to look at himself. Will she play coy and give Fortune's dog a run? If she's easy—just stands there and lets him, you know—then this scheme won't work."

Duncan laughed. "Well, hell, Grady, Candy here always gives all the boys a good run."

"Good." Grady grinned and pointed down the street. "There's a weight lifting contest down there, and Eric Jorgensen is showing off for Fortune. Ever since he showed up, I've been trying to think of a way to get rid of him *and* the dog. I think I've finally thought of something. It may not work at all, but if it does I won't be forced to share Fortune with the Swede at the dance tonight."

"Just tell me what you want me to do." Duncan smiled devilishly.

"What took you so long?" Fortune asked Grady when he shouldered Eric aside and squeezed in beside her.

"Miss me, Sugar?"

Fortune gave her head an exasperated shake. "You're incorrigible."

"I know," he drawled in her ear. "But then I *am* a rebel."

"It'll be my turn soon," Eric said, pointing at the judge's platform off to the side.

Fortune watched as a young man took his place next to a pulley device. The pulley's heavy rope was attached to a large anvil, and behind it a crude board with painted horizontal lines stretched up its entire height.

"Each man must pull the anvil as high as he can," Eric explained. "I've taken the prize for the past two years." He lifted Fortune's chin with a finger. "There isn't a Reb in town that can beat me. But then, everyone knows Rebs can't win at anything." He looked pointedly at Fortune then smirked at Grady, making his meaning clear.

Fortune scowled. Annoyed with his rude comment to Grady, she pulled her chin out of Eric's grasp. The competition between them was childish and was beginning to grate on her nerves.

Seething, Grady spun on his heel and stomped off toward the judge's platform. When he returned, he removed his hat and gunbelt, handing them to Fortune. "Hold this," he ordered, heading back to the platform.

"Wait a minute. Where do you think you're goin'?" Eric objected. "It's my turn next."

"Not anymore it isn't," Grady replied without looking back.

Irene, Laila and Ursula slipped through the crowd to Fortune's side. "Looks like they're at it again," Irene said, chuckling. "Ah, to be young again and have two handsome swains vying for my charms."

"It's not funny, Irene," Fortune hissed. "I feel like a prize cow."

Irene tried unsuccessfully to hide her mirth, then nudged Fortune. "Quiet," she ordered. "There's Grady. Oh, my, I never realized he was such so . . . so well-formed."

Fortune's head snapped around. Her breath caught in her throat at the sight of Grady MacNair, barechested, legs spread wide, hands resting on slim hips. She caught her breath. A light sprinkling of wheat-colored hair covered his chest nipple to nipple, then narrowed to an arrow that disappeared beneath his belt buckle. Fortune's eyes did a long, slow slide downward, and she suddenly felt cheated by the denim cloth that hid the rest of him from her appreciative gaze.

The people around Fortune cheered when Grady grabbed the iron rod knotted in the pulley rope and began to pull. But she paid no heed to the cheers or the rising anvil. She saw nothing but a perfect example of male virility.

Muscles, slick and glistening with sweat, rippled with the strain of the weight. Fortune suddenly felt hot all over. A tingling ache unfurled deep within her, and her fingers curled in a fist as she imagined caressing every powerful inch of Grady MacNair's magnificent body.

A cheer went up, and Fortune gave her head a shake. The anvil hung suspended just one line from the very top of the board. Grady slowly let the rope out, and the anvil hit the ground with a solid thump.

"I can beat that," Eric bragged, walking toward the pulley.

Fortune frowned at Eric's arrogance and silently prayed that Grady would come out the winner.

Grady stood by the judge's platform, putting his shirt back on as Eric stripped off his own and approached the anvil. A slow smile swept over the Southerner's face when he spotted Duncan waiting across the street with the bitch at his side.

Everyone's eyes were on Eric as he put his full weight into his effort. When the anvil was halfway to the top, Grady signaled Duncan by removing his hat and replacing it quickly. As the Reb hurried back to where Fortune and the other women stood, he watched Duncan stealthily work his way behind the pulley board to the judge's stand. Grady retrieved his gun belt from Fortune and was standing innocently between her and Irene when all hell broke loose.

Grumpy's head went up, and he sniffed the air. He darted after the bitch, nearly jerking an unsuspecting Fortune off her feet when he pulled the leash from her hand. Women screamed and children gave chase as the dog ducked under skirts and around trousered legs. Fortune looked up just in time to catch the look of horror on Eric's face as first a black dog and then her own big lummox of a pet tore a path directly between the Swede's widespread legs.

Distracted, Eric loosened his grip on the rope. The sudden slack flung him off balance as the anvil crashed to the ground. At the same time the iron rod flew up under his chin and knocked him out cold.

The crowd broke into uproarious laughter, finding this amusing mishap far more entertaining than the contest itself.

"Oh, poor Eric," Fortune cried as she ran to him.

While Fortune and the other women pushed through the crowd to Eric's side, Duncan meandered over to where Grady stood rocking on his heels. "How far will that bitch run," Grady asked with a chuckle.

"If that male don't catch 'er first, she'll run all the way back home," Duncan replied, hiding the bitch's leash in his trouser pocket.

Grady held out his hand. "I owe you one, friend."

Giving Grady's hand a shake, Duncan hurried up the street to meet his wife.

The excitement over, the people dispersed in search of new entertainment. Grady frowned when he saw Fortune sitting on the ground, cradling Eric's head in her lap. Shoving his hands in his pockets he directed his steps toward them.

"Dead," little Tish was crying. "Dead!"

"Now he ain't neither dead," Ursula told the child. "See there, he's wakin' up."

"Oh, Eric," Fortune apologized, "I'm so sorry. I've never seen Grumpy behave like that. I can't imagine what got into him."

"Ugh," Ursula grunted. "Dat dog ain't no different den the rest of male creation. He lost de good sense he was born with at the sight of a waggin' behind."

"Oh, Ursula," Irene said, laughing, "you're just awful. I love it!"

Grady offered his hand to Eric. The Swede hesitated, eyeing the Reb suspiciously, but finally grabbed hold and struggled to his feet. He groaned and rubbed his aching head but appeared otherwise unhurt.

Grady had hoped for, at the very least, a sprained ankle that would send the man home for the rest of the day. But it looked like he'd have to settle for getting rid of Fortune's bodyguard.

"Do you think Grumpy will come back?" Fortune fretted, gazing in the direction her dog had taken. "Maybe I should go after him."

"No!" both men shouted at once. They stared at each other in surprise, then quickly dropped their glances before Fortune could see the amusement that twinkled in their eyes.

"You'd never catch him now," Grady explained. "He'll come home soon as he's finished sparking his girl."

"That's right," Eric seconded. "Besides, we don't know who's behind the vandalism at Landry Freighting yet. I don't think you should be wandering around alone."

"I'm hungry, Ma," Tish said, pulling on her mother's skirts.

"I could eat a bit myself," Irene replied. "What say we all go over to the church stand and pick up that prize pie Book won, along with some other vittles? Eric, maybe they'll also have some ice for that head."

While they enjoyed a filling meal at the church tables, Jim Fetters, the Landry night watchman, appeared and shyly asked Irene and the children if he might escort them to the dance and fireworks display that evening. Irene happily accepted. Then, since Fortune had turned down Grady and Eric's offers of escort, the housekeeper asked Jim if he'd mind escorting the other three ladies as well. Jubilant over Irene's acceptance, the big man readily agreed.

After eating, Fortune and her entourage wandered over to Hassler's stable where the greased pig contest was to take place. Fortune was relieved when neither Grady nor Eric challenged each other on this one. Both claimed their bellies were too full. Book, however, had no such problem and promised to win them a pig.

Within a few minutes the squealing, greased pigs were turned loose in a corral, and a horde of little boys, sleeves rolled up to their elbows, ran yelling after them. Fortune had never seen anything like it in her life, and she laughed so hard her cheeks hurt. Book unfortunately didn't win his pig, but he did have a good time wallowing in the mud with his friends.

No sooner had they all drifted away from that competition than a rackety band struck up a tune. Two scandalously clad young women marched ahead of the band players carrying a sign that read *King of Pain Medicine Show*.

"Laila, you think dat dere King of Pain has somethin' for my rheumatiz?"

Laila rolled her eyes. "Ursula, they're all fakers. Why, who knows what they really put in those bottles? Besides, the medicine I make you works just fine. What do you want with that infernal stuff? It's like to poison you."

"Well, I ain't neber seen one of dem medicine shows. And I'm gonna have me a look-see, all the same."

Fortune, sandwiched between Eric and Grady, followed along behind the other three women. Tish hopped and skipped at her mother's side singing, "King of Pain, King of Pain," in time with the band music.

When the band reached the Medicine Show wagon it abruptly quit. The women in the crowd oohed and ahed when a handsome giant of a man with iron bands on his wrists appeared on a platform at the front of wagon and flexed shirtless biceps. Fortune laughed when she saw one man slap his hand over his wife's bugging eyes.

"Now that's what I call a man," Irene said next to her. The two women giggled, earning a scowl from both Grady and Eric.

Next, the band struck a bawdy tune and a young girl pranced out in tights, and little more, to perform contortions that Fortune would have thought humanly impossible. The men in the crowd hooted and catcalled when she lay down flat then arched into a backbend in a rather lewd display of her attributes.

Fortune felt herself being shoved forward and glanced up to find that the crowd had swollen considerably, mostly with men.

Standing on either side of her, Eric and Grady's hands accidentally touched behind her back as each tried to put a protective arm around her. When each felt the other's hairy hand, they jerked away and exchanged killing looks. Then Grady took her left arm, Eric the right.

Suddenly the band played a loud introductory fanfare, drawing their attention back to the medicine wagon. The pitchman, dressed in a fancy frock coat and top hat, stepped out on the platform and picked up a large, colorfully labeled bottle.

"Come closer, Ladies and Gents, gather round," the King of Pain proclaimed, waving his arms around in gestures of grandeur. Then he raised his hands for quiet.

"Ponder this! You are all dying! Yes, it's true—dying! From the moment we are born we are on our way to dying. No man can hope to escape the Grim Reaper. But . . ." He paused for effect and held up his pointer finger. "There is a logical course to pursue, my friends. Yes, all of you can delay the sorry day your name is written down by a skeletal hand in the book of death." He held his bottle high for all to see. "This secret recipe formulated by our very own Madame Rupa, famous Gypsy Queen, can prolong your life.

"And let me assure the ladies . . ." He wiggled his eyebrows naughtily. "Madame Rupa's Blood Tonic will put the vital sparks back into your bedrooms."

There were a few shocked gasps from the females in the crowd, but Fortune could see speculation running rampant. Rough laughter and bawdy jokes broke out among the men.

The handsome, muscle-flexing brute and the nimble-limbed contortionist reappeared at the spieler's side then. Extending his hand toward them, he continued in a persuasive voice. "These fine specimens of manhood and womanhood were raised on Madame Rupa's Blood Tonic! Proof, Ladies and Gents, of its genuine quality. Now who will be the first to invest in a longer and stronger life by buying this truly miraculous tonic?"

"By gum, I'll have me some of that there stuff," shouted a voice in the crowd.

"Who's that?" Eric asked. "I've never seen that old timer in Helena before."

"He's a shill," Laila answered with disdain.

"A what?" Irene asked.

"A shill," Laila repeated. "Someone who is part of the troop and is planted in the audience. They get the buying started, since no one actually likes to be the first to admit to needing or wanting the benefits of the tonic."

"How do you know about such things?" Grady asked with a curious tilt of his head.

Laila shrugged. "Medicine shows started in Europe years ago. Even the roving Gypsies use shills for one thing and another."

Fortune cast her Granny a warning glance and was relieved when the old lady added no more to her explanation. Then the King of Pain was speaking again, and she focused on the wagon platform where an ugly, middle-aged woman in a parody of Gypsy attire had joined him.

Fortune stared at the woman with frank amusement. Iron gray hair, long and witchy, stuck out from underneath a red scarf knotted at the back of her head. A huge wart grew out the side of her long, hooked nose, and a myriad of ridged wrinkles mapped her face. The strange woman wore a gaudily gold-embroidered bolero over a shabby, loose, long-sleeved blouse of red. The full skirt, made of scarves in various colors, came only to her ankles and displayed slim, sandled feet. It was the sight of those slim, youthful feet that made Fortune's brows knit in consternation.

"Ladies and Gents," the spieler announced, "you are truly in for a rare and wondrous treat. Madame Rupa has just informed me that the dark ones from the beyond are with her today. For a small fee, she will grant you an audience and amaze you with stupendous knowledge of your past, present and future. Just line up at the back of the wagon and you will be admitted inside for the experience of a lifetime."

"Another faker," Laila grumbled to no one in particular. "It's an insult to all good Gy—"

"Grandmother!" Fortune blurted sharply. "Well, Granny, you certainly are not in a holiday mood today, are you?"

Laila stubbornly crossed her arms beneath her bosom and stuck out her lower lip in a pout.

"Come on," Grady said, playfully tugging on Fortune's arm. "Let's get our fortunes told. I know it's all a bunch of hogwash, but it'll be fun all the same."

Ursula looked ready to burst with glee, and Irene tossed Fortune an amused wink.

Wearing a worried expression, Eric took Fortune's other arm and tugged in the opposite direction. "I'm taking Fortune to watch the horse race now," he stated flatly.

One look at Eric's face and Fortune instantly knew that Roc had disclosed far more than her penchant for magic to the man.

"The race doesn't start for another half hour," Grady protested, knocking Eric's hand away from Fortune's arm. He tugged the girl closer to his side, "Come on, Sugar, let's see what our futures hold," he teased.

Fortune barely had time to wonder where Ursula and her grandmother had gotten to when Eric again tugged her in the opposite direction. "The lady is with me for the rest of the day, Reb."

"Like hell, she's with—"

"Stop it, both of you! I'll not stand here and let you treat me like a rope in a tug of war game."

A commotion broke out at the back of the wagon, and the sudden surge of humanity in that direction separated Fortune from the two men.

The wagon walls literally shook. A loud crash was followed by an ear-splitting howl of protest. Fortune could see little from where she stood at the back of the assemblage, but she recognized all too well the acerbic repertoire of Romany castigations. Sweet Gaia, it was Granny in there causing that ruckus! She had to get up there and put a stop to it.

But just as she started to struggle forward, a loud authoritative voice bellowed, "What's goin' on here? Move aside, move aside." As the man rudely shoved Fortune against the chest of a burly miner, she saw the silver badge on his chest and gasped in horror. Granny was about to be arrested!

Thinking fast, she turned around and blinked up into the face of the burly miner she'd just bumped into. "Are you going to let that rude oaf get away with shoving a lady around just because he's got a star on his chest?" she demanded. The miner frowned, obviously torn between defending the beautiful lady in front of him and going up against the sheriff. Fortune leaned against his arm and managed to blink out a tear. That's all the inspiration the man needed.

"Come on, boys," the miner raged, setting Fortune gently aside. "Let's teach that lop-eared defiler of wimmin a lesson!"

"What's that you say?" shouted a freighter. "The sheriff hurt our boss's sister? Get 'im, boys!"

Pandemonium broke loose, and only a few actually saw Laila pull a bedraggled young woman out of the wagon by the hair of her head. Ursula followed and triumphantly held up the gray wig the fake Gypsy had worn. Then laughing with glee, she tossed it into the melee.

Over the heads of fighting males and shrieking females trying to escape, Fortune saw Grady and Eric lift Granny and Ursula down from the wagon.

"Come on," shouted Irene, suddenly appearing behind Fortune with Tish clutched in her arms.

Once away from the brawl, they slowed their pace. Irene set Tish down to walk on her own. "Where are we going?" Fortune asked.

"We're to meet the men with Granny and Ursula at the other end of town so we can hide out in the horse race crowd."

Book came running up to the two women then, Joe Billings puffing for breath at his side. "By jingo," Book said, laughing, "this is the best Fourth we've ever had. Did you see Eric and Grady rescuin' poor ol' Granny and Ursula? And did you see what happened to Madam Rupa?"

Irene grinned at Fortune then turned to her son, mimicking his excited tone. "And by jingo, did you see how Fortune started that riot so Granny and Ursula could escape the sheriff?"

As Jamie glanced at Fortune Bleu turned to her and, almost like she slapped her, "And he must, did you see Jamie Fortune told me she and no Granny and Gretch could or can see the story?"

Chapter Seventeen

She clutches his heart to her breast
And wings away on another quest
Only the wind hears Gajo's distress and emptiness

After the horse race, Fortune and the other women took the children and headed for the house on Cutler Street. Little Tish was put down for a nap, and Book helped his mother heat water for baths.

Upstairs Fortune knocked lightly on her grandmother's bedroom door.

"Come in, Fortune."

The young woman entered and shut the door behind her. She hadn't been in her grandmother's room since they had moved in, and she was amazed at the transformation. Granny had utilized her love for bright colors to decorate the small room in a tasteful, feminine manner.

Dressed in a purple wrapper, the old lady sat like a queen on a bed covered with pillows representing every color in the spectrum. In one hand she held a delicate silver hand mirror,

188

and with the other she applied a matching hairbrush to her long snowy hair.

"Irene told me that the tub down the hall is filled and waiting for you, Gran," Fortune said leaning back against the door.

Laila smiled knowingly and gazed across the room at Fortune. "Yes, well, I've been expecting you. Do come sit down. Looking up at you like this gives me a pain in the back of my neck."

Fortune obeyed, shoving a few pillows aside and sitting at the foot of the bed.

"Now what is it you came to say?"

There were times that Fortune felt she was the adult and her grandmother the child. This was one of them. "If you were expecting me, then you know that I am not happy with you. I'd like to know what you thought you were up to this afternoon. Good gravy, Gran, you could have been arrested for disturbing the peace."

"But dear, don't you see? I couldn't stand by and let that ridiculous woman represent herself as one of us. It's charlatans like her that give us Gypsies a bad name."

"But Granny, you could have given us away. What will Grady make of all this?"

"Oh, wasn't he grand helping us escape the way he did?"

"Granny, stick to the subject."

Laila pursed her lips and shrugged. "I simply told Grady that the woman tried to sneak her hand into my reticule when I wasn't looking."

Fortune shook her head. "You lied? What if that poor woman is thrown in jail?"

"It wouldn't be anymore than she deserves. But not to worry," she added lightly. "When Grady rescued us I heard that King of Pain man order his people to pack up so they could leave immediately. And since the sheriff hasn't come after us, I think we can safely assume he didn't see Ursula or myself leave that wagon. Grady, of course, won't breathe a word about it. I must say this Southern custom of protecting a lady's honor comes in handy."

"But Granny, you shouldn't have lied."

"Well, it's really no sin for a Gypsy to lie to a Gajo, is it? Anyway, that Madame Rupa, or whatever her name was, didn't even know how to read my palm." When Fortune cracked a smile at that, Granny pushed her advantage, "You aren't really mad at your old Gran, are you, dear? Why, it was the most fun I've had in years. And the way you distracted the sheriff . . ." She laughed. "Oh, you are your grandmother's blood, that's for sure."

Shaking her head, Fortune scooted closer to her grandmother and hugged her. "Granny, you are impossible. And you know I can't stay mad at you. But there is one thing."

"Yes?"

"Could you please stay out of trouble from now on?"

Laila sighed. "Yes, dear, I'll try. And I'm sorry for being so cranky earlier today. I didn't want to admit it in front of Ursula, but I have been rather upset about the failure of the last Riddance spell."

"Yes . . . the Riddance spell." Fortune frowned in consternation. "Lately, I've been wondering if there isn't a reason why our Riddance spells haven't worked."

Laila set her brush aside and gave her granddaughter a considering look. "I must admit that I've wondered myself. But maybe I'm just losing my touch. Don't tell Ursula I said so, but I am getting a little old."

Fortune smiled. Granny had never disclosed her true age, but "a little old" had to be between 80 and 85. "I don't think you're loosing your touch, Gran. But did you ever consider that there might be a higher power beyond our magic, a power that ordained Grady and I should be together?"

"Power? What power?"

"Call it destiny, if you will."

Laila cocked her head. "Hmm, interesting theory, that. I suppose it's possible. And the theory would certainly exonerate my failure with the Riddance spells. I don't mind telling you, my pride has taken a licking lately. But while the explanation is convenient, I have to be honest with you, Fortune. I know very little about this thing called destiny. As I've told you before, we Gypsies live for the moment. We believe we make our own fortunes or, as you call it, destinies. And when there is something we can't change we rely on our magic."

"But if there is some higher power . . ."

"This is all very confusing, dear, and I'm afraid I have no reliable answers for you."

Fortune stood. "I'm keeping you from your bath. You better go before the water chills, but I have to tell you that I feel very naked knowing my magic might be useless." She spread her arms in a helpless manner. "I don't know how to proceed, what to do."

"Now, now, we don't know for a fact that our magic is being usurped," Laila said, standing and retrieving her toilet items from a chest drawer. "But if it's true we are dealing with destiny, you must listen with your heart, first, your head, last."

"Then you're saying this thing called destiny is within me?"

Laila shrugged. "Who can say? That's something we must all decide for ourselves. As for me, I live for the day." She ushered Fortune to the door. "Now, you better see to your own bath as well. You'll want to look pretty for tonight's festivities."

Jim Fetters appeared before the house in a wagon at precisely 6:30. The ladies were pleased to see that he'd provided a couple of clean benches in the back so they wouldn't dirty their dresses. The children laughed and chattered about the fireworks, too excited to notice Fetter's polite considerations.

It was a short ride to the Kessler place on the outskirts of town. Fortune heard the music before the farm came into view. A shiver of anticipation surged through her. There was definitely a little magic swirling about in the mountain air this evening. Hadn't she, without setting out to do so, dressed especially for Grady?

Tonight he would whirl her around the dance floor in his arms. A little smile curved her lips as she fondly remembered that day in the mercantile when they'd danced around barrels and tables.

Finding both Grady and Eric waiting for her arrival came as no surprise. But to forestall an immediate confrontation, while the two young men were occupied helping Granny and Ursula from the wagon, she gathered up her skirts and jumped down on her own.

Book, holding his little sister's hand, ran ahead of the adults to the festively lit barn. "Just listen to that music," Irene enthused. "I hear they got the King Solomon Masonic Band to play for the dance. They sound real good, don't they? Oh, Jim, don't forget that basket of food under the seat," she reminded her escort. Jim reached for the basket, and she slipped her hand over his free arm. "Come on, handsome, let's crack some calico!"

Fortune followed Irene and Jim while Eric and Grady brought up the rear with Ursula and Granny on their arms. The Gypsy girl felt the heat of the men's burning eyes against her back and prayed both would behave themselves tonight.

A myriad of lanterns lit the barn, including a few delicate Chinese lanterns in the center of the room. Bright red, white and blue paper ribbons festooned the rafters between the lanterns and adorned the raised platform where the band performed. Wooden benches lined the walls, a few arranged in intimate circles. The hard-packed dirt floor had been swept clean of straw and was barely noticeable for all the colorful dress hems that skimmed above its surface.

Granny and Ursula immediately gravitated to a corner near the refreshment table and set up court. That left Fortune with Eric and Grady.

She glanced from one pair of blue eyes to the other, Grady's the deeper delft blue and Eric's the paler blue of his Norse ancestors. She sighed and smiled. "You two aren't making this very easy."

Grady grinned and produced a coin from his trouser pocket. "Shall we flip to see who gets the first dance, Swede?"

Eric nodded. "I get first call, Reb."

Fortune frowned, unsure of the honor of being a prize on the flip of a coin.

Eric won the toss. Grady stood on the sidelines, trying not to look as jealous as he felt. Since there were far more men at this affair than available ladies, he felt no compulsion to ask another woman to dance. He much preferred staying right where he was so he could keep an eye on Fortune.

At first sight of her in back of the wagon tonight, he'd decided that she'd dressed especially for him. His confidence in this conjecture grew when he smelled her sultry perfume. She hadn't worn it since their first kiss in the woods behind the Landry ranch house. Could she be sending him a subtle message?

Her jet hair was beautiful as always, parted in the middle and drawn up at the temples to the crown. Red ribbons were twisted among the long curls that dangled down her back.

Her dress, a Scottish plaid of red, blue and black, had a scooped neckline accented with a wide ruffle that ended just above her breasts. Her waist was accentuated by a bright blue sash with streamers that flowed down the front of her full skirt. Grady again wondered if her choice of the plaid held special meaning for him. He felt the warmth of her feline gaze transverse the dance floor and meet his eyes. He winked, and she blushed prettily.

Fortune couldn't keep her eyes from straying to the handsome figure Grady cut in his dark suit. His light hair was a perfect foil for the dark blue coat he wore over a crisp white shirt. She smiled when she noticed that rather than a tie, he wore his trademark black silk scarf loosely knotted at his throat. His trousers hugged his long muscular legs and fell over shiny black boots.

Eric snatched her full attention when he pulled her close and whispered, "May I hope that the faraway look in your eyes is for me, Fortune?"

She gazed up at the handsome Swede. He was not only attractive but also gentle and kind. She loved him, but only as she would a brother. Fortune reached up and brushed a lock of flaxen-blond hair from his brow then replaced her hand on his shoulder as he waltzed her into a fancy turn.

"Eric, I . . . I care for you deeply, but I can't lead you on. I'm—"

"You're in love with the Reb," Eric sighed resignedly. "I think I knew it all along, but I hoped I was wrong. Roc told me that you believed you were falling in love with the Reb because of some spell you cast over him during the war. But he was wrong, wasn't he, sweetheart? You really do love the man."

Fortune lowered her gaze from his and nodded. "I'm sorry, Eric. I think too much of you to be less than totally honest." She gazed back up at him and smiled. "You're a very handsome and wonderful man. You deserve the very best a woman has to offer. And as much as I wish that woman could have been me, it just wasn't meant to be. I think, dear friend, destiny has someone else in store for you."

Eric swallowed hard, and Fortune could see that it wasn't easy for him to keep dancing as if nothing of importance had been said. And that saddened her.

The music ended, but before leading her off the floor, he said, "If you ever change your mind about the Reb, I hope you'll give me another chance."

Fortune nodded, smiled and stood up on tiptoe to kiss his cheek.

Eric led her to where Grady MacNair stood anxiously waiting. The big Swede astonished Grady and Fortune when he reached for Grady's hand and placed Fortune's hand within it. "I was wrong earlier today," he said solemnly. "The Rebs don't always lose. Just know this, Reb—if you hurt Fortune, I'll make it my mission in life to hunt you down and kill you!"

He turned to Fortune then and smiled sadly, "I promised your brother I'd look out for you while he was gone. This doesn't change a thing. I'll still oversee the building of the new warehouse, and I'm available anytime you need me." He turned to Grady once again and added stonily, "Remember what I said, Reb. You hurt her and you're a dead man!" With that the Swede turned on his heel and stalked out of the barn.

Grady wasn't at all sure what had gone on between Eric and Fortune on the dance floor, but if it meant he now had Fortune to himself it didn't matter. Grateful that the band was playing a slower rhythm, he drew Fortune into his arms. She felt so good, so right. What was it about her tonight that seemed so different? She seemed more at ease, not only with him but with herself.

Fortune didn't protest when he gathered her much closer than propriety ruled proper. Something beyond her control was urging her to surrender her heart to this man, and she could no longer deny her own yearnings. Whether Moondance or destiny, she couldn't say. Perhaps the time had come to live moment by moment, as was the true Gypsy way.

Grady's intense gaze held hers, conveying a message that caused her heart to soar. As he swirled her about the room, he touched her forehead with a light inconspicuous kiss.

His hand on her back pressed her a little closer, and when they performed an intricate turn, the evidence of his desire glanced off her thigh. Her own desire, strong and demanding, flamed to life. Suddenly, she found herself remembering how Grady had looked earlier today without his shirt. Sweet Gaia! How she yearned to touch him, to see him, all of him. Her nails sunk into the fabric of his coat.

Grady's eyes widened with surprise and sudden understanding. His smile was as intimate as a kiss, and Fortune couldn't help the blush that washed her cheeks.

One dance led into another and another, and when Grady was obliged to allow another to partner Fortune, he politely asked Laila to dance. Laila loved to dance, but her body was not so young as it once was and halfway through she begged off. When he looked Ursula's way she shrank back and adamantly shook her head. "Ain't neber pranced about with a white boy," she said. "Ain't 'bout ta start now."

Unfortunately for Grady, Reva Wentworth, a pretty little featherhead, immediately hooked her arm through his. "I'll dance with you, Grady," she gushed.

Unable to refuse her without appearing ungentlemanly, Grady smiled and led her out on the floor. Reva immediately and quite shamelessly draped herself all over him. Grady stiffened his arms and held the girl off, all the time trying to think of a way to have some time alone with Fortune. He had to know if what he'd seen in her eyes tonight was real or if he'd just imagined it because he wanted her so badly.

When the music ended, Grady left Reva at her mother's side and searched for Fortune. Just as he reached her side, the mayor of Helena took the platform. "Ladies and Gents," he boomed over the pleasant chatter, "I understand that the Chinamen have the fireworks display ready for our pleasure. I invite you all to adjourn outside for a spectacular show. Later the dance will resume, and of course there's still lots of good eats."

As they left the barn, Grady slid his arm around Fortune's waist. His eyes drank her up and reflected his urgent need to be alone with her. Fortune shivered, unable to look away.

Irene hurried up to them, smiling and brimming with her usual enthusiasm. Behind her Jim stood with his arms full of blankets. "Here," she said, plucking one from the top of the pile and handing it to Grady. "I brought these to sit on so we wouldn't dirty our dresses."

Grady thanked her, but when Irene and Jim started up the hill he called them back. "Would you mind seeing Miss Price and Mrs. Fontaine safely home? I'd like to see Fortune home myself."

Irene winked at Fortune. "Don't you two worry 'bout a thing. Jim and I will see to them."

Laughing and joking, adults and children alike headed up the grassy knob above the Kessler farm, some carrying lanterns to light the way. Grady found a place a short distance from the main crowd and spread the blanket on the grass beneath an oak tree. They had barely settled themselves when the starry sky was lit by the crackling and popping of the colorful fireworks. Starbursts of red, white and blue bloomed against the dark sky then gently fell to earth in long sparkling trails of fairy dust.

Fortune clapped with delight, and Grady edged closer to her side. He chuckled, enjoying her excitement. "Amazing, isn't it?" he said staring at the panorama of color. "Some ancient Chinese cook accidentally dropped a little saltpeter into the fire with the sulfur that was used to make the charcoal burn hotter. The resulting explosion gave birth to gunpowder and then fireworks. Must have caused a lot of excitement way back then, too!"

Fortune turned her head to reply and found his lips only inches above hers. Her Gypsy blood stirred restlessly. "I think," she said huskily, "that it wasn't nearly as exciting as this." Her hand went to the back of his head, pulling him down to meet her kiss.

It was the first kiss between them that Fortune had ever initiated, and Grady knew he'd been right about what he'd seen in her eyes on the dance floor. Her mouth was soft and sweet, and when her small tongue ventured between her lips, he opened to her and deepened the kiss. Emboldened, she explored his mouth and eagerly partnered his tongue in a pagan love dance. The kiss went on and on until they both were gasping for air.

"Darlin'," Grady whispered huskily, "I've been wanting you to kiss me all night. Lord, woman, what you do to me!" His hands cradled her face, and he lowered his mouth to hers once more. He nibbled softly at her lower lip till she opened and welcomed his invasion.

One of his hands slipped to the soft nape of her neck. Fortune moaned softly, quivering in response to his sensual massage. The colorful bursts of light in the sky suddenly paled next to the shattering desire that splintered through her.

The chatter of surrounding voices finally intruded on the lovers' world. They looked all around, then at each other, and laughed. The fireworks display was over.

Many of the young people returned to the barn to dance the night away, but some families loaded up their little ones and headed for home. There wasn't a lantern left on the hill, and Fortune and Grady were alone in the magical moonlight. Neither one made a move to leave.

Grady was full to busting with wanting Fortune. Though they had kissed passionately, Grady hadn't gone so far as to touch her intimately. But now, alone with her in the cloak of darkness, his willpower reached the end of its tether.

"Fortune?"

Fortune knew what he was asking without hearing the question. *Follow your heart*, her Granny had said—and follow it she would. She lay back on the blanket and gazed up at the stars. Yes, this was the right place—high on a hill, by the light of the moon. It suited her Gypsy soul. She lifted her arms to him. "Love me, Grady."

He released a feral growl of desire and lowered himself onto the blanket. His mouth took hers in a branding kiss that made her burn to blend her body and soul with his.

As Grady made love to her with his mouth, his hands worked feverishly to free her of her clothing. God, he'd waited so long to sink himself into her sweet body. He lifted his mouth from hers and took a deep breath, trying to calm himself lest he frighten her with his animal lust.

Fortune took his mouth as feverishly as he'd taken hers and tore at the buttons on his shirt.

Grady shed his shirt and helped Fortune with the tiny buttons down the front of her dress. Then he loosened the sash around her waist, grasped the hem of the dress and lifted her slightly so that he could pull it off over her head.

Grady looked down on the corset ribbons and wanted to roar with frustration. Then he remembered the knife inside his boot. In a flash he sliced the obtrusive garment from her. The chemise quickly joined the growing pile of feminine lace and ruffles. Finally, but for the shell amulet pillowed between her breasts, she lay naked and vulnerable before him.

The arousing sight of her full, creamy breasts tipped with dusky rose nipples nearly undid him. But when she self-consciously covered herself, he was abruptly reminded of her innocence. Taking several deep breaths, he smiled down at her with tenderness. "Forgive me, lass. Your passionate nature made me forget that you're new at this." He replaced her hands with his own over her breasts. "I knew you would be beautiful, but you far surpass my dreams." He kissed her again then, long and languorous as he rolled one of her nipples between his thumb and forefinger. Then very slowly, he slid her drawers down, adoring every inch of flesh as it was revealed.

Fortune gasped as the cool air touched her steamy womanhood. But modesty surrendered to wanton abandon when Grady sucked a nipple into his mouth and cupped the dark triangle between her thighs. As he gently inserted one finger, then two, preparing her for his intrusion, waves of pleasure rippled through her. "Grady, please . . ."

"Easy darlin'," Grady soothed. "Is this what you want?" He massaged the sensitive kernel hidden within her soft slick folds.

"Oh, yes." Fortune eagerly pressed herself against his fingers. Suddenly his fingers were gone and only the night air touched her heated center. Her eyes flew open in dismay, but what she saw rendered her speechless. She watched in fascination as Grady rose and quickly discarded his boots and trousers. His phallus extended boldly from a thatch of hair a shade darker than that on his head.

Fortune wasn't completely ignorant of men. She'd accidentally caught glimpses of her brother when they were children. But the differences between a young boy and a man fully aroused was daunting. For the first time since she'd asked Grady to make love to her, she was frightened. This thing had to fit inside her, but it was impossibly huge!

Grady lowered himself at her side, saw the fear in her eyes and gently took her hand in his. "Touch me, Fortune."

Desire to know his body overcame her alarm, and she allowed him to wrap her fingers around his erection.

Fortune marveled at the feel of him. He was steel-incased in the softest satin, and when she moved her fingers over his staff, it reared like a lusty stallion. "Oh!" She would have pulled away, but Grady stayed her hand, tutoring her movements to show her how best to please him.

"Fortune, love," he said, finally removing her hand, "I can't hold on much longer. If we are both to enjoy this experience, I have to take you now." Nudging her legs apart with one of his, Grady covered her body with his. His mouth slanted across hers, and as he leaned into the cradle of her hips, her legs automatically wrapped around the back of his thighs.

Grady reached down between their bodies and massaged the taut bud at her threshold, reigniting her desire for him.

Fortune thrashed her head from side to side and offered up her hips. The sensual tension heightened till she thought she would explode with unappeased hunger. "Grady, please, now!"

Sweat broke out on Grady's brow as he forced himself to go slow. "Easy, honey girl," he soothed, easing his shaft into her wet heat. "Wrap you arms around my neck. That's it." Grady slid through her barrier then, smothering her sharp cry with a smoldering kiss. For a moment he lay still, allowing her body time to accustom itself to his.

Fortune relaxed as the burning sensation was gradually replaced with a feeling of fullness. Then Grady began to move slowly within her, gradually increasing his tempo. And to her surprise and delight the intense longing blazed to life again, stronger and more demanding than before.

Fortune's tight little canal clutched at Grady's member, and it was all he could do to hold back. But he did, because more than anything he wanted her to climb the pinnacle of satisfaction with him.

To Fortune, her entire existence seemed wholly centered in the secret place between her legs. As Grady stroked her harder and faster, she lifted her hips and met his deep thrusts with her own. The tension built. Up and up she climbed until she exploded into a flight of pleasure like none other she'd ever known.

Grady's cry joined Fortune's as he spilled his seed deep within her and collapsed atop her.

For a moment neither could speak. Fortune continued to clasp him tightly, unwilling to let this magical moment slip away into sweet memory. A single tear trickled down her cheek. She was unequivocally in love with Grady MacNair, but sadly, her love was utterly impossible. For if he knew the simple truth of her identity, he would hate her.

Grady rolled off Fortune, one leg and arm possessively wrapped about her. Fortune Landry had thoroughly bewitched him. Innocent that she was, she'd given all that his body demanded of hers and more than his senses could comprehend. Never had he experienced such a melding of souls.

From the moment he'd first seen her in the hotel, he'd made up his mind to have her. And almost immediately after that, he'd decided she'd make him a suitable wife. He'd connived and even lied to gain his end, but the joke was on him. He'd fallen in love with this enigmatic little vixen, and funnier yet, he hadn't even realized it until this very moment.

Grady felt a warm drop of moisture where his cheek rested on hers, and he raised his head. "Fortune? Are you all right, sweetheart? Did I hurt you?"

Fortune shook her head. "No, no, you didn't hurt me."

"Then what is it?"

Fortune smiled up at him tremulously. "I'm just so happy." It was true. She was glad she'd given herself to Grady MacNair. Maybe it was selfish, but she planned to grab all the happiness she could and store it away. Without a doubt there would come a time when that's all she'd have left of him.

"Do you know what I think?" Grady whispered. "I think we were meant for each other and that we shouldn't waste such happiness. I'm asking you to be my wife, lassie, and I want us to get married as soon as possible." He lifted her chin with a finger and brushed her lips with his. "Well, what do you say, darlin'? I've made you mine tonight. Will you be mine in the eyes of the law as well?"

Marriage? She hadn't expected the question of marriage to come up—at least not so soon! What to say, what to do? She'd give anything to be his wife, but once he discovered the truth . . .

Fortune opened her mouth to speak, but obtrusive voices and the jingle of tack drew their attention down the hill. She yanked a piece of discarded clothing over her breasts.

Grady sat up and scanned the small commotion taking place in front of Kessler's barn. "It must be very late," he said, turning back to her. "The band is leaving, and the lanterns are out."

"We better leave, too," Fortune said, gathering up her clothes. "Granny and the others might worry."

Grady sighed resignedly and began pulling on his clothes.

Fortune donned her dress over her naked body, then carefully collected her underthings and rolled them up in Irene's blanket.

When Grady saw she was ready to leave he took her bundle from her and let it fall to the ground.

"We . . . we should go," she said, nervously backing up a step. He followed and gathered her to him. Her lips parted in anticipation, and he didn't disappoint her. He kissed her passionately. Finally, he lifted his head, and even in the dark she could see the possessive light in his eyes.

"You haven't answered my question, love, and we're not leaving here until you do."

"Grady, I . . . I do love you. I love you terribly, but . . ." Her words snagged on a sob of anguish.

"Fortune, darlin', what is it? If you love me, that's all that matters. If there's a problem, we'll solve it together."

"Not this problem." She buried her face in her hands as he crushed her against his chest. "I . . . I want to say yes, but I can't," she sobbed. "I . . . I have to think. I need time."

Grady dropped his arms from around her. Hurt by what seemed her lack of trust in him, his words came more sharply than he intended. "It's that damn Yank brother of yours, isn't it? He thinks I'm not good enough for you!"

"No, that's not it at all. It's something else."

"Then share it with me. For God's sake, Fortune, if you love me then you must trust me, too. And I can't help you if you won't tell me what's wrong."

Fortune turned away, shaking her head. "It's not a matter of my trust and love for you, but of yours for me. I've asked for time, Grady. Can't you allow me that?"

Grady sighed deeply, the anger drained from him. "All right, darlin'. If you need time to straighten out whatever it is that's bothering you, then you got it. But Fortune," his voice turned stern, "I've just made you my woman, and if you expect me to keep my hands off you while you're solving your problem, you ask too much. I love you, lass, and I want you in my bed where you belong—ring or no ring." With that he kissed her long and hard.

Chapter Eighteen

Fortune stretched like a sleek cat sated on fresh cream. The movement made her aware of a slight ache between her thighs, a reminder of last night's tender initiation into womanhood. She smiled, remembering Grady's gentle solicitousness afterward.

He'd taken her up before him on his gelding and carefully arranged both her legs across one of his thighs. Then he cuddled her close and stole kisses all the way home. By the time they'd reached Cutler Street, it was with great reluctance that they parted.

With last night lying so sweetly on her mind, it was a good thing she wasn't working at the mercantile today. She doubted that she could look at Grady without blushing, and then surely someone would guess the intimacies they'd shared. It would be bad enough facing the women in her own household, especially Granny.

Knowing she'd feel less vulnerable to her grandmother's criticism groomed and dressed, Fortune threw the covers aside and rose to perform her morning ablution.

She'd just pulled her shoes on when two sharp raps hit the door. Not waiting for a reply, her grandmother sailed into the room. "'Bout time you got up, young lady," she said, sitting next to her granddaughter at the foot of her bed. "It's almost noon, and there's something we need to discuss before Ursula and I leave for the ranch tomorrow."

Finished lacing her shoes, Fortune sighed in resignation and rose from her bent position to face her grandmother. "What is it, Gran?"

"As if you didn't know," Laila replied, sounding vexed. "You were with the Reb last night, weren't you? I hope you didn't do anything foolish."

Fortune had known Gran's questions were inevitable and unavoidable, but what she and Grady had shared was too personal and new to discuss with anyone, even Granny. Since she didn't wish to lie to the dear old lady, she distracted her with half of the truth. "Gran, I'm in love with Grady MacNair, and last night he . . . he asked me to marry him."

Laila squeezed her eyes shut in an expression of pain and shook her head from side to side. "I didn't realize the enchantment had grown so strong. Fortune, please don't forget that neither of you is *truly* in love." Then almost as an afterthought, she asked anxiously, "You didn't consent to marry him, did you?"

Tears moistened the young woman's eyes. "Oh, Granny, I wanted to so badly. But no—I didn't say yes. I put him off. Grady won't allow me to elude the question for long, though. Then I'll be forced reveal everything."

Laila laid her hand over Fortune's. "Now don't be too hasty. There's still time to perform another Riddance spell."

"But what of the greater power we discussed yesterday? I have serious doubts that any Riddance spell will work."

"That destiny business is just a theory, and one that holds little water. Since we know all the terms of the Moondance were met, we must assume its magic is responsible for this mess you find yourself in."

"But you've always said that believing is half the magic. If that's true then my doubts will reduce a Riddance spell to nothing more than a useless ceremony."

"Well, perhaps another type of spell is called for, one in which your participation isn't necessary."

"What kind of spell are you talking about?" Fortune asked warily.

"Well, you might call it a reverse Riddance spell." Laila cackled slyly and smoothed a white strand of hair back into the knot at her nape. Now," she said, standing and preparing to leave, "I'll need something of a very personal nature from Grady to conduct this special spell. I'll think this out today and give you a list of the needed ingredients before Ursula and I leave for the ranch tomorrow."

The next morning, before departing, Laila handed Fortune a folded sheet of paper. "The recipe," she whispered with a wink. "Don't lose it."

Fortune nodded and tucked it into her skirt pocket just as Irene came running out the front door.

"Wait for me," she called. Puffing, she climbed into the wagon driven by Nubbins Smith, intending to ride only as far as the mercantile.

Fortune waved, then headed for the stable at the back of the house. As she walked around the house she took the list from her pocket and read it.

She halted abruptly. *Great crystal balls and tea leaves! Gran can't be serious!* She read aloud, "A garment soiled with Grady's perspiration, a lock of hair—and, if possible, blood. The blood may be on a cloth but must be fairly fresh. Bring Grady and the ingredients to the ranch for dinner two nights from now."

What is Gran up to? Fortune wondered. These items were the ingredients used in a love spell—a very potent love spell at that!

Fortune glanced up from the list as Book and Tish flew out the back door with Grumpy at their heels. "Grumpy's home, Grumpy's home," Tish shouted.

"We were goin' out the front door," Book explained, "and there he was sittin' on the porch."

The list momentarily forgotten, Fortune shoved it into her pocket and crouched down to hug her beloved pet. "I should be scolding you, you old rascal," she said ruffing his fur, "but I'm too glad to see you."

"Can he play with us today?" Tish asked.

"Of course," Fortune replied. "He'd probably rather play with you than come to the store all day." *And I don't need his protection*, she added to herself with a smile. "Why don't you and Book take Grumpy inside and feed him now. Otherwise he might try to follow me to the mercantile."

Book and Tish dragged Grumpy back into the house, and Fortune entered the stable to saddle Magic. The paper in her pocket made a crinkling sound when she mounted, and her thoughts returned to Granny's spell. During the short ride to the mercantile she pondered on how best to procure the needed items with Grady none the wiser.

Fortune was still without a solution when she arrived at the back of the store. After tying up her mare, she hurried into the back room. Finding it empty, she walked toward the front of the store, intending to let Irene know she'd arrived. As she passed the stairs to Grady's private quarters, it occurred to her that if Grady were out, now would be the perfect time to fetch a soiled shirt or handkerchief without his knowledge. But first she had to be sure that he wasn't anywhere around.

"I'm here," Fortune sang out cheerfully, as she joined Irene.

"What took you so long?" Irene asked, glancing up from a crate she was unpacking.

"Grumpy showed up before I left," the girl answered absently, as she looked around for Grady. "I was so glad to see him home safely, I had to take some time with him. Have you seen Grady this morning?" she asked offhandedly. "He told me we'd discuss the Fort Benton trip today."

"One of the mining companies is looking for a freighter to haul in some heavy equipment," Irene told her. "Apparently the mine owner didn't want to talk business with a woman, so Grady told me to tell you he'd check into it for you. He said he'd return late this afternoon."

Normally, Fortune would have resented not being included in a business deal, but since Grady's absence afforded her the opportunity to search his room, she held her peace. Besides, no business transaction could be completed without her approval and signature on the contracts, which meant that in the end the mining company would have to deal with her.

Thanking Irene for conveying the news, she escaped to the back room and hurried up the stairs to Grady's quarters.

The moment she set sight on his bed, she remembered the day he'd carried her up here and laid her on it. He'd been achingly tender with her and at the same time fiercely protective, vowing to find out who ever had run her down in the carriage. *I was falling in love with him even then*, she thought dreamily. She couldn't help picking up his pillow and bringing it to her face. His masculine scent clung to the pillowslip, and she hugged it close, wishing it were Grady in her arms. Then remembering why she'd come, she admonished herself for her girlish behavior and scanned the room for a soiled garment.

The shirts hanging on the hooks opposite the bed looked freshly laundered so she searched the nooks and crannies for a pile of dirty clothes. She'd almost decided she'd have to steal his pillowslip when she saw a shirt sleeve sticking out from under his bed. Sure enough, there was a small pile of dirty clothes under the bed. As she started to pull them out, a trouser leg caught on something that was dragged out from under the bed along with the clothes. It seemed to be a ledger.

She tossed the clothing aside and opened the cover. There, in Grady's neatly penned hand, were the records of all the receipts she'd just spent weeks itemizing in a new ledger. Turning one page after another, she stared in disbelief and growing ire.

"He lied to me! That dirty, rotten, contemptible coyote! Wait till I get my hands on him."

You're forgetting something, a little voice taunted. *You can't say a word to him about the ledger without explaining why you were snooping in his room.*

But why had he lied to her? By doing so he had delayed the opening of his store in Fort Benton. What could he have possibly gained?

She thought over the past weeks, all the time they had spent slaving over that messy box of receipts, all his nasty comments about her guard dog, all the arguments about retaining a businesslike demeanor between them.

And then it came to her like sunshine bursting out on a stormy day. Grady had wanted an excuse to spend time with her. She'd refused all his attempts at courting her in the normal manner so he'd resorted to chicanery.

She couldn't decide if she was angry or flattered. But then the humor of the whole thing struck her, and she started laughing. *Sweet Gaia, no wonder he was so furious when I showed up with Grumpy! Damn his Rebel hide, it served him right!*

Suddenly realizing how much time she'd wasted, she shoved the ledger back under his bed and searched through his laundry.

She found one of his black silk neckerchiefs. Perfect—easy to hide, easy to carry. He'd never miss it, not like he would a shirt or a pair of trousers. The neckerchief joined Granny's note in her skirt pocket, and she shoved the laundry back under the bed. Starting down the stairs, she paused halfway down to listen and make sure no one had entered the back room while she was gone. The coast clear, she proceed down the stairs and across the room to the desk.

All I have to do now, she thought, *is figure a way to cut off a lock of his hair. And then there's the blood. A haircut?* She hated the idea of causing him any pain, but if she was careful he'd receive no more than a nick. Then she'd have the hair and the blood. Yes, it just might work.

Several hours later Grady sauntered through the doorway. A handsome smile brightened his expression when he spied Fortune at the desk.

Her heart skipped a beat. Had it been only one day since she'd seen him? It seemed much longer. Like a magnet drawn to a lodestone, she left her chair and went into his arms.

One of his hands cradled her head, while the other lay just below her waist as his mouth took possessive command of hers. Desire, like liquid fire, instantly poured through her veins, and she leaned more fully against him.

"Hi, darlin'," he drawled softly against her lips. One big hand moved to cup her bottom and press her against the swelling in his snug-fitting denims. "God, I want you. Hot damn, Sugar! Let's go to my room." He took her hand and started for the stairs.

Resisting, Fortune laughed and extracted her hand from his. "Wait a minute. We can't go upstairs. What would Irene think?"

Grady shrugged and grinned roguishly. "Hell, she's probably wondering why it's taken me so long to get you there."

She cuffed his shoulder in mock disgust. "I believe we have some business to discuss, have we not?"

"Well, if you're going to be stubborn, I suppose we'll have to take care of business first."

"Irene said you went to talk to a mining company about contracting to haul in some heavy mining equipment."

"Yeah. You heard of the Whitehall outfit?"

"I've come across the name in Roc's book of accounts, but as I recall it's been a while since we've hauled for them."

"I heard Harry Whitehall was taking bids on a job. When I talked to him, I told him that I was just a minor partner and that any contracts would need your signature. But the old man is stubborn as a mule. Said the only place he conducted business with a woman was upstairs at the Red Dog Saloon. So I thought it best that I meet with him alone this morning." Grady reached inside his vest and extracted some papers. "If these meet your approval, all you need do is sign them and the deal is ours."

Fortune sighed, took the contracts and placed them on the desk. "Since Roc left, I've run into a lot of narrow-minded men. I suppose it will take time for some our customers to accustom themselves to doing business with a woman. But I think the only way to overcome this problem is to confront it head on. I'll read these papers over. If I like what I see, you can set up another meeting with the man. I'll attend with you and sign the papers at the meeting."

"Sounds good," Grady replied with a grin. "Once the men around here realize how business savvy you are, they should have no qualms in the future."

"I hope you're right. By the way, are you still planning to leave for Fort Benton at the end of this week?"

"Yeah. Just you and me—alone," he drawled softly.

Fortune knew she was setting herself up for more heartbreak, but she looked forward to the time she and Grady would be spending together. Then again, if Granny's spell worked, it might turn out to be nothing more than a platonic business trip after all. Though that would be for the best, she couldn't summon any enthusiasm for Granny's success. Still, she had to do her part or be prepared to suffer Grady's wrath later.

"Just you and me alone," she said stepping back into his arms. She urged his head down to hers, her kiss every bit as hungry as his. Her fingers tangled in the blond curls hanging over his collar, and then she slowly drew back and gazed up at him with a little frown. "Your hair is getting a little shaggy. Perhaps I should trim it for you. We'll need to make a favorable impression in Fort Benton."

He looked at her skeptically. "I don't know. You ever cut a man's hair before? There's a barber here in Helena I usually go to."

"Oh, no! I mean, well, barbers always cut off too much, don't you think?" She dazzled him with a sensual smile. "A woman likes to be able to run her fingers through a man's hair. Don't worry," she added, "I've cut Roc's hair lots of times." She tunneled her fingers through the hair at his nape, felt his neck muscles quiver and knew she'd won.

His voice gone husky, he aligned his body with hers in all the strategic places and whispered, "I'll let you cut my hair on one condition."

"Yes?" she replied, caught up in their sensual play.

"We do it upstairs in the privacy of my quarters."

"So where's the shears?"

Grady chuckled, pleased with her ready acceptance. "You go on upstairs. I'll find them and tell Irene we're going out on business and then to supper. She won't mind closing up for me."

Upstairs, Grady set an old straight-back chair near the window, arranging it so that Fortune could easily move all around it. Then he found a piece of linen to drape over his bare shoulders.

Fortune took the comb and shears he handed her and waited for him to sit down. She stood behind the chair and was about to drape his shoulders with the cloth, but first she couldn't resist running her hands over their breadth. When he commented on her soft hands she massaged his neck and shoulders, too.

"Mmm," Grady murmured. "My barber never did *this* for me."

Fortune smiled to herself and draped the cloth over his shoulders, knotting it at the front so it wouldn't slip off. She combed his hair over and over again, fascinated with the different shades of blond that blended into a rich wheat color. As she stepped to one side and raked the comb from temple to nape, Grady closed his eyes and smiled in ecstasy.

Fortune decided she'd better begin before he changed his mind about the haircut and tossed her on his bed instead. She ran a finger along one scissor blade, satisfied that it was sharp enough. Moving to the back of his head where his hair was longest, she snipped off a short lock and tucked it into her skirt pocket. Then she trimmed from the center of his nape to his left ear. Holding her breath, she let one sharp blade brush the thin skin of his earlobe. He didn't even jump, but ears being ears, the lobe started to spurt blood everywhere.

"Oh!" She feigned surprise. "I've nicked your ear."

Grady chuckled. "Well, I can't have lost an ear because I didn't feel a thing."

"It's just a nick, but it's bleeding all over the place." Still standing behind him, she pressed one corner of the linen drape over the tiny cut and applied a slight pressure. After a few moments, she released his ear, then with an expeditious snip, she cut the bloody corner off the linen and added it to her pocket. She bent and kissed his injured ear. "Just a little more trimming and we're all done."

The young woman edged around the chair trimming from back to front until she finally stood directly in front of him. While she held a lock of hair with one hand and snipped with the other, Grady reached up and began unbuttoning her blouse. She didn't realize what he'd done until she felt his warm hands cup her breasts through her chemise.

"Oh!" Fortune jumped and cut a knuckle on her left hand. "No fair sneaking up on me like that," she admonished with laugh. "And just look what you made me do!"

"Shall we press your cut to mine and let our blood run together the way the Indians do?" He chuckled.

"I don't want to be your blood sister," Fortune said huskily as he lifted her finger to his mouth.

"No, never my sister, love." He blew away any hairs that might surround the cut, then took the knuckle into his mouth and sucked away the blood. His tongue swirled about the hurt, then trailed up and down her entire finger until finally he took it deep into his mouth and back out again several times.

As Fortune watched his erotic foreplay, moisture gather in her nether region. The shears and comb fell to the floor forgotten.

Grady whipped off the cloth from his shoulders and stood to catch her up in his arms. Kissing her eyes, cheeks, mouth and throat, he anxiously fumbled with her clothing.

Impatient to be joined with him, she stepped from Grady's embrace and quickly removed the rest of her garments. Then, utterly naked, she went down on her knees and started unbuttoning his britches. She helped him remove his boots, then pulled the britches off after them. His phallus reared and bucked, begging for her attentions. She bent her head and caressed it with the softness of one cheek.

Grady growled, scooped her off her feet and turned to the bed. He followed her down, his hard muscles fitting against her softer curves. "Sweet God in heaven, you're even more beautiful in the sunlight," he whispered reverently. "Kiss me, love."

Fortune wrapped her arms around his neck, urging his mouth to meet hers. As she sucked on his tongue, she rotated her hips against his hard shaft, communicating an unmistakable message.

Grady grasped a breast in each hand, kneading and rolling the nipples until they puckered proudly. Then nibbling his way down her neck, he teased her taut rosy peaks with a swirling tongue.

His talented mouth didn't stop there. With his lips and tongue he worshiped every sweet inch of her. He tasted the deep indentation of her waist, nipped at the curve of her hip, caressed her belly. And as he kissed the insides of her thighs, his fingers found the sensitive kernel at their apex and massaged in a slow steady rhythm that raised all her senses to a screaming pitch. Fortune cried out, her hips writhing in time with his caress.

Then, very gently, Grady dipped a finger inside her and used her own creamy moisture to lubricate her threshold.

"Grady, please now!"

"Tell me what you want, darlin'," he insisted. He positioned himself between her legs, moistening the tip of his sex against her own.

Overwhelming desire claimed all her thoughts save one. "Take me!" she gasped. "I want you to take me—now!"

He merged with her, then reined in the compelling desire to quickly spend himself inside her. She was still new at this, and Grady didn't want to hurt her. But more than that, he wanted her to enjoy their coming together as much as he did.

When he felt her muscles relax he began moving in a slow pace that had Fortune undulating her hips against his. Lacing her arms under his, she hooked her hands over his shoulders and held him tight. Then bracing her feet on the bed, she lifted her undulating hips and met his thrusts.

Gradually, Grady increased his cadence until he pounded in and out of her like a man crazed—and in truth he was. Never had he wanted or enjoyed a woman as much as he did his darling Fortune. He hadn't thought it could get much better than their first time, but he'd been wrong. Loving Fortune promised a lifetime of discovery and pleasure, each better than the last.

She gasped, stiffened and cried out as the pleasure blossomed and carried her over the edge. Grady plunged hard and deep, then shuddered with his own release.

As they lay in each others' arms, Grady trailed his fingers through her loosened hair that now lay in wild disarray all about them. "Mine," he whispered.

Despite the stuffiness of the tiny room, Fortune nuzzled against his neck and cuddled closer, wondering how she ever would manage to let him go when the time came. She pushed the troubling thought from her mind as Grady began kissing and teasing her with little love words that detailed what he wanted to do to her. She started in surprise when she felt him harden again. Then his hand crept down between her legs, stimulating her to sweet rapture once more.

He loved her slowly this time. Rolling her over on her belly, he kissed her back and buttocks and tickled the sensitive skin behind her knees with his tongue. Then he rolled her over and performed the same loving ministrations to her front. When he finally entered her, he swept her to a shattering climax before he released his seed deep inside her.

When Fortune awoke the room was growing dark. She started, then realized where she was and relaxed. She lay on her side, Grady's body spooned lovingly around hers with one of his hands clasping her breast possessively. She smiled guiltily to herself. They'd spent the whole afternoon loving each other and then had fallen into an exhausted sleep.

Grady stirred and slowly sat up. "You hungry, darlin'?" he asked, brushing her cheek with a soft kiss.

"Starving."

He laughed softly and rolled out of bed. "Me, too. Loving you takes a lot out of man." Fortune stretched her slim, curvy body, and he groaned. "If you don't hurry up and dress, lass, I'm going to have to satisfy another kind of hunger before we leave this room."

Fortune sat up, surprised to see that he was fully aroused. She giggled, bent over, picked his shirt off the floor and tossed it at him. "Get dressed, Grady MacNair. You owe me a dinner for that haircut."

"Sugar, I owe you several dinners for *that* haircut." He laughed when his britches landed on top of his head.

Within a half hour the young lovers were enjoying a fine dinner at Chang's. The restaurant was small, crowded and lacked anything resembling an elegant ambiance, but the delicious aroma and wonderful food more than made up for it. Grady and Fortune sat at a tiny table next to a window that overlooked the street.

"When can we leave for Fort Benton?" Fortune asked, swallowing a bite of crispy-skinned duck.

"How's Friday sound to you?"

Fortune poured jasmine tea from a small pot that had been left on the table and smiled at the little flowers that floated to the top. "Friday is fine."

Grady sipped his tea and asked, "Would you mind traveling horseback? I hate the coaches, and a wagon will slow us down. Riding, we can make Fort Benson in two days."

"Almost anything will be better than riding in a slow-moving freight wagon for eight days the way Granny, Ursula and I did on our way to Helena. But I warn you, it's been a while since I've been in a saddle for more than an hour at a time."

Grady shrugged. "We can take our time. One day more or less won't make a difference."

"How long do you think we'll be staying in Fort Benton?"

"That's hard to say. I've already picked a location on River Street close to the Wells Fargo office. It won't take long to get the store built and furnished—three weeks, four at the most. When we're almost ready, I'll telegraph Angus to bring those crates I've been storing. The rest of the goods are coming in on your brother's wagons."

"Why didn't you have them shipped up the river?"

"The Missouri starts drying up and gets too shallow for the steamers to navigate this time of year. It's been an especially good year, and I hear the river is still plenty deep, but I had no way of knowing that when I placed the order."

Fortune shook her head in astonishment. "Just when I begin to think I've learned all there is to know about freighting, I learn something new."

"Fortune . . ." Grady started, reaching across the table and taking her hand. "I've been thinking, and . . . well, I think we should be married right away." He held up his hand when he saw her dismay. "Wait, let me explain. I know I said I'd give you time, but darlin', we're going to be alone together for better than a month. I don't plan on depriving myself of your company in my bed, but I don't want folks in Fort Benton thinking you're a low woman either."

Fortune leaned back in her chair, extracting her hand from his. "Grady, I can't marry you—not yet!"

"Damn it, Fortune, either you love me or you don't."

"I do love you, Grady, but I still need time to work things out. I know you don't understand, and I'm sorry, but we have to wait."

"Fortune, I didn't want to scare you into marriage," Grady reasoned, "but I can see I'll have to be blunt. Have you considered the possibility that you're already carrying my child?" At her sharp intake of breath, Grady leaned back and crossed his arms over his chest in triumph. "I see that hadn't occurred to you."

"I . . . no, I didn't stop to think. That is, I know it happens but . . ." Fortune thoughts suddenly were in a tangle. Should she blurt out the truth now? No, because that would be the end of everything between them, and damn it, she wanted these next few weeks alone with him. Besides, it would be better to wait until Roc had returned from Salt Lake City. That way, when the secret was exposed, Roc would be around to contain any damage Grady might inflict as a means of revenge.

But what if she were already pregnant? There were herbs a woman could take to end pregnancy, but they often had adverse affects. Granny once warned her against ever using them. Besides, the idea of destroying a child that she and Grady had made in love sickened her.

"Well?" he demanded.

"We'll cross that bridge when we come to it, Grady."

"Christ, you're stubborn!" He leaned across the table. "You leave me only one choice. I won't have you slandered so I'll introduce you to folks in Fort Benton as my wife."

"But . . ."

"No buts—*Mrs. MacNair*"

Chapter Nineteen

"But I can do it," Clyde Sheety whined.

"I said Bull will take care of it, and that's what I meant," Deke Tunney snarled, pounding his fist against the wall of the abandoned log cabin. "I only want the Landry bitch scared. I know you, Clyde. You'd get carried away and kill 'er, and I don't want her dead yet. Hell, you're lucky I'd trust you with anythin' after that trick you pulled at the warehouse fire."

"But how was I ta know the damn door would get stuck? You said you wanted her scairt, and I figured she'd come screamin' outta there."

"Well, you figured wrong. And what about that night watchman? Shit, you almost got caught. Now, because of your stupidity, the Reb and the Swede are askin' questions all over town."

"I'm leavin' now," said a brutish redheaded man waiting in the doorway.

"Remember, Bull," Deke cautioned, "stay away from the house. They've got men watchin' it. You got to catch the woman alone, and that won't be easy. Rough 'er up some, but whatever you do, don't kill 'er. Give her my message, too. Understand?"

Bull Durant nodded his grisly head and left without another word.

Wednesday's sizzling heat bore down on Fortune's head as she headed her horse toward the mercantile for the second time that morning. She chuckled to herself. On her first attempt Grumpy had escaped the children and come trotting alongside her horse, his tail wagging so vigorously that his hind parts looked like they might fly off.

Laughing at his antics, she'd nonetheless returned him home. She didn't need Grumpy at the mercantile any more, and with the trouble she'd had lately, she worried that her home and the people she loved might be the next target. Thus leaving Grumpy to guard them seemed the sensible thing to do.

When she returned Grumpy to the house, she ordered him to stay and asked Book to keep him inside until she was well on her way.

Tonight, after closing, she and Grady were going to the ranch to have dinner with Granny and Ursula. And of course Granny planned to perform her special Riddance spell. How Gran intended to do that with Grady present, she hadn't a clue. And though her head told her she'd better hope the spell worked, her heart had vastly different ideas.

Fortune started out her reverie when a man ran out from behind the Methodist Church, yelling and waving his arms.

"Ma'am, you gotta come help me," he pleaded as the young woman drew rein. "The preacher fell down in the carriage house and is rollin' round in some kinda fit. I don't know what to do."

Had Fortune had time to look into the burly man's calculating eyes, she might have thought twice before eagerly lending her help. But the man turned away quickly, and she followed him to the back of the church. Outside the carriage house, she dismounted and hurried inside after him.

Momentarily blinded in the dimness, she was unprepared for the hand that reached out and shoved her farther inside. She hit the ground hard, knocking the wind from her lungs. Barely had she lifted her head when a heavy boot planted itself on the middle of her back.

"Not so fast, Missy," the man chuckled menacingly.

Fortune spit a piece of straw out of her mouth and gasped, "What do you want? Where's the preacher?"

Again came the sinister laugh. "He ain't *here*, that's for damn sure!"

The man lifted his foot, and she quickly rolled over. But almost instantly, he fell on her, pinning her arms above her head with one of his hands. Shaggy red hair hung over a broad sweaty forehead, and cold eyes stared at her lewdly.

Furious and frightened, Fortune struggled vainly against her attacker's superior strength and weight. "What do you want?" she demanded.

"Can't you guess, honey," he snickered, bringing his broad, unshaven face closer to hers.

Fortune tried to evade his fetid breath, but he grabbed a handful of her hair and held her head immobile. When she yelped in pain, his mouth came down on hers with savage force.

Revolted, Fortune twisted her head, bucked and reared. Her actions only served to madden him. With one cruel swipe, his grimy nails bit into the skin at her neck and ripped her shirtwaist and chemise down to her waist.

Fortune screamed and tried to knee his groin, but he anticipated the move and rolled half off her. "Hold still, bitch!" He backhanded her, whipping her head to one side with ear-ringing force. As she lay there stunned, he mauled her breasts cruelly.

Finally managing to free one of her hands, Fortune clawed at his vicious face with a savagery she hadn't known herself capable of.

He roared angrily, one hand flying to the bloody cuts on his face. "Bitch! Try that again and, orders or no orders, I'll finish you off here and now." He raised up, straddling her. "Now listen real good, Gypsy whore. I got a message for you from my boss. The carriage accident, the fire, the poisoned mules and this . . ." He paused and pinched her breast painfully. They're just a taste of what he has in mind for you and that brother of yours. He wants you two to suffer like he had to suffer back in '64. Then, when you're both wishin' you was dead, he'll oblige you!"

Tears streaming down her battered face, Fortune could hardly credit what she was hearing. But it appeared this man's boss, who ever he was, knew her and Roc from the war. *Sweet Gaia,*

*if he knew they were Gypsies, then he knew something of their
spy mission, too!*

Her assailant reached for her breast once more, but this time
his hand never touched her flesh. A snarling blur of fur flew
through the air, knocking the man off her. Fortune scrabbled
to her feet, never so glad to see Grumpy as she was now.

Grumpy straddled Fortune's attacker, his huge canine jaws
snapping and snarling at the man's jugular. The man raised his
arms, trying to protect his face and ward off the dog's vicious
fangs. Man and beast rolled in the straw and dirt, and Fortune
cringed at the sight of blood streaming down her adversary's
mangled arms.

She knew better than to try stop Grumpy once he went in
for the kill, but when the man managed get hold of a thick
log from a wood pile and started swinging it at her pet, she
went into action. Circling round, she grabbed a log of her own
and swung. Her aim was slightly off, but the blow dazed him,
and he dropped his weapon. Then Fortune hit him again, and
he passed out cold.

Exhausted and bruised, all the girl wanted was to put a
safe distance between herself and the madman sprawled in
the dirty straw. Grumpy followed her outside and watched as
she struggled into Magic's saddle. "Come on, boy," she called
to the dog. "Let's go home."

Book was raking out the stable when a battered Fortune
trotted her horse to the back of the house and slid to the ground
in a weary heap. "Miss Fortune!" he cried, falling down on his
knees beside her.

The Gypsy girl waved the boy off to the house. Quick to
pick up on her meaning, he ran to the house calling his mother.
Wrapping her arms around her pet, Fortune rested her head
against his soft fur and waited.

Within moments Irene was crouching beside to her. "Lord,
girl, what's happened?" she asked anxiously. When Fortune
just shook her head, Irene turned to her son. "Book, get on her
other side and help me get her into the house."

They made it only as far as the kitchen door when Fortune
began to shiver violently. Then all went black.

Something cool soothed Fortune's brow and brought her up
from the depths of a dark void. She heard familiar voices and

opened her eyes. "Welcome back, young lady!" Doc Holly smiled.

Fortune blinked up at the kindly doctor and a harried-looking Irene. Then her hand went to the cool cloth resting on her forehead. She lifted the sheet and gasped at the condition of her clothing. The morning's events stormed through her with frightening velocity. She sat straight up in bed, her eyes frightened and wild.

"Whoa!" Doc Holly admonished. "Lay yourself back down there, girl. You've had quite a shock."

"How are you feeling, honey?" Irene asked, readjusting the sheet to cover Fortune. "Can you tell us what happened?"

"I . . . I'm fine, but there's a man behind the church. He hit me. He's still there. Please, Irene, get Grady. He has to find that man before he gets away."

"Grady's out in the hall," Irene said, stepping to the bedroom door. "Book rode Magic and fetched the Grady on the way to get Doc Holly. Grady beat them both back and carried you upstairs." Irene opened the door and motioned the waiting Reb inside.

He rushed in, gently folding her into his arms as he sat on the edge of Fortune's bed. "I'm here, honey girl," he said with a slight catch in his voice.

"Grady," she sobbed, "the fire, the mules . . . the man that did it . . . he's at the church up the street. Grumpy tore him up, and I knocked him out."

Grady leaned back from her and cocked his head, trying make sense of her disjointed words. "Do you mean the man that did this to you?" he asked.

"Yes, he's unconscious in the carriage house."

Grady was off the bed like a shot, and Fortune heard him thunder down the stairs and slam out the front door.

Irene approached the girl again, taking Grady's place. "Fortune, honey, I've got to ask you a delicate question. From the looks of things, the Doc and I didn't think you'd been raped, but he needs to know for sure."

Fortune gazed up at Doc Holly and blushed. "No. He just hit me and . . . and . . ."

"That's all right, Miss Landry," Doc Holly interjected, patting her shoulder. He poured a thick liquid into a spoon. "Take this. It will help calm you down and ease the ache in those nasty bruises."

Fortune did as he asked and within a few moments felt herself drifting sleepily. Before she surrendered to the medicine's effects, she asked after Grumpy, and Irene assured her that he was fine.

When Grady got to the carriage house behind the church, he found dried blood on the straw but no sign of the swine who had attacked Fortune. Cursing, he searched for anything that might lead him to the man's identity, but no clue had been left behind. Knowing that the doctor had probably given Fortune something to help her rest, he decided to inform Eric Jorgensen of this latest attack on the Landry's.

Eric led Grady to the office at the back of the furniture shop. "Care for a drink?" he asked, as Grady slumped down in a chair. "You look like you could use one."

"Yeah, I reckon I could at that," Grady replied dispiritedly.

Eric poured them each a drink, handed one to Grady, then sunk into a chair behind his father's desk. "So what's this all about? I hope Fortune hasn't had more trouble out at the ranch."

"Worse. She was attacked."

"God Almighty!" Eric cursed coming out of chair. "Why didn't you say so right away? Is she all right?"

"She wasn't up to talking much when I left, but other than a few bad bruises, I don't think she's seriously injured." Eric flopped back into his chair with a sigh of relief, and Grady continued. "Fortune told me she knocked the man out in the church carriage house, but by the time I got there he was gone. Near as I can figure, she was lured back there then attacked. Irene's kids must have let Grumpy out of the house, because he sniffed out his mistress and like to tore her attacker apart. There was blood all over the straw."

"Someone's walking around looking mighty chewed," Eric surmised sardonically. "Shouldn't be too hard to find him."

"My thought exactly, but if he's smart, he's holed up somewhere nursing his wounds." Grady sipped his whiskey, anger and determination hardening his features. "We've got to find out who's playing this vicious game with the Landry's before it turns deadly."

"Why are Roc and Fortune being targeted?" Eric wondered aloud.

"If we knew why, we'd probably know who," Grady replied. "I've got a feeling he only wanted to scare Fortune, otherwise she'd already be dead. Maybe he's trying to get her brother's attention, blackmail him into doing something. Don't forget, it was the warehouse he hit first, then the ranch. Could be that when those acts didn't achieve what he'd hoped, he decided to take drastic measures."

"Do you still think it might be one of the competing freight companies?" Eric asked, downing his drink.

"It's the only thing that makes sense, but I'll be damned if I can dig up any information. There's more freighters in the territory than flies on a dung heap, and it's impossible to check them all out. I have met most of the freight owners in Helena though, and none of them seem like someone who would stoop to these kinds of tactics."

"There's something else to consider," Eric said. "If it's a freighter trying to put the Landrys out of business, how come some of the other small freighters haven't experienced the same kind of trouble? Seems only logical that a man willing to go to such lengths would try to cut out *all* the competition."

"Which leaves us right back where we started," Grady stated disgustedly.

"I think I'll ride out to the ranch and inform Fortune's grandmother of what's happened," Eric said, getting to his feet. "More than likely she'll want to come back into town with me."

"That's a good idea. While you're doing that I'll check around town and see if anybody has seen a man who looked badly mangled. Maybe I'll get lucky."

The next morning, Grady was ushered into Fortune's house by a beaming Irene. "She's doin' much better," she assured him, answering the question in his eyes. "That girl has more spunk than anybody I ever met. And now that she's over the horror of the whole thing she's just plain mad."

"May I speak with her alone?" Grady asked. "I need to find out exactly what happened and see if she's up to leaving for Fort Benton tomorrow."

"She's alone in the parlor," Irene replied. "I think she's been expecting you. Don't worry about interruptions. It was late last night when Eric got here with the two old ladies. They're sleepin' in this morning. I'll just be in the kitchen if you need me." She started to leave, then added over her shoulder, "Watch out for Grumpy. We haven't been able to budge him from Fortune's side."

Grady thanked her and turned toward the garish parlor. At the doorway he was brought up short. Glancing through a book, Fortune sat with her feet stretched out before her on one of the settees. Even her dusky complexion couldn't hide the bluish bruise on her cheek.

He noted her high-collared dress and winced at the memory of the scrapes and bruises on her neck. Irene had done her best to preserve the girl's modesty by throwing a blanket over her before he'd arrived yesterday. But as he'd carried her upstairs, the covering had slipped, and he'd seen the full extent of her attacker's abuse. *God,* he thought, *what I wouldn't give to get my hands on that bastard!*

He started over the threshold but halted at Grumpy's familiar growl. The dog looked him over for a minute, then lay back down at the foot of the settee and closed his eyes.

Fortune watched the scene with amazement. "Congratulations, sir. It appears you've won him over."

Grady met her smiling gaze, and a great weight lifted from his chest. "Hi, darlin'."

She held out her arms to him, and in four long strides, he was at her side. As he settled one hip on the edge of the settee, Fortune felt herself being surrounded by the warm haven that was his embrace. "I wish you could have spent the night with me," she sighed against his chest. "I needed you to hold me."

Grady chuckled low. "I don't think that would have pleased your Granny much, love. But I'm here now."

She nodded, then leaned back against the settee arm. "I'm really all right," she said. "I just needed a hug."

"So did I, Sugar."

"You want to know what happened, don't you?" she asked, getting straight to the point.

"Only if you're up to the telling."

"I admit I was shaken up yesterday, but I'd rather be hexed than give that horrible man the satisfaction of accomplishing his goal."

Grady beamed and nodded his approval, proud of her fiery gumption. "And what was his goal?" he asked.

As succinctly as possible, Fortune recounted her ordeal, leaving out the part about the man referring to her and Roc as Gypsies and the fact that her assailant's boss knew them from the war.

At the end of her tale, Grady muttered an oath and stood to pace the room. "So revenge is behind all this. Damn!" He paused and turned to her. "Fortune, what has your brother got you mixed up in?"

Sweet Gaia, Fortune thought, *what should I tell him?* There were many who might harbor murderous feelings for herself and Roc, but none that she could immediately put a face or name to, save Grady himself. Any one of Grady's men who were captured that long-ago night could be out for revenge. Then, too, there were those deserters that they'd caught ransacking a farm. Unfortunately, she could reveal none of this to Grady.

Feeling trapped, Fortune's tone was sharper than she intended. "I can honestly tell you that neither Roc nor I have done anything illegal, if that's what you're implying."

"I'm sorry, I didn't mean to sound accusing, Fortune," he said, sitting next to her again and taking her hands in his. "But I want to protect you, and I can't do that properly if I don't who or what I'm protecting you from."

"I'm sorry, too." Fortune lowered her lashes, unable to look him in the eyes.

Grady sighed and took her hands in his. "Darlin', I know you've been through hell, but if you're at all able, I think we should leave for Fort Benton tomorrow morning. I want you with me and safely away from Helena. I've already talked to Eric, and he's agreed to keep guards posted here at the house."

"I was hoping you wouldn't want to postpone the trip to Fort Benton," Fortune said, smiling eagerly. "I'm as anxious as you to get the store built before winter. I understand that the cold weather sets in quite early in the territory."

Relief washed over Grady. He'd been afraid she'd balk at leaving the other three women alone. Enfolding her in his arms, he murmured in her ear, "I promise I'll not let anyone ever hurt you again, love. And like I said a while back, I take good care of what belongs to me."

"Are you sure you want to take me on?" she asked, only half-kidding. "You could have any woman you want—and without all the fuss."

Grady lifted her chin and lightly brushed her lips with his. A devilish grin deepened the dimple in his chin. "Honey girl, don't you know that's what I love about you most? Loving you is just one adventure after another. Though I'll admit, the adventures I like most are those that take place when I've got you naked and just oozin' with passion."

His slow Southern drawl rippled over Fortune like a passionate caress. "Grady," she whispered, "I wish we were having an adventure this very minute."

Laila was surprisingly insistent that Irene invite Grady to join them for supper that night, and when Eric showed up to inquire after Fortune, he was included also. Jim Fetters then showed up, turning the farewell dinner into a lively affair.

Laila and Ursula helped Irene in the kitchen, and Laila sent Book on a mysterious errand. Everyone was surprised when the boy returned with Miss Reva Wentworth in tow.

Fortune said nothing to her grandmother, but she couldn't fathom why her grandmother had invited that insipid blonde for dinner. She was even more astonished when Granny asked the girl for her assistance in the kitchen.

If Fortune was confused, poor Eric was downright worried. As he sat in the parlor, visiting with Fortune and Grady, he asked, "Do you think your granny is trying to match me with that girl? It's nice of her, of course, but Reva Wentworth isn't exactly what I have in mind."

Fortune could only shrug. But later, as they all gathered at the dining room table, she noticed that it wasn't Eric the girl had her eyes on at all. It was Grady!

Though Irene's meal was a simple one, she'd taken special care with its presentation. The table was covered with a crisp, white linen tablecloth, and the polished silver reflected beautifully against the sparkling glassware. Beef stew, fresh hot bread and greens adorned every plate. "There's plenty more food." Irene smiled proudly. "But there's so many of us tonight, Laila suggested I fill your plates in the kitchen, rather than clutter up the table with serving platters. And save some room for apple pie!"

"Irene, this is delicious," Eric said, taking another bite of beef stew.

"Thank you, Eric. It's my mother's reci—Grady! What's wrong?"

Grady was bent over his plate, his mouth working from side to side. Seeing he had everyone's attention, his ears turned bright red, but he couldn't seem to help himself. He gagged a couple times, opened his mouth and rummaged inside with his fingers.

Fortune glanced from Granny to Ursula. Granny was scowling, but Ursula was definitely smothering laughter behind her napkin.

"What the hell?" Grady held up a soggy strip of material. Then he stirred through his stew and fished out what looked like a small ball of hair.

"Oh, my Lord! How did that get in my stew?" Irene cried in dismay. "Oh, Grady, I'm so sorry."

At the other end of the table Ursula's laughter finally broke free and burst forth over the room. Reva Wentworth jumped from her chair and bawled, "I did what you told me to, Mrs. Landry. I swear!"

Fortune glanced at her grandmother, who was staring at Reva with disgust. "Granny," Fortune started accusingly, "what have you been up to?"

"Why, Fortune, I was only doing the girl a favor," she expounded innocently. "But I guess I shouldn't have trusted her with such a delicate matter. You see, things got hectic in the kitchen, and I had to divert Irene's attention so that Reva could add the magical ingredients to Grady's plate."

Ursula started laughing all over again. Eric stared aghast at the hair ball on Grady's plate and turned green. Jim Fetters started stirring through the contents of his plate with a squeamish expression. Reva stood in a corner weeping loudly, snorting into a handkerchief that Eric had handed her.

"Would somebody mind telling me what's going on here?" Grady asked.

"Granny?" Fortune prodded. Then glancing down the table at Reva, she added, "Hush up, Reva. I want to hear this."

"Well," Laila said, "you don't have be so rude. I only did it to help Reva."

"Did what?" Grady asked.

"It's like this," Laila started, avoiding looking at the Reb directly. "At the dance the other night, Reva told me how she wished Grady would notice her. I gave it some thought and talked to the girl again the next day. That's when I agreed to conjure a love potion for her. But things going like they have lately, there's been no time or opportunity to feed Grady the ingredients."

Grady shook his head in befuddlement. "You mean you were trying to perform magic on me?"

"Yes, a love spell. "You see it works like this," Laila explained. "Reva gave me a lock of her hair and a piece of material with her sweat and a drop or two of her blood on it."

"Jesus!" Eric gasped. "And you fed that to him?"

"That was the idea," Laila replied, "but Reva forgot to burn the ingredients first. Only the ashes are supposed to go into the food. Silly twit! She tossed everything in whole."

Fortune now understood everything, and she knew without a doubt that Reva had been given food containing the ingredients she'd collected from Grady. Actually it was a very strong love potion—so strong, that had Grady ingested the food, he probably would have fallen in love with Reva almost instantly. Oh, that Gran was a sly one! The negative forces of the Riddance spells hadn't worked, therefore it logically followed that a positive love spell was called for.

Irene jumped up then and grabbed Grady's plate. "I'll get you a fresh plate, Grady," she said, casting a disgusted look at Laila. "Reva, honey, sit down and stop crying. We've all been known to do fool things—even the old fools."

The rest of the meal went on without mishap, but Fortune couldn't help but notice that neither Grady nor Eric could bring themselves to eat any more stew.

After dinner, Eric volunteered to take Reva home, and Grady and Fortune retired to the parlor to discuss their early morning departure for Fort Benton. When everything was settled, Fortune walked him out onto the front porch. "I'm sorry about what happened at dinner, Grady, and I promise you, Gran will never play such a trick ever again."

"It's all right. Now that I've gotten over wanting to be sick, the whole thing seems pretty funny. I know you told me that you and your grandmother believe in magic and stuff, but I never realized to what extent."

"Grady, there is such a thing—as magic, I mean. I've seen it at work. And it's very bad luck to discount it."

Grady shook his head. "Oh, I don't discount it entirely, darlin'. After all, what we share between us is darn magical, if you ask me."

Great crystal balls and tea leaves! If he only knew!

Chapter Twenty

Fortune and Grady were on the road to Fort Benton long before sunrise on Friday morning. Grady, on his dark bay gelding, led a pack mule, and Fortune followed on her mare.

Fortune thought Grady looked handsome in a simple clerk's apron, but in the sturdy, fringed buckskins he'd donned for the trail he looked tough, lean and devastatingly male. The buckskin britches hugged his long, muscular legs closer than a lover's embrace, and the sight made her want to end the day before it had hardly started.

She, too, was dressed for the rugged trip, wearing a divided buckskin riding skirt and vest. Beneath the vest was one of her brother's old cotton work shirts, none too feminine but more practical than one of her dainty shirtwaists. Her jet hair trailed down her back in a single thick plait that bounced in time with Magic's gait.

They rode north on the Gillette and King stage road through Prickly Pear Valley, a dry area too barren for trees. At Prickly Pear River they passed a well-irrigated farm which Grady said belonged to a friend of his. Fortune could barely discern the farmhouse in the distance.

They nooned near a mountain rill, and afterward as he started to help her remount he paused. "If you don't mind riding a few miles out of our way," he said, "I'd like to detour west on the high water trail. There's some fine range land that would make a good place for our ranch. I'd like you to see it, darlin'."

Having made up her mind to let nothing spoil this time with him, Fortune didn't correct the assumption he made. "Lead on," she replied cheerfully. "If you like the place then I know it must be beautiful."

Grady grinned and helped her into her saddle. Then they directed their horses back onto the main road.

Instead of fording the Prickly Pear they traveled north a ways to a place called Morgan's ranch. There they crossed a small bridge and rode north again for several miles.

Two hours later, Grady reined in beneath a clump of trees by a lazy steam. "We'll camp here."

Despite the fact that her bottom was aching, Fortune felt compelled to ask, "Why are we stopping so soon? We could put quite a few more miles behind us."

Grady grinned and dismounted. "Darlin'," he said, raising his hands to her waist and gently lifting her down, "you don't have to put up a front with me. I know darn well that cute little bottom of yours is saddle sore."

Fortune blushed. "Is it that obvious?"

"For the last half hour you've been squirming around in the saddle like you had bugs in your drawers." He chuckled. "Besides, this is the place I wanted you to see. These ranges of bunch grass have supported buffalo for hundreds of years. I reckon cattle would do just as well."

"It's beautiful here," Fortune replied, scanning the rolling green horizon. "Over there," she pointed, "where the land dips between those two knolls might be a good place for a house, don't you think?"

"We can put the house anywhere you want it, darlin', but before we get too involved in house planning, we'd better set up camp. I'll take care of the animals while you gather wood for a fire."

Admonishing herself for mentioning a house she knew she'd

never share with him, Fortune nodded and turned to the task he'd assigned her.

Her experience on the trail during the war and her more recent eight-day trip by freight wagon from Fort Benton had prepared her well for the rigors of making camp. By the time Grady finished unsaddling the horses and unpacking the mule, she had a good fire going and a pot of water boiling for coffee.

Supper was a simple affair of beans, bacon, pan-fried bread and coffee to wash it down. Grady leaned back against a tree trunk and rubbed his lean stomach as Fortune returned from washing their tin plates and cups in the stream. "Fortune, you never cease to surprise me. Thought I'd be cooking all the meals on this trip."

Fortune hooted. "Well, don't get to used to it, because what you witnessed tonight is the extent of my culinary abilities."

"Still, most ladies don't take to the trail at all. You've got gumption, darlin', and that's important in these parts, because being a rancher's wife isn't easy."

Fortune shrugged. "I always helped Granny on the horse farm. I enjoyed it, and I felt like I was doing my part to make the farm successful, even if I didn't actually work the horses as Grandpa and Roc did.

"It was different when we went to live with my parents in the city though. They have a small army of servants to do everything. It was nice for a while, but it got pretty dull around there with nothing to do but dress up pretty."

Grady patted the ground next to him. She settled into the curve of his body, and he rested his arm around her shoulders. "You've never said much about your mother and father, Fortune. I'd like to hear more about them." He chuckled. "Are they as ornery and as eccentric as your grandmother?"

Fortune sighed and leaned her head back against his shoulder. "Are you sure you want to hear about them?" she asked pensively. "My grandparents were a lot like your parents, but my mother and father are very different."

Grady gave her shoulders a light squeeze. "I want to know everything there is to know about the woman I plan to make my wife."

"My mother's father was a younger son of a French nobleman, but he was disowned when he married Granny because she wasn't of his class. Grandpa had some money of his own so he came to America and started breeding horses. It's a very romantic story," she said dreamily. "You should get Granny to tell you about it sometime.

"Roc and I lived with Granny and Grandpa on their horse farm most of the time. My father traveled a lot while he was building his import-export business, and mother accompanied him. She's very beautiful, and Father always used to say she was the best business asset he had."

"Looking at you, I'm not surprised to hear your mother is lovely," Grady commented.

"I wish she were as pretty on the inside," Fortune replied sadly. "Granny says that even as a girl, Tshaya—that's Mama's name—acted above herself. And when Papa's business no longer required extensive traveling, Mama became infatuated with the *haute monde*. Papa was busy expanding an already lucrative business, and my parents started growing apart. Mama stopped smiling at him, and Papa stayed away more and more."

"That must have been difficult for you and Roc to understand. Did something bad happen between them?"

Fortune glanced away. She'd never been certain of the exact cause of the schism in her parent's marriage, but she knew it had something to do with her mother's Gypsy blood. Of course, she couldn't tell Grady this.

"I don't know what drove them apart, Grady. I guess parents don't discuss those things with their children. At least mine didn't.

"When Roc turned twenty-one," she continued, "Papa offered to make him a partner in his business, but he refused. It was no wonder; Roc hardly knew his own father. Also by the time Papa made the offer, Roc had grown to love working with animals. My brother probably would have been a horse breeder like Grandpa if the war hadn't come along.

"Grandpa died while Roc was off fighting for the North. Then soldiers came and raided the farm of all Grandpa's beautiful horses. We realized it was no longer safe to remain there without a man's protection. Granny sold the farm, and she and I moved in with my parents. After the war, Roc spurned Papa's offer once again, took the small inheritance Grandpa had left him and headed west.

"I asked Papa if he'd teach me the business, but he scoffed and told me women didn't have a head for such things. Then he promised to find me a suitable husband. I found out that by suitable, he meant a good business merger."

"Well, you've proven your father wrong. You're very good at running a business, Fortune. You should be proud."

"I am, I guess. Only I'd feel a lot better if my father was aware of how well I've done. Does that sound petty, Grady?"

"No, not at all. Every child wants his parents' love and admiration, Fortune. But tell me, does your parents' troubled marriage have something to do with your reluctance to marry me? Are you afraid you'll end up like them?"

How very easy it would be to lie, Fortune thought, but she simply could not build lies upon lies.

"My reasons for not marrying you have nothing to do with my parents, Grady. Actually, it would be a poor excuse, because I've seen the good side of marriage as well as the bad. My grandparents were bonded by a very strong love. Each of them made a great sacrifice and risked much to be together."

"Then what is it that's troubling you, darlin? Does it have something to do with your recent problems?"

"Please, Grady, don't press me. Just hold me."

Grady felt angry and frustrated over her refusal to let him help her. *Christ! Doesn't she know that she can trust me, that I'd do anything for her?*

Her eyes gazed up into his, and Grady was lost. Pulling her across his lap, he gathered her into his arms. "I've been wanting you all day," he confessed, inhaling her erotic scent. "You can't imagine the fantasies that have gone through my head." One corner of his mouth twitched in amusement as he remembered one in particular.

"Tell me." She grinned mischievously. "I want to fulfill all your dreams in and out of bed."

"You'll think I'm crazy," he warned.

"Tell me."

He leaned his head back against the tree and urged her head to his shoulder as one hand played lightly over her breast. "I fantasized plucking you from your saddle to ride *me*, while I rode my horse."

Fortune blinked. "Ride you? You mean . . . ?"

He grinned down at her rakishly and nodded his head.

The young woman in his arms blushed. "Is that possible?"

Grady was delighted by her innocent shock. His hand slowly moved to her other breast, tweaking her nipple through the material. "Well, I've never tried it, but I don't know why it wouldn't work."

Unconsciously, her hand drifted to the open vee of his shirt. Lifting desirous eyes to his, she begged, "Tell me more about this fantasy."

Grady felt his shaft swell and lengthen at her breathy request. I daydreamed that while riding I unbuttoned my britches and took you up on my horse, facing me. Then I lifted your skirts and filled you with myself."

Fortune closed her eyes and pictured the erotic scene. Her breathing became ragged, and her breasts arched into his questing hands. "Go on," she rasped.

"As you rode me I opened your shirtwaist, then licked and sucked your breasts until your nipples were hard as pebbles." His fingers pulled at her swollen nipples through her clothing, and Fortune began to squirm on his lap.

She felt his responding arousal straining against her bottom, and her body instantly readied itself, making her slick and wet for his eventual penetration. "Is there more?" she asked, barely able to breathe normally.

"Yes, darlin'. I kicked my spurs into my steed's sides and let him into a sharp trot. You bounced up and down on my lap, and the pleasure of it made you throw your head back in wild abandon and cry out my name. I urged my horse faster. You clung to me and screamed when you reached the peak of your pleasure. Then I exploded inside you."

Fortune opened her eyes, silently begging him to take her.

The desire Grady saw there stoked his lust to towering heights. Wait here," he said getting to his feet. He unrolled their bedrolls and laid them side by side. Returning to her, he pulled her up into his arms and pressed his mouth to hers in a searing kiss.

Her tongue entwined with his, its sweet urgency setting him afire. Grady cupped her buttocks in his hands and lifted her against his grinding hips. He groaned with the pleasure of the intimate contact.

"Grady, love me. Fill me!" Fortune cried, tugging at his

buckskin shirt. Her fingers worked the buttons and lacings
on his pants, while he unfastened her shirt and skirt. In no
time they were both naked. Then Grady reached for her long
braid and slowly unraveled the raven tresses. For a moment
they parted and just stared at each other's bodies silhouetted,
in the pinkish blaze of the sunset.

Fortune reveled in Grady's masculine beauty. The light brown
pelt on his manly chest made her long to feel its abrasiveness
against her nipples. With that sensual thought her rosy peaks
swelled and pointed, as if daring him to possess them. But
she refrained from instantly flowing into his arms, inherently
knowing denial would arouse them to even greater heights.
Instead she cupped and lifted her breasts, her exotic, emerald
eyes confirming her erotic invitation.

Grady's greedy gaze feasted on Fortune's dusky beauty. In
the sunset's glow her skin was the color of burnished copper,
her nipples a dark brownish rose. His glance slid down her
sleek body, past her flat stomach to fasten on the dark triangle
beneath.

Suddenly he could hold back no longer. The long, arousing
rendition of his fantasy, her hot gaze, the sight of her naked
flesh—all burned away the gentleman and left only the feral
male.

With a low growl, he scooped her into his arms, lowered her
onto their joined bedrolls and plunged into her hot, wet canal.
Consumed by pure animal lust, he paused for a moment to get
a hold on himself.

But Fortune was a wild thing in his arms, arching her back
and gyrating her hips madly, and Grady forgot about restraint.
Rearing back on his knees and lifting her hips in his hands,
he savagely pounded into her body. He watched as her breasts
swayed violently with each thrust, and when her eyes went wide
with the shock of her shattering climax, he roared her name and
spewed his seed deep inside her. They collapsed in a tangle of
arms and legs and fell into an exhausted sleep.

Later, they trotted down to the stream and bathed each other
in the silvery light of the moon. When they returned to their
bedrolls, he loved her slowly and worshipfully, kissing every
square inch of her body and murmuring sweet endearments.

Grady's tongue swirled around her breasts, feathering over
her nipples before taking them deep into his mouth. His tongue

mapped out her body, leading him down her belly and then further.

Fortune begged him to take her, but when he lifted her legs to rest on his shoulders and dipped his mouth to her sex, she gasped in shock and surprise. "Grady, what are you doing?"

"Easy, darlin'. There's lots of ways for a man and woman to love each other. Let me teach you."

His tongue swept her sensitive kernel, and Fortune lost the will to protest. He lapped and nibbled at her until she thought she might die with yearning. Time and again his tongue dipped inside her and tasted her feminine nectar until finally she exploded with a shattering orgasm. "Oh Grady! Yes! Yes!"

Before she descended from the sensual heights, Grady raised up and sank his hard staff into her tight sheath. With a will-power born of his love, he sent her spiraling to climax again and again before coming himself. As his seed washed her in its warmth, he clutched her to him, arched his back and lowered his head so that he might suck her breast. And though she wouldn't have thought it possible, Fortune took flight again and joined him in heaven.

It was late the next morning before the exhausted lovers woke. Grady was up first and left to water the horses and the mule downstream. When he returned Fortune was reaching for her clothes. The sight gave him pause. Her hair was wildly tangled from their night of lovemaking, and her lips were still a bit swelled from his kisses. Possessiveness surged through his every fiber. She was every man's fantasy—a lady out of bed, a loving, passionate wanton in it. But she'd become so much more to him.

In his mind's eye he saw this same woman running into the street and throwing herself into the path of a runaway carriage to save a child. He saw her give Irene, a virtual stranger, a home for herself and her children. He saw her ignore the irritating crankiness of two old women out of love and respect. He saw a beautiful woman, who was both intelligent and quirky as hell. And she was his! Damn, why wouldn't she marry him?

Fortune and Grady made the long tortuous ascent up Medicine Rock hill then descended on the other side. Riding at a fast trot they soon rejoined the Gillette and King road, and Fortune noted that the closer they got to Fort Benton the busier the road seemed to get.

At one point they passed the Diamond R wagons, one of the largest freighters in the territory. Seeing the pretty young woman riding by, the rough mule skinners called out and waved greetings.

Coming upon a patrol of soldiers escorting a stage traveling in the opposite direction, Grady commented, "Last year a few freighters lost everything to Indian attacks. But since the arrival of the Thirteenth Infantry, things have been fairly quiet."

Fortune gave an exaggerated shiver. "I'm glad to hear it."

Because of their late start that morning, Grady kept them at a brisk pace, but rather than travel the last ten miles in darkness they camped that night near the Coolie stage stop. Exhausted, they hit the bedrolls that night and were instantly asleep.

In the semiconscious state between sleep and wakefulness, Fortune felt a gentle tug on one of her nipples. A sensual stirring unraveled and flowed from her breasts downward. Her moan of pleasure fully awakened her. Grady was suckling her breasts. He must have sensed her gaze, for he raised his head and cast her a rakish smile. "I like waking up next to you in the mornings," he said, his voice rough with desire. Two of his fingers entered her below, testing her readiness for him.

Fortune gasped and reached for him. He moved over her, grasped his sex and teased her threshold before surging into her.

Her moist sheath welcomed and gripped his thick erection, and Grady's eyes squeezed shut with the ecstasy. "God, darlin', you're so small and tight." Her muscles contracted, inadvertently massaging his phallus from within. "Oh, Sugar, do that again."

"Do what?" she asked innocently.

"Massage me by flexing your muscles and then relaxing them," he replied.

Wanting to give as much pleasure as she received, Fortune did as he asked, amazed at her ability to grip and hold him within her.

Crooning soft love words in her ear Grady began a slow, tantalizing rhythm of thrust and retreat. On and on he went, until Fortune was mindless with yearning.

Growing impatient, she lifted her hips, dug her heels into the blankets and met his thrusts with her own. As their mutual need escalated, their movements became faster and faster, until together, they both achieved release.

Later, as they rode toward Benton, they smiled at each other continually, like lovers do, and their conversation jumped from topic to topic in their eagerness to know everything about one another.

They arrived in Fort Benton at midmorning. Grady led the way down River Street. The smell of rotten fish, animal dung and garbage, made worse by the summer heat, assaulted Fortune's senses, reminding her of the trip up the Missouri from St. Louis the past spring.

Though slightly less busy, the port was still chaotic. Better than 15 ships, the captains hurling profanities at one another across the water, jockeyed for docking space. On shore freighters with mules and oxen vied for the unloading ramps, trampling everything that got in their way. Curious, solemn-faced Indians idled along the riverbank, gawking at the crazy whites; dirty-faced young hooligans darted around beer kegs and flour bags, looking for discarded treasures or trouble, whichever came first. Near the docks, a horde of half-wild dogs barked and sniffed through the odorous refuse littering the entire area.

As soon as they were past the docks, Grady halted his gelding and turned in his saddle to face her. "Don't forget—while we're in Fort Benton, you're Mrs. MacNair."

Fortune had forgotten that he'd planned to tell everyone they were married. She sidled her horse alongside his. "Grady, I don't think that's a wise thing for us do. What if we meet someone from Helena?"

He tipped his hat back on his head and grinned. "Nothin' says we can't be newlyweds."

"Grady, people travel back and forth between Helena and Fort Benton all the time. Just what do you think I'm going to tell everyone when we get back to Helena and they discover we're not really married? I'll be ruined!"

"Why, I guess I'll just have to talk you into marrying me before that happens then, won't I?" He tapped his hat back down over his forehead and dug his heels into the bay's sides.

Knowing the impossibility of his suggestion, Fortune quickly caught up with him. "Can we discuss this Mrs. MacNair thing?"

He head swiveled in her direction, and he cocked a brow. "I thought we finished that discussion."

"You did. I did not. Grady, I plan to be with you as much as possible, but to be honest, I don't think the problems keeping me from becoming your wife are going to disappear any time in the near future. I can't play your wife in Fort Benton and then return to Helena as a prim and proper business woman."

"You just spent two days alone with me on the road," Grady reasoned. "Why aren't you concerned about that?"

"It would be my word as a proper lady against anyone who might say otherwise. But sharing a room with you here in Fort Benton would be flaunting our relationship in everyone's faces. And don't forget, my brother has a warehouse here in town. What will he say when he learns we've lived together without benefit of marriage?

"Aw, hell!"

"What's that suppose to mean?" she asked.

"It means that we've arrived at the Overland Hotel," he grumbled.

They stopped their horses in front of the unimpressive two-story structure. Glowering, Grady dismounted and tied his horse to the hitching post. She knew the full extent of his ire when he lifted her from her horse and practically planted her into the hard-packed road. Catching his arm as he pivoted away, she blurted, "Grady, wait! Please, don't be mad."

The rigid lines in his face relaxed. "I'm not," he said. "Just disappointed." He took her arm as they gained the boardwalk, then turned to her again. "Fortune, I'm sorry. I've been acting like a selfish bastard. I said I'd give you time to work things out, and I've been bullying you ever since. I don't want anyone saying bad things about you or what we have together. If you want separate rooms, then that's the way it will be."

A loving smile on her face, Fortune brushed his cheek with a kiss. "I love you, Grady MacNair."

"And I love you, lass." His hand rested at her waist as they passed through the open doors of the Overland Hotel.

As it turned out the only accomodation available was a suite, two rooms connected by a smaller room used for dressing and bathing. Fortune played the part of a prim and proper business woman, demanding a key to the door that connected the dressing room to Grady's room. The clerk led the way upstairs and didn't see her drop that key into Grady's hand. The smile on Grady's face told Fortune he was extremely pleased.

Chapter Twenty-one

Grady left Fortune to enjoy a long hot bath and a nap while he contacted the man he hoped to hire to build the new store. By the time he'd finished making a deal with the carpenter, it was nearly time to meet Fortune for dinner.

Back at the hotel he ordered up a bath and hurriedly prepared to join her. Then, for the sake of appearances, he left his room and knocked on her hallway door.

When she opened the door a familiar herbal and floral scent wafted toward him. "You brought your sweet-smelling house herbs with you." He grinned.

Fortune smiled and left the door open wide while she retrieved her reticule off the bed. "I seldom stay anywhere for long without them."

"You wouldn't happen to have any left over, would you?" he asked.

"Why, Grady MacNair," she said, returning to the door, "are you taking my magic to heart?"

The way she smiled up at him made his heart somersault in

his chest. "Not exactly, Sugar. I just asked because my room smells like dirty feet."

Fortune laughed as he wrinkled his nose. "This room was pretty bad, too. I swear I could smell the docks from here. And the answer is yes, I do have some extra herbs." She stuck her head out the door and glanced up and down the hall. Then she tugged him inside and closed it.

"Fortune, what . . . ?" Grady started.

"Shush." She rummaged through the small chest of drawers next to her bed and retrieved a good-sized, flower-printed cotton bag. Reaching inside, she pulled out several tiny lace doilies filled with dried herbs and flowers and tied with ribbons. "I'll put these in your room now. It will only take a moment, and by the time we return your room will smell as nice as mine."

Without a word, Grady followed her through the connecting door and watched as she carefully set the fragrant sachets in every corner of his room, under the bed, and even inside the battered chest of drawers. The last one she tucked beneath the pillows on his bed.

"There!" she said, turning away from the bed. She glanced up to find him grinning ear to ear. "What are you thinking, Grady MacNair?"

"Only that you looked like a lovely, little fairy flitting about my room with your magical pouches."

"How do you know that I'm not?" she teased. "Fairies and goblins often take human form to play pranks on unsuspecting humans."

Grady tapped his finger to his chin in mock thoughtfulness. "So that's how you did it."

"Did what?" she asked, clearly enjoying the nonsensical banter.

"Made me fall madly in love with you, of course."

The smile slipped from Fortune's face, and she suddenly looked so sad he took her in his arms. "Sugar, what is it? What did I say?"

Fortune stood back, her green gaze locking with his concerned one. "I'd never intentionally use a love potion or love spell on you or anyone else, Grady. Maybe that's hard for you to believe after what Granny tried to do to you, but you must believe me. I want a man to love me for me, not because he's under my spell."

Grady shook his head. "You little goose. I don't believe in that love spell nonsense, and you know it. I'm a strong-willed man, and no one could make me fall in love if I didn't want to in the first place. I love you because you're a beautiful, kind, intelligent and thoroughly loveable little witch." He yanked her into his arms and kissed her long and thoroughly. "Understand?" he asked huskily.

"I understand so well that if we don't get out of this room this very minute, you can forget about having any supper tonight. Come on, Reb, let's go to supper. I'm starving!"

"All right, little witch. But once we satisfy our hunger for food, I'm going to satisfy another." After checking the hall, he guided her out of his room.

"By the way, did I tell you yet how fetching you look this evening? That shade of lavender sort of makes those green eyes of yours turn turquoise." From his taller vantage Grady peered down at the enticing view of cleavage revealed by her low-cut bodice.

Fortune saw where his gaze was fixed and cuffed his arm. "Rogue!" She laughed. "It's not my dress you're admiring."

Grady wiggled his brows at her and whispered in her ear. "You've found me out. But tell me, lass, would you have me any other way?"

They had a leisurely meal in a quiet corner of the hotel restaurant, and since a couple hours of daylight remained, Grady decided to show Fortune the location he'd picked out for the new store. They walked down the boardwalk past the Wells Fargo stage office and a small café. The next lot was vacant, and it was here that Grady halted.

"It's a huge lot, Grady," Fortune commented. "Will we need all this space?"

"You bet," he replied emphatically. "Benton is growing even faster than Helena. As a port town, it's a stop off for everyone that takes a steamer into the territory. Fur traders have used this port for years. Though the fur trade isn't what it once was, you'll still see a lot of trappers passing through, not to mention the miners pouring in from all over.

"Most everyone provisions themselves here before setting out to the more remote areas, and at the end of the season many pass through on their way east for the winter. With the comings and goings of so many people, we'll need a large stock of supplies on hand all the time. The new mercantile will have enough room to store goods that can be sold in both stores all winter long."

"Operating such a large store sounds like a full-time task, Grady," Fortune reasoned. "How will you manage it *and* the store in Helena?"

Grady loosened a button on the clean cotton shirt he'd donned for dinner. "It won't be easy, but I've had a couple of ideas I thought I'd run by you, partner. Angus will be bringing up some the new merchandise from Helena. I could have him stay here and run the place for me. He knows how I operate, and I trust him. But there's another possibility, too. I've noticed how often your night watchman, Jim Fetters, has been at your place paying court to Irene. If she were to divorce her no-good husband and marry Jim, I could eventually let them have the Benton store to manage and transfer Angus back to Helena. Since the Benton store is bigger than the one in Helena it would provide them with a good stable income."

"As much as I'd miss Irene and the children, it would be a wonderful opportunity for them. And perhaps when you're settled on your ranch, they might like to buy you out."

"*Our* ranch," Grady corrected with a grin. "And yes, your thoughts on the eventual sale of the mercantile match my own."

Our ranch, he had said. Fortune smiled to cover the pain his innocent words brought to her heart. Her time with Grady was so short.

Back at the hotel, Grady left Fortune at her door and entered his own room through the hall door. He gave her a half hour to complete her ablutions then tapped on the connecting door. "Fortune, honey, may I come in?"

She opened the door, and the sight of her rendered him speechless. Lamplight filtered through the diaphanous peach confection she wore.

Fortune's smile was sultry as she tugged him over the threshold and closed the door. "Have I succeeded in rendering you speechless, love?"

Grady reached for her. She laughed low, her long hair floating around her as she pirouetted out of his grasp. Entranced, he took two steps farther into the room but stopped abruptly as a memory flashed to mind. For a moment the lamplight became firelight, and it shimmered through a veil of red over the lower half of a woman's face. The tilted green eyes above the veiling dared him to touch her. Midnight tresses swirled about inviting hips as the Gypsy girl danced out of his reach.

Stunned, for one terrible moment Grady eyed Fortune with suspicion and hatred.

"Grady, what is it?" Fortune asked, backing away from his frightening countenance.

The loving concern and fear he saw on Fortune's beautiful upturned face finally broke through his trance, and he gave his head a shake. *Christ! What's gotten into me? This beautiful lady couldn't possibly be one and the same as the Gypsy whore who had danced so wantonly before my men and me.* "Sorry, darlin', for a minute the way you danced away from me reminded me of an unpleasant experience. But I assure you, I find you not only lovely but irresistible."

He divested himself of his clothing where he stood. Then approaching Fortune, he picked her up in his arms and deposited her on the bed for a long night of loving.

The next morning Grady delivered Fortune to Roc's warehouse. After introducing themselves to the manager, a young man by the name of John Adair, Grady took his leave with one last warning. "You aren't to leave here unescorted, Fortune. Fort Benton is ten times rougher than Helena. It's a port town. Every ruffian in the territory passes through here. Besides, trouble may have followed us here."

Fortune promised Grady she'd be careful, and he left to tend to his own business.

She was pleased to learn that Roc had written and informed John that he was to give her his full cooperation. The warehouse was twice as large as the one in Helena, and having just received its last river shipment of the season, it was a beehive of activity. John proudly showed her around, and she was impressed with his orderly organization of the inventory.

Later in his office, Fortune filled him in on Landry Freighting's recent problems in Helena and asked if there had been any problems or suspicious happenings here in Fort Benton. She was relieved to hear that all was running smoothly.

John then left her in his office to go over his records and bills of lading. At noon he invited her to accompany him home to meet his wife, Luanne, and their new baby daughter. Immensely pleased that he didn't seem the least upset about taking orders from a woman, she readily accepted.

Fortune liked Luanne Adair on sight and knew it would be especially nice to have a female friend in town. After sharing lunch with the happy family, she returned with John to the warehouse office.

That evening when Grady returned to escort her back to the Overland, they had a lot to tell each other. They went straight to a restaurant across the street from the hotel to exchange news over their meal.

After the waitress cleared away the dishes, Grady laid the drawings for the new mercantile on the table. "The carpenters will start first thing in the morning," he told her. "The counters and shelves will be constructed at the carpentry shop while the building is going up. That way, they'll be finished and ready to install the minute the building is ready."

"It sounds like we'll be open for business much sooner than we anticipated," Fortune replied.

"Unless something unexpected happens, we may be in business in less than a month's time." Grady said, rolling up the mercantile plans.

"Fortune, did you warn John that he might want to put an extra guard on night duty?" he asked. "We certainly don't want a repeat of what happened in Helena."

"Yes. In fact, he called all his men into the office, explained what happened in Helena and warned them to keep an eye peeled for trouble. I was really quite touched by all the men's concern for me." Fortune blushed and added, "John told the men that I had been threatened, and they all swore that they would let no harm come to me. Honestly, Grady," she said, chuckling, "I feel like I've got five full-time bodyguards. John even put a guard on the office door. Like Roc's office, John's has two doors—one opening into the warehouse and one that opens on the side of the building. The guard will be posted at the outside door whenever I'm present. That way no one can sneak in on me."

Grady nodded his approval. "John Adair sounds like a very capable young man."

"Oh, he is. I was so impressed with his inventory methods

that I've asked him to come to Helena and organize the new warehouse in the same manner. I invited his family to stay at my house because he said it would take a couple weeks to organize the new inventory and train a man in the new method."

Grady grinned and stood. "You're getting to be quite the business woman, aren't you?" he said, helping her from her chair. "Sure am glad you're my partner and not my competitor."

As they stepped out onto the boardwalk of River Street a breeze caught at Fortune's dark skirts and exposed her petticoats. But rather than subdue her garments, she grasped her amulet instead and mumbled something to herself.

Grady, who had been occupied untwisting her skirts from around his legs, laughed and asked, "Now what are you up to, little witch?"

"I'm no witch, Grady MacNair. Witches are evil creatures."

"Then what were you muttering over that funny little shell you wear?"

"It was just a protective chant. Granny always says, *'The devil never sent the wind, but he would sail with it.'* "

Grady laughed then licked his finger and lifted it into the air. "Well, the devil may travel on a wind, but my father used to say, *'The wind in the west suits everyone best.'* And this one is definitely a west wind."

"Well, your father was right, but Beng can ride a good wind as easily as a bad."

"Beng? What's that?" Grady asked, taking her arm and starting them across the street.

Fortune hadn't realized she'd used the Gypsy word for devil and thought quickly. "It's an ancient druid term meaning devil," she improvised. "Granny always calls the devil Beng, and I sometimes forget and use the term myself."

As they made their way upstairs to their rooms, Fortune doubted there was anyone in the whole territory of Montana that knew Romany. Still, too many slips might invoke Grady's suspicions. She'd have to remember to be more careful.

"It's early yet," Grady said when they stopped before her door. "Why don't you slip over to my room when you get inside, and we'll play some poker."

"All right, but you'll have to teach me. I've never played it before."

"Sure, if you promise to teach me some of your magic," he quipped.

Fortune grinned mischievously. "I'll teach you only the good things, Grady."

"Such as?"

"Such as how to keep your lover from straying, and how to keep her fires burning."

"Hell, darlin', I don't need magic for that."

"Conceited oaf!" She opened her door, stepped inside and turned around. Glancing up at him with a distinctly seductive gleam in her eye, she pulled a long hairpin from her chignon and shook her hair loose. She ran her tongue along her full bottom lip suggestively. "See you . . . lover." She shut the door.

Grady was through his own door and in her room in a flash. She yelped in surprise when he caught her from behind and carried her into his room. When he set her down, he captured her in his embrace. "Kiss me, you little hussy, and give me some of that naughty little tongue, too."

Fortune pressed her curves against the hard planes of his masculine body and threw her arms around his neck. As she stroked the inside of his mouth with her tongue, she felt his burgeoning heat through her clothes.

He moaned and reached for the buttons on her dress, but she broke away and put a short distance between them. "You promised to teach me poker, Grady MacNair."

"Now?" he almost squeaked.

"Yes."

"All right, but only on one condition. The first three games won't count because you'll just be learning. But after that, we play five games. The winner of three or better takes the prize."

"Which is?"

Grady wiggled his brows. "The loser has to pleasure the winner in bed tonight. Do we have a deal, Sugar?"

"Oh, yes!"

"Good." He threw the sheets back on the bed. "We'll have to play here since there's no table," he said. "Very appropriate, though, don't you think?" He went to the chest of drawers and found a pack of playing cards. Then they slipped their shoes off, climbed onto the bed and sat cross-legged across from one another.

Grady shuffled the cards. "Now in poker," he began, "certain combinations of cards beat other combinations. For instance, a royal flush beats a straight flush."

"Grady, stop right there." Fortune laughed. "Why don't you lay out the different types of hands in order from best to least best."

"I suppose that might be an easier way to explain it." With the dexterity of a seasoned gambler, he set about showing her eight types of poker hands.

"I think I understand," she mused, looking over the different combinations. "Five of a kind, say four kings and a joker, beats most anything else. Next comes the royal flush, one ace, one king, one queen, one jack, and one ten, all of the same suit. Am I right?"

"You're a quick learner, darlin'."

The first three hands, as Grady promised, were practice games, and Fortune caught on quickly, delighting in the game.

"You're doing great, love," Grady complimented, "but you must learn to keep a poker face. Don't giggle and squirm every time you get a good card, or you'll tip off your opponents."

"You mean I can be sneaky?" The Gypsy part of her loved that idea, and her green eyes snapped with impish delight.

Grady laughed at her mischievous expression. "I think sly might be a better word. Sneaky implies you're a cheat, and in the game of poker that's no laughing matter."

Grady won the first two games, and Fortune the next two. "I've never seen anyone pick up on poker so fast," he said.

"But this last hand is the one that decides the victor, right?" She grinned, then picked up and studied the cards he'd just dealt her. Bluffing, she smiled at him. "Prepare to spend the night pleasuring me, my handsome slave."

"We'll see who pleasures who," Grady replied with equal confidence.

As the game progressed, Fortune's hand improved very little. Still she kept up her very provocative smile. Very subtly, she played with the buttons on her dress until the top of her cleavage was clearly visible. Frowning at her cards, she ran her tongue along her bottom lip and fiddled with the lace edging at the top of her chemise.

Grady retained his poker face, never letting on he knew what she was up to. Despite his stoic facade, however, he couldn't help feasting his eyes on the swell of her breasts, and when she ran a nonchalant finger down her cleavage, his britches suddenly became uncomfortable.

But in the end, Fortune's wiles didn't help. When she slapped down her hand displaying four of a kind, Grady grinned and covered her cards with his royal flush. He laughed, flopped back on the pillows and stretched out his long legs. "Get to work, little love slave," he commanded.

Fortune never liked losing, but as she eyed his virile body, she decided that *she* was the real winner. "A love slave like a harem girl, perhaps?"

Grady grinned and nodded eagerly.

Struck by a sudden inspiration, she slid off the bed and bowed subserviently. "I must first prepare you and myself, O Great One. Please, wait here and do not move. I promise to make this a night of a thousand delights."

Fortune picked up her shoes and slipped into her own room. She then put them on and hurried down the stairs to the clerk's desk. "I would like a bath sent up please, and I want the biggest tub you have. I don't like being cramped."

"It'll be just a few moments, ma'am," the clerk replied. Fortune nodded and returned to Grady's room via her own. "Have patience and you shall be rewarded," she said, slipping back into the pretense. She kissed him long and languorously. Then there was a knock at her bedroom door, and she disappeared back into her own room, shutting the connecting door.

When the tub was brimming with hot water she sprinkled a few drops of scent into the tub and laid out towels and soap. She pinned her hair off her shoulders, then returned to Grady. At her approach, he lifted an inquiring brow but remained on the bed.

Without a word, she began unbuttoning her dress. It slipped to the floor and pooled around her ankles. Taking her time with each remaining garment, she splayed her fingers over her flesh in provocative places. When she was completely naked she stepped out of the pile of clothing and performed a slow turn. "Does the Great One approve?" she asked.

As an answer Grady leapt out of the bed and reached for her.

Fortune agilely eluded his hands. "Have patience, O Anxious One. At least let me undress you."

Falling in with the fun, Grady nodded and crossed his arms over his chest in the arrogant manner of a great sultan.

The Gypsy girl unfastened his shirt. As she pulled it down his arms she slowly circled around him, rubbing her nipples across his chest and then his back. At Grady's sound of pleasure, she smiled to herself. She added his shirt to her pile of clothing. Then she lathed his nipples with her tongue as he'd so often done to her.

Grady grasped her head, squeezed his eyes shut and let his head fall back in abject pleasure. She moved from his grasp, her lips burning a sensuous trail down his belly. He inhaled sharply when her hands suddenly released his belt buckle. He would have helped her, but she softly brushed his hands away.

Falling down on her knees before him, Fortune tugged his britches down. When his erection sprang free, she paused and touched her cheek against its heat. Then returning to her chore, she helped him step out of his pants and socks.

Willing himself to remain still, Grady waited to see what this fascinating woman would do next. He was surprised when she led him into her room and urged him into a prepared bath.

Grady eased into the hot, exotically scented water, now truly feeling like some kind of pampered Arab chieftain. He watched expectantly as Fortune took soap in hand. "One might think you had all this planned." He chuckled.

She shook her head. "I like winning too much. But before I'm done with you, Grady MacNair, you may question who really won, because I plan to thoroughly enjoy myself."

"Going to have your way with me, are you?" he asked huskily.

Her lashes lowered over her eyes. "Wait and see, O Great One."

He leaned against the back of the tub and shut his eyes. "Will you join me, little slave girl?"

Grady's eyes flew open when she quickly complied. Sitting on his naked lap and facing him, her breasts brushed his chest, and a delightful idea occurred to her. She soaped her breasts and her hands. As she reached around him and soaped his back, her lathered orbs did the same for his chest.

He inhaled sharply and clasped her buttocks, but when he would have set her down on his staff, she shook her head. "Not yet, O Master of the Long Staff." She gingerly scooted backward off his lap, wrapping her legs over his in the narrow confines of the tub.

She then soaped her hands and washed each of his legs in turn, as best she could in the awkward position. At last, her hand circled his throbbing shaft. Holding and gently massaging the sacs beneath it with one hand, she applied her soapy hand to his slick, hard length. He reached out and tutored her hands, showing her how to move the foreskin so that her slick fingers massaged the sensitive vein on the underside. She worked her hand up and down till he growled and abruptly sat up, splashing water over the sides of the tub.

"No more, love," he begged raggedly, "or you'll finish me off too soon. Lord, I'm beginning to see what you meant about winning."

Fortune laughed softly and disentangled herself from him. Reaching for one of two buckets setting outside the tub, she asked him to stand while she rinsed him off. He did so, then stepped out of the tub and repaid the courtesy by pouring the second bucket of water over her. After quickly drying each other off, Fortune led him to her bed and let down her hair. "Thy couch of pleasure awaits," she said, smiling and bowing.

More like an eager slave than a chieftain, Grady stretched out on his back and awaited her ministrations with a devilish smile.

She stretched out over the top of him. Mimicking what he'd taught her, she kissed and touched him everywhere. Her tongue skimmed down his lean torso, exploring every masculine inch.

Fortune was shocked to realize that in seducing him, she was seducing herself as well. Her opening was hot and wet, and her longing manifested itself in the increasingly passionate caresses she plied on her lover.

The Reb's hands grabbed the sheets as his desire grew beyond any reckoning. His heavy sacs ached to be relieved of their burden, and his shaft reared and bucked like a randy stallion. Then he felt her hands bridle the lusty fellow.

"Is it as good for a man as it is for a woman to be kissed here?" she asked, cupping his heavy sacs.

Grady's speech was husky with desire. "Yes, but darlin', you don't have to . . ."

"I know. But I want to give the same kind of pleasure you gave to me. Will you guide me and show me what pleases you?"

As an answer he gently pressed her head down. She again became the aggressor and took him into her mouth. He held her head between his hands and gently guided her in and out motions. At the same time she instinctively applied her swirling tongue to the sensitive vein he'd told her about earlier.

The pleasure was so great, Grady thought he might very well die of it. Never had a woman pleased him so much, so selflessly. And when he tried to pull her atop him she'd have none it. Within minutes she brought him to a climax bordering on the mystical.

When Grady came down from off his cloud, he realized Fortune was curled against his side. He adjusted their positions so that they lay on their sides facing each other. Pulling her close, his sated gaze locked with hers. "God, woman, I love you so bad it hurts." He kissed her deeply, raking his hand through her long tresses. And when he finished that kiss he began another and another, until finally he was ready to fulfil her needs.

Chapter Twenty-two

Sitting on a crude cot inside his cabin hideout, Deke Tunney swore, "Damnation, Bull, she's been gone over a week. Somebody must know where she got to."

"If they do, they're keepin' their mouths shut, boss," Bull Durrant said, leaning against a rough-hewn log wall. "We did find out the Reb, Grady MacNair, is gone, too. As chummy as them two been, I bet they took off together."

"How about Eric Jorgensen? You been able to learn anything from him?"

"Not a damn thing."

The two men heard a horse gallop up and drew their guns. Deke positioned his wooden leg, then stood and joined Bull at the blanket that served as a door. The two men peered out cautiously. "It's Clyde," Deke said, shoving the blanket aside and hobbling outside. "Maybe he has news." Bull lumbered after his boss.

Clyde dismounted and turned to Deke with a gleeful grin on his weasely face. "I know where the Landry bitch is," he said excitedly. "I talked to one of them kids what lives with 'er. The little gal was playin' with that dog out backa the mercantile. I pretended I had a real 'portant message for the Landry woman, and—"

"Just get on with it," Deke yelled. "Where's the Landry bitch?"

"Her and that MacNair feller took off for Fort Benton. The kid said somethin' 'bout them buildin' a new store."

"Is that so?" Deke laughed. "For once in your life, Clyde, you did good. That was real smart askin' that kid."

"How did you get around that damn dog?" Bull snarled, staring down at his scarred arms.

"Well, see, I just sat myself down at the back of the buildin' not movin' a muscle. Then along comes the kid and the dog. The dog, he growled somethin' fierce, but I just sat there. The kid calmed 'im down. Then I said I was waitin' to give a message to the pretty lady that works in the store, and that little gal up and told me everythin'."

"You did good, Clyde," Deke said. "Bull, you and I are going to take a couple of the boys and head for Fort Benton. We're gonna put a good scare into that Landry woman. I heard tell the Landrys have a warehouse in Benton, too. I want it destroyed."

"The boys are gettin' restless, boss," Bull warned. "They said they're not doin' any more of your dirty work less they get something for their trouble."

Deke tugged at his shadowed chin thoughtfully, then glanced up at Bull. "We'll steal a couple wagons and the men can rob the costly stuff out of the warehouse before they burn it. Will that suit the greedy bastards?"

"Should."

"Good. Now get to Helena and fetch the supplies we need for the trip."

"There's just one thing I got to do before I leave town, boss," Bull replied determinedly.

"What's that?"

"I got to settle a score with that damn dog."

Deke chuckled evilly. "Good idea, Bull. Anything that will hurt Fortune Landry is fine by me. Now, if all goes well, by sometime next week Eli and Frank will hit Roc Landry and his freight wagons at Blood Rock." Deke stretched his arms out, clasped his hands and cracked his knuckles. "Yep, everythin's lookin' good."

Later that day, Bull sneaked up on the guard watching Fortune's house and rendered him unconscious. He then took the man's place behind the tree across the street and waited.

When the Tabor woman and her kids pulled up in a buckboard, he raised his rifle and drew a bead on the dog trotting alongside.

A shot rang out. The dog staggered then fell to the ground. A satisfied smile slashed Bull's ugly face. He hurried away amidst the children's frantic cries. He had supplies to gather for the two day ride to Fort Benton and knew just where to go to get them.

Three days later Fortune and Luanne Adair were shopping.

"Sure will be glad when Grady gets his new store built," Luanne commented to Fortune as she rummaged through several bolts of dress material. "They never have much of a selection at this small place. Do you like this one?" She held up a bolt of royal blue calico. "Think I should buy it?"

Fortune glanced up from the baby she held for Luanne and nodded. "It matches your eyes perfectly, Lu. It will look pretty with your blond hair, too." The six-month-old baby girl cooed, and one tiny hand patted Fortune's cheek. The young woman laughed. "I think April likes it, too."

Luanne smiled at Fortune as she laid the bolt of material on the counter and told the clerk how much to measure off. "You're good with children, Fortune. When are you and Grady going to get married and have some of your own?"

Fortune flushed and glanced down at the baby. "I . . . I didn't know Grady told you about us."

"Uh oh. Was it suppose to be a secret? Well, don't be too upset with Grady for mentioning it. John and I were curious because he seems to dote on you so. And, to be honest, we got kind of nosy and pried it out of the poor man."

Fortune didn't know what to say. She liked Luanne but didn't feel she knew her well enough to confide her problems. "I'm afraid I've had to put Grady off for a while," she confessed. "There are some problems I have to clear up before we can be married."

Luanne paid the clerk and picked up her package. "Wanna trade bundles?" she asked, holding her arms out for the baby.

Seeing her mother, little April's arms flailed the air excitedly. Fortune chuckled, handed over the little girl and took possession of Luanne's purchase.

"I know all about obstacles to marriage," Luanne said as they headed for the door. "John was one of the Yankees that occupied my parents' plantation during the war. We fell in love during his stay, but duty soon called him away. When he returned after the war to marry me, my brother chased him off the property with a shotgun."

"Oh, no!"

"Oh, yes! Finally, John got a message to me, and I sneaked out to meet him. We got married that same night, then went back home to tell my mother and brother. It wasn't very pleasant for John, and in the end we decided to head west and start a life of our own. Maybe you and Grady will have to do the same," Luanne advised as they stepped outside on the boardwalk.

"I wish it were as simple as that, but—" Fortune dropped the package and grabbed for Luanne as two large men barged past, nearly knocking the woman and her baby flat. She felt her reticule snag on something, but she was too intent on catching hold of the other woman to pay it any mind.

"Of all the nerve!" Luanne snapped angrily after the departing men.

"Are you and April all right?" Fortune asked anxiously.

"Yes, thanks to you. How about you?"

"Yes, I . . . What's this?" Fortune held up her reticule into which a large scrap of paper had been haphazardly stashed. As she opened it up and read the scribbled note, her hands began to shake.

F.L. Did u think u cud run from me. I wil hunt u down wherever u go.

Fortune whipped around to get a look at the men that had brushed past them, but they were nowhere in sight. "Luanne, those men, did you see where they went?"

"No. They probably ducked into one of the saloons. Why? What's that note say? Did one of them shove it into your bag?"

"I think so," Fortune replied distractedly. "If you don't mind,

I'll walk you home now. This note is a threat from the man I told you and John about, and I must find Grady right away."

"Then let's stop at the warehouse first. John can see me home, then escort you to the mercantile."

"I really don't want to take the time."

"Fortune, you have no business going anywhere alone."

"All right, but let's hurry. From the looks of this note, my troubles have followed me to Benton."

John Adair glanced up in surprise when his wife and Fortune tore into the warehouse. "Luanne," he said, taking the baby from his gasping wife, "what is it? What's happened?"

Fortune tugged the note out of her reticule and read it to John. "Someone shoved this into my bag just a few minutes ago." She told him about the men that had barged past them on the boardwalk. "I think it was one of them that put the paper in my reticule. I'm worried, John. I think we should find Grady right away."

A line creased John's forehead as he handed the baby back to Luanne and called two of his men over. "Hank, Billy, I want you two to take my wife home and stay with her until I return. Fortune, let's you and I find Grady." With that John gave his wife a quick buss on the cheek and loaded Fortune up in his buckboard.

Ten minutes later, they found Grady on the building site of the mercantile. "And to what do I owe this unexpected pleasure?" he asked, climbing over a pile of lumber to join them.

John helped Fortune from the buckboard, and without a word she handed Grady the letter.

"Damn!" Grady cursed, looking up from the note. "How did they find out?"

Fortune shook her head. "I don't know. I know none of our friends would have told anybody. Grady, I'm worried. Whoever is doing this might try to kill you to get to me. I think it might be best for everyone if I went back to Helena while you finish building the store."

"Like hell you will, woman. Do you think I could stay here knowing some madman is stalking you?"

"But Grady—"

"No buts about it, Fortune. You're staying with me. Where did you find this thing?" Grady asked, handing the paper back to her.

Fortune repeated the incident on the boardwalk. "I was so busy catching Luanne, I didn't see their faces."

Grady glanced over at John. "If you haven't put a guard on your home, I suggest you do it right away."

"It's been done," John replied.

"Good. Let's leave Fortune with your wife and hit the saloons. You're acquainted with most of the men in this town, aren't you?"

"Those that live here. But you know as well as I do that dozens of strangers pass through Benton everyday. Unless you have an idea what these men look like, I'm afraid trying to find them will be impossible."

"Fortune described the man who attacked her in Helena," Grady explained. "I'm betting he's one of the men that followed us here. He's a big man, about my height but built like an ox. He has dirty red hair and is uglier than sin. Fortune's dog chewed his arms up pretty bad, so we'll look for a man with scars on his arms and hands."

"Grady," Fortune said, "I can't stand pacing the floor for hours while you're out endangering yourself on my behalf. Why don't you let me go along? I'd recognize that varmint anywhere, but you two might miss him. What if he has his arms covered?"

Grady sighed impatiently. "They don't allow ladies where we're goin', darlin'. And even if our man has his arms covered, there's still his hands. He can't very well go round wearing gloves all the time." He took her arm and gently maneuvered her toward the buckboard. "The best place for you is with Luanne."

Fortune grudgingly obeyed and allowed him to help her into the buckboard. John climbed up on one side of her, Grady on the other.

A half hour later John and Grady started their search of the saloons. In each one they took a table in a shadowy corner, where they could discreetly study the patrons that came and went for a time. John pointed out the strangers, but they found only two red-haired men in the entire town. One was a mule skinner with the Diamond R outfit, a big man, but fair in looks and not a single scar visible on his forearms. The other was a small gangly man who didn't fit Fortune's description in the least.

It was after midnight when the two men admitted defeat. Since they supposed the women had probably gone to bed, Grady decided not to fetch Fortune back to the hotel until the next morning.

Disappointed and exhausted, he trudged up the hotel stairs. He didn't notice the man coming down the hall from the direction of his and Fortune's rooms until it was almost too late. The red-haired man spotted Grady and drew his gun.

Grady looked up at about the same time the man's gun cleared leather. A bullet whizzed past his head just as he fell to the floor. Rolling and drawing his own gun at the same time, Grady took aim, but the man had already turned tail and headed for the backstairs at the opposite end of the building. Several doors up and down the hall flew open but slammed shut when they saw Grady race past with his Remington in hand.

Grady heard the man's boots thump against the wooden stairs on the outside of the building. Unfortunately, by the time he made it to the stairs himself, his quarry had disappeared below into the dark alley. Chasing him would be inviting an ambush.

Cursing his ill luck, Grady retraced his steps to his room. He quickly discerned that his room was undisturbed and went through the connecting door to check Fortune's room. Everything appeared to be in order, and he was about to return to his own room when he spied a folded piece of paper laying on the floor, where it had obviously been shoved under her door.

The message was so vile that he was very glad Fortune had not found it herself. He struck a match and burned it. For her own protection he would have to tell her of the threat, but he wouldn't subject her unnecessarily to such filth.

God, if anything happened to her . . . What was his love hiding from him? She'd said Roc had involved her in nothing, but more and more he suspected she was lying to him. And he suspected that those lies had something to do with her refusal to marry him. There had to be some clue to this mystery, something that he'd missed.

He'd promised to give her time to work out her problems, but he prayed she'd come to her senses and confide in him before it was too late.

Fortune shared an early breakfast with John and Luanne, while John regaled both women on his and Grady's fruitless search. After the meal, John took Fortune back to the hotel.

Grady was on his way to fetch Fortune when she and John stepped into the lobby. He thanked John, then hustled Fortune up the stairs to her room. Taking her key, he unlocked the door and unconsciously pocketed it as they entered the room. The minute the door closed behind them, Grady pulled Fortune into his arms.

Melting in his embrace, she lifted her mouth for his kiss. "I missed you last night, partner," she said.

"And I missed you." He kissed her then, almost desperately, holding her as if she might disappear at any moment.

When he drew back, Fortune's expression was concerned. "Something has happened. Tell me"

Retaining his intimate hold on her, he cupped her chin and smoothed back a loose ebony strand. "Fortune, I hate to greet you with bad news, but I found another letter in your room last night after running into the messenger in the hall. It was the red-haired man. He saw me and took off in the opposite direction. I tried to catch him, but he got away."

"And the message? I want to read it."

"I burned it, darlin'. I couldn't bear for you to see it."

"Grady, no matter how bad it is, I have a right to know what I'm up against. What did it say?"

"Suffice it to say that whoever is after you has promised to give you to his men when he's done with you himself."

Fortune shivered. "Sweet Gaia, the man must be insane. He . . . he wants me to worry, to anticipate . . ." She buried her face in the comfort of Grady's brown cotton shirt.

Grady hugged her for a moment then set her away so he could scrutinize her face. "Fortune, I think you know who's terrorizing you and why. Don't you think it's time you trust me with an explanation?"

Tears welled up in her eyes, and she wrenched out of his arms.

He was right behind her. Taking her arms in a gentle but firm hold, he forced her to turn around and face him. "If I'm going to be shot at, woman, I'd like to know why!"

She stiffened at his harsh tone and this new revelation. "He tried to kill you? But why?" She grabbed his arms, her eyes searching him for injury. "Are you all right?"

"He didn't even come close. But to answer your first two

questions, he probably shot at me because I'm interfering with his boss's plans. Fortune, I know you're hiding something from me."

There was no way Fortune could tell him the whole truth, and she resented his tone of voice. "I've told you everything I know."

"There has to be more," Grady asserted. "The bastard obviously wants you to guess who's doing this to you and why."

Fortune heaved a defeated sigh, tossed her reticule on the chest of drawers and sank down on the edge of the bed. "Perhaps I should catch the next stage back to Helena after all. I'm not only endangering you but John's family as well."

Grady clenched his fists and growled a curse. "Damn it, woman, how many times do have to tell you that I protect what's mine?"

"But I'm not yours. I'm not your wife, not your responsibility."

"You're mine just the same." Grady inhaled a deep breath, and his next words were softer. "We love each other, darlin'. That's why we belong to each other." He took three long strides and stood before her. "Talk to me. Tell me what's going on here."

"I can't!" she cried, hiding her face in her hands.

Frustration stoked Grady's temper anew. "Can't or won't?" With that he slammed out of her room and into his own.

Grady stood in the middle of his room, his fists opening and closing. Didn't she know that he'd gladly slay all her dragons if she'd just trust him? With a growled oath, he grabbed up the building plans for the mercantile and stormed out of his room. Then remembering her threat to grab the stage for Helena, he paused outside her door, fingering the key in his pocket with indecision.

Fortune heard Grady's door slam. His footsteps paused outside her door, and she froze, waiting. She'd never seen him so furious as when he slammed out of her room. Would he come in now and apologize? She heard a key rattling in her lock, gasped in outrage and ran to the door, trying to jerk it open. But it was no use. "A hex on you, Grady MacNair!" she yelled through the door. "Let me out of here this very minute or I'll scream so loud that I'll bring the roof down!"

She heard his roguish chuckle, and the sound of his retreating footsteps. She ran to the door connecting their rooms, but it had locked behind him when he slammed it.

At noon a key rattled in Fortune's door. She quit her pacing and turned as the door eased open. "Grady MacNair, you've got a lot of nerve, com . . ."

It wasn't Grady at the door at all! Blushing profusely she stepped back from the door and stared at a man she recognized as one of the guards of the mercantile building site. One hand held the side of a tray of food, the other balanced it from beneath. Only when she politely took the tray from him, did she notice the hand under the tray held a small pistol.

At her look of horror the poor man turned several shades of red. "Sorry, ma'am," he said. "I didn't mean to scare you, but Mr. MacNair said you was a feisty one and that he locked you in here for your own protection. He said I wasn't to let you get past me, or I'd lose my job."

"Oh, he did, did he?" Fortune exploded angrily and slammed the tray down. Tea sloshed out of the cup, staining the napkin, but she paid it no mind. Caging a Gypsy was like walling up one of nature's fiercest elements, and Fortune's temper had blown itself into a raging tempest.

"Yes, ma'am, he did." The man's head bobbed up and down, as he started backing out the door.

"Wait a minute," she said, stalking him. "I'm Mr. MacNair's partner so I'm your boss, too, and I demand you leave that door unlocked, Mr . . ."

"Randall, ma'am," the man replied, looking utterly distressed. "Heck, ma'am, you're puttin' me in a terrible spot."

"Then take me to Mr. MacNair, sir. Now!"

"But ma'am . . ."

"I'll put a terrible hex on you if don't do what I say this very minute!"

Randall's mouth fell open. "You can do that?"

"The last man I hexed lost all his teeth and went gray overnight."

Balanced on a roof beam high above the ground, Grady spotted Fortune marching down the street. A veritable storm cloud at full sail, her long hair waved through the air like an ominous pirate's flag on the high seas. And though he couldn't yet see her eyes, he knew they'd be spitting lightening bolts. A defeated-looking Randall trailed behind her, looking as if he'd not weathered the storm at all well.

Muttering an oath, the Reb started to climb down, then thought better of it. If he stayed where he was, she'd have to shout up at him, and he doubted she'd make a scene in front all his men.

Fortune stopped in front of the skeleton of the new mercantile, jammed her fists on her hips and glanced around. "Where is he, Mr. Randall?" she demanded.

Randall pointed up to the rafters and slunk off.

"Grady MacNair, get down here! I want to talk to you!"

"Damn," the Reb muttered under his breath. Deliberately ignoring her, he made his way to the opposite end of the roof. But when he looked back down to where she'd been standing, she wasn't there.

"Hey, lady," one of the builders shouted, "you can't go up there."

What Grady saw made him grit his teeth in fury. Her skirts bunched up over one arm, her legs exposed from the knees down, Fortune slowly made her way up a ladder leaning against the framework. Every man on the premises, and some passers-by as well, stared in awed appreciation at the young woman's shapely calves. It wasn't everyday they were treated to such a sight.

Grady walked across the rafters as neatly as a cat and sat down next to the top of the ladder. "For God's sake, woman," he hissed when she reached the top, "put your skirts down."

Fortune complied, then leaned against the ladder and glared up at him. "How dare you lock me in my room, Grady MacNair!" she blasted without preamble.

"Keep your voice down," he replied tersely and leaned closer. "Fortune, you threatened to catch the stage to Helena. I couldn't let you do that. Don't you realize by know that your every move is being watched? You'd be kidnapped off the stage within an hour."

"I doubt it. Whoever is doing this wants me to suffer and worry a little longer. If my enemy wanted me that bad, he could have taken me the day his hireling accosted me behind the church in Helena."

Seeing that they were gathering curious stares, Grady suggested, "Why don't we climb down and discuss this in private."

"There's nothing more to discuss. I just wanted you to know that you can't treat me like some kind of criminal and keep me locked up. I won't have it. You're not my husband, and you're not my brother. And even if you were, you have no right to act like a bully."

"Then I want your promise that you won't try to leave town on your own."

"Very well, you have it."

"Good, now get down that ladder and let Randall take you back to the hotel."

"I've been cooped up in that hotel room all morning, and I'm not going back. I have work to do at the warehouse."

"Fine!" Grady said, throwing his hands up in exasperation. "Now will you get down off that ladder. People are staring, for God's sake! And make sure Randall escorts you to the warehouse."

"All right," she acquiesced.

Grady gingerly stood up, but when Fortune didn't immediately start down the ladder, he asked, "Is there something else?" Fortune looked down the ladder, then back up at him. He noted her white-knuckled grip on the ladder and her sudden pale pallor. "Fortune?"

"I forgot," she said in a trembling voice.

"Forgot what, Sugar?"

"I'm afraid of heights."

"You're afraid of . . . and yet you . . ." He broke off with a burst of laughter.

"You're cruel to laugh at me," she scolded. The sternness she strove for was ruined by a smile that quivered at the corner of her mouth.

Grady shook his head. Lord, but he loved this bewildering little baggage! Taking hold of one side of the ladder, he swung one of his long legs around the girl, placing his foot on the rung beneath the one she stood on. The other leg followed. Then forming a cage around her with his own body, he slowly moved down the ladder with her.

Chapter Twenty-three

Though Grady had exhausted Fortune with his passionate love-making, she lay next to him, restless and unable to sleep.

The last three days had been peaceful enough, but she surmised that it was her enemy's way of drawing out the torment, making her guess when and where he'd strike next. To a certain extent he'd succeeded. She jumped at every little noise and felt compelled to look over her shoulder every five minutes; now she couldn't sleep either.

As if that weren't enough, there was a subtle strain between Grady and herself. He knew she was hiding something from him, and from time to time she caught him looking at her strangely. At those times, she felt sure he'd guessed her secret and would hold her breath, praying for just one more night in his loving arms.

A thunderous pounding at the door made Fortune start. Grady sat straight up in bed and grabbed his gun out of its holster where it hung on the bedpost. "Stay put, darlin'," he whispered. "I'll see who it is." He crept to one side of the door and asked, "Who is it?"

"MacNair?" a voice called through the door. "It's me, Hank, from the warehouse. John sent me. We got trouble."

Responding to the urgency in Hank's voice, Grady yanked open the door. "What is it?"

"The warehouse has been robbed, and it's afire!"

From the bed, Grady heard Fortune's sharp intake of breath. "Thanks, Hank. Tell John I'm on my way." Grady slammed the door shut and grabbed his pants.

Fortune threw the sheet aside, jumped out of bed and lit a lantern. "I'm coming with you," she said, tugging her dress over her head.

Knowing there was little he could do to prevent her from following, Grady nodded. "Fine, just stay close. We don't know what we'll find." He strapped on his guns and grabbed his hat. "You ready, partner?"

Fortune finished tying her high-top shoes. "Ready."

By the time Grady and Fortune got to the warehouse only a few ribbons of wispy gray smoke remained to testify that there truly had been a fire.

"We're lucky," John said, meeting them out front of the building. "We caught the fire before much damage could be done. The guards weren't killed, only knocked unconscious and tied up. Near as we can tell, the thieves stole what they wanted and drove off with it in a couple of wagons. They left one man behind to start the fire, and he's dead now. I think it's the red-haired man you've been looking for, Grady. When Hank arrived to relieve one of the guards he surprised him. Unfortunately, Hank had to shoot him or be killed himself."

Grady's fingers furrowed through his hair. "Damn, too bad we couldn't have taken him alive. I'm grateful, though, that none of our men were seriously hurt."

Grady fixed a grim gaze on Fortune. "You up to having a look at the thief, darlin'? We should make sure he's the same man who attacked you in Helena."

Fortune swallowed hard, but it wouldn't be the first time she'd seen a dead man. She'd witnessed death during the war. Still, it wasn't something she thought she would ever get used to. "I'll be fine. John, let's have look."

Grady kept a supportive arm around her shoulders as they followed John to the back of the building. The warehouse manager pulled aside a blanket that had been tossed over the thief and held a lantern close to the still face.

"It's him," Fortune gasped, turning her face into Grady's shoulder.

Grady nodded. "It's the same man I ran into in the hotel the other night, too."

John threw the blanket back over the dead man, then turned to point out the damage to the warehouse. "The fire was barely started when Hank came on duty," he explained, "but he had to get past that culprit lying over there before he could put it out."

Fortune studied the damage, thankful that she would not have to go to the expense of rebuilding. One corner of the building was blackened, and a hole big enough for a man to crawl through had burned through to the inside of the building.

"Thank God, we were prepared for trouble this time," she said. Turning to John she asked, "What about the two guards that were knocked out? Will they be all right?"

"'Cept for a headache, they'll be fine," he replied.

A man of medium height and build with a sheriff's badge on his chest strode up and joined them. "Tom." John greeted the man, shaking his hand. "This is Miss Fortune Landry and Grady MacNair. They're partners in Landry Freighting. Fortune, Grady, this is Sheriff Tom Stanton."

"Ma'am, Mr. MacNair." The sheriff tipped his hat. "Hate to keep you folks, but I need to ask some questions 'bout that dead man over yonder."

It was nearly dawn when Grady and Fortune returned to the hotel. Neither thought they could go back to sleep so they retired to their respective rooms to clean up and dress for the long day ahead of them.

A half hour later Grady tapped on Fortune's door. "Ready for breakfast, darlin'?" he asked, entering her room.

Sitting on the edge of her bed, Fortune tucked a hairpin into the neat chignon at her nape. "I don't know, Grady. I really don't think I could eat anything. Perhaps I'll just go downstairs with you for a cup of coffee." She stood, tucked her hairbrush into her valise and smoothed the old green calico she'd donned to work in.

"You should eat something, Fortune. We've got a long hard day ahead of us at the warehouse."

"You aren't going to the mercantile today?" she asked.

"They'll get along fine without me today. And I'm sure John can use an extra pair of hands to clean up the mess made by the fire."

Fortune nodded. "I'll have to take an inventory to determine what was taken," she responded perfunctorily as she threw the blankets up over the bed.

Grady watched her move about the room like a busy little mouse. He reached out for her arm when she passed by for the third time and turned her to face him. "Fortune, what's wrong? I mean, besides the obvious."

Fortune gazed up at him through watery eyes and moved into his arms. "Everything is wrong." she said. His old blue plaid work shirt was soft from many washings, and the warmth emanating from his broad chest was inviting. She laid her cheek there and circled his neck with her arms. "I don't know what to do any more, Grady. If this keeps up, there may not be a Landry Freighting for Roc to return to. How do I deal with a man who won't tell me who he is or why he wants revenge?"

Grady's arms enfolded her. "You're shaking like a leaf, darlin'," he said against her hair. "Don't you know I'll take care of you, that I'd never let anything happen to you?" His husky Gaelic burr was pronounced by his obvious love and concern.

Fortune nodded against his chest. In the shelter of this big man's arms, she felt very small and vulnerable, yet very safe. "I'm scared, Grady. Not so much for myself, but for others that may come to harm because of me. One of John's guards could very well have been shot." She tilted her head back and gazed up into his blue eyes. "I'm especially worried about you."

Grady smiled and shook his head. "I've the luck of my Irish mother, remember? I survived the war, survived prison, survived savages who coveted this yellow hair of mine. I've got plans for the future, and you're a very big part of them. I'll let nothing interfere with those plans. Do you hear me? Nothing." He chucked her under the chin and grinned. "Now buck up, darlin'."

Fortune smiled sadly. "My magic seems to have deserted me lately. What if your Irish luck runs out, too?"

"It can't. Irish luck runs in the blood, love. Since I've not developed any leaks lately, I reckon I'm plumb chock-full of luck."

Fortune smiled, heartened by his teasing.

"Now," he said, "are you ready to tackle the warehouse and show our enemy that he can't get a good man or woman down?"

Fortune nodded. Then feeling the hot throb of his arousal through her clothes, she grinned. "I know of another good man that can't be kept down." Her hand slid down his body to find the hard ridge of flesh beneath his clothing.

Grady groaned and lifted her hand from his britches to his lips. "Any more of that, and we'll never get out of here today. Come on, minx," he said adjusting his britches. "We've got work to do."

Roc Landry rode alongside his 17-wagon freight train. Not a mile behind him was a smaller competing outfit of at least 13 wagons. As the wagons snaked over mountain trails and through green valleys, they churned up a cloud of dust that could been seen from miles away. The dust settled on the sweaty skins of drivers and the few guards on horseback. Well used to the harsh life on the road, the crusty mule skinners took little notice of a little dirt.

From beneath his dusty, black shirt, Roc retrieved the amber amulet he'd found in his saddlebags the first night on the trail. He'd immediately recognized it as Fortune's talisman and knew that for her to have parted with it she had to have been truly upset. He frowned, remembering how shaken she'd been after that horrible nightmare. He fingered the thing absently, wishing it really did have powers of good luck. Heaven knew he could have used a little on this trip! It had been nothing but one mishap after another.

Slim Pittman, his trail boss, trotted his horse alongside Roc's. "Well, it's been one hell of a trip, hey, boss?" He chuckled, surveying the northern horizon through eyes narrowed against the sun.

The amulet forgotten, Roc glanced over at his trail boss with a wry grin. "I was just thinking the same thing, Slim. We've never had equipment go bad like we have on this trip. Hell, I checked all the wagons myself before we left Helena. Yet we still had two axles break and two wagon wheels crack. And one of those axles was brand new!"

"Don't forget them three mules that just up and disappeared," Slim added. "And each one was part of a different span. It's dang hard to pair up the remaining mule of each span to an unfamiliar partner. All these accidents kinda makes a body get suspicious like, don't it?"

"Sure does. Especially now that I know what's been going on in Helena since we left. Hell, first Fortune sends those men to tell me my warehouse burned down; then I arrive in Salt Lake City to a telegram that says my mules have been poisoned."

"Sounds to me like somebody's tryin' to put you out of business, Roc."

"That's what I've been thinking, Slim." Though he didn't voice it aloud, Roc wondered if the Reb had somehow discovered his and Fortune's secret. It would certainly explain this sudden run of bad luck his company was having. But wouldn't the Reb have waited until the new mercantile was well-established before seeking revenge? Maybe not. A man seeking revenge was operating on emotion, not good sense.

And if the Reb was behind the sabotage, then Fortune could be in danger. For about the tenth time since leaving Salt Lake City, he wondered if he should ride ahead of the freight train and make sure she was all right. The girl put entirely too much faith in her good luck charms and magic.

Slim interrupted Roc's thoughts. "Could be we got a couple skunks amongst the men. There's four new fellers that signed up this trip."

"Yeah," Roc returned musingly, "there's Dan Townsand, Big Ears Johnson, Frank Mundy and Eli . . ."

"Eli Holms," Slim supplied.

"I think you and I better keep a close eye on those four," Roc suggested. "I got a gut feeling we haven't seen the end of our troubles yet."

"I thought your sister might be jumpin' to conclusions when she sent those extra men to help guard the wagons, but I gotta tell yuh, Roc, I'm damn glad she did."

"Yeah, me too, old friend, me too."

*   *   *

"Pssst! Frank, you awake?"

"Keep it down, Eli, or somebody'll hear yuh," Frank replied, rolling over in his bedroll to face his partner.

"How we gonna fix a wagon to break down tomorrow?" Eli asked. "Landry has extra guards stationed tonight. And if we start tappin' skulls he's gonna hear about it in the mornin' and be lookin' for trouble."

Frank chuckled low. "Remember cook saying somethin' about having a small bottle of laudanum in that little medicine bag of his?"

"Yeah, what of it?"

"Well, when he was out takin' a piss this afternoon, I sneaked into the chuck wagon and stole it. While ago, I got myself a cup a coffee, then poured some of the laudanum into the pot."

"Did all the guards have some?" Eli asked.

"Can't say for sure, but, hell, everybody has a cup to help keep 'em awake when they got guard duty."

"What we waitin' for, Frank? Let's get this job done so we can get back and get some sleep before mornin'."

The sun was straight overhead when the Landry freight train started to wind uphill through the pass at Blood Rock. Roc rode point, and Slim rode flank along with a couple of the men Fortune had sent to help guard the wagons. The first few wagons were already through the pass when a loud crash and the curses of mule skinners shattered the calm. Roc galloped back from his forward position to see what the hullabaloo was about.

What he found made him roar with fury. The back left corner of one of the wagons rested on the ground, and its 200 pound wheel was rolling down the incline of the road at an escalating speed.

Slim rode up and gave a loud whistle of astonishment. "Well, if that don't beat all," he said rubbing at a stubbly chin. "Cotter pin musta worn through."

The air was sulfuric with foul language as the driver who had crawled under the wagon to check the damage rose to stand next to Roc. "The guldanged cotter pin didn't wear through. It was loosened so as how the wheel wouldn't come off till we hit a good incline like this one."

"Well, that cinches it. It was done apurpose," Slim declared.

Roc slapped his hat against his thigh in disgust. "We can fix the damn thing, but we'll be laid up for a—"

Gunfire rang out and zinged off the surrounding rocks. "Dry gulchers! Take cover!" Roc shouted.

Drivers leaped from their lofty perches atop the wagon seats and dove under and behind their wagons. Curses fouled the air as the mule skinners found their guns and returned fire. Roc yelled, ordering them to conserve their ammunition as the dry gulchers had the advantage of being on the boulder-strewn ground high above the pass.

The big Gypsy turned to Slim who was hunkered down next to him. "Cover me the best you can, Slim. I got a feeling those boys up there let us get a few of the wagons through the pass for a reason." Slim nodded, and Roc started to creep alongside the wagons toward the front. He made it as far as the sixth wagon back when five men, guns blazing, galloped down the trail toward the wagons.

The bandits above the freight train peppered the trapped mule skinners while their cohorts leaped from their steeds onto the seats of the wagons already through the pass. Two burly drivers tried to prevent the theft of their wagons, but both were immediately killed and booted to the ground.

Roc managed to get a shot off at the bandit that leaped into the fifth wagon. The man pitched off the wagon seat before he could set it in motion. Roc fumed in helpless outrage as the other four wagons disappeared down the road. The bandits in the rocks kept the freighters pinned down for another two hours.

"How long you reckon they'll keep this up," Slim asked, slipping up behind Roc.

"I don't know, but their gunfire seems to be letting up some. They were probably told to keep us pinned down long enough to give the wagons a good head start."

A few minutes later the gunfire stopped completely. The men waited for a while to make sure it was safe to come out from cover. Gradually they ventured forth, and Roc hurried to check on his two drivers. Unfortunately, there was nothing that could be done for them. Cursing, Roc stomped over to the bandit that he'd shot off the seat of the fifth wagon. Using his boot toe, he nudged the man over on his back.

"You recognize him, boss?" Slim asked.

"No, afraid not."

"Hey, Mr. Landry," another driver called running up the line of wagons. "Frank and Eli aren't with their wagons. Are they up there with you?"

"Maybe they was shot," Slim suggested.

Roc's eyes narrowed as he scanned the wagons and the surrounding rocky terrain. "Remember what we were talking about yesterday, Slim?"

"You think Frank and Eli sneaked off with them other coyotes?"

A driver named Dooly sauntered up then and, hearing Slim's reply, added, "When we stopped the train to check the breakdown, Eli jumped down from his wagon. Said he was gonna water the bushes. Frank said he might as well do the same. Then the shootin' started and that's the last I saw of 'em."

"I reckon that answers our question." Roc's voice crackled with anger. He turned abruptly to the congregating drivers and rapped out orders. "Two of you men start digging graves for George and James. Jenkins, Dooly, get that wagon jacked up. Couple of you men go find that damn wheel. Slim, you stay here with the train and get it on the road again as soon as possible." Roc glanced at three of the five men his sister had sent to him. "Watson, you and Fuzzy drive George and James's wagons. You other three come with me. We're going to track down those wagons."

Roc took Slim aside then. "I'm going to try to get our wagons back, Slim. Since my mules are wearing the Landry brand and the wagons bear my name, they're gonna have to stop somewhere along the way and make some changes before they risk driving them into a town where my outfit is well-known.

"I probably won't see you till after you've arrived at Helena. Even if the warehouse is finished, go straight to the ranch. The men can rest up a bit, and the wagons will be safer. As soon as I return, we'll head on up to the Fort Benton warehouse."

"Be careful, Roc," Slim warned. "Them no-goods is probably expectin' you to follow 'em."

Roc gave his friend a slap on the shoulder. "Don't worry about me, Slim. Just get this train to Helena safely."

Differentiating his own wagons' trail from those of so many others that traveled the freight road was next to impossible. But because of the large amount of stock he owned, Roc employed his own blacksmith, and he easily recognized the blacksmith's mark on the shoes of his stock. Still, tracking took time and the thieves already had a good head start.

Roc lost the trail once and had to backtrack. When he found it, he realized the bandits had left the main freight road and turned west toward Bannack. He wasn't too surprised. The mining in Bannack had dwindled after '65, and the town was no longer the center of activity it once was. Also its merchants were on the hungry side these days and didn't ask too many questions as long as they were able to make a dollar or two. Now that he knew their destination, Roc and his men urged their horses into a gallop and headed for the small mining town. It was near sunset when they skirted Yankee Flat on the south side of Bannack. To the north, a snowcapped Mount Baldy stood guard over the rolling green hills around Bannock. But Roc and his men were too weary to notice the beautiful, scenic surroundings.

The town livery was located behind Skinner's Saloon, and it was there that Roc stopped first. From the owner, he learned that a man had brought in five teams of horses two days ago. And just that afternoon, four wagons had been driven to the livery. There the mules had been quickly exchanged for the horses. The man who bought the mules had paid the fake mule skinners the difference in price between the cheaper horses and the more expensive mules. Then he took the mules and immediately left town, heading west.

The livery owner told Roc that he heard one of the wagon drivers say something about heading for Virginia City.

Roc now had two choices. He could try to track his mules, or he could take the chance on locating his wagons in Virginia City. He chose to do both.

He and his men put up at the Mead Hotel that night, but the next morning two of his men headed west. Roc and the other man rode east toward Virginia City in hopes of recovering the valuable freight.

Chapter Twenty-four

Dressed in a simple brown skirt and white shirtwaist with a faded blue scarf tied over her hair, Fortune stood in the storeroom of the new mercantile, cleaning sawdust from the many shelves that lined the walls and formed three isles across the large room. The whole place smelled of newly cut wood and fresh paint.

Two weeks had gone by since the Fort Benton warehouse had been robbed, and not a trace of the stolen merchandise had been found. John told Fortune that their chances of locating the stolen property weren't good. Benton was full of freighters and their wagons were parked all over town. She could walk by the very wagon containing the Landry merchandise and not know it.

There were, however, some disgruntled merchants in town whose merchandise had been taken in the robbery. A few went so far as to accuse the Landrys of arranging the fire and theft so that the new Landry, MacNair Mercantile would have an advantage over its competitors.

The last thing Fortune needed on top of her other problems was to have the town of Fort Benton boycotting the new mercantile and Landry freighting. Grady suggested a way she might rectify their opinions, and she'd immediately set about doing just that.

Calling the merchants together for a meeting at the warehouse, she assured them that Landry Freighting would reimburse them for their losses. And to prove her goodwill, she offered to freight their next order of merchandise at a reduced charge. Her gesture had been well-received, and confidence in Landry Freighting had been restored.

Her one consolation in the midst of all this havoc was that there had been no more mysterious missives nor any more frightening incidents. She knew she'd not heard the last from the mysterious avenger, but she was glad for the reprieve, however temporary it might be.

"Fortune?" Grady called from the front of the store.

She set her cleaning rag aside and peeked around the end isle. "Right here, Grady."

He followed the sound of her voice and came down the isle of shelves, a hammer dangling from one hand and a big grin on his face. "Angus and a hired hand just arrived out front," he announced. "They're bringing the wagon round back so we can unload the supplies."

"Oh, Grady, that's wonderful. We'll soon be open for business."

He nodded and did a quick survey of her. "Hot damn, darlin', you do look good today."

Fortune rolled her eyes. Though she and Grady could hardly keep their hands off one another, the past two nights they'd been too tired to do anything except sleep. This morning, however, she'd recognized a randy glint in his eye, and it had remained there all day. "Grady MacNair, your eyes must be going bad. I'm wearing my oldest clothes, my hair is straggly, and I'm covered with dust."

"And you're not wearing a thing under that shirt," he said huskily. Laying one hand over her breast, he squeezed gently as if to prove his statement.

"It's . . . it's too hot for so many clothes," she said, desire glowing in her eyes.

"I'm glad. And I don't mind the dirt on you either. At least I don't have to worry 'bout getting you mussed when I toss you down back here and have my way with you."

"Aren't you forgetting something?"

"What's that, honey girl?" The dimple in his chin deepened with his smile, as he lowered his head to steal a kiss.

"Angus? The supplies? You've been anxious for them to arrive all week."

"Aw, hell."

"Come on, Reb," she said, taking his philandering hand and tugging him along to the back door.

Reluctantly opening the door, Grady ushered Fortune outside and hailed Angus McPheany. He curled an arm about her waist and pulled her close while they waited for Angus and his companion to set the wagon brake and climb down.

The gangly young clerk took Grady's proffered hand and shook it heartily. He then introduced Robert Bradford, the young, robust freighter, who had accompanied him.

"How was the trip, Angus? Any problems?" Grady asked.

"Nope, none at all. I was glad I had Rob with me though. I'm not much of a hand with them stubborn mules."

"Why don't you boys go wet your whistles and have a bite to eat across the street," Grady suggested. "When you get back, you can help me finish unloading the wagon and fill me in on what's been going on in Helena."

Fortune was anxious for news from Granny and Irene, but she held her tongue. The two men had been on the road with the heavy wagon for better than a week, and they did look tired and hungry. As they hurried off, Grady was already untying the canvas that protected the goods from dust and weather.

While he hauled in crates and bulky parcels, she opened them and wrote down each item on prepared inventory sheets, then put them on designated shelves.

Tomorrow she'd help Grady stock the front of the store, and when Roc arrived with the rest of the order, the tedious process would start all over again. But not all the merchandise would immediately go into the store. Much of it was stock that would serve to replenish the store all winter long.

Angus and the freighter were back within the hour, and the unloading of the wagon progressed faster than Fortune could unwrap and inventory. When the wagon was empty, Grady sent the two men off to find a hotel room while he helped her finish with the inventory.

She was writing down the last item when Grady came up

behind her, relieved her of paper and pencil and folded her into his arms. "We make a good team, don't we, darlin'?"

She smiled into his devilish blue eyes. "Yes, but why do I get the feeling you have something else on your mind, Grady MacNair?"

His answering laugh was low and husky as he centered her within his wide-legged stance. One hand around her waist, he used the other to cup her head and snuggle her closer. "You smell so good, Fortune, darlin'." He nuzzled the soft hair at her temple.

"I think you're just feeling frisky, my dear. I'm not wearing my perfume, and I'm covered with sawdust. I can't possibly smell good."

"You smell damn good to me, lady. It's your own womanly scent I'm speaking of."

As his lips teased one small ear, his warm breath sent thrilling little goose bumps down her neck. Fortune shivered. "And you find that scent appealing?"

"Yeah, I do." He pulled the scarf off her head. One hand slid down to cup her buttock and press her against his arousal. "Let's hold a private christening of the new store, shall we, darlin'?"

Fortune pushed back slightly so that she could see his face. "Are you suggesting that we . . . here, in the store?" she asked, incredulous.

He grinned wickedly and cocked a challenging brow.

Suddenly, the daring Gypsy emerged in blatant abandon. The risk of making love in such an unlikely place evoked a sense of the erotically forbidden, and she realized she was already wet with anticipation. Her sultry gaze answered his challenge.

With a feral growl, Grady scooped her into his arms and carried her to the back door. He set her down, pressed her against the door with his body and captured her lips in an earth-shattering kiss.

With a terrible fire in his loins, he stripped off her shirtwaist, carelessly tossing it on a pile of yard goods. He took each of her breasts in his hands and again claimed her mouth. As his tongue dueled with hers, his fingers teased her nipples into hard little pebbles of sensitivity. In a fever of lust, his tongue and lips licked and sucked until her pearly globes were shiny and wet with his loving.

Holding his head to her breasts, the wild Gypsy thrilled to the magic performed by his swirling tongue. She cried out and pressed her hips against his erection. Her knees went weak, and she grabbed his shoulders for support. "Grady, I need you, but how . . . ?"

His breathing erratic with excitement, he rasped, "Trust me, baby." He gave her no time to guess his intentions. Bunching her skirt up between their bodies, his knowing fingers found her dark triangle of curls through the slit in her pantalets. And as his thumb pleasured the kernel hidden in her moist folds, his tongue did the same for her nipples.

Fortune's head twisted from side to side as Grady worked her into a wild frenzy of need. Never had she lusted for him so strongly. Just when she thought she might explode, he withdrew. She cried out, and he hurriedly unbuttoned his britches and released himself.

Her hand immediately wrapped around his hard throbbing shaft. "Grady," she whispered, "please, I want you inside of me."

Grady levered her shoulders flat against the door, grasped her buttocks and glided into her slick heat. Fortune took him into her to the hilt and cried out in instantaneous climax.

Grady watched her face as she gave herself up to the pleasure and was quickly drawn into the same vortex. He pounded into her, faster and faster. Her nails dug through his shirt, her head writhed. Grady threw his head back, his cry of triumph joining hers as he sunk himself deep and washed her with his seed.

For a moment, he held her there, their bodies still joined. Then he slowly let her down to her feet. Fortune would have collapsed but for his arms circling her waist. When she lifted an incredulous gaze to his, he placed a tender kiss on her swollen lips. "Forgive me, darlin'. I didn't mean to be quite so . . ."

"Wild? Abandoned? Decadent?" she offered dreamily. "It *was* quite a christening, wasn't it? You may think I'm a loose woman for saying so, but I loved every minute of it." She reached out for her shirtwaist as he handed it to her.

"A loose woman." He chuckled, stepping back to adjust the britches he'd never gotten around to removing. "Honey girl, you're every man's dream." He crushed her to him. "There's nothing to be embarrassed about between two people who love each other, Fortune." He was quiet for a moment. Then taking her shoulders he set her away, looked down into her exotic green eyes and added, "Nor should there be any secrets between us. Marry me. Tell me what's troubling you, and I'll make it right. We love each other too much to let anything come between us."

A tear trailed down Fortune's cheek. "Grady, please understand. I can't marry you. You say you love me, but if you knew . . ."

"Damn it, Fortune!" He gave her a shake. "If I knew what?"

She shook her head and lowered her eyes, unable to bear the sight of the anger and hurt in his relentless gaze. She heard his deep sigh of exasperation, then to her surprise, he gently pulled her into his arms again. "All right," he said, taking a deep breath, as if to control his emotions. "I'll not push you now. But when we get back to Helena, I want some answers, lady. Deal?"

Fortune smiled up at him and nodded. "Grady, I love you so. You're the gentlest, the most patient, the most . . . most . . ."

"The most handsome, smartest?" he suggested with a smile of reconciliation.

"Yes, that and more." She threw her arms around his neck and pulled him down for a kiss that told him, like no words could, how much she loved him.

Anxious for news from home, Fortune asked Grady to invite Angus and Robert Bradford to dinner in the hotel restaurant that night. During the meal the clerk seemed a little nervous, but she mentally waved it off. After all, Grady had just asked the young man to take over the temporary management of the Benton store. He was naturally flustered and anxious to show his boss that his trust was well-placed.

"How is Irene?" Fortune asked. "She isn't working too hard, is she?"

"No, ma'am," Angus replied. He faced Grady then and said, "I hope you don't mind, Grady, but I hired young Book to help me make deliveries and help load customers' wagons. With you and Miss Fortune gone, I was having a hard time keeping up with everything. The boy works hard, and his ma says the work has helped to keep him out of trouble."

Grady leaned back in his chair and smiled. "It's a great idea, Angus. I'm sorry I didn't think of it myself."

Angus looked visibly relieved. Then Robert elbowed him in the ribs and jerked his head at Fortune, indicating there was something more to be revealed.

"Is something wrong, Angus?" Fortune asked, frowning. "My grandmother and Ursula are all right, aren't they?" Angus swallowed and looked away, alarming Fortune even more.

"Spit it out, Angus," Grady urged. "Can't you see you're upsetting her?"

Angus's freckles stood out starkly against a face sudden gone pale. "I . . . I'm sorry, ma'am. Mrs. Fontaine and Miss Price are doin' fine. But it's about your dog, ma'am."

"Grumpy?" Fortune exclaimed, exhaling a sigh of relief that Granny and Ursula were all right.

The clerk lowered his eyes to the white linen tablecloth. "I'm sorry, ma'am, but you see somebody shot him just a few days after you left town."

Grady watched in alarm as Fortune's face drained of color, and her hand flew to her mouth to suppress a cry. His arm went around her shoulders, and she turned her head unabashedly into his shoulder.

Angus glanced at Grady, his expression commiserating. "Perhaps we should go now," he said softly. "Come on, Rob."

"No, wait!" The raven-haired young women glanced up at him, her pretty green eyes misted with tears. "Do you know who killed him?"

"Not really, ma'am. Irene and her children were returning home from the mercantile when it happened. Grumpy was with them, runnin' alongside the carriage." Angus shook his head in wonderment. "You see, the dog never let them out of his sight after you left town. It was real strange the way he guarded that little family. Anyway, someone stepped out from the trees across the street and shot him. At first Irene thought someone was shootin' at 'er and the kids, and they ducked low. She thought she saw a red-haired man runnin' away, but all she could think about at the time was protectin' 'er kids. By the time she realized that they weren't in danger, the killer was long gone. I'm real sorry, Miss Fortune. I know you loved that dog."

Fortune's breath caught on a heart-wrenching sob. "Thanks for telling me, Angus," she said barely above a whisper. "I know it's not pleasant to be the bearer of bad news. Thank

heaven, though, Irene and the children were unharmed. I never
could have forgiven myself if they had been hurt."

When she turned her head into Grady's shoulder once again,
the young clerk and his companion took their leave. Grady left
money on the table and guided Fortune upstairs to their rooms.
The key he pulled out of his pocket was his own so he let
them into his room and urged Fortune down on his bed. She
immediately curled into a tight ball and gave into her grief.

"I know Grumpy was just a dog," she sobbed, "but I loved
him so much."

"And he loved you, darlin'," Grady assured her, brushing
damp tendrils from her cheeks. Not knowing what else to do
or say, Grady sat down on the side of the bed and slipped her
shoes off. Then he kicked his boots off, crawled into bed next
to her and wrapped himself around her quaking body. With
soft murmurs of comfort, he held her until she fell into an
exhausted sleep.

Carefully, so as not to disturb her, Grady left the bed. As
he did every night, whether they shared her room or his, he
checked the door to make sure it was locked. Finding his own
secure, he entered Fortune's room. As he stepped to the door
and rattled the lock, his foot slipped on something on the floor.
He bent and lifted a folded sheet of paper. Taking it with him
to his room, he read it next to the dimly lit lantern.

U kilt Bull but he got yore dog first.

Grady cursed under his breath, but he was glad that he'd
been the one find the note rather than Fortune. He glanced at
the tear-stained face on the bed across the room. The last thing
the girl needed was to be reminded of the madman responsible
for her pet's death. He pivoted round, locating his saddlebags
in a dark corner. Lifting the flap on one of the deep pockets,
he shoved the missive to the bottom, intending to tell her
about it after she'd had time to recover from this evening's
emotional blow.

Chapter Twenty-five

Roc Landry finally arrived in Fort Benton a week later. Though late, he was all in one piece, and that was all that mattered to Fortune. The minute he dismounted from his horse in front of the mercantile, she threw herself into his arms, nearly bowling him over. "Oh, Roc, I was so worried for you. Are you all right? Everything went well? I have so much to tell you."

"Slow down there." Roc laughed, hugging her tight to his bearlike frame. He signaled to the men waiting in two wagons in the middle of the street. "Take them on around back, boys."

Grady came forward, offering his hand to Roc. "Glad to see you made it, partner."

Roc looked taken aback by the Reb's obvious friendliness, but he rapidly recovered and took the man's hand in a hearty shake.

"Come on inside," Grady invited. "The store doesn't look like much yet, but now that you're here with the rest of our order, we'll be in business in no time."

Slinging his arm around Fortune's shoulders, Roc grinned. "Lead the way, Sister Mine."

At Roc's familiar name for her, Fortune beamed up at her brother's handsome face, thankful that her amulet had protected him well. She couldn't resist giving him another quick hug as they entered the new store.

Inside, she and Grady proudly showed off all their hard work. "As soon as we get the shipment you brought inventoried, we'll be able to fill up the rest of these counters and shelves and open up for business." Fortune pointed out excitedly.

Roc ran a finger over a shiny new cash register. "Very nice," he said. "This place should turn quite a tidy profit."

Fortune took her brother's free hand, anxiously dragging him along to the storeroom. Her grin widened with pride when he gave a low whistle of appreciation. As the freighters and Angus bustled in and out with crates, she briefly explained John Adair's inventory system and how she'd customized it for the mercantile. "I plan to use John's system at the Helena warehouse, too," she added. "By the way, how is the new warehouse coming along?"

"It's finished," Roc replied. "I was able to store part of the merchandise I brought from Salt Lake City there."

"Is there a problem, Angus?" Grady asked as his clerk approached hesitantly.

"Beggin' your pardon, but, yes, there is. I could be wrong; there's still a lot of unloadin' to be done, but it looks to me like some of your order is missin'."

Roc cleared his throat, drawing their attention. He tipped his hat back on his dark head with a swarthy hand. "McPheany's got the right of it, MacNair. My freight wagons were attacked at Blood Rock on the return trip. The varmints got away with four wagonloads of freight. Slim took a quick inventory during our stopover in Helena, and I'm afraid half of what was in one of those wagons was part of your order." He glanced down at the small feminine hand that had suddenly gripped his arm, and he lifted his gaze to his sister's worried countenance.

"Was anybody hurt, Roc?" she asked.

He started to speak, then halted. "We better go someplace where the three of us can talk without being overheard."

"Roc," Fortune interjected, "perhaps we should send for John Adair. There's been trouble here in Benton, too."

Roc nodded solemnly. "John said there was news when I left a few wagons there earlier, but he said he'd wait till we could talk privately. I reckon he might as well get in on this powwow so we don't have to waste time repeating ourselves."

"Why don't we all head over to the warehouse office?" Grady suggested. "John's office should be private enough." At Roc's nod, the Reb turned back to Angus and issued a few last instructions.

As they walked the short distance to the warehouse, Roc put his arm around Fortune. "I heard about Grumpy from Irene," he said. "I'm sorry, honey. I know you loved that ol' dog. Hell, I even had a soft spot for him."

"We're fairly sure Grumpy was shot by the man who attacked me behind the church," she replied sadly. "Irene did fill you in on what happened, didn't she?"

"Yes, but I'd like to hear all about it from you, in case she left anything out."

Fortune nodded. "I think our meeting at the warehouse will be a long one. We need to piece together everything that's happened to both of us since you left Helena."

At the warehouse Roc disclosed all that happened on the way to and from Salt Lake City. "And did your men find your mules, Roc?" Fortune asked.

"No. Apparently the man who bought them sold them off to individual miners who took off for God knows where. I found my wagons in Virginia City, but they were empty, and nobody seemed to have any information about the men who drove them into town."

"I suppose this means we'll have more angry merchants on our hands," Fortune sighed. "I had quite a time pacifying the ones whose goods were stolen out of this warehouse. Thank heaven, the Helena warehouse was practically empty when it was burned down."

"You'd have been real proud of your sister, Roc," John interjected. "She's a fine little diplomat."

"I can't take all the credit," she objected. "It was Grady's idea."

"But it was your diplomacy that made it work, Fortune," Grady put in.

Roc's brows knit in a grim expression. "Well, we can't last long, if this sort of thing keeps up. It's getting damn expensive. You've not received any more of those letters from the culprit?"

"None," Fortune replied. "Everything's been quiet now for three weeks."

"Maybe that red-haired bastard that Hank killed was the real culprit all along," Roc mused, leaning his chair back on its hind legs. "He could have lied about working for someone else."

Fortune wondered at the odd way her brother was looking at Grady. She waved it off and responded to his comment. "I don't think we've heard the last of this, Roc." She knew she had to tell her brother about the rest of what the red-haired man had said, but she didn't dare say a word in front of Grady.

Grady sat on the opposite side of the room, thinking about the note he'd found a week ago in Fortune's room. The note proved the Landrys' problems hadn't died with the red-haired bandit, but he couldn't bring himself to reveal its existence. Fortune's painful loss of her pet was still too fresh in her mind, and the poor girl had just begun to relax a little. If he could, he'd get Roc alone and turn the missive over to him. He pulled his watch fob out of his pocket and flipped the lid to check the time. "It's getting la—"

Roc's chair hit the floor abruptly. "Where did you get that?" he demanded, pointing an accusing finger at the bracelet attached to Grady's watch.

Great crystal ball and tea leaves! Fortune had never told her brother that she'd lost one of Granny's bracelets that night in the Virginia countryside. Nor had she thought to mention that Grady had found and kept it. *Sweet Gaia, don't let Roc give us away! Not yet!*

"This thing?" Grady asked, obviously bewildered by Roc's belligerent tone.

Seeming to come to his senses, Roc sighed and stared down at his toes as if ashamed of himself. Then he did a very Gypsy thing. He lied to the Gajo. "I'm sorry, Grady. I didn't mean to jump on you like that. You see, ah . . . I bought a special girl a bracelet much like that one during the war. As things turned out, she jilted me for one of you Rebs." He chuckled self-consciously. "With you being a Reb, I guess it just struck me as strange there for a minute."

Grady's grin was cynical. "I doubt it's the same bracelet. I got this off a little Gypsy whore during the war. The traitorous little bitch lost it after she and the rest of her lot tricked my men and myself into getting captured. I found it tangled in my leg shackles the next morning." He chuckled mirthlessly. "I kept myself sane all those days in prison by devising ways I might punish her if I was ever lucky enough to get the opportunity."

Fortune suddenly felt sick inside. She weaved unsteadily and grabbed the back of her brother's chair.

All three men jumped up and made a grab for her.

"No, please." She stayed them with an upraised hand, "I'm all right."

"She's been jumpy as heck," Grady commented. "She hasn't been sleeping well either."

Fortune grimaced at Grady's careless disclosure of his knowledge of her sleeping habits. And seeing Roc's burgeoning fury, she did a very uncharacteristic thing. She fainted.

Fortune woke to find herself back in her hotel room. The glare of the setting sun told her she'd slept for several hours. As she rose from her bed, she was startled by a snore in the corner of her room. Reaching under her pillow for the small handgun she'd recently purchased, she stood and slowly turned up the wick of the lantern on the bedside table.

She exhaled an audible sigh of relief. There in the corner of her room, her brother was curled up on his bedroll, sound asleep. Tucking the gun back under the pillow, she went to him and gently nudged his shoulder. "Roc, wake up. It's late. You should get something to eat."

"Son-of-a-bitch!" His hand suddenly flashed out, grabbed her wrist in a painful grip and jerked her off her feet. With a loud shriek, she landed up against the wall behind him.

As her brother sat shaking his head groggily, Fortune struggled to a sitting position and rubbed her bruised wrist. "Looks like I'm not the only one that's been nervous lately," she muttered.

Plowing a hand through his thick black hair, Roc stared at his sister, befuddled. "Sorry, Sis, I'm dead tired, and I've been on the alert for trouble for so long, it's becoming habit."

"It's okay. Sorry I startled you." She stood up, noticing how wrinkled her clothes were from sleeping in them. Remembering the circumstances that caused her to be in bed at this time day, she sent out a cautious probe. "I take it I fainted in the office."

"Yeah," Roc said, getting to his feet. "How are you feeling?"

"Fine. A little embarrassed though." She nonchalantly set about finding her hairbrush, then sat down on the edge of her bed to groom her hair.

"And in case you're wondering," Roc said studying her carefully, "Grady explained his statement about your sleeping habits."

Fortune's face flooded with color.

"He said," Roc continued, "that what with his room next to yours, and the walls being paper thin, he heard you up nights."

"Yes, I suppose he did hear me. Roc," she rushed on, anxious to leave the subject, "I'm sorry you found out about the bracelet that way you did. I guess I forgot to mention it to you." She paused and winked. "That was some mighty fast thinking, coming up with that tale of a girlfriend the way you did. But actually, I'm glad we have this time alone. There's a few details I need to fill you in on, things that I couldn't mention in front of Grady."

"Like what?" he asked curiously. He sat down on the foot of the bed and watched her stroke the brush through her long hair.

"The day I was attacked behind the church. The man did say his boss wanted you and I to suffer before he killed us, but I left out the reason why. He also said he wanted us to suffer like he did back in '64."

Roc jumped off the bed at that. "My God, Fortune, that's more than a little detail you left out!"

She turned a disgusted look on him. "I know, but I couldn't very well blurt it out with Grady present, could I? He'd ask questions and figure out who we are."

Seeming to calm down, Roc leaned against the wall, holding his chin thoughtfully. "This bit of news certainly corroborates with a piece of information I was able to pick up in Helena. But before I get into that, tell me, how much longer will it take to get the mercantile open and operating?"

"Only a few days, now that you've arrived."

"You think you can be ready to leave for home by Monday?"

"I suppose so."

"Good. I think you and I should get back to Helena as soon as possible. I have a feeling our enemy will show his hand very soon now."

"But what about Grady?"

"What about him?" Roc arched a quizzical brow.

"Well, I just thought . . . that is . . ." Fortune glanced away from her brother on the pretense of reaching for a hair ribbon. "You know about the Moondance, Roc. Well, things being the way they have been, I needed someone to . . . well, you know. I needed someone whose shoulder I could cry on. And . . ."

"And you're in love with MacNair," Roc filled in.

Her head jerked up in surprise. "You talked to Eric, then?"

"Did you think that I wouldn't?" he asked enigmatically.

"I suppose I should have expected it. Are you angry?"

"I should be," he said sternly. Then sitting down next to her, he wrapped his arm about her shoulders and exhaled a deep sigh. "But mainly I'm just concerned. Fortune, I can't say as I've ever been deeply in love, but I'm not a fool. I know it's something no one has any control over. That's not to say I'm happy about this situation between you and the Reb. I'm just saying, I understand how it could happen."

"Thanks for that, at least." Emotions that she hadn't dared to let Grady see welled up inside Fortune, and she buried her face against her brother's chest. "Oh, Roc, what am I going to do? I love him terribly, but I can't marry him with this secret hanging over our heads."

Roc gazed down at her, as if debating the advisability of voicing his thoughts. "Fortune," he finally said, "I discovered a little detail I couldn't reveal in the office this afternoon in front of MacNair. Remember I mentioned the two men that hired on in Helena, the ones responsible for all the accidents we had on the trip?" At her nod, he continued. "As I said, they disappeared after the raid at Blood Rock. When I got back to Helena I started asking around to find out if anybody in town knew anything about this Frank Mundy and Eli Holms."

"And?"

"A few weeks before your arrival from back east, Eli Holms was working for Grady MacNair. Supposedly, the Reb fired the man soon after hiring him."

"Supposedly? Roc you can't be implying that . . . No, I don't believe it! He wasn't the man in my dream. I know he wasn't."

Roc took her by the shoulders and forced her to look at him. "Contrary to what you may think, I don't *want* to believe that MacNair is the one responsible for what's been happening.

Christ, we're talking about the man my sister is in love with, but, Fortune, who else could it be?"

"Not Grady! I know it's not him." She twisted out of his hold to pace the room. "He loves me. I know he does. If he wanted me dead, he had the perfect opportunity on the trip up here from Helena."

"You said yourself that the man wants us to suffer for what happened to him during the war. You seduced his men into getting themselves captured. Maybe, in his sick mind, seducing you and then revealing that he's the one that wants you dead is the perfect revenge. You heard what he said in John's office. And I saw the way you reacted. He struck a nerve."

Fortune stopped pacing and stared into the recesses of her mind. Could it be true? Everything Roc said made perfect sense. Was she a fool not to believe such condemning evidence?

She pivoted round on Roc. "No, it's not Grady. My magic may not have served me well of late, but my dreams have ever been true."

"Damn it, Fortune!" Roc jumped up and would have grabbed her shoulders again, but she sidestepped him. Knotting his fists at his sides, he reasoned, "Your dream wasn't entirely true, little Gypsy. You thought I was shot, remember? Well, as you can see, I haven't so much as a nick."

"Destiny can be altered," she argued. "I'll wager you were wearing the amulet I gave you. Yes, I see in your eyes that you were."

"And the cabin in your dream? What of that?" he persisted.

"Yet to come," she answered.

"Of all the mule-headed, stubborn . . ." He halted his tirade with a sigh of exasperation. "I'm wasting my breath here."

"I'm glad you at least realize that."

"There's just one more thing, Fortune. Don't breathe a word of this to MacNair. If he is the bastard that's trying to ruin me, I want to get the proof, and then by God, I'll see him hang for it!"

"I haven't told Grady of my dream. And I can't tell him your suspicions without revealing who I am."

"Ha! As if he doesn't already know."

"He doesn't!"

Roc grabbed his hat and headed for the door. "I need some fresh air. There aren't any more rooms to be had, so if you don't mind, I'll bed back down there in the corner when I get back."

"Roc, wait!"

"What is it?" he snapped.

"Did you talk to Granny about your suspicions?"

"Yeah. She didn't believe me either."

Fortune smiled in satisfaction. "She's never wrong, you know."

Grady, Roc and Fortune had been on the road to Helena for only a few hours, and already Fortune wanted to scream with the uneasy tension that was her constant companion now.

Part of the problem could be summed up in the old adage, "Two's company, and three's a crowd." With Roc's constant presence, she and Grady hadn't had a moment alone in or out of bed. Fortune found out very quickly how accustomed she'd become to sleeping in his arms every night, and she missed him dreadfully.

And if she didn't miss her guess, Grady was suffering the same malady. He'd been short-tempered with everyone, ever since their first night apart. To make matters worse, he was well-aware of Roc's constant scrutiny and resented her brother's suspicious attitude.

Roc's behavior wasn't any better. Still angry with her for not accepting the damning evidence against Grady, he'd scarcely spoken to either one of them.

So here they were—Grady leading a pack mule, Fortune second in line, and Roc bringing up the rear—all afraid to open up a conversation for fear of getting their heads bit off.

Despite their irritable feelings toward one another, the opening of the mercantile had gone remarkably well. Customers had flooded into the store and seemed pleasantly surprised at the variety and quantity of goods offered. MacNair's Mercantile was without a doubt a huge success.

It was apparent from the onset, however, that Angus would need to hire help. And when they left Fort Benton this morning, he was already interviewing a few eager men and women for the position.

"Let's rest and water the horses here," Grady called over his shoulder, breaking into Fortune's reverie. He reined in at a small mountain rill.

Fortune slid out of her saddle before Roc could think of a reasonable protest. Not that he necessarily would have, but since her bottom was sore, his foul mood precluded taking chances.

After refreshing herself at the stream, she left the men to seek a moment of privacy in the bushes. When she started out of the trees she stopped short at the sound of their voices tangled in argument.

"Why in the hell don't you just say what's on your mind, Landry?" Grady groused. "I'm sick of your sullen, suspicious looks. Come on, out with it. What's sticking in your craw?"

"All right, since you asked, I'll tell you, Reb," Roc tossed back caustically. "Does the name Eli Holms sound familiar? Yeah, I can see by the look on your face it does."

"So what's your point, Yank?"

"My point is, Eli Holms is one of the men who sabotaged my outfit and set me up to be dry gulched. I know he worked for you just a short time ago. Maybe he *still* does!"

Grady regarded Roc with icy disdain. "You're insinuating I'm the one trying to ruin you? That would be kinda stupid, don't you think, considering we're partners and all? What would I have to gain?"

Alarm bells went off in Fortune's head. *Great crystal balls and tea leaves! What if Roc in his anger gives us away? Think fast!*

Ruffling her hair into a frightful tangle, she ran out of the brush screaming and waving her arms. "Bears! Run for your lives! They're coming!" With a running leap she hit her mare's back. The horse reared on her hind legs, pawed the air and landed in a running gallop.

Cursing, both men leaped into their saddles and chased down the road after her.

Fortune kept Magic at a sharp gallop for almost a mile before halting. Since Grady had the mule tethered to his horse, Roc was the first to reach her.

"What in the hell was that all about?" he exploded. "There were no bears after you."

"Yes, there were," Fortune replied indignantly. "Is it my fault if you left so fast you didn't see them?" Haughtily, she slid off Magic's back and poured a little water into her hand for her mare.

Grady rode up then and reined to an abrupt halt. When he tipped his hat back on his head his angry expression was clearly visible. "What got into you? I didn't see any bear back there."

"Well, there were bears—two great big ones. Didn't you hear them, growling and snarling at one another? It was just awful."

"Fortune," Grady started, "I heard no such thi—" He stopped short, and gazed over at Roc, seeing that the man had just reached the same conclusion he had. They'd both been had. "So we sounded like bears, did we? You little minx, I ought to wallop you for that." He tried to maintain an angry face, but it was useless.

Roc managed not to laugh, but a telltale twitch developed at the corner of his mouth. "You've got one coming, Sister Mine. Remember that."

"Roc," Grady sighed, in a conciliatory manner, "Eli Holms does *not* work for me. He lasted only two days in my employ. Angus caught him stealing out of the till, and I fired him the same day."

"Well, you have to admit, it looked mighty suspicious, Reb," Roc replied grudgingly.

Grady's saddle leather creaked as he shifted forward to look Roc right in the eye. "I get the feeling there's more to this accusation than meets the eye. If you've got another more valid reason for suspecting me, speak up. Otherwise, I suggest we put this incident behind us and hit the road."

Fortune could see that her brother itched to disclose the most damning evidence of all, but he nudged his horse and headed down the road without a word.

The September night was brisk after sunset. Fortune curled into her bedroll by the fire and heartily wished it were possible to join Grady in his. His gaze, as he stared at her across the campfire during their scant meal, had been so hot she thought she might go up in flames.

She smiled mischievously up at the stars. She'd repaid him tit for tat by brushing her breast against his arm when she had collected his dirty dish. His eyes had blazed, and if her brother hadn't been chaperoning, Grady would more than likely taken her right there in the dirt.

Now, as she watched him tossing and turning on the other side of the campfire, she doubted very much either one of them would get much sleep.

Breakfast the next morning was a hurried affair. Fortune rummaged in vain, trying to locate the bar of soap she'd tucked into her saddlebags.

"Get a move on, Fortune," Roc ordered impatiently. "If we make good time today, we'll get to Helena late tonight."

"I'm not going anywhere until I've found my soap and washed up," she replied, her voice muffled as she bent over the saddlebags.

"Use mine," Grady said, pouring the last dregs of the coffee-pot into his cup. "My saddlebags are there by my saddle. Soap's in one of those big pockets."

Exhaling in defeat, she tossed her own bags aside and got to her feet. She strolled over to Grady's gear and sat down. "It's not in this one," she mumbled to herself, after searching one pocket. She opened a second, pulled out a shirt, then ran her hand along the bottom. "Got it," she said.

Grady grinned, threw out the last of his coffee and picked up his saddle. "Take your time washing up, darlin'," he said softly so as not to be overheard by Roc. "I'll saddle Magic for you." He gave her an intimate wink and hefted the saddle over his shoulder.

Fortune pulled the soap out of Grady's bag, frowning impatiently at the paper that stuck to it. Careful not to tear it, she separated the paper from the soap. As she started to return the paper to the bag, she noted something written on it. Frowning, she smoothed the crumpled note and read, "U kilt Bull but he got yore d . . ." The rest was smeared, but she knew exactly what it had said.

She went still. Then turning on her heel, she stalked up to Grady.

He tightened the cinch on his bay and glanced at her askance. "What's the matter? Couldn't you find the soap, darlin'?"

She slapped the smudged paper flat against his chest. "When did you get this, and why wasn't I told about it?"

Grady made a grab for the paper before it fell to the ground and grimaced when he realized what it was. "The night I found this Angus had just told you about Grumpy. I figured you'd had enough hurt for one night and stashed it in my saddlebags."

"What's wrong, Fortune?" Roc interrupted.

Grady handed him the note and explained what he'd just told Fortune. "I'm sorry, Sugar," he said turning back to Fortune. "What with the rush of opening the mercantile and all, I just forgot about it."

"Maybe you wrote this yourself, then decided it wasn't necessary to leave it in her room after Angus told her about the dog," Roc said accusingly.

Grady drew back his fist and landed a solid blow to one side of Roc's cheek.

Fortune screamed and grabbed the front of Grady's shirt. "Stop it! Stop it, now." Shoving away from him, she fell on her knees at her brother's side as he slowly sat up. "Are you all right?" she asked in a tone that pronounced her every bit as angry with him as she was Grady.

Wiggling his jaw back and forth, Roc nodded and got to his feet, glaring at the Reb.

His legs spread wide and his fists at the ready, Grady glared right back. "You're a damn fool, Landry. If I'd written that letter, I wouldn't have been stupid enough to keep the evidence. Use your head, man! I'm in love with your sister."

"You *claim* to be in love with her," Roc shot back. "How do I know you're not lying? You could be using her as a cover."

"Then tell me why I asked her to marry me."

A stunned expression glazed Roc's eyes as he turned to Fortune. "Is this true?"

"You didn't tell him?" Grady asked in angry disbelief.

"I . . . I told Roc that I was in love with you." Fortune's defense sounded weak even to her own ears. "I haven't really accepted your proposal, Grady. I thought it best to wait. Besides, you and Roc haven't exactly been getting along, and I didn't want to add fuel to the fire."

Roc studied Grady for a moment, sighed and shook his head. "Believe it or not, Reb, everything you've been telling me suddenly makes sense. I may be a fool, but I'm willing to give you the benefit of the doubt—for now."

"Then would you mind telling me what it is that's keeping your sister from accepting my proposal? She tells me she's got some problems to straighten out, but I can't help feeling that those problems have something to do with what's been happening to your company."

"Will you two stop talking about me as if I weren't here?" Fortune fumed.

Ignoring her, Roc looked thoughtful then shook his head. "I'm afraid I can't help you, MacNair. When Fortune is ready, maybe she'll tell you. But it's not my place to butt into her affairs."

"How nice of you, brother, considering you're the one who—"

"Fortune," Roc interrupted, his voice low with warning, "shut up while you're still ahead."

Because Roc was anxious to get back to Helena and make sure that nothing else had gone wrong in his absence, they pushed hard that day and rode on into the night.

None too happy with either man, Fortune refused Grady's first offer to take her up on his saddle before him. But when she fell asleep and nearly fell off her horse, he simply reached over and dragged her from Magic's saddle.

By the time Roc glanced back to see what had slowed them down, the deed was done. Grady shrugged at his partner. "She nearly slid out of her saddle," he explained over the exhausted girl's head.

Roc nodded and faced front again without a word.

Feeling as if he'd just scored a coup, Grady cuddled Fortune within the folds of his buckskin jacket. He smiled to himself when she sighed and buried her cold nose against the heat of his chest. Now that they were returning to Helena, he knew the opportunities to hold her like this would be few until after their wedding day—if there was a wedding.

He couldn't fathom the young woman's complicity in anything amoral or illegal, but he was still of the mind that Roc had involved her in something that had come back to haunt to them. Whatever it was they were mixed up in, Fortune obviously didn't want him to know about it. Maybe she trying to protect him, but then again, maybe she just plain didn't trust him. And that hurt.

Damn, he never should have let himself fall in love with her. All he'd wanted was a tolerably attractive woman to be his wife—well, maybe a little bit more than tolerably attractive. That aside, if he hadn't fallen for the little vixen in his arms, he could be courting a more willing candidate right now! *A*

andidate like Reva Wentworth? a little voice asked mockingly.
God Almighty, no!" he muttered under his breath.

He kissed the top of Fortune's head and hugged her pos-
essively. His pa had sorely loved his ma, and he'd grown
p surrounded by that love. When it came right down to it,
e supposed he'd only been fooling himself into thinking that
e didn't need love in a marriage. He remembered what Fortune
ad told him of her own parents. He knew now he could never
xist in that kind of relationship. And if he could ever get
ortune to say yes, he'd never have to.

Roc reined in on the edge of town. "How 'bout I take her
ow," he said. "You needn't detour out of your way."

"If you don't mind, I'd like to take her on home," Grady
eplied. "No sense jostling her around when we're almost
ere."

"You really do love her, don't you, MacNair?"

"More than you'll ever know, partner."

Roc nudged his horse off Main Street toward Cutler. "Too
ad," he muttered more to himself than to Grady.

"Why's that?" Grady asked, following close behind.

"Huh? Oh, I was just talking to myself. Pay no mind to me;
y mind's wandering. I'm so tired I could sleep for a week.
ure am glad tomorrow is Sunday."

Chapter Twenty-six

When Fortune woke up and saw herself in the mirror over he
bed, she started, not realizing at first where she was. The la
she remembered, Grady had pulled her out of Magic's saddl
to ride with him.

She stretched and threw back the covers, nearly jumping ou
of her skin when a giggling little body squirmed under th
blankets that had just been tossed over it. "Tish?"

Another giggle. Then the covers flew off in the other direc
tion. Tish Tabor's brown hair crackled and stood on end. Fo
tune laughed, and the little girl looked up at herself in the gian
mirror. "I'm the Rupa Gypsy!" She laughed, pointing at he
wild hair.

"What are you doing in here, you little rascal." Fortun
chuckled. "Come over here and give me big hug. Oh, hov
I missed you!"

"Shh, Ma will fine me." Tish crawled onto Fortune's lap an
gave her a big wet kiss on the cheek.

"Are you hiding from your Ma, Tish," Fortune whispered.

"Uh huh. But I'm not sposta be here cuz yer seepin'."

"Well, I'm not sleeping now." With that the young woman tumbled the child back on the bed, tickling her and demanding she surrender.

"Never! Never!" Tish shouted, rolling away and grabbing a pillow.

"By jingo, a pillow fight!" This came from Book as he burst through the bedroom door.

"Pillow fight?" Fortune yelped, just before Tish clobbered her over the head. "Why, you little devil, I'll get you for that!"

The fight was on. Pillows were wielded left and right amidst the laughing and hollering. "Book's the mean ol' sheriff, Fortune," Tish yelled. "Git 'im!"

"You're under arrest," Book shouted. *Thump.* Tish went rolling across the bed, and Book turned on Fortune.

Laughing as hard as Tish, Fortune rolled away and bounced to her feet on the bed. *Thump.* Down she went.

"I win, I win, I—"

Whomp. Tish let him have it across the rump, and thousands of feathers exploded into the air. "Goodie, it's snowin'," Tish squealed in delight.

"Can't a man get any sleep around here?" Roc said, wandering sleepily through the doorway. "What the hell!"

Thump "I got 'im, Fortune," Book yelled. "I got 'im real good!"

Fortune, her hair now white with feathers, burst into laughter at the dumbfounded look on her brother's face.

"I'll teach you not to wake up a tired man in the middle of the day," Roc growled in mock ferocity. He grabbed Book's pillow and swung it backward in preparation for a mighty blow. *Whomp.* As feathers filled the air like a January blizzard, Roc realized he'd whacked an innocent bystander who had just entered behind him. He whirled around to apologize to the unfortunate victim. "Oh, God! Honest, Irene, I just got here," he blurted.

Book spit a feather out of his mouth, and his eyes got big. "Oh, shit, it's Ma!"

Tish and Fortune immediately quieted down as they stood still on the big bed.

Laila and Ursula then sauntered in to stand behind their stunned housekeeper. "Slitherin' serpents," Ursula exclaimed.

"Will you look at dis! Looks like a hen house de fox got inta."

"Looks like a heck of a lot of fun to me," Laila muttered with a wry wink at Fortune.

Fortune tried to keep a straight face but burst out laughing. "Don't be mad, Irene. I've always wanted to have a pillow fight and never got to. And I've never had so much fun in my life."

A loud sneeze precluded Irene's comment.

"Featers make Ma cry and sneeze," Tish said.

"Oh my," Laila said, "we better get her out of here, Ursula."

Irene held up a hand for silence. "I'm glad you *children*"—she eyed Fortune and Roc—"had fun, and I—ah-ha-choo—hope you have just as much fun cleaning the—ah-ha-choo—the mess up." With that she pivoted and left the room, Laila and Ursula trailing along, brushing feathers out of their hair.

"Well, hell, I just got here in time to get clobbered," Roc protested. "I'm not helping clean this mess up."

"Come on in," Irene said, opening the door that evening to Grady.

"Thanks, Irene. I hope I'm not intruding." He tossed her a dimpled smile. "I was sitting over there in that little room of mine and realized I was feeling kind of lonesome. Rather than just sit there and feel sorry for myself, I decided to visit my favorite people."

"Favorite people, or favorite gal?" Irene teased, ushering him into the entryway. "Come into the parlor, Grady. You're just in time for the fun. Laila talked Roc into getting his fiddle out and playing us a couple tunes."

Beautiful silvery notes of a violin floated out of the parlor. "Have you ever heard the like?" Irene asked in awe. "That boy sure can saw a fiddle. He and Twig ought to get together, don't you think?"

Before Grady could comment, a woman's beautiful voice broke into the song *Aura Lea*. As if in a trance, he walked to the parlor doors and halted at the sight of Fortune standing at her brother's side. Her voice was clear and beautiful, soft yet strong, and the song was sung with a depth of feeling the likes of which he'd never heard before. Or had he? An eerie sense of *déjà vu* suddenly overwhelmed him.

As Grady stood frozen next to Irene, everything and everyone in the parlor seemed to swell to the forefront as if the entire room were under a giant magnifying glass. He noticed Roc sitting on a straight chair, facing into the room. Fortune stood a few feet away, her back to Grady as well. Hair, black as sin, hung long and loose past the waist of her full skirt. And as he listened to her sing, pictures from the past flashed in his mind.

He saw the garlic over the doors of Gypsy caravans and saw it again over the doors of this very house. He saw the Gypsy dancing by the light of the flickering campfire as she beckoned him, then twirled out of his reach. He saw Fortune in her diaphanous peach nightgown as she swirled away out of his reach and beckoned him to bed. He saw the Gypsy's unusual green, tilted eyes above the red scarf covering her face and saw those same eyes light with lust as he made love to Fortune. He saw Laila Fontaine getting upset over a fake Gypsy. He saw Roc practically fall out of his chair at the mere appearance of a watch fob. He could hear the Gypsy's entrancing voice as she sang to his men by the firelight, and he listened to Fortune sing now with that same lovely, distinctive voice.

The magic, the superstitions, his initial shock upon first meeting Fortune—it all made sense to him now. It dawned on him that he now knew what Fortune Landry had been hiding from him. God, but he'd been a fool! He'd asked the Gypsy whore to be his wife, for Christ's sake, the same whore who had sent him to a living hell!

Grady's hands slowly knotted into fists, and his blood pounded through the veins in his spinning head. His heart beat faster and faster, pumping him into a burgeoning rage.

Fortune and Roc ended the song, and Book and Tish clapped and clamored for more. But one person's loud, incongruent clap continued longer than the rest.

Fortune turned and stared as Grady strolled into the room, clapping his hands loudly. The hatred on his face made the color drain from her face, and she reached for the back of Roc's chair to steady herself.

Instantly, Grady's hand shot out, grabbed her wrist and roughly jerked her against his chest. "Bravo, Gypsy whore!" He then laid savage claim to Fortune's mouth in a kiss that was meant to degrade.

Irene looked aghast and shuffled the children out of the room.

Out of the corner of his eye, Grady saw Roc lay his violin aside and make a grab for his shoulder. He shoved Fortune away, then drove his fist into the Yank's jaw with a superior strength borne of killing rage. Roc hit the floor, out cold. Laila cried out, but before she could go to Roc, Grady ordered coldly, "Leave, Mrs. Fontaine. Your granddaughter and I have something to discuss."

"Ursula," Fortune begged, "please take Gran upstairs. I need to talk to Grady alone."

Grady stood fuming as Ursula practically dragged a protesting Laila from the room.

"And now, Gypsy," he sneered, turning on Fortune, "I believe I have something that belongs to you." He slipped his watch out of his pocket, unfastened the bracelet and threw it at her feet.

Tears brimming in her eyes, Fortune cried, "Grady, please, I was going to tell you."

"It's a little late for explanations, Fortune. My God, woman, you sent me and my men to a living hell. And I bet you and your brother had one hell of a good laugh when you managed to pull the wool over this Reb's eyes for a *second* time, didn't you?"

"Grady, it wasn't like that at all. Please, I—"

"Well, you may have kept your identity from me," he interrupted, "but there's one thing you didn't keep from me, and we both know what that is, don't we?" He laughed, his leering gaze traveling the length of her body. "Baby, I've got to give credit where it's due. Now that I've got you broken in, I'll bet you're the hottest piece in town. But I guess it just comes natural to a lying, conniving, Gypsy slut! Hell, it's little wonder you chose to live in a whorehouse. I suppose after tonight, I'll have to pay for your services."

The force of Fortune's hand cracking across his face turned Grady's head. "The truth hurts, doesn't it, Gypsy?" he sneered.

"Stop it! Hate me if you will, but don't discredit a people you know nothing of."

"What's there to know? In the rank and file of the human race, I reckon Gypsies are the filthiest, lowest form."

This last statement opened an old wound, and the pain escalated Fortune's anger tenfold. "Oh, how could I have ever thought myself in love with such a narrow-minded bigot?" she asked, berating herself aloud. She pointed a trembling finger at the door. "Get out! And stay out!"

Grady's upper lip curled in contempt. "Gladly. But before I do, let me give you fair warning. I'll be selling my interest in your brother's freighting business just as soon as I can find a buyer."

"I'm sure Roc will be more than happy to take it off your hands."

"Not a chance, Gypsy. I aim to sell it to anyone *but* Roc. Hopefully your new partner will be a real ass."

"We could do the same, you know, sell our interests in the stores," Fortune threatened smugly.

Grady laughed derisively. "You either missed or failed to remember the fine print on my bank loan and partnership agreement. You can't sell your shares in the mercantile until I pay off the loan on the Benton store."

"I'm sure Roc's lawyer can find some solution," Fortune replied with more confidence than she felt.

"He's welcome to try, but come what may, I don't want any of you thieving Gypsies in my store. If you care to have a look at the books on occasion, I'll send them home with Irene."

"I believe I just ordered you to get out. Go, now!" she hissed.

The Reb, turned on his heel and stalked out of the house.

Roc groaned and rolled over. Rubbing his jaw, he slowly got to his feet and stumbled to Fortune's side. "Where is that bastard?" he growled.

Still staring at the door Grady had just walked out of, Fortune's reply was toneless and perfunctory. "Gone."

"Well, what the hell got into the man? What did he mean by jerking you around like that?"

"He knows."

"Knows wh—?" Roc's question halted as her meaning dawned. Fortune lifted her gaze to his then. Never had he seen anyone look so desolate. As his arms drew her close, the tears she'd been holding back spilled down her cheeks. Roc pulled her onto his lap as he sat down on one of the settees. For a while he just let her sob her heart out. Then haltingly, she revealed the details of what had taken place.

"Oh, Roc," Fortune cried at the end of the telling, "I knew he'd be mad when he discovered the truth, but I'd hoped that he'd eventually forgive us. I didn't count on his horrible opinion of Gypsies. I realize now that even if he forgave me for having him imprisoned, he could never overlook my Gypsy heritage. Sweet Gaia! He called me a Gypsy whore and said now that I was . . . was broken in, he'd probably have to pay for my services."

"I'll kill the bastard for that," Roc raged. Then more softly, he added, "Don't cry any more over him, sweetheart. He's not worth one of your precious tears."

Roc glanced up and noticed Laila standing on the parlor threshold. Strain radiated about her mouth and eyes, adding new lines to her wrinkled face. "How much did you hear?" he asked, as the old woman came to stand before her grandchildren.

"Enough," she replied, taking Fortune's hand and helping her off her brother's lap.

Fortune seemed to come out of her trance then. "I need to be alone for a while," she told them. "I'm going to my room."

As she started away, Roc ventured, "Fortune, will you be all right? Maybe you shouldn't be alone right now."

She smiled sadly. "I'm all right. I feel very tired, though. Maybe sleep is my body's way of allowing me to step back and calm down before I try to look at what happened tonight in a logical manner."

"Go on, dear," Laila interjected. "I'll be up to check in on you in a while."

As soon as Fortune was gone from the room, Roc leapt to his feet, barely restrained fury burning in his dark eyes. "I'm going to kill MacNair for what he's done to Fortune," he vowed.

"No," Laila said softly but firmly. "You will do no such thing."

"Granny, I—"

"Listen to me, Roc. Don't let your anger lead you to do something you will come to regret later as Grady MacNair most surely has done tonight. The man has been harboring a bitterness that I'll wager even he did not know the proportions of. In time he will come to sorely regret his words, and living with that regret will be punishment enough."

"But Granny, MacNair has . . . he's compromised Fortune. No man, Gypsy or Gajo, wants a woman that has been sullied by another."

Laila sank heavily into a purple chair. "So what would you do, kill him? That wouldn't make Fortune any less sullied. Or would you force him to marry her? Then he would never come to his senses, and Fortune would be condemned to a life of hell."

"But what of her honor?"

"Fortune obviously gave herself to the man because she loved him. There is no dishonor in that, and I doubt she would thank you for insisting otherwise, Roc."

"But he's threatened to sell off his portion of my freighting business. He'd probably delight in selling to some unscrupulous scum."

"So hire some unscrupulous scum to act on your behalf and purchase it yourself," Laila suggested.

"It's a good idea, Gran, but I've suffered the loss of a great deal of money of late. I need the cash I have left just to survive the winter."

"Then we'll just have to think of a way to keep anyone from buying Grady's shares."

Roc sat down on a settee across from Laila, and though his mood was far removed from joviality, he found amusement in watching his Granny's rumination. Nobody could conjure up mischief as well as his little Gypsy grandmother. But when she abruptly stood and made to leave the room with a pleased smile on her face, he began get worried. "Granny, wait," he said, jumping up to go after her. "What are you thinking of doing?"

Rather smugly, she grinned. "Don't worry, dear. All will be well. There are only a couple things I would ask you."

"What's that?"

"If anyone asks you if it's true you are a Gypsy, you should strongly confirm it—and with a great deal of pride, too. You must also confirm that I am a Gypsy shuvani."

"Is that wise?"

"Well, the only man who you didn't want to know about it now knows anyway. What possible harm can it do now? You haven't grown ashamed of being Gypsy, have you?" she asked slyly.

"Of course not. In fact, I've already told Eric Jorgensen."

"Good! I know Fortune told Irene Tabor, too."

"So what do you have planned, Gran?"

She cackled and wagged her finger back and forth. "You'll see soon enough. And wipe that worried look off your face. I guarantee you'll be happy with the results." She continued out the door then, leaving Roc to stare after her.

It had to happen. Fortune knew it would, yet she hadn't visualized it happening in quite the manner it had. Carelessly tossing the bedcovers aside, she dimmed her lamp, and crawled between the cool sheets.

The Moondance enchantment—if that *truly* was the force that had bonded her to Grady—had finally been broken. The handsome ex-Confederate captain now hated her.

There was only one problem. She, too, should now be free of the enchantment, but she wasn't. Instead her heart ached for the loss of Grady's love and respect.

She could put no faith into destiny taking a hand in this mess either, because even if Grady changed his mind about loving her, he would never respect her. He made it quite clear that he held Gypsies in the lowest contempt, and she doubted his ability to ever ignore that sentiment. And even if he could, she could not.

She'd always hated people's prejudices against Gypsies. It was one of the more important reasons she'd come West. She could never be happy with a man who couldn't respect her heritage. Sweet Gaia! If she were to marry Grady now, she'd be putting herself in the same position her mother had when she'd married Bonner Landry, and look at how that marriage had turned out.

No. Somehow, she must learn to get over Grady MacNair. It wouldn't be easy, but her proud Gypsy spirit demanded that it be so.

Of course, now that the burden of hiding who and what she was had been lifted, she and Roc could openly pursue their enemy. Not that the fact was much of a balm to her savaged heart, but it was, nonetheless, one positive result of the night's events.

And beyond a doubt, Grady wasn't involved in the assaults on Landry Freighting. His angry revelation tonight had been too real. No one could have faked that kind of reaction. Even Roc had to be aware of that truth.

Perhaps, helping her brother discover the real culprit's identity would help keep her mind off Grady. She certainly hoped so because if it didn't, she didn't think she could survive the horrible emptiness his defection had left in her heart.

Chapter Twenty-seven

Many friends question Gajo's sad smile
As they offer solace through his trial
But their advice falls on a soul turned ice

"Morning," Irene greeted Laila and Ursula as they entered the kitchen.

"Mm, looks and smells like you been busy, gal." Ursula smiled, eyeing the pie dough Irene was crimping round the edges of a pan.

Irene dusted the flour from her hands on her bibbed apron and reached for the coffeepot. "I couldn't sleep," she confessed, pouring coffee for the three of them. "I couldn't get Fortune and Grady off my mind. At four o' clock this morning, I gave up." Reaching into a cupboard she pulled out a plate of cinnamon buns. "I occupied my time making these for breakfast," she explained, setting them on the table.

"Irene," Laila began, as she took a seat and helped herself to a roll, "how much did you hear last night?"

"Nothing really. If you'll remember, the minute Grady yelled

308

'Gypsy whore,' I hustled the children upstairs."

"I'm sorry they had to witness that," the old Gypsy said.

Irene nodded. "Me, too. They may be just kids but they figured out a long time ago that Grady was sweet on Fortune, and they were pretty upset by his name-callin' last night. At least now I understand why Fortune was adamant about my not telling Grady that she's a Gypsy."

"Ugh," Ursula grunted, "dat's only de half of it."

"What do you mean?" Irene asked as she tucked the pie into the oven.

"Come sit down and drink your coffee," Laila said. "This is a long story."

"Laila, you don't have to tell me, if you think you shouldn't. I've always thought right highly of Fortune, and though Grady is a good friend, too, I'd never think less of either one because of their rift."

"Oh, I know that, Irene," Laila assured her. "But I came into this kitchen with every intention of telling the whole story, because, you see, I'm going to need your help. But before I get into that let me get this story told."

Irene settled down in her chair and listened intently as Laila told of Fortune and Roc's adventure during the war. Several times her eyes widened, and she looked as if she might interrupt with a question, but to her credit she kept quiet until Laila's story ended with the previous night's events.

"Well, if that don't beat all," the housekeeper finally exclaimed in astonishment. "Fortune, a spy. I always knew that little gal had spunk, but by jingo, she's a real hero, ain't she?"

"You won' convince her of dat," Ursula interjected. "Dat gal had nightmares for months when she found out de prisoners was a dyin' in dem prisons."

Laila confirmed Ursula's statement with a nod. "She dreamed of Grady MacNair. And though I doubt she'd admit it, I think she knew she'd meet him again." At Irene's raised brow, she explained. "Though she's sometimes called it more curse than gift, nonetheless Fortune has the ability to see the future in her dreams. She is also highly sensitive to people's emotions. At times she is so sensitive that she must retreat from everyone to find herself."

Irene covered her mouth and stared at Laila sheepishly. "And here I told her I thought her magic was a bunch of nonsense."

"Fortune's gift has nothing to do with magic," Laila said, shaking her head. "It is what it is, and that's all. Generations of women in my family have been Gypsy shuvanis. We each have had our particular gifts."

"What's a shuvan . . . ?"

"Shuvani," Laila finished for her. "It means wise woman. You might compare a shuvani to an Indian medicine man, and in many ways Gypsy beliefs parallel those of the Indian."

"Well, fancy that!"

Laila chuckled at the housekeeper's awe-struck face. "Now to get to my reason for telling you all of this. Grady has threatened to sell his share of Landry Freighting, and right now Roc hasn't the money to buy it back himself. With all this trouble he's had, Roc would rather know the devil he's dealing with than one he doesn't. So we must try to prevent Grady from selling his share in the business. I think you can help us in this endeavor."

"I don't know," Irene said doubtfully. "I'm a friend to both Grady and Fortune, and it sounds like you want me to jeopardize my friendship with Grady. I owe him a lot, Laila, and I won't repay him by stabbing him in the back."

"If you were that kind of person, Fortune would never have trusted you enough to invite you to share her home," Laila replied. "And I think what I have in mind will benefit both young people in the end."

"Well, I would like to see them kiss and make up," Irene said. "Anybody with two eyes can see those two was made for each other."

Laila smiled. "Irene, I think you and I are going to get along very well together." With that, Laila quickly outlined her plan. "Now remember, as a member of Fortune and Roc's household, you'll be called on to vouch for this bit of gossip, but you must let on that I am the one who dreamed of the fire and that I also possess the ability to hex. You needn't jeopardize your relationship with Grady by saying that I will hex anyone who buys his share of Landry Freighting. I'll give that job to another."

"Who?" Ursula asked, clearly as curious as Irene.

"Why, Eric Jorgensen, of course. He'll be delighted to lend his help, I'm sure."

Irene rolled her eyes. "Laila Fontaine, I shore am glad you're my friend and not my enemy!"

Fortune stood at the front of her house whacking away at the rose bushes. Ursula had been right about one thing. The disreputable rose garden was more a briar patch. They had become tall and woody with horribly thick thorns. Before she'd left for Fort Benton, one of the customers at the mercantile had told her that if she waited till fall and cut them down to the ground, they'd bloom in beautiful lush bushes the following spring. She hoped they were right because, right now, they looked totally butchered.

Roc had wanted her to hire a man to do the job, but she needed the work to keep her mind off Grady and what had happened two nights ago.

Not an hour went by that she didn't think of him at least once. At night in her dreams she relived their passionate love-making with his teasing, tender endearments in that wonderful low Southern drawl that resonated with a Scot's burr. She still loved Grady MacNair, but he hated her with every fiber of his being—hated her for what she'd done and for the blood that ran in her veins.

"Fortune," Tish called, running into the yard and interrupting the young woman's ruminations. "A man gived this to me. Said it was for you."

Fortune took the envelope, but when Tish would have run off, she asked the child to wait. With trembling hands she opened the letter and pulled out a single folded sheet.

Yore time is short. My men want u Gypsy. And I want u and that brother to pay for my brother dyin' and makin me loze my leg.

With a cry of outrage and fear, Fortune grabbed Tish's hand and hauled her into the house after her, calling for her grandmother.

"Sweet Gaia!" Laila cried hurrying down the stairs. "What is it, Fortune?"

Fortune handed Granny the note and waited the few seconds it took the old lady to read and comprehend its message. "It's starting again, Gran," Fortune gasped on the verge of tears.

"And they used Tish to deliver that filthy thing."

"Calm down, dear. Book's out back. I'll have him hitch up the buggy, and we'll take this to Roc at the warehouse."

Fortune nodded and turned to Tish as Laila hurried to the back of the house. "Honey, do you know the name of the man that gave you this letter?"

"No." Tish's eyes moistened. "Did I do somethin' bad?"

The young Gypsy knelt down and hugged the child. "Of course not, love. But the man who gave you this note is a very bad man who might try to hurt you. If you ever see him again, you should tell me or your mother. All right?" At Tish's nod, she added, "And never, never go near that man. If there is no grownup with you, run away and come home or go the mercantile if that's closer." Still trembling, Fortune rose and took the child's hand. "Come on, Tish. I think it's best if you and Book come with Granny and myself to the warehouse."

"Will Ursula come, too?"

Fortune smiled. "Yes, honey. I'll go fetch her."

At the warehouse the women and children flooded into Roc's office. It still smelled of new wood and paint, and his rickety furniture had been replaced by sturdy masculine pieces made of mahogany. "Well, well, out and about, are we." Roc grinned, setting his pen down. "You're just in time to join me at the hotel for lunch."

Fortune rummaged in her reticule, found the despised letter and placed it on the desk before him.

Roc glanced at her in askance then picked up the letter. "Gran," he said, after reading it, "would you and Ursula mind taking the children out to wait for us in the carriage?" As soon as he and Fortune were alone, he asked, "Where did you find this?"

"I didn't find it. A man gave it to Tish while she was playing up the road with her little friends. Oh, Roc, when I think that she could have been abducted or hurt, I . . ."

"Calm down, Sister Mine. This may be the clue we've been waiting for. We now know the villain has only one leg."

"But Roc, he says it's our fault. What can he mean?"

"A lot of men lost limbs during the war, Fortune. Perhaps he's one of the men we captured. He might have had a wounded leg that got infected in prison." He stood, tucking the note into his coat pocket. "I'll get my horse, and we'll all ride over to the Jorgensen's."

"Why the Jorgensen's?"

"Eric and MacNair have had guards put on the house for some time now, but I think it's time we take a few extra precautions. I don't want any of you women or the children left unguarded at any time. I'll need a few more good men. Most of my men have left on another trip to Salt Lake. I'm going to see if Eric can recommend any of the men that work for him."

"What about the sheriff?"

"He's shorthanded right now, and I don't think you'd want to chance his recognizing you, would you?" At her questioning expression, he added, "Eric told me what happened at the Fourth of July celebration. He said the sheriff is still madder than hell."

Fortune bit her lower lip, looking sheepish. "I couldn't very well let him arrest Granny, Roc. And he did shove me out of his way."

Roc shrugged. "I'd just as soon keep the sheriff out of this anyway. He's a Confederate, and if he found out what we did during the war and the problems we're having now, I doubt if he'd be too sympathetic." Coming out from behind the desk, he took her arm. "Come on, let's go see Eric."

"Irene," the Widow Harkins whispered leaning over the mercantile counter, "is it true that the Landry's are Gypsies?"

"Why, yes, it is, Marian," Irene replied. "Why do you ask?"

"Well, I heard that Sarah Barkly said the ol' woman was some kind of . . . oh, what was that word?"

"Shuvani?" Irene asked, smiling broadly.

"Yeah, that's it! It means she's like a witch, I think. Ain't you afraid to live there and work for those people?"

"Of course not," Irene said, shaking her head. "Laila Fontaine, that's Fortune's grandmother, is the shuvani, and she's not there much. Besides, I've always found them to be perfectly respectable. Of course, I'm on their *good* side!"

"Do you know anybody who's been on the shuvani's bad side?" the widow asked, wide-eyed with curiosity.

Irene leaned forward, whispering herself now. "My poor boss, Mr. MacNair," she confessed. "But you mustn't tell anyone I told you. See, he found out they were Gypsies, and for some reason he hates Gypsies. Anyway, he was so mad that he decided to sell his twenty-five percent interest in Landry Freighting. Well, I'll tell you, the Landry's ain't takin' kindly to the slander."

"Then it's true that the ol' shuvani said she'd hex whoever dared to buy MacNair's share?"

Irene shrugged.

"Can she really do that? I mean, there really isn't any such thing, is there?"

"Well, now, I'll tell you, Marian, I didn't rightly believe such, but now I ain't so sure. You heard Miss Fortune's dog was kilt, right?" At the woman's nod, Irene continued. "Well, Laila dug the bullet out of that poor hound and said some words over it. Then she buried the bullet and walked over that spot everyday. Next thing I know, the man what did it turned up dead in Fort Benton."

The poor Widow Harkins nearly swooned. "Oh, my! I must warn my friends immediately. Some of them wanted to ostracize Fortune Landry from their doings. Oh, I must hurry!" With that the woman flew out of the store, leaving the thread she just purchased sitting on the counter before a grinning Irene Tabor.

"I don't understand, Henderson," Grady said to the man who had offered to buy his share of Landry Freighting. "Yesterday, you seemed real anxious to buy me out. What could have possibly happened since then to change your mind?"

Aaron Henderson shifted uncomfortably at the table he shared with Grady MacNair in a back corner of the Gaiety Saloon. "It's my wife, MacNair. She won't let me."

"I beg your pardon, your wife?"

"My wife heard that ol' Gypsy shuvani, Laila Fontaine, said she'd hex whoever bought you out."

"What?" Grady exclaimed. "Surely you don't believe that mumbo jumbo?"

"Of course not," Henderson blustered indignantly. "But my Martha said she heard there was positive proof of the old woman's powers. And further more she said if I bought you out, she'd leave me to suffer the hex on my own and head back East to her ma."

"That's the most ridiculous thing I ever heard," Grady scoffed.

"The Landrys have put that gossip out to prevent me from selling my share of the company, that's all."

Henderson shrugged. "That may well be, but my Martha swears it's true. And though Martha ain't much to look at, I'd miss her cookin' fierce if she left me. So," he said, getting to his feet, "I'm afraid the deal is off."

Grady slugged a swallow of whiskey down and watched Henderson leave the saloon. This was the second man that had backed out of buying his share of Landry Freighting. He could hardly credit people's gullibility.

Cursing, he left his chair and headed back down Main Street to the mercantile. He wasn't in the place two minutes when Old Man Twig walked in.

After looking around the store and finding only Irene and Grady working behind the counter, he slammed his fist down on the counter and bellowed at Grady, "So it's true!" You got rid of my pretty, little Kitten. "Well, that does it, you narrow-minded son-of-a-bitch. I ain't comin' in here no more! That little gal might be Gypsy, but by gum, I say that's what put that special twinkle in them purdy cat eyes of 'ers."

"Now, Twig," Grady started, "you don't know the whole . . ."

Twig slammed out the door without looking back.

Grady gritted his teeth and stalked into the back room. For no other reason than to work off some steam, he started rearranging crates and stacking them against the opposite wall. The whole time he cursed Fortune Landry's sultry, green, cat eyes.

When next he glanced up, Irene was standing in the door- way with Eric Jorgensen. "Quitin' time," she announced. "I've locked the front door. Eric and I will leave by the back."

"What's he doin' here?" Grady growled.

"Not that you'd care, Reb," Eric spoke up, "but as I've just explained to Irene, a man gave her little girl one of those filthy notes to give to Fortune today. It informed her that her time was short. I'm here to see that Irene gets home safely."

Fear for Fortune pierced Grady's gut, but he ruthlessly shoved it aside. "Why not just tell the shuvani to put a hex on the man," he growled peevishly.

Eric strolled casually up to Grady. "You know, I once told you that if you ever hurt Fortune, I'd kill you. But you aren't even worth hangin' for, you bastard!" With that, Eric hauled back a fist and plowed it into Grady's face. As Grady shook his head and sat up off the floor, Eric added, "Watch yourself, Reb. Men are found in dead in dark alleys all the time. And who's to say who did it?"

Grady watched as Eric took Irene's arm and squired her out the back of the mercantile. Fortune's beautiful face flashed to mind, and he flopped back down on the floor and stared at the ceiling.

He'd thought his love for her had died two nights ago in the Landry parlor, but when Eric announced she was in danger, his heart had leapt, and his first thought had been to run to her. Christ, what was wrong with him? He hated her, but he loved her.

He really hadn't meant the insulting things he'd said about Gypsies though. Truth to tell, the nomad-like Gypsies were as misunderstood as the American Indian. These past three years he'd not known for sure if the spies who had maneuvered his capture had actually been real Gypsies at all. Nonetheless, he'd come to associate that misfortune with everything bad he'd ever heard of Gypsies. And in his anger he'd thrown the slander in Fortune's face.

Since Sunday night he had replayed that night in Virginia over and over in his mind, and there was one detail that always stuck in his mind. It was a trivial thing really, and yet now after all that had happened it seemed to hold a special significance.

The Gypsy temptress had danced up to him, an invitation in those teasing, green eyes of hers. He remembered how he'd caught her hand, how their gazes had locked. It had been as if their very souls had reached out to one another and met in a jolt of unexplicable excitement.

Incredibly, it had been almost the same way upon their meeting that first night in the hotel. He realized now that something within him had recognized her. But the lady sitting at the table that night had seemed far removed from the daring bare-legged Gypsy whore, and he'd pushed the ridiculous thought right out of his mind.

He chuckled mirthlessly. Whore? Perhaps in mind, but not in deed. He knew for a fact that he'd been her first man. Damn, the woman was an enigma! Had he actually known the real woman? What was she—Gypsy or lady?

The face of an old comrade who had died in the Yankee prison flashed to his mind, and he remembered that first winter as a Galvanized Yankee. They'd all nearly starved to death. "Curse the deceitful bitch!" He got to his feet and headed out the door, intent on getting laid and getting drunk though not necessarily in that order.

A few days later, the Landrys sat gathered at the breakfast table. "I hate having a bodyguard in the house all the time, Roc. If I didn't fear for the children's safety so much, I'd make you get rid of him."

Roc looked at Fortune for a moment, then asked, "Why not load everyone up and head out to the ranch for a while? I'd still have to have guards on you, but perhaps you wouldn't feel so confined. There's really not much for you to attend to at the freight office right now anyway."

"The children have school," Irene protested, "and I still work at the mercantile. Of course Fortune, Laila and Ursula are welcome to go on out to the ranch. I don't mind."

Fortune shook her head. "As much as I'd love going out to the ranch for a while, I think it's best if we all stay together as much as possible."

"We can go der on de weekend," Ursula suggested from the opposite end of the table.

"Yeah, can we, Ma?" Book piped up.

"I don't see any harm, if it's all right with everyone else." Irene grinned. "I've never been to the ranch. It might be fun."

"Can you leave the mercantile a little early on Friday?" Roc asked. "That way you can have all day Saturday and most of Sunday to enjoy yourselves."

"I'm sure Grady won't mind," Irene answered.

"Do you ride, Irene?" Fortune asked excitedly.

"It's been a while since I owned my own horse, but I used to be a very good rider."

"Good. I can hardly wait."

The next few weeks an easy routine was established. The week was spent in town, the weekends out at the ranch. The children were learning to ride and seemed to love helping with the chores that involved the animals.

Though Fortune was never allowed to be completely alone, she was allowed to visit her favorite spot by the river with a modicum of privacy. The men Roc had hired seemed to understand her need to be alone and stayed just close enough to be within calling distance. At this very moment, a friend of Eric's sat on a rock upstream a ways, barely visible through the trees.

She sighed deeply and leaned her head back on the tall aspen. It was the first of October, and the weather was growing chilly. The leaves were starting to fall and cover the ground with their brilliant gold, and the mountain stream was much too icy now to go wading in. But the clean, crisp air and the scent of pine was more than enough to sooth Fortune's senses.

Today as on other days when she'd come to this special place, she reflected on her and Grady's relationship and the magic that had supposedly brought them together. The loss of her handsome Confederate was still a raw wound, but she was coming to terms with it, deciding that it was one of life's harsh lessons. She should have told Grady who she was before they'd fallen in love, but she'd been so sure she and Granny could break the Moondance's spell. She'd worried about his revenge, too.

Fingering her shell amulet, she smiled sadly. Had there been any magic involved, she would now be free of the love that the enchantment had brought upon them.

Irene had been right that night in the kitchen when she'd declared, *"Trust in yourself, I always say."* And what of the trouble she and Roc now found themselves in? Shouldn't her magic have protected them from that, too? No, there was no magic, at least not of the proportions she'd always believed in. Perhaps in Granny's efforts to preserve her Gypsy heritage through her granddaughter, the old lady had inadvertently exaggerated. Right now that seemed to make more sense than anything else did.

She wasn't angry at Granny. How could she be? The old woman had filled her childhood with tales of fairies, demons and monsters, and what child after all doesn't enjoy a good fairy tale? The only problem was that to Fortune they had not been fairy tales, but reality. In a way, discovering that magic was only a figment of fairy tales was sad. It reminded her of the time she'd caught Granny and Grandpa, rather than St. Nick, filling her sock on Christmas Eve.

Well, at least she was left with the knowledge that her and Granny's Gypsy gifts of foresight were not a figment of magic.

Those gifts were as real as the Gypsies themselves.

"Fortune?"

She glanced up to see Roc's big body crashing through the trees and brush. He was rather like a bull moose at times, she thought with an amused smile. "I'm over here, Roc," she called. He changed direction and headed toward her. His face, when she finally glimpsed it, made her rise to her feet in alarm. "Something has happened."

He reached for a piece of paper in his pocket, and Fortune thought that another threatening note had been delivered. "I just received a telegraph from Salt Lake City," Roc said gravely. "Fortune, honey . . ." he started hesitantly.

Fortune had never seen her brother look so defeated. Reaching out to grasp his arms, she asked, "Roc, what is it?"

"We're in for some hard times. My freight wagons were attacked by a large party of road agents. Four of my men were killed, three badly wounded. Nine wagon were taken. Some of the men have deserted the wagons, saying my fight isn't theirs and that the pay isn't worth their lives. It could start snowing any time now, and if those wagons don't arrive soon, they won't make it back till spring."

Fortune threw her arms around her brother and hugged him tightly. "Oh, Roc, I'm sorry. Will you be leaving soon to fetch the wagons?"

He set her back and shook his head. "I won't leave you and the others unprotected. I have a feeling that whoever is doing all this wants me out of the way for while. It's been quiet in Helena, and the very fact that you haven't received any more of those messages makes me think the bastard is wanting us to drop our guard."

"But who will bring those wagons home? Roc, you must go. This could ruin you."

"I'm sending Eric."

"That's crazy! He doesn't know anything about freighting."

"I know he doesn't, but right now I have to be careful who I trust. I trust Eric, and he asked to go. I had to pay triple wages, but I finally found some mule skinners willing to go with him and drive those abandoned wagons back to Helena. I've given Eric instructions, and he'll see to it that my orders are carried out."

Chapter Twenty-eight

"Why don't you admit it, Grady MacNair," Irene said as she neatened the yard goods table, "You still love Fortune, and you're miserable without her."

With a belligerent look on his whisker-shadowed face, Grady slammed the money drawer shut and stuffed a few bills into the pocket of scruffy trousers. "Look, Irene, I know you mean well, but I think you better keep your nose out of this."

"I can't keep out of it; you're my friend, Grady. I care about you, and the past few weeks you've been goin' from bad to worse on a fast train to nowhere. You don't eat, you don't sleep. And you look like the very devil!"

Grady went to the front door of the mercantile and twisted the key in the lock. "All right, damn it! So I love her, so what? For God's sake, Irene, the little witch was the Yankee spy who sent me to Point Lookout Prison!"

"And you were one of Mosby's raiders. If memory serves me right, I recollect that Mosby had spies planted all over the North. Ain't that right?"

"Yes, how else were we to get the information we needed?"

"My point exactly," Irene bit out. "Both sides had their spies. Laila told me Roc Landry had a special talent for it. When he got orders to infiltrate Confederate territory and put an end to Mosby's raids, he came up with idea of posin' as Gypsies. He told Fortune she'd be doing her country a great service if she'd help him pull off the ruse.

"She was only seventeen, Grady, full of dreams of heroism and adventure. Then too, her Granny admits she'd filled the girl's head with all matter of notions 'bout the glorious life with a Gypsy caravan. Now I ask you, what youngun wouldn't jump at the chance to live out one of her fantasies?"

"All right, Irene, I see your point. But that still doesn't account for her failure to fess up when we met in the hotel that night."

Irene hooted at that one. "Oh, no? Tell me, Grady, what do you think was goin' through that girl's head when she saw you sashaying up to her and Roc's table? I imagine she was shocked spitless, don't you? On top of that she then learned that you were her brother's new partner.

"Stop and consider that Fortune didn't really know what kind of man you was. As far as she knew, you might try to kill her and Roc or, at the very least, destroy their business."

"She could have told me later, after she knew me better."

"Did you stop to think that maybe she thought she'd lose you and that she loved you too much to let that happen?"

"People who love each other don't keep secrets."

"That's true, but Fortune had more than herself to think about. Her brother was sure you were guilty of setting the fire and everything else that was happenin'. He forbid her to say anything because he wanted to get evidence against you. I 'spose she did as she was told cuz she wasn't too crazy 'bout tellin' you in the first place."

"Well, that explains a few things, at least."

"There's more." In as few words as possible Irene explained that Fortune had withheld the crucial part of the message the red-haired man had given her the day he attacked her behind the church. "Then there was a dream she had, too," Irene added.

"I can understand why she might doubt me after learning she and Roc had met the suspect during their spy mission, but a dream?" Grady exclaimed with a harsh laugh.

"I don't pretend to understand it exactly. Fortune has what

Laila calls a gift. The girl sometimes dreams of what's to come in the future." Irene quickly explained about the fire and the faceless man in a gray uniform.

"So that was one more thing in my disfavor," Grady concluded, frowning in consternation.

"No, not in Fortune's eyes, it wasn't. She remained your defender throughout this whole mess. Roc, however, wasn't easily persuaded of your innocence, especially after he found out that Eli Holms had worked for you."

"And then there was that damn note Fortune found in my saddlebags," Grady said, thinking aloud.

"Yeah, I think I did hear Roc mention that a couple weeks ago when Eric Jorgensen stopped by," Irene replied.

"I suppose Jorgensen is back to courting Fortune," he interjected peevishly.

"Why shouldn't he? You've made it perfectly clear you don't want her."

"And I suppose she's loving every minute of it." .

"I couldn't say," Irene replied with a knowing sparkle in her eyes. "But in any case, Eric is no longer in town." Once again, she filled Grady in on what had been happening in the Landry household.

"Damn it, I'm a partner. Why wasn't I informed? Surely they don't still suspect I'm behind all this?"

"I think any suspicions they had were gone the night you walked in and heard Fortune sing. Your reaction couldn't have been faked. Also, that last note Fortune received stamped out all doubts."

"Why's that?"

"The man revealed that he has only one leg. He holds the Landrys responsible for that and the death of his brother."

"The bastard must be a madman."

Irene nodded gravely. "I'm very frightened for Fortune, Grady."

Just then there was a pounding at the storeroom door. Grady went to the door and opened it. "Evenin' Jim," he greeted Jim Fetters. "I reckon you're here to fetch Irene, huh?"

Jim grinned and nodded. "She 'bout ready to leave?"

Irene joined them, draping her increasing girth with a shawl. Before leaving, she turned to Grady. "You think on what I've just told you."

Grady locked up behind the couple, turned around and leaned against the door. For the most part, Irene had done her best to remain neutral in the rift between Fortune and himself. But today his surliness had most definitely rubbed the lady the wrong way.

He hadn't wanted to listen to Fortune's side of things at all, but now he was glad he had. During the past miserable weeks, he'd never once stopped to think about how young and impressionable she'd been during her stint as a spy. It had been dark the night she performed for his men, and she'd been as shapely and beautiful as any mature woman. Now that the truth of the matter had been brought to his attention, he realized he'd like nothing better than to strangle that brother of hers for risking Fortune's life. Because, had things gone wrong for Roc and his band of Gypsies that night, it could very well have been Roc and Fortune that found themselves in a prisoner of war camp. The thought of Fortune in one of those hell holes sickened him. He realized with a sudden jolt of surprise that he was glad it was him and not her that had gone to prison.

He knew then that he'd come full circle and forgiven her for the nightmare she and her brother had put him through. It was, after all, war. And though he didn't fully understand her reticence to trust him enough to reveal the truth to him, he forgave her that, too.

He stiffened suddenly and pulled away from the door. *My God, what have I done? Will she ever forgive me for those horrible things I said to her?*

There was only one way to find out. He marched upstairs to shave and change clothes. When he glanced at his image in the mirror, he cursed. Irene was right; he looked like the very devil. And damn, when had he last eaten? Suddenly he felt like he could eat a bear. He laughed at himself then, feeling as if he just awakened from a long self-induced stupor.

Roc nearly dropped the gun in his hand when he opened the front door and found Grady MacNair standing on his doorstep. "What do you want, Reb? I thought Fortune made it perfectly clear she didn't want you around here anymore."

"I'd like to talk with you, Roc. I won't take up much of your time."

Something in the Reb's voice gave Roc pause. He holstered

his gun and step back from the door to allow him inside. "We can speak in the library."

Grady followed him into the small room across the hall from the parlor. Roc noted Grady staring at the stark walls and the clutter. He cleared his throat and commented, "Fortune has been bored. She's got this whole goddamn place torn up. There's not a flat surface to sit on. Now, I advise you to say your piece and get, before Fortune discovers your presence and brings the roof down on my head."

"Why did you let me in?" Grady asked.

"Damn if I know, MacNair," Roc replied, running his fingers through his tousled black hair. "I should shoot you for what you said and did to Fortune. But I guess I'm hoping you're here to remedy that situation before she decides to tear the place down and rebuild it. You see, she thinks if she keeps busy enough, she won't hurt so bad."

"I could tell her from my own experience that it won't help," Grady replied solemnly. "I tried drowning my sorrows, and when that didn't work I tried working myself to death. When that failed I just got plain mean with everybody around me." One corner of Grady's mouth lifted in a half-hearted smile. "Irene finally got her stomach full today and gave me hell. I'm glad she did.

"I love your sister, Landry, and I want her for my wife. Will you ask her if she'll at least hear me out?"

Roc inhaled a deep breath and let it out on a sigh. "I can ask her, but that's as far as I'll go. If she says no, then it's no. She's upstairs. Stay here, and I'll go speak with her."

Roc closed the door on the library and bounded up the stairs two at a time. He rapped on Fortune's door. "Fortune, can I come in?"

The door opened, but at seeing her brother's grim face, Fortune's smile died. "What is it, Roc? Not more bad news, I hope."

"No, it's not what you think. Grady MacNair is downstairs. He's asked to—"

"I want that man out of my house now, Roc," she snapped bitterly. "I thought you understood that he wasn't welcome here."

"I think you should give him a chance. He wants to apologize. And Fortune, he said he loves you."

Her facial muscles tightened, and Roc could tell that she was doing her best to control her emotions. Despite her efforts telltale moisture gathered in her eyes. "He can't love me and hate what I am. It doesn't work that way. Tell him to go away."

"Fortune, ple—" The door slammed in Roc's face.

Grady had become anxious and was waiting in the hall when Roc returned from upstairs.

"I'm sorry, MacNair," Roc intoned grimly, "but it's no use. When you maligned Gypsies, you hit a sore spot with Fortune. I don't reckon she'll ever forgive you for that."

"Did you tell her I love her?"

"Yes. She said you couldn't love her, yet hate what she is."

"What I said was said in anger. Doesn't she realize that?"

Roc held up his hand. "I'm sorry, MacNair. I did what I could. Now you'll have to leave."

Grady straightened and donned his hat. "Tell her I'm not giving up on us, even it takes till I'm old and gray." With that he showed himself out the front door.

The next morning, Grady was loading a miner's supply wagon when he saw Fortune, dressed in a pretty apricot frock, come out of the stationer's shop across the street. A guard who had been waiting for her just outside the door followed unobtrusively.

Without a second thought he pushed the shovels he held into the miner's hands and hurried into the mercantile. "Book," he called, "where are you?"

"He's out back, cleaning out the stable," Irene answered.

"Irene," Grady said, tearing his clerks apron off, "do me a favor and have Book finish helping Kramer load his wagon. I just remembered something I have to take care of."

Irene answered in the affirmative, but Grady was already out the door.

Damn, where is she? he wondered, as he headed down the boardwalk in the direction she'd taken. Just as he started to pass by a ladies' dress shop, he caught a flash of apricot skirts through the window.

"Why, hello, Mr. MacNair," the dressmaker greeted as Grady rushed in. "Is there something I can help you with?"

Grady startled the poor woman when he grabbed her arm and

whispered, "The lady in the apricot dress, where did she go?"

"Why she just stepped into the dressing room to—Stop! You can't go in there," she shrieked.

Grady yanked back the curtain on the dressing room. "Fortune, I—"

A shattering scream nearly split his eardrums, and for a moment he was too stunned to do anything but stare. There, standing in front of a mirror, naked as the day she was born, was the mayor's chubby little wife.

"Sweet Jesus!" He yanked the curtain back in place and ran for the door. Back outside on the boardwalk, he tried to look as nonchalant as possible and stuck his shaking hands in his pockets.

It was then that he spied Fortune coming out of Whyler's Mercantile, and he forgot all about the mayor's wife. He watched her stroll down the street and enter Bremer's General Store before he started after her.

Ernest Bremer raised his eyebrows when his competitor rushed in, stopped and scanned the store, then strode toward the back corner where he kept various types of hardware.

A familiar prickle at the back of her neck alerted Fortune, and she glanced up from the paint brushes she'd been examining to find Grady MacNair bearing down on her. Not wishing to create a scene, she demanded in an ill-tempered whisper, "What are you doing here? Go away and leave me alone. Didn't Roc give you my message last night?"

For each of his steps forward, she took two backwards until she bumped into a wheelbarrow, lost her balance and nearly fell in. Grady reached out and caught her arms just in time to save her dignity.

"Take your hands off me," she hissed, squirming in his grasp and glaring murderously. When he failed to comply, she jabbed in him the belly with her parasol.

He immediately let her go to rub his abused middle. "Fortune please, I have to talk to you, Sugar."

"I am not your *Sugar!* Now step aside, and let me pass."

His smile did not indicate compliance. "I'm not budging until you listen to what I have to say, hellcat." She opened her mouth and he slapped his hand over it. Her brows shot up over eyes gone wide with surprise. "Damn it, darlin', I love you! I forgive you for what you did to me and for keeping quiet about it al this time. Irene filled me in on a few things and I—Ao-o-o-ow!" Grady doubled over, holding his private parts.

Fortune stepped around him, lingering just long enough to whisper, "I don't need your forgiveness, Gajo. This lowly Gypsy slut was helping to win a war, just as you were." Then holding her head high and proud, she wove her way through the cluttered store and whisked out the door.

Still bent over in pain, Grady turned to watch her go and realized Bremer and his customers had witnessed his humiliation.

That night, Grady was drowning his troubles in one of a succession of drinks at the Gaiety, when his blurred eyes fixed on the stony-faced mayor coming his way. "Now, Mayor, I kin 'splan eberthin'," he slurred, rising clumsily to his feet.

Normally, the Reb was three times the man the mayor was, but in his inebriated state, he wasn't half the man little Book Tabor was. The last thing he remembered was an amused cowboy yelling, "Timber!"

The next morning Grady paid a fine to the sheriff and nursed his aching head all the way up the street to the mercantile. Once there, he applied cool rags to his swollen eye.

In the week that followed Grady attempted several times to get Fortune to listen to reason, and he had all the bruises, bumps and trough dunkings to prove it. Miners, freighters and businessmen alike began placing their bets on whether or not the stubborn Scotsman would win back his feisty Gypsy.

Wearing an old pair of her brother's britches and one of his old work shirts, Fortune tied a red scarf around her constrained hair and set to work in the cramped library. Dipping a paint brush into the new premixed paint that had just been introduced that year, she furiously swathed the walls in white.

"Are you painting that wall or clubbing it?" Laila asked from the doorway.

Fortune stopped, flashed the petite old lady a churlish expression, then turned back to her painting. "Was there something you wanted, Granny?"

"Yes, I want to talk to you about Grady MacNair."

"If you mention that Gajo's name to me again, I'll scream! He's made me the laughing stock of Helena."

"If you had let him talk to you in the first place, that wouldn't have happened," Laila admonished.

"There's nothing to talk about. He's a Gajo who hates Gypsies. I'm a Gypsy. End of story."

"Fortune, any man who's gone through what that one has this week is a man in love! And don't forget your grandfather was a Gajo, and our marriage was wonderful. Now, I know I haven't always felt charitable toward Grady, but mostly that was because you came to me and begged my help to get rid of him. At the time, it seemed the thing to do. But he knows everything now, he's not taken revenge, and sweet Gaia, he's told half the world he loves you!"

Fortune dropped the brush into the pail. "That doesn't change the fact that he has a very low opinion of Gypsies, and I don't believe a bigot can become unbiased overnight."

With a screech of exasperation, Laila threw her hands up in the air. "Oh, but you're a stubborn Rom!" She turned on her heel and stalked off.

Fortune turned angrily and bent down to pick up the brush, but it had sunk into the thick depths of the paint, handle and all. She sat down on the floor, crossing her legs Indian style, and let the floodgates open on her dammed-up tears. "A hex on you, Grady MacNair, for making me love you!"

Heaven knew, it hadn't been easy turning Grady away, but every time she considered giving in to him, she wondered what would happen when the newness of love and passion wore off their relationship.

Her father had loved her mother once. He had thought he could overlook her lowly background if she agreed never to let it touch their lives. And so her mother repudiated everything Gypsy. But one cannot entirely wipe out what is in the blood, and when her father became successful, he worried constantly that he might be looked down on because of his Gypsy wife. In the end, love turned to resentment, and though they lived together, each had a separate life.

In turning Grady away, Fortune felt she was doing what was best for both of them.

Chapter Twenty-nine

The Landrys, the Tabors and Jim Fetters headed out of Helena late Friday afternoon for another weekend at the ranch. Jim Fetters manned the reins of the wagon with a verbose Irene cozied up next to him. Book was teaching his sister a bawdy song he'd just learned, and Laila and Ursula were arguing the virtues of Gypsy magic versus voodoo. Fortune and Roc rode their horses alongside the wagon.

"You look very Gypsy today, Sister Mine," Roc commented surveying his sister's attire. "Quite fetching, really."

Depressed by her inability to put Grady MacNair from her mind, Fortune just shrugged and gazed down at the full russet skirt she wore with a matching shawl over a light blue shirtwaist. "I probably should have worn my riding skirt. My petticoat shows, but I was just too lazy to change."

"Ha!" Roc scoffed amusedly. "Lazy? You, the girl who has practically painted the entire house on her own, rearranged every stick of furniture and hung new kitchen curtains?"

Before Roc could bring up the reason behind her recent flurry of redecorating, she interjected, "The house is beginning to look very nice, isn't it? Just two more bedrooms to go and—"

The lovely day suddenly erupted in gunfire, dust and masked riders. Fortune screamed as she was torn from her horse and roughly slung astraddle one of the outlaws' mounts.

"Don't make a move or the woman gets it!" shouted her captor.

Roc and Jim's hands froze a hair from their gun butts.

"Nice and easy like, throw them guns down. Landry, get off your horse." Again this came from the man that held Fortune before him, and she assumed he must be their leader.

When Roc and Jim hesitated, the leader shoved his gun barrel into her ribs, making her cry out. "Any tricks and the girl dies."

Roc and Jim threw their guns down, and Roc dismounted. One of the outlaws slid from his saddle to retrieve their weapons. Another man slapped the rump of Fortune and Roc's horse and sent them in a dead run towards town.

The outlaw leader laughed, reached up and pulled down the bandanna covering his face.

"You!" Roc shouted angrily. "It's been you all along, hasn't it?"

Glancing over her shoulder, Fortune gasped. She remembered the man's evil face well—the bulbous nose, the greasy brown hair, the large thick body. Three years ago, Deke Tunney, his brother and several other Confederate deserters had been about to rape a young farm wife and her sister after ransacking their home. Roc, Fortune and their Yankee band of Gypsies happened along in time to spare the frightened young women. The deserters were promptly subdued and turned over to the first company of Union soldiers they ran into.

Deke Tunney took in Fortune's horrified expression and laughed fiendishly. "Clyde, take this bitch on your horse." A slightly smaller man nudged his horse through the others and hauled Fortune onto his saddle.

"Leave my sister out of this, Tunney," Roc demanded. "She just happened to be along with my men and me when we caught you and the rest of those bastards."

"You don't get off that easy, Landry," Tunney replied smugly. "You see, I heard all about you and your damn Gypsy spies. Some of them prison guards thought you was quite a hero. They didn't know who the woman was you had with you, but

hey said it was thanks to her that you caught up with some of
Mosby's men. So, I reckon the slut is as guilty as you for all
ou done.

"I shore was pleased to see her show up in Helena. And when
found out she was your sister . . . well, it couldn't of worked
ut better."

"What is it you want, Tunney?"

"I want ten thousand dollars and your life for your sister's
reedom. You're gettin' off cheap considerin' it's your fault my
rother died, and I got me this." He lifted his wood leg from its
pecial stirrup.

"You're mad, Tunney," Roc snarled. "Fortune and I had
othing to do with you losing that leg or your brother's death."

"You're responsible for turnin' us over to the Yanks. My
rother, Cal, died in that stinkin' prison. And if not for you I
vouldn't have got my leg blasted to pieces tryin' to escape. I
owed that if I ever found you, you'd pay. The man that shot
ne in the leg is dead, and so is the sawbones that whittled it
ff. Now it's your turn."

"You'll never get away with this, Tunney."

Deke chuckled. "Sure I will. You got two days to get the
noney, Landry. I'll send a man to the warehouse with the time
nd place you're to deliver. If you ain't where you're 'sposed
o be with the money, I'll give the girl to Clyde and the boys.
Her death won't be pleasant."

Roc roared angrily and lunged at Deke's horse, but the out-
aw merely lifted his wooden leg and kicked him into the dirt.

"Remember, Landry, you and the money for the girl." He
eined his horse around and called to his men. "Let's ride!"

Roc watched helplessly as Fortune was carried off, her long
hair streaming like a banner behind her. In the wagon little
Tish sobbed quietly against her mother's shoulder, and Laila
nd Ursula clutched each other.

Roc turned to Jim, all business. "Jim, help me unhitch one
of the horses. Then head this wagon back to town, and make
sure no one gets near the house."

As soon as a horse was unhitched, Roc climbed on bareback
nd galloped back to town ahead of the slow-moving wagon.

The outlaws rode hard, going first south then west into coun-
ry Fortune was unfamiliar with, and one by one the outlaws

removed their masks. Their lack of concern for hiding their identities forced her to acknowledge what she'd unconsciously known from the first. Deke Tunney had no intention of freeing her as he'd promised Roc. Her brother would undoubtedly know this, too, and try to rescue her. She had to help him in any way she could. Because if Roc saw no other choice, he'd sacrifice himself to save her. There was no way she'd allow that to happen.

As they pounded down the trail, she clutched her handkerchief to her mouth for a while as if to protect her face from the dust. Along the way she discreetly lost it on a bush.

Out of the corner of her eye Fortune curiously studied the man on whose horse she rode—Clyde, Tunney had called him. A set of missing and rotting teeth nested in a shaggy beard. There was something frightening about the vague expression in his small eyes. She judged that he wasn't any too bright and hoped it might later prove useful.

When they finally stopped to water and rest the horses, Fortune begged a moment of privacy. After answering Mother Nature's call, she removed her amulet and dropped it into her skirt pocket. Then she tore off a long strip off her petticoat, and ripped that into two separate pieces.

"Hurry it up, woman," Clyde called, "or I'll come in them bushes after you."

Fortune stuffed the strips of material into her pocket with the amulet and rejoined her captors. She dawdled getting a drink at the stream until Clyde had mounted. When he held out his hand to pull her up before him, she asked to ride pillion instead. He shrugged indifferently and hauled her up behind him.

For a time, they traveled north through the shallow stream itself. Fortune surmised this was supposed to cover their trail, and she knew she was right when one of the outlaws took pains to erase the evidence of their departure from the stream. No one noticed when she let the amulet catch on some low branches. They entered a densely forested area, and she feared that Roc wouldn't be able to track them over the leafy forest floor. Thus she snagged a strip of petticoat on a tree and hoped Roc would spot it.

When they broke through the trees they rode on another open trail road headed north. Not 20 minutes later they left the road to head cross-country. It was here Fortune dropped her last trail marker.

She soon spied a log cabin located in a vale surrounded by hills of sage brush and greasewood. Other than a copse of cottonwoods at one corner, the crude structure stood out in the open. It struck her that the outlaws hadn't chosen an easily defended hideout, but then she realized that anyone approaching could be easily spotted at a considerable distance.

Within moments of arriving, Clyde dragged her from his saddle and shoved her to the dirt floor inside the cabin. Deke followed them and jerked her to her feet. "Hand over your skirt and shirt," he ordered. "And them boots, too."

"Please, no," she pleaded, hating the quiver of fear in her voice. *Sweet Gaia, were they going to immediately rape her?*

As if reading her thoughts, Deke gestured at the hanging blanket that served as a door. "There ain't no real door in this place, and I gotta make sure you don't try to get away. Now, do as I say or I'll make you strip down to nothin'."

Fortune didn't see that she had much choice. She hesitated, waiting for them to leave, then realized she would be granted no privacy. Turning her back, her trembling hands slowly peeled off her skirt and shirtwaist. Thankfully both men seemed too intent on staring at the cleavage above her chemise to notice the torn hem of her petticoat.

She handed her clothes to Deke who tossed them at Clyde. "Burn 'em," he ordered. Then leering at Fortune he added, "She won't be needin' 'em any more."

Fortune breathed a sigh of relief when both men left her alone then. She turned in a small circle, scanning her prison for a possible means of escape other than the doorway. The only other opening was a tiny window above a rickety cot. On sighting it, she came to a startling and terrifying realization. She knew this place! She had visited it in her dreams.

Fortune and Roc's horses had returned to the stable at the back of Fortune's house. After stabling the old wagon horse, Roc mounted his black and headed for MacNair's Mercantile.

The store was closed when he arrived, but he pounded on the door until Grady left his quarters to investigate the racket and let him in. "How much do you love my sister?" he asked the Reb without preamble.

With an expression of surprise and consternation, Grady shut and locked the door after Roc. "I told you I want to marry her, and I meant it. What's this about? My God! Is Fortune in some kind of trouble?"

"Yes, and I need your help. Our enemy has finally made himself known. His name is Deke Tunney, a Confederate deserter my men and I had a run-in with while escorting Fortune back to Philadelphia in '64. He and four other men waylaid us today on our way to the ranch. They took Fortune."

Grady went very still as first shock and then fear for Fortune reverberated through his entire being. His voice was low and tightly controlled. "What does he want?"

"Ten thousand and my life in exchange for hers," Roc replied succinctly.

"Christ in heaven!"

"There's little chance he'll keep his end of the bargain, but I don't see that I have any choice but to meet his demands—or appear to meet them. You see, I don't have the money. Tunney has already worn my finances thin. The most I can roundup fast is four thousand. I could sell off mules and wagons, but there's not enough time for that."

"What I've got is yours, Landry, but it isn't enough. And if what you say is true, money or no, the bastard plans on killing you both. How long before you hear from him again?"

"Two days. I'm worried that Tunney won't keep his word and keep Fortune safe until then. His plans for her were pretty clear in those letters he tormented her with."

Grady's mouth pulled in a tight line. "Then we have no choice but to find her as soon as possible. I became a fair tracker during my Indian-fighting days, but it'll be dark soon. We'll have to wait till first light."

"I'll see about rounding up some men."

"No! Too many men muck up a trail. Besides, we can't charge in with a bunch of men or they're liable to shoot Fortune first thing. We need to get a lay of the land, then decide how to get her out of this mess unharmed."

"We'll be outnumbered," Roc reminded him.

Grady's smile was mirthless. "I'm a Reb, remember? We're

used to being outnumbered. Five to two is nothing. Besides, we'll have the element of surprise."

Roc nodded. "I'll be here just before dawn."

Grady let Roc out the door and leaned back against it. Alone now, his cool reserve slipped. Swallowing over the lump in his throat, he blinked back the moisture in his eyes.

The past weeks had been hell without Fortune, but in the back of his mind he'd been sure he would eventually win her back. Now, though, it seemed the choice had been taken away from both of them.

Of all the stupid bastards in this world, he surely took the prize. Christ, if he hadn't been so quick to condemn her maybe she'd be here right now, safe in his arms. He straightened and slammed his fist down on a countertop. Unfortunately, the jarring pain did little to ease his heart.

Once before, he'd lost everything that had been precious and good. He'd survived that and rebuilt his life. But everything he'd done would be an empty success if he lost the most precious thing of all, the woman he loved.

Fortune lay hungry and shivering in the dark, drafty cabin, when Clyde ducked inside with a single moth-eaten blanket. She jumped up quickly, not wishing to be caught in a vulnerable position with this man.

He snickered at her obvious fear of him, tossed the blanket on the cot and started backing her into a corner. A small sound of alarm escaped her when her back hit the wall.

"Let's you and me get acquainted, girly," he said rubbing his stinking body against her.

Though sickened, Fortune somehow managed to keep her head. She'd watched and listened at the way Deke Tunney had treated Clyde and was convinced that her first assumption had been right. Clyde was definitely short on smarts. Perhaps she could trick him into helping her escape.

Forcing herself to relax in his groping embrace, she circled his neck with one of her arms. "You know Gypsies have magical powers, don't you, Clyde?" she cooed.

He licked her neck, yanked her shawl off and roughly pulled her chemise down, baring her breasts. "I heard talk that old Granny of yours was some kind of witch," he answered distractedly, loosening her petticoat ribbons so he could shove his hand down the back of her drawers and pinch her bottom. Fortune flinched, and he chuckled. "I like my wimmen real scared."

Fortune swallowed back the bile raising in her throat. "It's true," she finally managed to reply. "Gran is a witch, and she taught me everything she knows, including how to please a man. If you were to help me escape, I could be all yours, Clyde. You wouldn't have to share me with the other men."

Abruptly he jerked her down on the dirt floor and fell over her, holding both her hands in one of his. "Why should I help you? Deke said I get ta have you after your brother brings the money. 'Sides, iffin' I was to help you escape, Deke would kill me sure." He started fumbling with his britches. "Maybe I'll just have a little taste of you right now."

"Take your filthy hands off me, or I'll hex you!" she hissed, struggling against his oppressive weight. "Your man's part will shrivel up and fall off, if I but say the words."

Clyde leaped up with a look of horror. "You wouldn't do that to a feller, would you?"

"Shall we find out, Clyde?" Fortune asked, sitting up and forcing herself to eye his rapidly deflating member with menace. She smiled wickedly. "See, it's already beginning, Clyde. By this time tomorrow you will look like a woman. If you want me, Clyde, there is a price—my freedom."

Clyde backed toward the door, stuffing his shrinking male member back into his pants. "Don't hex my poker, you hear?"

Fortune pulled her chemise up, stood and brushed the dirt off her underclothes as best she could. Then rolling her eyes wildly, she started mumbling nonsense. When next she glanced at the doorway Clyde was gone.

Shivering now more from fear than cold, she replaced her shawl, then wrapped the blanket around herself. No time for self-pity now, she told herself. She had to think! Hopefully she could keep Clyde frightened enough so that he'd be incapable of attacking her again.

Fortune paced the cabin like a caged lioness. If she was to keep Roc from riding in here like some kind of knight in shining armor and getting himself killed, she had to initiate a plan of escape by tomorrow night.

This time of year weather in the Territory got contrary as hell, but Grady hoped that Mother Nature would hold up on winter's inclement onset for at least one more day. If it began raining or snowing there would be little chance of tracking Deke Tunney's gang.

"This is where it happened," Roc said, pulling up on his steed's reins. He pointed south and added, "They took off in that direction."

Grady nodded and dismounted. He spent a quarter of an hour carefully walking the area and checking for signs that might help him follow the outlaw trail. He noted an unusual S-shaped marking on one of the horseshoe prints and found the tracks of the horse that carried two riders. "This isn't much to go on," he said, gazing over at Roc's worried face, "but it will have to do"

"Damn," Roc cursed, gazing off in the direction the bandits had taken, "I wish we had Grumpy here. He'd find her in short order."

"Believe it or not, I kind of miss that ol' dog myself," Grady replied, rising from his crouched position and gathering his horse's reins.

As they mounted up, Roc tipped his hat back thoughtfully. "You know, I've never met a dishonest man that wasn't basically lazy. I got a hunch Tunney's hideout isn't far from Helena."

"I hope you're right. We don't have much of a trail to follow, and if we don't find where Tunney is hiding by this evening, we may not find it at all."

Grady and Roc lost the trail twice when the tracks mingled with those on a well-traveled wagon road. The two men had split up then. The first time Grady found the trail, he signaled Roc by shooting his gun twice in quick succession. Then Roc found Fortune's embroidered handkerchief.

"Poor darlin' must be scared to death," Grady commented anxiously. "You reckon she'll try to leave us any more signs?"

"No doubt she is scared, but she held up under some gruesome experiences during our mission to Virginia. She'll be all right, and if I know Fortune, she'll help us as much as she can. I just hope they don't catch her at it."

The terrain became more hilly and rugged then, but the trail was easily followed until they reached a clear shallow stream, where the outlaws had obviously rested their horses. When Roc would have crossed it, Grady told him to stay put while he scouted the area on foot.

"Well?" Roc asked impatiently. "Which way?

Grady sighed. "I don't know. Looks like they decided to cover their trail here by keeping the horses to the stream bed. Sometimes in shallow water you can tell the direction taken by the way the moss and rocks have been torn up, but this is a fast-moving stream. There's little moss here, and the trail is relatively cold."

"So we've lost them." It was a statement rather than a question.

"Maybe. We traveled south, then west," Grady said, thinking aloud. "If your theory is right about their hideout being close to Helena, I'd say they walked their horses through this stream, heading back north."

"And if we're wrong, Reb?" Roc bit out in angry frustration.

Grady shrugged. "We'll backtrack south. Let's move, daylight's wasting. Maybe Fortune left us a sign that will help."

"Are you sure you know what you're doing?"

"Your testy attitude is getting on my nerves, Yank," Grady snapped, growing short-tempered himself. "I spent my whole stint with the Galvanized Yankees fighting or tracking Indians. We had Indian scouts working for us. I listened and I learned. It's how I survived. Now you got any other bones to pick?"

"You bedded my sister and hurt her real bad, Reb," Roc replied stonily. "Am I supposed to love you for that?"

"Let's get something straight. I asked Fortune to marry me the first time we were together, and she refused me. Only thing was neither one of us could keep our hands off each other. Hell, man, I even tried pointing out to her that she might be carrying my child. Stubborn little vixen said we'd cross that bridge if and when we came to it.

"Don't get me wrong, Roc. I'm not proud of the spiteful things I said to her, but a man can build up a lot of hostility in three years. I found out exactly how much that night in the parlor. It was like a dam busting loose, and when that happened . . . It's hard to explain. It was almost as if I wanted to blame Fortune and you for the whole goddamn war. Can you understand that at all?"

"Yeah, I guess I can," Roc answered, seeming to pull in his horns.

"Then tell me, how do I get through to Fortune, Roc?"

"Believe it or not, if I knew I'd tell you. I love my sister, and I hate seeing her miserable."

"I won't give up on her."

"I'm not surprised. You Rebs are all alike, tenacious as a dog with a bone. Hell, you wouldn't admit defeat until we Yanks practically burned and starved out every last one of you."

"I've got to think of a way to prove to her that I care," Grady muttered more to himself than Roc. "Damn it, she won't even hear me out."

"If we get out of this with our hides, talk to Granny," Roc suggested. "If anyone knows how to get through to that stubborn sister of mine, she does."

Fortune was scared spitless. She'd played a dangerous game all morning, both taunting and tempting Clyde every time he came near her, and still she wasn't sure if she could trick him into helping her escape. But this last time Deke had come in to hear her threaten Clyde with the hex.

"Don't listen to that claptrap, you damn, gullible fool," Deke yelled, belittling Clyde. "Can't you see what she's trying to do?" He grabbed Fortune and angrily jerked her to her feet. "Sly little bitch, ain't you? Well, you won't feel so cocky when my men are done with you."

Fortune began to struggle against his hold as he dragged her out of the cabin into the chill of the autumn morning. He called for a rope, and within moments she found herself bound to the hitching post out front. "'Bout time you start sufferin' for what you done, bitch."

Deke pulled Clyde aside but called the other three outlaws to gather round her. "Don't be rapin' 'er yet, boys," Tunney called laughingly. "I want that brother of hers to watch us make his sister into the camp whore. For now, just get good and acquainted with that sweet little body of hers. Get 'er all hot and wantin' you." He laughed at his lewd joke, and Fortune realized Deke was every bit as twisted as Clyde. The difference was that Deke was cunning. That, combined with his sick mind, made him twice as dangerous.

Her hands tied behind her, Fortune was totally helpless and watched in horror as the men, their eyes gleaming with lust, stretched out pawing hands to her quaking form. She squeezed her eyes shut as her shawl was torn away and her chemise raked aside by ungentle hands. Another set of hands tore her petticoat off, and yet another pair yanked impatiently at the ribbons on her pantalets. *Sweet Gaia,* she prayed, *help me be strong. Don't let them steal my dignity.*

Using a craft Granny had taught her to escape within herself, she slowly sank into a trance-like state. Chanting an age-old Romany protective spell, she divorced herself from the hands partaking of her body. She began to sway to the cadence of the mystical words. At first she wasn't aware that the marauding hands had abruptly stilled.

Deke screamed at his men, who had moved back to fearfully stare at the Gypsy girl's swaying figure. "What's the matter with you damn men? Go on. Touch her. Make 'er feel like dirt."

"Hell, she ain't right in the head, Deke," one of the men cursed. "'Sides, I ain't much on hurtin' wimmin no how."

"She's too damn spooky fer me," the second one chimed in, adjusting Fortune's clothing with trembling hands. "I don't think she even knows what's happenin' to 'er."

The third man turned stark white and grabbed his crotch. "Oh Lord, boys, I think she done to me what she done to poor ol' Clyde. My log pole's plum shriveled up!"

Fortune gradually became conscious of what was being said, but her face remained still as death except for her lips which continued the incantation.

Deke let go a foul oath and cut Fortune free from the hitching post. Her trance had been so deep that she collapsed weakly, and he was forced to catch her and carry her into the cabin. As if her body burned his, Deke dumped her ignobly on the cabin's dirt floor and made a hasty retreat. Only then did she cease the Romany chant.

Roc and Grady found Fortune's amulet on the west side of the stream and found signs of the outlaws passing in the forest. Having thought their trail well-obliterated at the stream, the outlaws hadn't bothered to cover their passage through the forest. Still, the tracking wasn't easy by a long shot, and when they found a strip of Fortune's petticoat, both men breathed a sigh of relief. They found her last marker easily enough and also found where the kidnappers had left the road and headed cross-country.

Near dusk, Roc and Grady stood inside a small copse of trees on a hill. Below them was a narrow valley where the cabin sat out in the open. Several men milled around a campfire, one with a distinctive limp.

Montana, her and Candy stood inside a small copse of trees on a hill. Below them was a narrow valley where the cabin sat, set in the bend. Several men milled around a campfire, one with a distinctive limp.

Chapter Thirty

Fortune paced her gloomy prison and brooded. It grew darker by the moment, but no one deigned to bring her a lantern. Unlike the previous night, no raucous laughter of male triumph drifted to her—only the low, subdued rumblings of men who'd lost the heart for their sport. But the girl knew hers was a hollow victory.

She'd heard Deke talking to his men earlier, and knew that another contingent of road agents, the ones that had recently stolen nine of Roc's freight wagons, were due to return with their booty sometime tonight or tomorrow morning. Therefore, any attempt at escape had to take place within the next few hours or not at all.

Her plan was extremely flimsy, but even a bad plan was better than meek acceptance of the fate Tunney had planned for her. Today, she had been lucky, thanks to her Gypsy teachings, but she couldn't count on that luck to hold. Out of the many outlaws due to arrived, there was bound to be at least a few who would have no scruples or qualms over defiling her.

A shiver that had nothing to do with the chill of the night suddenly feathered up her neck, setting Fortune's hair on end. She halted her pacing, chafing her arms to chase away the goose bumps. *Sweet Gaia! It was almost as if . . . No, it couldn't be! Grady doesn't even know I'm here. Does he? No, I'm just nervous and scared. My imagination is running away with me.*

Closing her eyes and forcing her breathing to slow, the Gypsy calmed herself. But the prickly sensation that she always felt when Grady was near continued to play havoc with the hairs at the back of her neck. *He must be here! And if Grady is here then Roc must be here, too!*

But how was it she could still sense Grady MacNair's presence? The Moondance had been defeated or destiny cheated, depending on how one chose to view it. And yet, the tie binding herself and the Reb was obviously still intact. It shouldn't be, but it was! That was the only reasonable explanation for her continued sensitivity to Grady's presence.

Now that she thought about it, she remembered sensing him the day he'd accosted her in Bremer's General Store. She'd been too angry at the time to lend the occurrence a second thought, but now . . .

She gave her head a shake. This phenomenon could be sorted out later. Right now escaping was more important, and with Roc and Grady out there someplace her flimsy plan had just gained a better chance at success. Fortune glanced out the window, and silently urged the sun to set a little faster.

An hour later she stepped to the doorway and called out to Clyde. As his silhouette rose against the light of the campfire, she mentally prepared herself for what she must do. *Sweet Gaia, don't let my plan backfire on me.* She backed inside the cabin to allow Clyde room to enter.

"Whatdayuh want?" he growled.

It was pitch dark inside the cabin now, but Fortune let Clyde's voice and ordurous body guide her as stepped close enough that her breasts brushed his shirt front. She heard his sharp intake of breath and smiled to herself. "Clyde, I need to go to the trees again," she said softly.

"Just took you a couple hours ago," he growled. His hand found her upper arm and half-dragged her from the cabin.

As they passed the campfire, Deke called out, "Where you takin' that bitch, Clyde?"

"Says she's gotta go to the bushes again."

"All right, but bring 'er right here on your way back. You girls may not be man enough to rough 'er up, but I ain't got any such fears." He laughed lewdly. "While you're back there, make 'er hand over the rest of them clothes. The rest of the men will be here soon, and they'll be anxious to have a look at the camp whore."

Deke's uproarious laughter sent a cold chill down Fortune's spine but served to renew her determination as well. Once in the small copse of cottonwoods at the corner of the cabin, she turned to Clyde and pulled his disgusting, bearded face down to hers. "Kiss me, Clyde," she begged as her free hand inched toward his gun.

Clyde grabbed her arms and shoved her away. "Deke said to watch out for your whore's tricks."

Desperately Fortune reached for his hand and placed it over one of her breasts. She made her voice go sultry and low. "Clyde, I won't hex you. I promise. You see, I know what's going to happen to me, and I'm really scared. But I thought it might be easier for me later if you took me first."

Clyde's fingers closed over her breast hurtfully. He chuckled. "Yeah? You're really scairt? That's good. I like my wimmen scairt. Hell, I can feel myself gettin' hard just thinking of you screamin' while I put it to you." He grabbed one of her hands and rubbed it over the enormous bulge in his britches.

Playing along with him, Fortune snatched her hand away and whimpered, "I'll probably be too worn-out to be afraid after all those other men get done with me. Then you won't get to have any fun at all."

Frowning, Clyde appeared to be turning that over in his demented mind. Then, without warning, he grabbed her around the waist and hauled her close for a sloppy kiss. He pressured her lips apart, then spiked his tongue inside.

Fortune wasn't acting when she gagged and struggled to free her mouth and body from his savage onslaught. He rubbed his arousal against her, becoming more and more excited by the sound of her muffled cries against his mouth.

"I think you was right, little whore," he said, breathing heavily. "I better take you now, before the rest of the men get here." Crushing her against his side with an arm about her waist, he used his free hand to start unfastening his britches.

Quickly regaining her senses, Fortune rubbed the back of her hand across her mouth and gasped for fresh air. This was the chance she'd hoped for when she initiated this nightmare, and she knew what had to be done. Carefully, her hand edged toward Clyde's gunbelt. She grasped the gun butt just as the holster fell to the ground.

"Ah, here we go," Clyde said, as his pants fell around his ankles.

She struck out. Fortune watched in relief as the outlaw slid to the ground in an unconscious heap. Not wasting a second, she pivoted round to run and nearly bounced off a dark visage skulking into her path. Strong arms caught her, and a callused hand squelched her scream. She pounded and kicked out at her captor, tears of defeat streaming down her cheeks.

"Ouch, God damn it! Stop that, darlin'," a wonderfully familiar voice whispered in her ear.

Fortune went still.

"You going to be quiet now?" he asked. At her silent nod, Grady took his hand from her mouth and turned her around to face him. "Are you all right, honey girl?"

Fortune nodded, then crumpled into his arms. "Oh, Grady, thank God it's you." At the moment the problems that remained between them seemed like nothing. She was in the arms of the man she loved, and she was safe.

Grady smoothed her wildly tangled hair from her face. "Listen, Fortune, we don't have much time. Roc's waiting on the other side of the cabin. You and I are lighting out of here and heading round back. If we're spotted, Roc will start firing and cover us." He set her away from him and lifted her chin. "Are you ready?"

"Hey, Clyde, what's takin' you?" Deke yelled, winding his way through the trees.

"Shit!" Grady cursed under his breath. "Lay down next to that bastard you clobbered," he ordered.

Fortune didn't waste time asking questions but did as she was told. She heard Grady grunt with effort, and a scream of horror caught in her throat as he rolled Clyde's half-nude body over hers.

"Quick! Cry!" he ordered, melting into the darkness.

Fortune did. It was easy.

Peering through the dark, Deke stopped short a few yards away. "Damn it, Clyde, I told you to wait!"

Deke stumbled through the underbrush and bent to grab Clyde's shoulder. At the same time, Grady slipped out of the stygian shadows and tapped Deke's skull with the butt of his gun. Deke dropped, and with an economy of motion the Reb rolled Clyde's inert body off Fortune and lifted her to her feet. "Two down, darlin'. This evens the odds a bit." He grabbed her hand. "Here we go!"

In the time it took to temporarily dispose of Tunney, the other three outlaws had become suspicious. All three were headed for the cottonwoods when Grady and Fortune streaked into the open. "Over there!" one of them yelled. "It's the girl. She's gettin' away!"

All hell broke loose then, as Roc stepped around the side of the cabin, guns blazing. Grady shoved Fortune to the ground and covered her with his own body, as he drew his gun and added his gunfire to Roc's. It was over in a matter of minutes, and all three outlaws lay dead.

Grady rose and gently aided a wobbly Fortune. Roc joined them, and she fell into her brother's welcoming arms. He allowed her to sob out her ordeal, then gently set her at arms' length. His anxious gaze raked her dirty face and what was left of her scant clothing. "They didn't . . . ?"

Fortune shook her head adamantly. "No."

"Thank God!" Roc exhaled deeply and gave her another hug.

He reached around her, and her gaze followed the gesture to find Grady offering his buckskin shirt. As Roc began tugging it over her head, she started to protest but stopped as the shirt, still warm with the Reb's body heat, wrapped her scantily clad body in a cocoon emanating his manly scent. She hugged it to her chilled body and glanced over at Grady. "Thank you."

Her gaze took in his bared upper torso. Memories of nights spent in those strong arms hurtled back at her, and she was nearly undone by her body's instant flare of yearning. But when her gaze lifted, the answering fire in his eyes recalled her reason for withdrawing. Abruptly, she turned her back on the Gajo. Grady MacNair might lust for her body, but he hated Gypsies, the very fabric from which she was made.

The two men left Fortune by the fire and returned to the cottonwoods to deal with Deke Tunney and Clyde. When they returned, the unconscious men were tied belly down over the saddles of two horses.

Her brother's countenance became brisk as he banked the campfire. "We better hightail it out of here, before those road agents you mentioned show up. Grady and I will fetch the sheriff and a posse and return as soon as we see you safely home."

Grady led three other horses up, and Roc tossed Fortune into the saddle of one. The shirt rode up her thighs, exposing her slender legs to the night chill. But there was no time dwell on it as Grady and Roc mounted and set a sharp pace away from her nightmare.

Clyde and Deke's horses were tethered to the back of Grady's horse. Fortune followed close behind, her brother bringing up the rear. As the reality of her safety settled over her, she began to relax, and the exhaustion held at bay for so long took its toll. By the time they reached the place where Roc and Grady had hidden their own horses, she was sagging in the saddle like a rag doll.

Not wishing to be caught here by the road agents, conversation was kept at a minimum. Fortune roused herself when Roc shoved a pair of britches into her arms and told her to get into them quickly. He helped her down and went about exchanging the outlaw's horse for his own. Too exhausted to give modesty more than a passing thought, Fortune tossed the ragged petticoat aside and hurriedly yanked the overly large pants up her legs. With a sigh of exasperation she wondered how she was going to secure them about her tiny waist.

"Here," Grady said, cutting off a piece of leather rein from an outlaw's horse. "Tie them up with this." As she followed his directions, he bent down at her feet and rolled up the pant legs. She noted that he'd retrieved a jacket out of his saddlebags and put it on. "Better?" he asked when he stood up.

"Yes, much. Thank you." For a moment she thought he meant to say something more, but instead he hoisted her back into the saddle and mounted his bay. She was both hurt and relieved by his reticence.

Chapter Thirty-one

Then comes a Gypsy shuvani so wise
She hears Gajo's loud forlorn cries
She chants, heed my song, to right this wrong

To capture Gypsy fairy's hand
You must love her Gypsy band
Only then will cupid's dart claim her heart

Under Fairy's pillow, Gajo secrets his hair
So of his love, she'll be aware
Two rings in his ear proves him a Gypsy sincere

Grady leaned over the desk in the back room of the mercantile, staring at his accounts without really seeing them. In the two weeks that had passed since Fortune's rescue, much had happened.

The people of Helena had been outraged over Fortune Landry's kidnapping. Women were precious and rare gems

348

in places like the Montana Territory, and crimes against them were punished with expedient ruthlessness.

Deke and Clyde had been duly jailed, but neither lasted till the trial date. Under suspicious circumstances the two men were broken out of jail one night. The next morning their castrated bodies were found swinging on the road just outside of town, a visual and harsh warning to any who might harm one of Helena's gems. As a civilized man, Grady knew he should be horrified by the outlaws' manner of death, yet he could not but think that the punishment suited the crime.

As for the rest of Tunney's gang, he and Roc had some satisfaction there, too. Along with the sheriff and his men they returned to the cabin hideout. As they had during Fortune's rescue, the men waited for nightfall then surrounded the bandits. In the resulting shoot-out, three of them were killed including Frank Munday and Eli Holms.

Roc was able to claim the money the road agents had received selling the stolen freight and mules, and the sheriff was pleased to find several bank bags full of money from recent stage robberies.

None of these victories, however, had been capable of curing the terrible pain in Grady's heart. He'd tried countless times to see Fortune and had been turned away as many times, always with the same message. *Fortune thanks you for your part in her rescue, but she prefers you not try to see her again.*

"Grady?"

Grady shook off his thoughts, glanced up at Irene's very round figure and smiled. This past week she'd announced that she'd seen a lawyer about divorcing her runaway husband. If all went well, she and Jim Fetters planned to marry in the spring.

He got to his feet and rounded the desk. "You need something moved or carried," he asked solicitously.

As an answer, Irene stepped aside, ushered Fortune Landry's tiny grandmother into the room, then disappeared.

"Mrs. Fontaine?" Grady said in surprise. "Please come in." He guided the purple-garbed old lady to his desk and pulled out the chair he'd just vacated. Sitting on the corner of his desk, he regarded the wrinkled face framed in snowy hair. "Is there something I can do for you, ma'am?" he asked curiously.

Her sharp retort made him jump and belied her fragile appearance. "Of course not! *You* sent for *me.*"

"Excuse me, ma'am, but I don't . . ."

"There is no excuse for you, you young nitwit! No need to scowl like that either." She set her reticule down on top of his ledger and gazed up at him with snapping dark eyes. "If it makes you feel any better I've called my granddaughter a nitwit almost everyday the past two weeks." She sighed in exaggerated impatience. "Young people!"

"I'm afraid I don't understand."

"Of course you don't. That's why I'm here. Roc told me he'd advised you to come see me, but did you come to me by the light of day? No, not you. You pestered me in my dreams, interfered in my card readings, and even had the gall to show up in my tea leaves."

"I did?" Grady chuckled.

"Don't be patronizing, young man—not if you want my help making that stubborn granddaughter of mine see reason. You do love her, don't you?"

Grady sobered and reached for her knarled hand. "Mrs. Fontaine, I'll never love another. Your granddaughter holds my heart and soul.

"I think you know that I'm not a fanciful man, but recently I came to the conclusion that both our fates were sealed three years ago in a moonlit grove in Virginia. Ours is no ordinary love. Unfortunately, Fortune doesn't share my opinion."

The old lady snatched her hand back. "She told you of the Moondance then?"

Grady's brows met at the center of his forehead. "Moondance? No. What's that?"

"It's a love spell. In fact, there is no love spell stronger than that of the Moondance enchantment." In a few words she explained the legend of the Moondance and the part it had played in bonding him to Fortune.

"You mean she avoided my courtship to give you time to try to reverse this Moondance thing?" he asked incredulously.

"Yes, but that's neither here nor there now. The question is, are you willing to do whatever it takes to win Fortune?" When he opened his mouth to immediately reply, she held up her hand. "Think carefully."

"I know she loves me, and I love her."

"That's true," Laila replied with a twinkle in her eyes, "but she *is* a Gypsy."

"I wouldn't have her any other way."

"She believes otherwise. You opened a raw wound in Fortune's heart when you slandered her Gypsy heritage, Grady MacNair." Briefly Laila explained Fortune's reasoning.

Then Grady asked, "The problems she mentioned between her mother and father—are they related to her mother's Gypsy blood?"

"Unfortunately, yes. You see, my daughter, Tshaya, let slip once to one of her husband's business associates that her mother was Gypsy. It was of little consequence to the business deal that followed, until that same man later insulted her by asking her to share his bed. You see, the scoundrel considered her a woman of hot blood and easy virtue. And he led Bonner, Tshaya's husband, to believe that she had invited his attentions. Bonner's acceptance of Tshaya's Gypsy blood had always been tenuous, and this incident ended even that. Then of course, there was the scandal that followed when Bonner called the man out. After that, Bonner never looked at Tshaya with respect. To this day, my daughter strives to deny her Gypsy blood to protect her Gajo husband and try to win back his respect. But it will never be."

"Does Fortune know all this?"

"Not all the details, but the reasoning behind her father's rejection has always been all too clear. After the incident, Bonner didn't want much to do with the children Tshaya had borne him. He did finally deign to trust Roc, when he realized what a fine young man he'd become. But as for Fortune, he considered her just another Gypsy woman who would no doubt disappoint him."

"My God!" Grady closed his eyes and shook his head. "All those horrible things I said to Fortune—the hurt I've caused her!"

"Exactly. Now you understand why love alone is not enough for my granddaughter. If you want her, you'll have to embrace her Gypsy heritage as well."

"Tell me what to do?"

"It won't be easy."

"Nothing worth having comes easy," he returned pointedly.

In the next few days he would repeat those very words to himself many times.

I can't believe I'm doing this, Grady thought as he stole up to Fortune Landry's home. *And couldn't the old lady have at least unlocked the back door for me? Why is it so important that I break into the house?*

He'd waited for an hour and a half after all the lights had gone out in the house before venturing forth. Tied on his belt was a small cloth bag containing a lock of his hair, a sweaty black bandanna, a piece of linen dabbed with his own blood, a few dried rose petals and a couple of acorns. According to Laila Fontaine the acorns not only attracted a lover but guaranteed fertility.

Using the tools he'd brought along, Grady jimmied the kitchen window open and stealthily climbed through it into the house. He stopped there to remove his boots, making sure he left them exactly below the window so that he could find them easily on the way out.

Straightening, he turned and immediately stubbed his toe on the leg of the kitchen table. Clutching his toe in one hand, he did a one-legged jig in silent agony. Then he froze, expecting Irene to waddle out of her bedroom across from the kitchen at any second. When she didn't, he breathed a sigh of relief and groped his way through the house to the stairs.

Cringing every time one of the steps creaked under his weight, he nonetheless made it to the top of the stairs without mishap. He stopped there to get his bearings, silently cursing the old Gypsy once again. *Damn, she could've at least left a candle somewhere.*

Remembering that Fortune's room was the last one to his right, he cautiously started down the hall. At her door, he wrapped his fingers around the doorknob, furtively inched it open and crept inside. Thankfully, the moon shining through her windows lent a modicum of light.

The sight of the lovely young woman curled on her side in slumber gave Grady pause. Her jet black hair spilled over the pristine white pillow like rolling black velvet, and above the bedcover her breasts were outlined by a ruffle on the modest nightgown she wore.

He ached to reach out and caress her, kiss her. Oh God, it had been so long! He felt himself growing hard and cursed his lack of control. Deciding he'd better accomplish what he'd come to do before he climbed into that bed with her, he untied the cloth bag at his waist and gently edged it under her pillow.

He'd almost made it back to the door, when a sleepy, childish voice asked, "Grady?"

He whirled round to see Tish Tabor emerging from a mound of covers on the opposite side of the bed. Feeling like a total idiot, he tiptoed across the room in a flash and planted a finger over the child's lips, indicating that she should hush up. To his dismay the little rascal followed him out of Fortune's room.

"Whatcha doin', Grady?" she whispered.

"I'm pretending to be a fairy godmother, what else?" he groused in a whisper.

"You're too big, Grady," she replied, seemingly unaware of his frustration. "And you're a boy. Boys can only be elves."

"Okay, so I'm an oversized elf. Don't you think you better go back to bed now?"

"Uh huh. I'm seepin' with Fortune cuz she said I could." She yawned. "Elf, did yuh bring Fortune a 'sprize? Elves and fairies always do, you know."

"Yeah, I left a 'sprize. Now will you go back to bed?"

She nodded sleepily. "Night night, Elf Grady."

Grady bent down and brushed a kiss on the top of her little head. "Night night, Tish."

Tish was nowhere in sight when Fortune awakened the next morning. Taking advantage of the reprieve, she lay back against her pillows to relax a while longer before getting up to greet the day.

As she had on so many other nights, last night she again had dreamed of Grady. Only last night's dream had gone off on a tangent the others hadn't taken. Her face heated with the mere memory of it.

"Good gravy," she muttered to herself, "what's the matter with me? I might as well get up. The longer I stay in this bed the worse my yearning for that rogue becomes."

Later that day, as Fortune headed down the boardwalk, Twig rushed up behind her. "Kitten, wait!" he said, huffing and puffing for breath.

Fortune halted and smiled down at the old man. "What's the matter, Twig? I've never seen you move so fast."

"Ma'am, I think someone you care about has cracked his nut."

"Cracked his nut?"

"Yeah. I saw Grady MacNair this mornin' and—"

"Twig, whatever MacNair is about I'm sure I don't care."

Twig tisked in disgust and took her arm.

"Wait, where are you taking me?" the young woman demanded, digging in her heels.

"I wantcha to see somethin'. It ain't far, and bein' as how I nearly kilt myself catchin' you, least you could do is oblige me."

Fortune let him guide her in the direction from which she'd just come. He halted across the street from Grady MacNair's mercantile. "See thar." He pointed.

"What? I don't see anything."

"Above the door—that bunch of garlic hanging there—see it? When I asked 'im what it was for, he said it kept the blood suckin' monsters away. Now kin you feature that?"

Fortune couldn't feature it at all, and yet that was definitely a bunch of garlic hanging over the mercantile door. *What on earth is the man up to?*

"Well?" Twig prodded persistently. "What do you think?"

"I don't know what to think, Twig, but you see, it really doesn't matter. Grady and I are no longer friends." With that she left the little man gawking after her.

Over the next week, gossip began to run rampant, all of it involving Grady MacNair's strange new behavior. If that weren't enough, Fortune's dreams were becoming more and more frequent and real. Every night, she awoke sweating and burning with the need to have Grady inside her body. Whenever she passed his store it required every ounce of her willpower to keep from walking through his door, throwing him down and making mad passionate love to him. She'd even gone so far as to reason that once she'd had her way with him, she could walk away satisfied and never have to see him again. Thankfully, she always came to her senses before acting on that ridiculous notion.

Friday, Irene asked her to join her for lunch at the restaurant across the street from the mercantile. The place had advertised that they'd just received a shipment of cocoa, and Fortune wasn't about to turn down a cup of hot chocolate. She did, however, forbid Irene to talk of Grady. Instead they discussed Irene's divorce, the baby and the wedding planned for spring.

"How does Book feel about Jim becoming his father," Fortune asked Irene, savoring the whipped cream floating atop the chocolate.

"Well, at first he didn't seem too excited about it," Irene replied, sipping carefully from her own steaming cup. "But Jim has made a real effort to befriend the boy, and they seem to be gettin' on well now."

"I'm glad." The younger woman smiled. "I sure am going to miss you and the children when you move to Fort Benton after the wedding. I've come to love you all like my own family, Irene."

"And we'll miss you, honey," Irene said, patting her hand. "But you can come stay with us when you visit your brother's warehouse, can't you?"

"Of course. I'll look forwa—" Fortune's attention was suddenly captured by something outside the window. Grady MacNair had just emerged from his store, carrying a customer's purchases. There was nothing unusual about that except he wasn't wearing his usual black bandanna. Instead he wore a red one. She might have shrugged that off, but she caught the gleam of something on one of his ears, too.

Irene followed her line of focus and smiled. "What is it, Fortune?" she asked innocently. "That's only Grady helping that farmer friend of his. You know the one, Duncan Lawson."

"But what's that on his ear? I can't quite tell from here, but it looks like he might be wearing an earring."

"Oh, that. Actually he's wearing two gold rings in one ear. Says that one of the rings will go on his wife's finger when he marries."

Fortune's head jerked in Irene's direction. "He said what? But that's a Gypsy custom!" She turned back to the window. "I wonder what's in that basket Lawson is handing over to Grady? He's handling it like were made of glass."

"Don't know. Want to go find out?"

"I . . . No, I don't care what Grady MacNair is about," Fortune lied.

"Oh, come now, Fortune Landry, you can't fool me. You're positively glowing with curiosity."

"No, I . . . I have to go home now." The Gypsy jumped up abruptly and headed for the door.

"Fortune," Irene called after her, "you didn't finish your cocoa."

"You finish it, Irene. I feel a headache coming on."

That night Fortune lay in bed wide awake. The house had gone completely quiet over an hour ago, but still she couldn't sleep. She wished Irene would have let little Tish sleep with her again tonight. The rambunctious child loved Fortune's big bed, and the two of them always wore each other out telling ghost stories in the dark. It had served well in past weeks to keep her mind off Grady—until she fell asleep, that is. Then she dreamed of the incorrigible rogue all night. And what dreams they were!

The melodic whine of a violin tuning up for a song suddenly broke the night's silence. Fortune recognized the rich notes of her brother's playing immediately. But it sounded like he was tuning the thing below her window. What was he up to?

She heard a harsh scraping sound against the house and threw her legs over the side of the bed. Quickly, she lit her bedside lamp. Just as she cracked her window open, an out-of-tune voice began singing in mispronounced Romany. She opened the window wider and leaned over the windowsill into the cold night air. Grady MacNair's head suddenly popped up over the edge of a ladder leaning against the house.

Though Grady MacNair's speaking voice was wonderfully seductive, he couldn't carry a tune to save himself. Yet here he was beneath her window, trying to croon a Romany love song. And not just any song, but the lovely Moondance enchantment.

Fortune wanted to be mad. She wanted to rant and rave. But she couldn't stop laughing. When Grady at last finished the song and she backed out of the window to close it, he brazenly climbed the rest of the way up the ladder and into her room.

She reached out and touched the two earrings in his ear then, remembering herself, yanked her hand away. "What are you doing here? I think you better leave at once."

"Darlin', I know the significance of the Moondance, and in case you haven't noticed, I've just sung it to you by the light of the moon. I'm wearing red, and you, my heart, have just reached out of your own free will and touched me."

Her hand flew to her mouth. She gave her head a shake. "No, I . . . I don't believe in magic any more. You have no hold on me, Grady MacNair."

"Oh, but I do," he insisted. "*We* are magic, Fortune—you and I together. We're a magic unto ourselves. Please, darlin', don't give up on the magic. Not ever!"

He moved closer, and she couldn't back away without falling into her bed. The very thought made her pulse race and her traitorous body go moist with anticipation.

"You've been dreaming of me every night, have you not, love?" he drawled low and sensual.

"No, I . . ."

"I see the truth on your beautiful face. Don't lie, Sugar. It's forbidden to lie to a fellow Gypsy. Besides," he added, bending and tugging something from beneath her pillow, "I know you dreamed of me because of this."

She watched in amazement as he emptied the contents of a small cloth bag on the bedside table. She recognized the contents and their significance immediately.

"I broke into your house and put this bag under your pillow myself," he explained. His arms came around her, and he swallowed her reply in a soul-stealing kiss, as he slowly lowered her to the bed.

Grady's tongue explored her mouth hungrily, and Fortune heard herself moan. One of his legs was between hers and she couldn't help arching herself against it, seeking the satisfaction she'd yearned for these many nights.

Grady continued to kiss away her reason. His hand caressed her naked thigh as he bunched up the hem of her gown. When her hips bucked in response to his touch, he took advantage of her upraised bottom to skim the gown up and over her head.

She knew she should put an end to this, but her body was already writhing with a desire too intense to deny.

His hands and mouth were all over her at once, and when he stood to discard his own clothing her cry protested the separation. But in the next moment she sighed as his warm masculine body fitted itself to hers. Ignoring her pleas, he took his time with her. He suckled her breasts, titillating their sensitive tips with his flicking tongue till they stood up red and impudent. Then he moved down her satiny skin, lingering at her tiny waist and nibbling at the turn of her feminine hip.

He parted her and took her with his mouth, tasting her sweet woman's nectar as his thumb set a slow steady rhythm against her sensitive bud.

Fortune's bottom squirmed on the bed, and she cried out not once but three times as his unrelenting mouth and hands played her like a finely tuned violin.

Grady brought her to the edge of ecstasy once again, then rose above her, his randy stallion butting its lustful head against her threshold. He paused there, kissing her thoroughly.

Fortune tasted herself on his lips and reveled in the intimacy they had just shared. But now she needed to feel him inside her and be one with him. She reached between their bodies and wrapped her fingers around his throbbing heat. Her touch brought a low growl of pleasure from deep within his chest.

"Careful, darlin'," he rasped, "I'm almost there. I wouldn't want to waste the magic of those fertility acorns, now, would I?" He kissed her again, his fingers continually massaging the sensitive bud between her legs. She moaned and cried, bucked and writhed against his talented fingers.

"Grady, please, take me. I need you, love."

"Do you? I mean do you truly need me?" He leaned back on one elbow and reached for one of the earrings piercing his ear. He removed it and clicked it closed. "You know the significance of these earrings, Fortune," he said huskily. "If you need me, truly love me, let me put this ring on your finger now. If you cannot allow me to do this, then I'll leave your bed now and never bother you again."

"You'd do that? Leave, when our bodies are so hungry for one another?"

"Yes. I want more than your body, Fortune. I've lost my heart and soul to you. Will you give yours to me? I want us joined, mated for life in the Gypsy fashion. Will you be my wife, Fortune?"

Tears of joy filled her eyes. "You . . . you really don't mind being married to a Gypsy."

"Honey girl, why would a Gypsy have anything against marrying another Gypsy."

"But you're no Gypsy."

"Oh, but I will be, darlin', if you but give me your Gypsy heart and soul."

Fortune held her trembling hand up and spread her fingers to receive his ring. Grady lowered the ring over her finger, then embraced her. "My wife," he whispered hoarsely into her hair. And then he sank into her silky warmth, praying his seed would truly find fertile ground this night.

Tinkling bells whisper in the breeze
Gypsy fairy chants Gajo's heart ease
Thy virtue is shown, you shan't be alone

Come unto me
Come unto me
Dance with me
Dance with me
That we may one till the end of time

Epilogue

Fortune and Grady were formally married three days later in the Methodist Church. The whole town of Helena celebrated with the young couple.

That night, in one of the International Hotel's finest rooms, Fortune carefully arranged herself atop the bed she would share with her husband. Grady had graciously disappeared to allow her a few minutes to primp, and she'd taken full advantage of the time.

She'd dabbed on her erotic jasmine and almond oil perfume and donned a lovely diaphanous nighgown of pale yellow. The sheer gown was meant to tease Grady's senses as it covered yet revealed all of her feminine attributes. She smiled knowingly. No doubt her randy husband would have the gown off of her the minute he returned to their room. He was determined that nine months from now she'd give him the first of many sons.

Hearing his key rattle in the lock she fluffed her freshly shampooed hair and waited anxiously.

Still wearing his dark wedding suit, Grady came in smiling and set a basket down by the door.

"What's that?" Fortune asked.

"Patience, darlin'." He grinned, already discarding his clothing.

Fortune relished watching him undress, her hungry gaze taking in his broad furry chest, his muscular arms and his powerful thighs. He chuckled when her eyes widened on the ardent proof of his desire for her. Since the night of their Gypsy wedding they had abstained from bedroom activities so that tonight their coming together would be all the sweeter.

Unabashed by his naked state, Grady retrieved the basket from beside the door. He lifted the latched cover as he sat down on the edge of the bed next to her. "This is a special wedding present from my friend Duncan Lawson, darlin'." He reached inside the basket and withdrew a wiggly, butternut ball of fur. "Honey, this is—"

"Oh, Grady, Grady!" Fortune cried, taking the pup from him. "I'd know that ugly little face anywhere. He's Grumpy's baby." When Fortune glanced back up she was surprised to find tears of joy in her husband's eyes.

"It's all right then, darlin'?" he asked. "He doesn't make you so sad?"

"Oh, no. How could he possibly? I adore him!" She set the puppy down and reached for her husband. "Thank you, Grady."

"But the pup is from Duncan, honey."

"But only you could have known how much this little dog would mean to me. How did I ever have the good fortune to find you, Grady MacNair?"

Grady simply replied, "Must have been magic, Sugar."

That night, Fortune MacNair had one of *those* dreams. She saw cradled in her arms a handsome baby boy with hair black as sin and eyes of heavenly delft blue.

LEGEND OF THE MOONDANCE

When night's veil comes on gossamer wings
The moon is full and the nightingale sings
The Gypsy fairy enchants with the Moondance

She lures poor Gajo man with sultry voice

Stealing from him any other choice
Her incantation becomes his damnation

Come unto me
Come unto me
Dance with me
Dance with me
That we may be one till the end of time

She clutches his heart to her breast
And wings away on another quest
Only the wind hears Gajo's distress and emptiness

Many friends question Gajo's sad smile
As they offer solace through his trial
But their advice falls on a soul turned ice

Then comes a Gypsy shuvani so wise
She hears Gajo's loud forlorn cries
She chants, heed my song, to right this wrong

To capture Gypsy fairy's hand
You must love her Gypsy band
Only then will cupid's dart claim her heart

Under Fairy's pillow, Gajo secrets his hair
So of his love, she'll be aware
Two rings in his ear proves him a Gypsy sincere

Tinkling bells whisper in the breeze
Gypsy fairy chants Gajo's heart's ease
Thy virtue is shown, you shan't be alone

Come unto me
Come unto me
Dance with me
Dance with me
That we may be one till the end of time